# BEGUILED

CYLA PANIN

AMULET BOOKS • NEW YORK

PUBLISHER'S NOTE: This is a work of fiction. Names, characters, places, and
incidents are either the product of the author's imagination or used fictitiously,
and any resemblance to actual persons, living or dead, business establishments,
events, or locales is entirely coincidental.

Cataloging-in-Publication Data has been applied for and may be obtained
from the Library of Congress.

ISBN 978-1-4197-5267-4

Amulet Books are available at special discounts when purchased in quantity for
premiums and promotions as well as fundraising or educational use. Special
editions can also be created to specification. For details, contact
specialsales@abramsbooks.com or the address below.

Amulet Books® is a registered trademark of Harry N. Abrams, Inc.

**ABRAMS** The Art of Books
195 Broadway, New York, NY 10007
abramsbooks.com

*To Misha, Luka, and Dominik—*
*my wish come true*

# Author's Note

I've shortened the weaving process for the sake of narrative in this story, but I want to acknowledge the vast amount of work weavers past and present put into creating a bolt of cloth. Many people were involved in the creation of a single garment of clothing in the seventeenth century—the time period I've pulled from for this fantasy world—including spinners, dyers, weavers, finishers, seamstresses, and tailors. Each step required a highly skilled tradesperson. Every person in this chain would have contributed to something like a court dress, and yet, they would have never been able to afford to wear their own creation. While some of their work has been immortalized through paintings of historical figures, they themselves have mostly been lost to time. This story is about one of those tradespersons, a young woman time would have forgotten.

# Chapter One

The sequins glinted in the sun like the edge of a knife. And these trimmings always were a weapon, in a way. Dazzle the viewer so they couldn't see any cracks underneath.

These silver disks weren't adorning a dress though. The trimmed cloth butterflies hung in the window, twirling in the breeze from the open pane. A parody of freedom.

"Beautiful," I said. I usually had eyes only for bolts of fabric, but I couldn't stop myself from admiring anything truly enchanting.

"Thank you. The lady who does them is just brilliant."

My client, Odina, caught one of the butterflies in her palm. She did it with such reverence, barely letting the iridescent fabric touch her skin.

The bundle in my arms, however, she pulled free without hesitation. No reverence there. The callouses on my fingers caught at the fine wool as I let go of hours of work, supplies bought on credit and the hope of a sale. All that work was Odina's now, and what she thought of me would be weighed by the pattern I'd woven, the skill I'd shown.

"It's nice," she said after a moment.

I swallowed, and it was like forcing down a ball of raw wool. I'd worked hard on that piece. My own blood had gone into it, actually—I'd had to scrub and scrub to get it out. *Nice.* Not *beautiful.* Not even *lovely.* My stomach soured. *Nice* wasn't good enough and I knew it. Plenty of cloth shops sold *nice* things. I had to make breathtaking, gorgeous fabric to make sure clients kept coming back. My father used to say that's what could set us apart from all the others. Being the best weaver in the city was the most important thing to him, and I'd understood why from the time I was very small. We were two of many in the square of buildings so old they seemed to ache as they leaned against each other. Most of the people there were the same—scurrying from place to place in an effort to outrun the hunger clawing at their backs. Like ants in a hill or bees in a hive. But our weaving was a rope that could pull us out of there. It was the only thing that gave us a chance for more. A talent we could sell.

Odina held the blue wool up to her warm brown cheeks, and even I could see it didn't set off her complexion as it should have. It wasn't quite the right shade. I pressed my thumbnail into the palm of my hand and cursed myself for not weaving in more green to give it a rippling, teal hue.

She'd notice the fabric wasn't very becoming when she looked into a mirror—I needed to complete the sale now while she stood in the middle of her parlor. She was my only chance at any money this week and I desperately needed coin.

"It brings the color up in your cheeks," I lied. "And the wool itself is from a village in the mountains where the sheep are said to graze in faerie rings."

Odina caught her lip with her teeth and ran one hand over the wool. Would she have any dry patches it would catch on? Probably not. She likely owned more pots of cream than she needed.

My whole body clenched, waiting, and my stomach took another sickening turn. If she refused to buy, I'd have no way to pay back the debt for supplies. I'd have to take the fabric to market and pray to all the gods someone would stop for a girl standing in the street without a stall.

"It'll make a handsome day dress," Odina said.

I took a breath and dropped my shoulders. My muscles burned from how tightly I'd been holding them.

"But Ella, look, I need to bring you into my confidence."

Odina took my white hand and I almost snatched it back. I didn't want her to feel the nervousness in my damp palms, but it would be rude to refuse her touch. In any other situation, I might have welcomed it. She was one of those people who drew others into them, who were lovely—yes—but more than that, compelling. Something about her made me want to look at her, want to hear the laugh she'd let loose one time that was much deeper and freer than anything I expected. But as it was, she was my client. And from the too-sweet smile on her face, I suspected she was about to give me bad news. I clenched my stomach and firmed my shoulders again, trying to make myself sturdy against whatever blow was to come.

"My dress allowance is fully spent this month, and Kiju simply won't give me any more silver. My mother doesn't understand. But I *need* a new dress. I'm going to a . . . a party next week and

3

everyone has already seen everything I own. Can you imagine if I show up in an old dress?"

I owned exactly three dresses made of my own cast-off fabrics. What I couldn't imagine was having more options than that. And I knew she wasn't talking about just a garden party, but I nodded anyway. The party would likely be with the Chieftain of our city and with the Players. I knew that, even though she seemed to want to keep up the pretense of a secret. Perhaps she thought she kept a veil of mystery over them, but there really was no need for it. People in town knew the influence the Players had over the Chieftain and his council. A group of young, wealthy people, the Players had sprung up around this Chieftain a few years ago, though there's always been a group of them hanging around each prince, playing to each of their desires. They were meant to be his eyes and ears in town, reporting the trends, the people's sentiments, advising him on how to please and gain loyalty, but it was them who really set the trends. They got to choose what people wanted to wear next, what patterns and fabrics and hats, where they'd spend their money. And they got richer by just being close to the Chieftain, it seemed.

"I can't imagine," I said, my words dripping with a sweetness that was as fake as the smile Odina wore.

"Exactly. So I want to buy this wool but I'll have to give you something else for it. Silver still! Just not coins."

Her smile fell into a hard line.

*No, no, not again.*

My heart sank like a stone. This had never happened with Odina. Before Papa was taken, I'd sometimes sold cheaper fabric

4

to farmers and mill workers and their families, and they'd offer something else for payment. A thing I couldn't take to market and trade for something to eat: a cracked earthenware pot painted a fading blue, a black plate that would reveal itself to be pewter if I just scrubbed it enough, a dress two sizes too small that smelled of someone else under the arms.

None of these things did me much good, but I took them anyway because I couldn't look at the faces of the children and think of them going without warmer clothes for the winter. Odina, though, was certainly not going without.

"I'm afraid it'll have to be coin, Miss."

I had a debt to pay, for the supplies to make this bolt, as well as many others. I had to deliver some money to Gregory today, or he'd call on the debtor's prison to come take me away too. Odina had to pay coin or I'd have nothing.

"But Ella! Just wait until you see."

Odina took a little brown box off a side table and pulled out a necklace. The pendant was a leaf with three points wrought in silver, darkened around the edges by time. It was beautiful in a way so few things I saw were. Made for no other purpose than to be admired. Like the butterflies in the window.

But it wouldn't pay off anything. She didn't realize how that felt, not when she lived in this beautiful house. Panic gripped my insides like a blacksmith's clamps, and I tried to steady myself enough to make my words clear.

"I can't take that, Miss."

Odina waved a hand. "Oh, don't worry, it's not that sentimental. I have others like it that we brought from back home."

I wasn't worried about its sentimentality at all, but she couldn't know that. She had to continue thinking I had money from other clients, that I was successful and she was buying from a known weaver. It was the perception I'd worked hard to cultivate. If I begged for coin now, I'd shatter it. But Gods, I needed the money.

"Please, Ella. I promise I'll come back to you right away when I have my dress allowance for next month."

Odina was the only one I had right now—my only client. People didn't feel any loyalty toward the ones who make their goods. We were interchangeable. The only thing that mattered to clients is who wove the most beautiful silk at the best price. I flushed, shame creeping into my blood. It was why I couldn't stop, couldn't make mistakes—like weaving the wrong shade of blue for Odina.

"What if your mother noticed it was missing? You don't want that, do you?" I asked.

Odina batted my comment away and smiled.

"Look, I'll even tell everyone at the garden party where I got the fabric from! They'll all be rushing to you after that!"

With more clients, I wouldn't have to rely on Odina. I wouldn't have to worry about my debts anymore. If Papa were here, I could explain it to him and it would make sense and he would nod his head with a wink and a glimmer in his eye. Hope. Plus, he wouldn't want me to show Odina any weakness—or have me scraping for coin.

With a sour taste on my tongue, I held out my hand for the necklace, and her eyes lit up with a smile.

"You've saved my reputation, you know that?"

I stared at her, at her lovely dark eyes and her full body and her long, scented hair. She didn't need me to save her. I swallowed the rancid phlegm in my throat and forced a smile.

"Happy to, Miss."

I could only hope this trade bolstered *my* reputation. But first, I'd have to go to the market and try to sell this old necklace and avoid Gregory so he couldn't ask for the money I wouldn't have enough of.

"I'm working on something lovely for you, and I'll bring it soon. I promise you've never seen anything like it," I said and left the stifling, cluttered parlor.

# Chapter Two

I turned the necklace back and forth in my hand, wondering who might buy it. Wisps of white chased each other across the sky and parted long enough for the sun's light to touch the silver. The clouds always looked higher here. They'd hung so much lower over my old village in the mountains. I used to play a game as a young child and run into the patches of grass lit up by the little bit of sun showing through a break in the clouds, trying to catch them before they faded away.

That was before I'd realized we were poor. Papa had somehow kept it from me, probably sacrificing his own portions of food for mine. I tried to remember how that felt, the levity of it, but it was always just out of reach. Like the sunlight.

The road kept on toward the market, but I slipped down the path to the river. A big rock beside the bank offered the perfect seat, and I was certain Gregory wouldn't be here. I breathed in the rich smell of water plants and dampened earth and my stomach settled. Others were scared to come because of the Bean-Nighe haunting its edges. They were terrified they'd see her and she'd trick them into reciting a wish—then extract payment for it. To me, other people's fear was actually all the more reason to come down to the water, since I often got to be alone here. The old, cursed washerwoman didn't scare me, really. She only came through the veil if you called her in some way, and I was careful never to say anything out loud on the bank.

Two barges, rowed by four strong backs, made their way through the water on the other side of the river. They held mysteries from the rest of the world, items packed carefully in barrels from places I would never see.

*Was there anything from Odina's homeland?* She'd told me she was Mi'kmaq from across the sea. Sometimes milliners would go through stacks of beaver pelts in the marketplace, looking for the best material for their hats, and I always wondered if there'd been beaver fur on her ship when she first traveled here. Odina had seen many places with her voyager mother before they landed at Eidyn Crag. She'd told me about some of the animals where she'd lived, huge horned beasts taller than any stag, and she'd once shown me a fruit from a warmer shore—deep red with seeds like jewels. A pomegranate. All the things she'd seen, the experiences she'd had, and yet she still hungered for more of everything. Perhaps after having anything you wanted, satiation wasn't possible anymore. My throat burned as her hard smile flicked through my mind. She'd expected me to give in to her, and I had.

I wrapped my arms around myself. The smells of the city didn't stretch down to the riverbanks, and neither did the harsh stares of people better than me wondering why I dared step into their path or breathe their air. My own clothes marked me out as *not good enough* to people like Odina. It was only because of what I could make—my fabrics—that I was allowed in her house at all.

Once the cold from the rock I sat on seeped through my skirt and petticoat, I stood and brushed away the dirt and pine needles clinging to my hem. It was time to go, but longing already sang in my heart. Here, I was safe from Gregory. Here, it was lovely and quiet. But I couldn't stay.

There was only really one chance left to make the money back I owed, or at least enough of it to satisfy him for a while. A purple silk sat half-done on my loom, and I knew Odina would want it as soon as she saw it. I'd begun a floral pattern of the likes I'd never seen before.

It was late enough now, probably teatime, and Gregory would most likely be gone from the market, back in his little shop to be served a meal by his wife. I'd sell the necklace for something, anything, whatever I could get, then I'd go home and weave.

I grabbed a thick root and pulled myself up the side of the embankment, loose soil falling around my shoes. After one last look at the way the falling light rippled over the river, I started down the road.

Butchers and vendors with stalls of country-grown produce dominated the lower side of Greenmarket. I didn't mind the tangy scent of blood or the way it pinched my tongue, and Gregory wouldn't be in this part of town either. He had a housekeeper to do his shopping. Even so, my stomach was as riled up as a mouse caught in a glass jar.

Vegetables lined up in baskets on crude wooden counters soothed me, made me smile. All those colors . . . I loved to just look at them. Purple carrots and deep-red beets and orange turnips. Red and green apples. The colors of wool and silk skeins I dreamed about buying. But dye was expensive. Beautiful things were expensive. Like the necklace should be. But no one would believe it was mine, not with the dress I was wearing, so I doubted I'd get as much as it was meant to be worth.

I'd have to walk up the hill to find a jeweler. The road twisted as it climbed, the stone buildings pressing against each other on either side. A statue of our patron goddess, Nemain, stood in front of the big temple. A man left a sack of oats by her feet, no doubt praying for some gift he hoped to receive from her—a good harvest or healthy fruit trees. I stopped to look, hiding myself in the corner of a wooden gate. Gregory *could* be near here now, away from the blood and rotted vegetables that sour the air in the marketplace. I glanced over my shoulder, to the other side. Nothing. But that didn't stop my heart hammering.

The foot of the statue wasn't as crowded as I was used to seeing it though. Maybe people were frustrated with getting nothing back. Papa always said we were better off keeping our oats and honey than trying to give them to a god. Nemain was strong enough anyway, what with all the images of her carved around the city and all the prayers she received. We didn't need to add to her strength with gifts she would never return.

I could use any help Nemain would give now though. Maybe she'd smile on me if I offered her something good enough. I stepped quickly to the gates and rubbed the necklace in my hand. I never had anything to gift the goddess—nothing extra. But the necklace might be appealing to her. *Would her help be worth more than the coins I would get for it?*

A woman dressed in a long robe of unbleached linen came through the temple's doors. A Protector of the gods, not that they needed it. The gods were the strongest of the fae, and the fae were the only holders of magic. The lesser ones didn't venture to this side of the veil very often—why would they? From what I'd heard of their world in the tales my father told me, the fae world seemed so much more filled with possibilities.

The gods came here much more often though. They needed to maintain and grow their power here, with our worship. Enough worship and they truly became immortal, unable to be killed.

But worship had to be willfully given or it wouldn't work. Would Nemain feel my hesitancy if I gave her the necklace? Papa had been a bit bitter because Nemain didn't stop my mother dying from a poison tooth when I was small, but he'd only given her a loaf of stale bread then. It was all he was willing to part with.

The Protector shuffled toward the statue in wooden clogs, a silver bowl cradled in her arms. She bent to pick up the bag of oats and emptied the sack into the bowl. I clicked my tongue. Instead of Nemain benefiting from them, they'd probably be the Protectors' dinner. If she stole my necklace too, I'd be giving it away for absolutely nothing.

I dragged my eyes away from the temple and searched up and down the street again for the bulk of Gregory's body. I needed to move further into the city. Faces blurred together as I tried to take in features, see him before he saw me. My heart thumped, heavy, in my chest. Sweat dampened the neckline of my dress. A swirl of people enveloped me, but no Gregory. I blinked and counted out three breaths. He probably wasn't here—he'd be at home, eating something rich and delicious. If I could just calm myself, I'd do a better job of selling the necklace.

People crammed together, hems of dresses brushing against one another. This place always made me itchy. Everything was up for the taking here. I bent in on my own body, lowering my shoulders and tucking my fist away, the necklace safe inside.

Shops petered out into stalls on top of the Chieftain's road. A woman stood behind a table glinting with stones and silver. A man leaned against the wall behind them and spat onto the cobbles. He watched the people going by, shifted his position, and reached out a hand to pinch the woman's bottom through her dress. My blood flamed for a moment, but the woman smiled and batted his hand away before giving him a quick wink. Lovers, then. Husband and wife maybe. She drew the customers in and he kept an eye out for thieves.

A team. And I'd have to tackle them alone, hoping they'd take some kind of pity on me. My stomach churned.

The silver necklace didn't catch the light this time because there was no sun to be had—it was swallowed up by those low, puffy clouds that look like wool before it's been spun. I cursed them. The silver just looked better, more enticing, more *expensive* when it glinted in the light. I held it out to the woman anyway, nestled in my damp palm.

"Where did you get that?" The woman leaned her elbows on the counter, letting her dress pull against her breasts.

She wanted me to stare, but I darted my eyes back to the necklace in my hand.

"It was given to me," I said, though I was certain she wouldn't believe me.

"No stones or anything, just silver in the shape of a leaf . . . it's not worth much."

My heart fell. This woman had a table full of near-worthless stones, little more than polished rocks, and yet she glared at me like I'd brought a river pebble to her stand. I reached out a finger to touch one of the blue stones, feel the cold smoothness of it against my fingertip, and my sleeve caught one beside it. It slipped to the ground. The man behind the stall grunted. His eyes burned into my back as I bent to pick it up, heat creeping up my neck.

Another man stepped in front of me with shining brown leather boots while I was low down to the street. Next came a pair of heeled satin slippers utterly impractical for the cobbles beneath them. The hem of the woman's blue silk dress landed just at her ankles to better show off her shoes and the purple feather fastened to them with a paste jewel. I sat back on my heels and stared at the couple's legs.

I had a paste jewel of my own, and when it was given to me I'd thought it valuable. It was the day the magistrate came for Papa, when they dragged him loudly out into the square in front of our building. Every person on the busy street to the left stopped to stare. Papa went quietly, but the soldiers wanted to make sure everyone knew his shame. I was twelve and couldn't help running after him, trying to memorize the lines of his face and touch the dry skin of the back of his hands.

Papa was never as successful as he wanted to be. There were many weavers in this city for the wealthy clients to pick from and Papa was rarely chosen. I hated that, because his fabrics were the most beautiful to me. When a young man grabbed me by the shoulder that day, he gave me the little purple gem and told me he was a Player. I was awed. I thought, if only he'd been here before, when Papa was selling his silks, the young man could have bought some and brought them before the Chieftain to show him how worthy my father's work was. We could have had customers, too many customers to deal with. Demand. A shop. It was only after I went to the market that day, to try to sell the jewel to save my father, that I found it was quite worthless to anyone else.

But I kept the jewel to remember that the Players existed, and maybe one day they'd choose my work to wear to a party and make my business successful in a single night. They'd done it with others—the dyer who made the purple hue they favored and the lace-maker who'd done a pattern like a spiderweb that was so in fashion a couple years ago. Both of those craftspeople had had customers lined up outside the doors of their new shops. Neither would have had to face the thought of empty bellies or debtor's prison. For now, I was still on the outside of influence. My name, my fabrics didn't mean anything to anyone. Shame flooded me. I should have been further along by now, a better-known weaver. Papa would have wanted that for me. *I* wanted that. But as it was, I had to stand at this booth, hawking a bit of old jewelry for a fraction of the coins I needed to pay off my debt.

The necklace still in my hand, I pressed it down on the table and pinned the jewel-woman with my stare. She couldn't shrink me. Not her. Not after Odina.

"How many silvers for it? And don't try to play with me, I'm not green."

"Two silvers, and it's a fair price, so take it or leave it."

I couldn't leave it and this woman knew. Her tongue skittered over her yellowing bottom teeth as heat flared in my cheeks.

"Fine."

She smiled, revealing a missing upper tooth, which I suspected would soon be followed by others, and slapped two coins into my hand.

"Now, on with you. You're bad for attracting customers."

My underarms prickled and my dress grew damp there. I wrapped my arms around my body and slipped back into the crowd like a small stone sinking into the river. People flowed around me, busy, families to be getting home to. I'd sold the necklace; now I had to get back to work.

I hurried away, back down the sloping road, in the direction of the river, but a glimmer in a window caught my eye, and I moved toward it. Papa's voice in my head told me I was being silly. We couldn't afford things like little enamel buttons with purple flowers painted on them. But imagine if every coin didn't have to go to survival. To Gregory, to the baker for the burned loaves. If I could buy those buttons, wear the purple of the Players, I might feel just a little bit special—like them. I even knew just the fabric scraps in my basket to go with them.

The leaded shop window sparkled as if someone had just scrubbed it with vinegar. Inside, the buttons leaned against an old velvet-bound book. The owner had placed a pick hat on a stand just above them—a suggestion.

*See how lovely the hat and buttons look together? Don't you want to look that lovely?*

I knew the tricks, saw them plainly, even though they sometimes worked on me. My fingers were almost transparent in the reflection on the glass as I reached toward the pretty purple buttons.

A heavy weight fell on my shoulder and I glanced behind me, heart in my throat.

Gregory's sour breath leeched over my shoulder. I'd let myself slip for one moment, let myself imagine I was a person who could stop and peer into a shop window like I had nothing else to do. Foolish. A cold sweat broke out on my hands and my upper lip. Men like Gregory could make decisions that would wreck my life. He could send me to the same prison Papa died in if he wanted to. I stuck my hand in pocket and rubbed the two silver coins together. It wasn't enough. Not even close.

"Ella. What you looking at, girl? You can't possibly have money for something in that window and not be paying me for that wool thread first."

"I can give you a little now and more later," I said, muscles coiled, ready to spring away. "I have something special, truly. I just need to finish it."

He smiled. "I've been kind to you, Ella. Given you lots of chances. More than most get. I'm not interested in your promises. I want to be paid. Now."

"I don't have it! Not yet."

Lying wouldn't get me anywhere. I couldn't magic coins out of thin air. He had to know there was nothing to gain from me now, but there could be. If he'd just give me time, I could make him back his money threefold.

"Listen," I continued. "I have a client with lots of money and I'm making something just for her. She's going to love it and she'll pay a pretty coin for it. You'll get your money back."

Gregory shook his head, and my throat went dry. He took two steps toward me, pushing me against the wall of the shop. People moved past us, not even glancing in our direction. We were nothing, not worthy of attention. I wasn't worthy of helping. Fear lodged in my throat, and I couldn't get a yell out.

Gregory's hot breath plumed over my face as he leaned toward me. "There's another way to pay, you know."

I squeezed my stomach muscles to stop the queasy writhing. "You like coin, don't you, Gregory? I'm telling you, I can get much more."

"You talk too much for your own good."

He grabbed my upper arm in his thick fingers. In a blur of adrenalin, I jammed my elbow into his soft belly. Gregory gasped and grabbed at me as I ran away, but I wove through the crowd as expertly as I shuttled thread through my loom.

# Chapter Three

I flicked my eyes between my pounding feet and the road ahead. Wherever space opened up, I filled it. Elbows and wide skirts and hats—nothing got in my way. My chest heaved, and fear pulsed through me down to my toes. I put distance between us but it wasn't enough.

Gregory's footsteps would sound like any other man's in the crowd, but I swore I felt them reverberating beneath my feet. I swung down a side street and doubled back, ducking under linen shirts and caps left out to dry on the line. One house had a crude painting of Nemain leaning against a window. I tried not to catch her eye as I fled.

The sound of the river's rushing water drowned out the heavy footsteps I couldn't get out of my ears. Clover slicked with mud gave way under my feet and I slid down the hill to the bank. Gregory was a big man, not a fast man—not even a particularly smart man. He wouldn't have followed me this far. I *knew* that, and yet my heart beat out of tune and my breath accompanied it with jagged wheezing. Fear was like a scab; it dried up and you thought it was almost gone, but one fresh scrape and the wound was bleeding again.

My papa had been hauled off to debtor's prison five years ago and died three years ago, and in my mind I could still see his face when the constables took him. Sadness, yes—tears had welled on his bottom eyelashes when his fingers slipped through mine—but there had been something else shadowing his face. Terror. He'd been very, very scared. I'd realized in that moment I'd never let them take me away to a place that could make my papa look like that. There wasn't anyone else who would sell supplies to me though. Not with the legacy of my father hanging over my head.

I bent over, arms clasped around my knees. Weaving was my only talent, my only way to make money at all. I couldn't do it without supplies. But I couldn't do it from prison either.

People like Odina knew nothing about need, real need. She'd said she *needed* a new dress, but absolutely nothing would happen to her if she didn't get one. She'd still have food to eat, a warm bed to sleep in. Her Kiju, her mother, had joined the North Men when they'd arrived on her country's shores. She'd made a fortune by trading with them before bringing Odina here on a big ship. Now they had everything. The worst thing that might happen to Odina was her friends thinking a teeny, tiny bit less of her. It served me best to keep her illusion intact, but Odina didn't want to know what my life was like or imagine her fabrics coming from a dark, dingy room in a collection of crooked flats. She based who I was on the beauty I could create, and it was best if she—if everyone—saw that as the product of something special, something other than desperation.

A magpie called and no one answered. Wind scattered golden leaves, and I glanced up to the birch behind me. It was only the beginning of the season, with lots of green left on the trees. A big oak shielded me from the little game path leading back to the street, and I sat in the twist of its roots so Gregory wouldn't see me if he did make it down here.

The Leithe flowed by, uncaring about the uneven pounding of my heart. I was just another unfortunate on its shores. It already had a resident one.

I glanced toward the opposite bank, not so far away in this narrow part of the river. There was no sign of the Bean-Nighe, no indication that she existed at all. Just dirt and trees and water and birds.

Mrs. Under, the old woman in the flat above me, first told me about the cursed washerwoman when I was younger, and I'd asked her why washing a shirt was supposed to be a curse.

*"She has no choice, Ella. Don't you like to choose?"*

*"Choose what?"* I'd asked. *"Can we be someone else, go somewhere else?"*

Mrs. Under had sighed and shaken her head. I wasn't saying the things she wanted me to. Papa used to give me a choice when I'd asked. We had so few things to pick between though. No choice between venison or rabbit, carrots or turnips, because none of those things were within our reach.

*"Well, you can choose whether we have porritch with honey or porritch with cream for supper."*

I'd picked both—the honey and the cream—and Papa had winked at me.

I'd never spoken of her with Mrs. Under again, but there was another reason I thought of the Bean-Nighe sometimes. Other children in our courtyard knew about her too and said she gave wishes to anyone who called on her, but because of the price of those wishes, no one tried it. The cursed washerwoman had magic, so she had to be one of the fae. Which meant she was powerful. I wanted to feel that kind of power in my own hands, wanted it to live inside me, under my skin.

I'd never called on her though. In the end, I was always too scared. She was a bringer of death, a trickster, not to be trusted. If you were close enough, she was said to emit a scream only you can hear when a family member is going to die. Bad things happened to people who sought her out for her wish—no one seemed to know exactly what, but the others talked about her in shuddering whispers anyway. I glanced at the trees where they bent over the river, leaves kissing the rippling water. If the Bean-Nighe was anywhere, she was here. A cold drop of fear slid down my spine as rain began to fall, pinging on the top of the river.

I sheltered under the canopy of oak leaves, but my dress grew wet anyway as I leaned against the thick trunk. I'd spent too much time here, let myself get wrapped up in my own stories. The truth was I had been talking to myself too much in my own head since Papa was taken. Sometimes I spun my thoughts like a web, only I wasn't the spider scuttling expertly around—I was the fat fly caught in the middle. Wrapping myself up like that did me no good at all though. I had work to do unless I wanted Gregory banging down on my door in the night. The purple silk needed to be finished right away. I could work through the evening and into the morning and bring what I could to Odina, even ask her to put a deposit on it. She'd see the pattern and the colors and she'd fall in love, I just knew it. There was a chance for me if I could keep myself awake in the company of the moon and finish the silk.

Home was a teetering building cut up into shabby flats. It was covered in once-yellow plaster that the sun had bleached cream. Wood beams crisscrossed the lower level, and the whole structure leaned so heavily against the next building that those on the third floor could reach out their windows and touch their neighbors' hands.

By the time I got home, my dress was heavy from the rain and my hair sent droplets rolling over my nose and cheeks. My whole body trembled, trying to keep itself warm. I was foolish to go down to the river with gray clouds overhead. Now it would take me all night wrapped in my one blanket on the loom bench to get warm.

I pushed the common door open and climbed the stairs up to the second floor. My key was smooth from years of fingers gripping the iron and turning it in the lock. I copied the movements of all those who came before me and opened the door to the one room that contained my whole life.

The loom took up so much space, we'd never had a table to eat at. Papa and I had taken our meals sitting cross-legged on his bed. Now it was my bed, and I leaned against the pillow to eat with my legs stretched out in front of me. I liked to take up the space. It was easier than being constantly reminded of how empty everything was.

My supplies and fabric scraps filled woven baskets beside my loom. I packed everything carefully and made sure never to touch any of the wool or silk thread with greasy hands. Everything had to be pristine when I delivered it to clients. I walked to the well twice a day to fill my bucket with fresh water and paid more than I should have for soap made of pig fat to keep my hands soft. They were my tools, after all.

The loom itself was old though. Papa bought it secondhand when I was small. I kept it polished with beeswax when I could get some. A little cushion made of scraps rested on the wooden bench. I had a good view out the diamond-shaped panes of my one window from the bench, so I could take little breaks and watch the birds dip in and out of the street.

My project sat half-finished on the loom. A purple silk threaded with a pattern of green roses. It was complicated—my most intricate piece yet. The purple shone just the right tone, almost exactly the shade I'd seen the Players wearing in the street when Papa was taken. Odina would love this so much, she might even tell her friends I was the one responsible for the gorgeous gown. They'd all gasp and come to me and ask me to make them new dresses too. My work would finally have the real attention of the Players and everyone else in the city, and I'd never owe Gregory money again. All I had to do now was be quick.

I peeled off my wet clothes and slipped on another shift before picking up my shuttle loaded with a spool of thread, the wooden tips pointed to slip easily under and over the lengthwise warp yarn. Again and again, I made the same movements, until the light faded and I was forced to light a candle. The smell of burning fat filled the room and I prayed to Nemain it wouldn't make the silk stink.

My stomach rumbled in the quiet of my room, and I forced down piece after piece of stale bread on my dry throat. I had no ale and the water in my bucket would give me a bad stomach if I drank it. No matter. I had a task, a focus, to distract me from the thirst. Eventually I'd forget.

I worked the shuttle and brought the green thread into the purple, forming the petal of another rose. Yes, Odina had said she was out of dress allowance, but I knew that was a lie, and she wouldn't be able to resist this.

Another dip of the shuttle, a tug, a dip, a tug. The silk caught. *Dammit.* I plucked at it, trying to free the thread. *Just work! Why couldn't anything just work the way I wanted it to?*

I tugged harder, my vision turning black on the edges. *Why did everything have to be so hard?* I never wanted this, any of it. Papa gone and an old loom and one single client and only one way to be useful to anyone at all. There had to be more than this.

The weft needed to be pushed up. I yanked on the reed. It splintered. I stared at it, shards around my feet, and held my breath, because if I didn't continue to breathe, this moment couldn't pass into the next where this would all be real. A scream built in my chest, tore through my throat. Everything stung, my skin burning as though flayed. My papa's loom. My livelihood. The only reason I was worth anything at all. Broken.

# Chapter Four

The silk threads hung limply across the loom, my intricate design of flowers fading into clumps of purple and green where I hadn't yet finished the bolt. I wrapped my arms around myself. If I could just step into the past, go back to moments ago. But I couldn't. This was here and now and real. The realness of it shivered through me. My throat hurt. A sliver stuck out from my thumb, but I left it in. I didn't deserve to be fixed if my loom was broken.

I'd pulled too hard in anger. But I couldn't afford to be angry. Hadn't I learned that yet? Anger was for the rich because they could do something about it. I had to swallow back whatever hot bile lived in the pit of my stomach and smile at my customers so they'd buy from me again. Even here, in my own small room, I didn't have the coin to pay for frustration.

But without my loom, I had no livelihood. Nothing to sell, nothing I could put a price tag on except what Gregory wanted and I couldn't, *wouldn't* do that.

A knock sounded at my door, and I spun round on my bench, the shuttle still glued to my hand. Who would come in the night? Fear zipped through me, shaking me from my shock. If Gregory had found out where I lived, I wouldn't be able to keep him out of my room. He was too big, too strong. I dropped the shuttle and grabbed the chamber pot—the heaviest thing I could pick up. If I swung it hard enough, it might stun Gregory for the time I needed to slip around him and down the stairs.

I tiptoed, the chamber pot cradled in my arms and my throat tight and tingling like that feeling before throwing up. The wood of the door showed its age in the dry whorls and cracked boards. I peeked through one of the spaces between the boards.

A face lined with disapproval filled up the space. I breathed, drooping over the chamber pot, a laugh at my lips.

"Mrs. Under," I said and swung back the door.

"What in the gods' imaginations are you doing down here? Are you bringing that out now?" she asked, looking at the pot in my arms.

"No." I set it down. "I'm sorry for the noise; I was weaving, that's all."

The old lady crossed my threshold, nose first.

"Weaving's normally a quiet activity."

I fell back and let her in. She showed up at my door sometimes, asking about the price of turnips in the marketplace or whether I'd bought one of Nelson's eggs and if I thought it smelled off. Chatter, that's all it was. She came, I assumed, when she could absolutely no longer stand being alone in her little room. I had to admit, I didn't mind how my own room felt with two people in it again.

"I pulled too hard on the shuttle and this split," I said, showing her the splintered wood and gulping down the tears. My body shook as I lowered myself down onto the stool.

Mrs. Under leaned over and bent down so close I almost pulled her back before she pierced her own eye with a sharp fragment.

"It'll need fixing; you better pray to Lugh."

"I don't need the craftsman god. I need a person who'll be willing to fix it for two silvers."

Desperation panged in my stomach. What was I going to do? A whimper escaped my throat.

Mrs. Under held up a finger to quiet me and I noticed how swollen her knuckle was. I wiped at my eyes and tried to pull the frayed ends of myself back together. I still had use of my hands, my body. She barely did. I should go up and help her more often—build her fire, cut up her bread.

"Don't shun the gods," she said.

"They aren't usually much practical help, though, are they?" I shook my head but softened it with a smile. "What do you think of the damage?"

I held my breath. She knew her way around a spinning wheel and a loom. She said she used to take peculiar colors of wool together, colors you might think would look ugly all combined, and woven beautiful patterns from the chaos. I wished I could have seen a bolt of her work, but she'd long since given up spinning and weaving. Gnarled fingers were a risk of our trade, and Mrs. Under's were worse than most.

She used one of those fingers now to prod at the loosened strands of purple silk.

"Why'd you choose this color? The silk thread must have cost you a fae's hoard of coin."

Heat crept up my neck. I tucked my chin into myself so Mrs. Under couldn't see.

"It'll be worth it. I have a buyer who I know will love the color."

Mrs. Under made a noise in her throat. "Mhmm, they're not the first to love purple. Don't buy on trust, Ella."

Heat flared in my belly. "You know I have to."

Mrs. Under shook her head, her white braid thumping her back. "I do know that, but it's still a bad idea."

I picked up the shuttle from the floor and sat back at the bench. There had to be some way to fix this. I was making such good progress with the bolt that I could have had most of it done by morning. By afternoon, I could have had enough coin in my pocket to put Gregory off, for gods' sake, and now everything was so much further away.

Mrs. Under ran her fingers over the loom and pushed a fingertip into one sharp shard of splintered wood.

"Mr. Robinson is a good craftsman," she said. "You should go to him, Ella. He'll be able to right your loom."

"He's dead, Mrs. Under."

The old woman sucked her four top teeth. "I wish they'd call out names when they ring the bells at the temple. I can't keep track."

I didn't know if I'd want to be reduced to a name drowned out by the sound of peeling bells, but I couldn't bring myself to say anything. The first of the day's muted sunlight streamed through the window. Little motes of dust floated through the rays, unhurried. *Faeries*, I used to say to Papa. He never corrected me.

"I need more than a mender," I said. The weight of everything that had happened settled in my chest and made it hard to breathe. "I wish we had magic."

"It would be more trouble than anything, if humans had magic," Mrs. Under said, staring at me. Her eyes were a washed-out blue, like someone had added too much water to paint.

"Maybe, but at least if I had enough for a good offering to Nemain, she might lend me some of hers."

I looked around at the near-empty room. My bed with its multicolored quilt of fabric scraps, my earthenware ewer and bowl, Papa's bone comb on the mantle over the little grate. Nothing anyone would want, least of all a god.

Suddenly Mrs. Under took up far too much of my space. I wanted to be alone with this heaviness in my lungs, my stomach. If my loom was broken, I had no way to pay the rent on this room, to even buy food. The only road open to me would be the one straight out of Eidyn Crag—and then what? I couldn't do much with only two silver coins in my pocket. It was too much, and I needed to wade through it alone.

"Why don't I help you back upstairs?" I said.

She waved a hand at me.

"I don't need your help."

Mrs. Under retreated through the doorway. I listened for her slow steps on the stairs, but she must have tread lightly.

Cool morning air slid in around the window casement. I had a little peat left, but it wasn't cold enough to warrant using it yet. Instead, I wrapped my quilt around my shoulders and picked up the discarded shuttle again. Even if I'd known how to fix my loom, I didn't have any tools. The bolt of silk wasn't complete enough to try to sell. I wanted more to show Odina, to make her yearn for it so much she couldn't say no to whatever price I named. I sat on the bench, the thin legs creaking against the floorboards.

The Players would never be in this situation. They were all interconnected, like the strings of a net, and they caught each other should one of them fall. Parent to child, friend to friend. No one would put their arms out for me, so I had to do it for myself.

I took a coil of string and pinched the wood splinters together to hold them in place. The string wouldn't work to hold the reed together for long, but if I could just finish this piece . . .

When the knot seemed strong enough to me, I tried to push the weft up again. Carefully, breath captured in my lung, fingers barely touching the wood. But the splinters fell apart, the string looped loosely around them. This wasn't going to work.

I sank down on the bench and rested my arms on the windowsill. A child emerged from the building carrying a bucket. Another emerged and grabbed the rope handle to help hold up the other side. It wasn't so long ago that chores were my only worry, but now I had to survive. I let my tears dampen my sleeve. Each one was a tiny release of worry, and once they were out, I'd make a plan.

The gods were out of the question without a good enough gift, but there was someone else who was said to have some magic. The Bean-Nighe. She might drown me instead of granting my wish, or the cost might be so high I die anyway. But the smell of Gregory's breath came to my mind. Whatever happened, it was better than that.

# Chapter Five

That night, cool air bit into the bare skin at the back of my neck. The tangle of the birch trees on the outer side of our courtyard unfurled themselves into the inky black sky. I liked this time of silence. Even though Papa hadn't wanted me to go out at night, there was a safety in the shadows he'd never understood. The dark corners let girls hide from people like Gregory. I passed through the gloom like a ghost, casting my gaze back and forth, making sure there were no faces peering from windows, no heavy footsteps behind me. My neck relaxed and I rolled my head around on my shoulders. It was just me and the insects humming their night song.

A little wooden bridge ran over a trickle of stream, and I kept my footsteps light so they wouldn't echo. Trees and bushes drained of color stuck their clinging arms into the path and scratched at me, as if trying to hold me back. Did they know about the Bean-Nighe too? Did they understand she was a harbinger of death? Maybe her song whistled through their limbs and tickled their leaves. I'd never heard the Bean-Nighe sing myself, but others in the courtyard said they had. Now I hoped everything I'd ever heard about the Bean-Nighe was true.

The riverbank itself was my place. A space that helped me breathe. But I always made sure never to say anything out loud there so the Bean-Nighe wouldn't think I was calling to her.

I tried to imagine what it would be like if life wasn't so hard—the empty purse, Gregory chasing me in the streets, the broken loom. With the wish, I could make sure I was never, ever in this position again. The Bean-Nighe's magic could help me if I was willing to pay the price, and of course I was. I had no other way forward.

Earth moved beneath my boots, and I stumbled over the mud and raised roots of the riverbank. Water, its color robbed by the night, moved past me at a low surge, the grumble of it deep in my ears. I leaned down and dipped my fingers in, and they numbed in the space of a couple breaths. I wondered what it felt like to live beneath the surface and never be able to escape the cold.

*How do I do this? Just call her name?* That seemed far too easy, but it was worth a try. My heart hammered in my chest, louder even than the wind in my ears.

"Bean-Nighe?"

The wind carried my voice away, but no mysterious woman appeared on the banks. I shoved my whole fist into the water and grabbed a handful of stones. I needed to be closer to her, to draw her attention.

"Blast!"

My index finger throbbed where a little sharp-edged pebble had lodged itself. I picked it out and a bead of red welled. I dipped the finger back in the water to wash the blood away and let the cold numb the prick of pain.

The water turned around my finger, spinning in a dark pool. I yanked my hand away and cradled it against my chest, leaving spots of wetness on my dress. The river gurgled and spat and I fell back in the mud of the bank. The air loosened into mist and the tang of wet dirt mingled with the moisture. I scrambled back against the thick roots that wound through the dirt wall of the bank like giant white worms. At least they were solid, no wriggling, not like the mass of unease churning in my belly. The river always calmed me, but now, in the dark, it seemed like a black hole that would swallow me up. The mist drifted away, and suddenly I understood why most people only spoke about the Bean-Nighe in whispers.

There, on the other side of the water, a woman emerged from the mist, crouching on the bank. Her hair fell from her head like river weeds. Her skin glowed white in the little light the moon provided, and her eyes shone like the pebbles beneath the surface of the water. She held a shirt and scrubbed it against a large stone, but it wasn't as dirty as I'd thought it would be. How awful to forever clean a shirt that barely needed it. A useless task.

A humming rose from her throat, delicate and frayed as old cobwebs.

I'd never seen anything like her before. I couldn't even claim to have ever seen one of the gods' messenger sprites. And she was worse, far worse, than anything I could have conjured up in my imagination. Dead, but living. That's what it seemed like. A corpse brought to life when she should be in a box under the ground. I grabbed hold of a root and pulled myself to my feet. If she was somehow miraculously quick, I wouldn't be squatting in the mud when she came after me. The best thing to do now would be to pull myself up the side of the bank and run, run, run all the way home. But all that was at home was my broken loom. My only way to feed myself, my only way to *be* someone— a wreck of useless wood.

The lines of the Bean-Nighe shimmered in and out of focus. She blurred and sharpened as I stared at her, as if she was only half here in my world.

I shifted in the mud and her pale gray eyes gripped me with a stare.

The breeze carried her words across the river, drawn long and thin. *"What do you want?"*

I suspected, somehow, she knew already. My livelihood. That's what I wanted. What I needed. That's why I was here when my heart screamed at me to get away. But my words wouldn't reach her from here, not across the wide expanse of silver water and the drifting mist. Not even if I screamed.

I took one step forward. And then another. The water slipped around my toes as I stepped into the river. The hem of my dress grew heavy with water. Across the way, the corpse-woman watched me and crooked a finger, ushering me closer. Her knobbly knuckles reminded me of Mrs. Under's.

The cold shot into my legs like needles, but I couldn't stop. The only way to make it across the river was to dive in. I bent my knees and let the water pool around my shoulders. My dress clung to my limbs, but I struck out against the slow current that rippled across the river. The Bean-Nighe went back to her work, dipping the shirt in where the water met the mud at the shore.

As I got closer to the woman, her soft song twined around me, caressing my damp shoulders. I hauled myself out of the water at her feet and took in her patched gray dress and cracked fingernails. Deep lines engraved her face with sorrow, but her pale eyes, when she lifted them, weren't watery like Mrs. Under's—they were clear, hard, bright. Shivers pulsed through my body, making my teeth clack together. I drew a breath and tried to steady myself, find some shred of warmth inside so I could stop shaking. I wanted to face the Bean-Nighe as still as a stone statue—and as impenetrable as one too.

*"What do you want?"* she asked again. This time the words were clearer, but it was still like hearing something with my head dipped under the river's surface. Muffled and strained. Not like it should have been with her right in front of me. She opened her mouth again and the smell of damp earth, like graves dug in the rain, wafted out.

She'd addressed me twice now. There was no point in waiting. I already knew I was going to do this, had already decided before coming to the river. I wanted more, and *this* was a way for me to get it.

I held up a cold, stiff finger. "I want a wish."

Her grin spawned new wrinkles around her mouth. "Yes."

"Will you grant it?"

The Bean-Nighe cocked her head and rubbed the fabric she was washing against the stone at her feet. Red trickled down onto the damp shirt—her fingers rubbed raw and bleeding. There was a price to looking clean and good, and some people could afford for others to pay that price. Girls going blind from embroidering in dimly lit shops, spinners and weavers with cramped fingers that never uncurled. Washerwomen with bleeding hands that never healed.

The washerwoman's limp hair slapped her bare back and she swung it over her shoulder. Her dress was torn and raw—made from undyed wool. The leftovers. I wondered if she felt the cold as I did. My wet shift and skirt stiffening around my legs, my sleeves clinging to my arms. The night air sank its teeth into my skin, and I held my teeth clenched together to stop them chattering. When I opened my mouth to speak, my jaw popped, and I knew it would be sore tonight.

"I'm a weaver," I said. "My loom is broken . . . I want you to fix it."

I had no idea if this was in her power or not. The Bean-Nighe lived behind the veil with the gods and fae. What did she know of looms in my world? In fact, none of the stories I'd heard about the Bean-Nighe had given examples of wishes. None of the gods had ever answered my prayers either, so I didn't know what it looked like when they did. Mrs. Under said the gods answered prayers loosely, but I'd asked this washerwoman for something very specific.

The old woman didn't raise her head or acknowledge my wish in any way. She dipped her stained shirt in the river and let fingers of blood trail away from it in the current.

"Can you do that?" I asked, one violent shiver wracking my body and corrupting the solidity of my words before I could stop it.

*Could she do any of this, or am I stupid with hope in coming down here?*

My shivering was no longer just the cold. This creature's grave-earth breath stuck in my nose. Her dark mouth stretched open again and I couldn't see the back of her throat. There was a void inside her—was that why people heard her scream when their loved ones died? Did she open wide to swallow their souls?

I stumbled back into the water, my boots filling through the hole at my heel. Cold and fear numbed me. I rubbed my hands together, trying to feel them, trying to remind myself that I was still here, in the world, feet safely on this side of the veil.

The Bean-Nighe's tongue darted around two broken teeth. The old woman nodded and wrung out the shirt in her hands.

"I want something too."

The price. I was about to see if I could afford my wishes.

"What?"

The old woman grinned, and her wrinkles multiplied. "Just a little blood. The prick of a finger before you use your loom."

A drop of my blood? A drop wouldn't cost me anything, so how could it be enough?

"What will you do with it? My blood?"

The grin faded. "Blood is life, isn't it? I want you to give me something important, valuable."

It was a tribute, a gesture more than anything. I could live with that.

"All right."

The Bean-Nighe's eyes snapped up and she tilted her head to the left, her gaze roaming over my face. Her lips fell at the sides, almost into a frown.

*Now what?* The water continued to flow around my sodden boots. The air remained sharp and still around me. The Bean-Nighe slapped the shirt she'd been scrubbing on a rock.

I took a step closer. I wanted her to look at me again, tell me what would happen. Did this really work or was it all for nothing? Would she grant my wishes or swallow me up?

The old woman stretched one gnarled finger out toward me, closer, closer, until her yellow nail tapped my chest.

I fell. The Bean-Nighe didn't push me. I didn't trip. I just fell backward as if the river wrapped invisible arms around me and pulled me in close. My ears and nose filled with water, muffling everything. I opened my eyes to the velvet dark of the water around me. My hands clutched at a floating reed, anything to give me purchase. The river wasn't deep and the bottom couldn't have been far beneath me, but I couldn't stretch to push up against it. I hung suspended in the black of the river and wondered if this is what it felt like to be untethered from the earth. To float away into the darkness with no one to pull you back.

# Chapter Six

I struggled against the magic that held me. My muscles strained against invisible bonds, but the black water wrapped me like a shroud. I pressed my lips closed to avoid making the fatal mistake of trying to breathe.

The Bean-Nighe's song twined around me, lilting notes falling over my shoulders and twisting around my waist. I was beyond fear now. I couldn't even tell if my heart was still beating. Everything was stiff, frozen. *Was she singing for my death? Was I already gone?*

The river water stung my eyes, so I closed them. At least I could do that, shut away this horror. I prayed to any god who would listen to let this be a dream. Let me wake in my bed with that profound relief of those whose nightmares stay blurred at the edges. This was much too sharp, too painful.

My lungs burned. I wouldn't last much longer. I'd have to pull in a breath, but it would only be water and it would fill up my body until I sank to the bottom.

*Please, please let me go. I'm not done yet.*

I had plans. The tiny room in a leaning building wasn't my final landing place. I wouldn't die the poor girl with the broken loom. I'd have a shop. People from all over the city would come to see my fabrics. The gilt from my woven cloth of gold would shine on me, dazzling the world.

The Bean-Nighe's song drifted away with the current. This was it. She'd left me to die—but I wouldn't do it. I wouldn't fade away. I focused on the ball of heat in my belly, my anger and fear all mixed and tangled together like unspooled silk. The heat sped through my veins. I saw it all in my mind—the white-hot determination shooting through my body down to my fingertips and toes. I begged my muscles to move.

One fingertip flinched. I could do this. My big toe on my left foot wiggled in my boot. With every tiny scrap of strength left in me, I pushed my legs down and moved through the water, hitting the bottom of the river with my feet and springing back toward the surface. My first breath ached—my lungs shocked and angry at what they'd just been through. I moved my arms around, keeping my head above the surface, and spun myself in the direction of the shore. The old washerwoman was gone, but she'd left behind the pink-tinged shirt on the scrubbing rock.

I struck out toward it, my numb limbs fighting with the water to get to shore. The shirt was as real as I was, rough and wet in my hands. I pulled myself up to standing and balled the shirt up. I wanted proof of what had happened, even if the linen would mean something only to me. Even if she'd just trapped me in the river instead of granting my wishes, I'd come here. I'd done *something*, even though it was scary.

Now I could go home and prepare to face Gregory. I knew I had it in me, could fill my veins with metal if I wanted to. He'd try to make me quake, but I'd stand like a stone before him and tell him he had to wait for my money. I'd show him the half-finished purple silk and ask him to imagine just how many coins that would fetch, and then I'd trade my skills for those of someone who could fix my loom. It wasn't unheard of—sometimes craftspeople would do that. I just had to make a very good case for myself. I couldn't promise anyone a silk bolt for their expertise—the supplies were just too expensive. But I might be able to weave them something with wool-ends.

My jaw ached with the effort of holding my teeth together, and the linen shirt grew stiff under my arm. Fall didn't care how much you trembled—it would blow as cold as it wanted. Well, so would I. I'd do what I wanted, what I *needed*, to get by.

The darkened shapes around me changed from the grabbing limbs of trees to the worn lines of the buildings on the edge of town. Under my feet, the wooden bridge groaned and the smell of sewage chased away the clean, icy scent of the air near the river. A dog barked in the distance. A child cried. I nearly slipped on the cobbles where someone had emptied their chamber pot. The city sharpened as the mist fell away, and reality set in. *What had just happened? Had she been real?*

I squeezed the wet shirt in my hands and water dripped onto the cobbles. The Bean-Nighe *had* been real. She hadn't granted my wish, but she'd been there on the bank. And if she didn't give me anything, there was no reason for her to take anything from me either, right? I nodded to myself. That made sense. There might have been a price to the wish if she'd granted it, but now I was free. Everything would be all right and I could just move forward with a plan.

I shivered all the way home from my wet clothes and the crisp night. The birches flanking the courtyard cast it in shadow, and my building rose up, the dark wood beams crisscrossing the lighter plaster. My legs didn't want to climb the stairs, but I made them. The door to my flat always swelled and stuck when there was moisture in the air, so I yanked at it and hoped Mrs. Under wouldn't hear. I really didn't want to explain to the woman why I was soaking wet and coming home after dark. She'd ask questions I was too tired to answer.

As soon as I was inside, I stripped my wet clothes off and let them fall to the floor. My skin ached with cold. I'd have to use the peat in the scuttle whether I wanted to or not or I'd get sick.

I took three steps toward the scuttle when something shiny caught my eye. The purple fabric woven with green flowers. It was finished and hung over my bench in a lilac waterfall. The petals of the roses winked in the moonlight with tiny sequins. I hadn't finished the piece, and I definitely hadn't added expensive and time-consuming sequins. They were rough under my fingertips.

A familiar smell niggled at my nose and I bent to sniff the fabric. Rich, wet earth. The Bean-Nighe.

My naked body trembled. She'd been here somehow. Did that mean . . . ?

I raked my eyes over my loom. It was whole. No splintered wood or loose threads. The loom shone like I'd just rubbed beeswax into the frame.

*It worked.*

Gods' fangs, it worked! The Bean-Nighe granted me my wish! My loom was fixed.

I spun around with the purple silk in a little dance, toes catching on the uneven floorboards. But I didn't even care. I had a chance again now. My plan could work.

And so what if the fabric smelled a little of the temple yard? No one would really notice. I mean, maybe a little, but they'd be distracted by the sparkling roses if I showed them in the right light. Odina loved glittering things, and I was certain she'd be drawn to this. I'd never brought her something so beautiful before.

My fingers burned with excitement. I had to move them, create something with them. I pulled on a shift so I'd stop shaking and went to inspect my basket. A spool of dark blue wool sat ready, and I loaded it into the loom. The shuttle fit in my hand exactly, smoothed down where the skin between my index finger and thumb stretched over it. Perfectly suited to me. I threaded it through the first line, over and under, over and under and . . .

I dropped the beat. My hand stopped moving. I searched through my mind for the next bit, the next thing my body should have known how to do by heart, but I couldn't find it. I couldn't remember how to weave.

My skin prickled and my limbs shook. Fear skittered down my back. I couldn't weave. That was all I was, all I had, and I couldn't make it work. Was this what the old washerwoman had taken from me in exchange for the loom? My skill?

It was horribly twisted. Why give me my loom back and leave me without proficiency to use it? I was more condemned to poverty than I'd been with a broken loom. At least I'd always held the majority of my worth in my fingers—skills that could be turned into profit. Now I had a great wooden machine and no way to use it.

She'd been smart, the Bean-Nighe. *This* was the way to hurt me, if that was what she wanted. Not almost drowning me in the river. No, that was nothing compared to this.

I sat riveted to my stool and stared out the warped panes on the window. The moon pressed down on the city, hanging low in the sky. Its light made the green roses in my lap sparkle. What a teasing way to crush me—giving me the most beautiful bolt I'd ever seen and the loom that made it, only to make sure I'd never create something so lovely myself.

Tears collected on the rims of my eyes and blurred the purple silk and the loom and the already wavy window panes. I wiped the back of my hand across my eyes. The moonlight struck one arm of the loom, winking on some piece of metal.

I bent to examine it. A perfectly pointed tip like a well-made sewing needle attached to the arm with an intricately carved holder. Flowers crawled up the stem toward the needle, their wooden petals deceptively soft.

The drop of blood. I'd forgotten to give the loom my blood.

I stretched my finger toward it, letting the needle press into me until there was a tiny pinch and my skin gave way.

# Chapter Seven

Blood welled bright red, but I didn't suck it away like I normally would when I poked myself with an errant needle. I stared at it while the tip of my finger stung. My mind cleared as easily as the sun burns away the night's mist. I knew how to weave again.

The steps laid themselves out behind my eyes: pick up the shuttle, thread the silk in and out, pull tight, shuttle the thread back across. Relief swelled in my belly, up, up till my lips pulled into a smile. I was all right. Everything was going to be all right. I could still weave and sell my creations. The long silver needle hadn't been part of my loom before, so the Bean-Nighe had to have put it there. Red tinted the sharp point of it. I'd given my blood and I'd gotten back my skill.

This was the price of the wish, and it wasn't so bad. A tiny drop of my blood for a working loom? The cost was much less than what I would have paid a craftsperson. A giggle bubbled up in my throat. It had all been worth it. The washerwoman and her song, the river rushing up around me. I'd gotten through all of it and now I had my loom and future back.

I stood and let the purple silk slide off my lap. My legs screamed, the muscles as sore as if I'd walked through town all day. My hands hurt too, sore with the pulling of threads and guiding of the shuttle. Even though everything had worked how I wanted it to, a lot had happened since I'd stepped out of bed that morning. Suddenly, I ached to wrap myself in my quilt and close my eyes on the world.

⌒ℰ◯

A knock on the door tapped its way into my half-formed dreams. I rolled over and slipped my foot out of the quilt to feel the coolness on my toes. I wasn't ready to get up yet, and it was probably Mrs. Under looking for a bit of chatter. After last night, I wasn't sure I had enough energy to string together even the tiniest bit of gossip.

Another rap on the door. Louder this time—too loud, in fact, for Mrs. Under's swollen knuckles.

I slid out of the quilt and padded across my room in my bare feet. The cold lapped at my toes and nipped at my ears. Had I ever really warmed up during the night? Whatever heat I'd stoked had drained from me now.

I peered through the eye-level gap in my door to see who was bothering me so early in the morning.

There was no one there.

I pulled open the door to see if I could catch the tail of them running down the stairs. Gregory wouldn't have run away, so it couldn't be him.

"Hey!"

I almost tripped over the packages at my feet, bundles wrapped in dull brown cloth piled up just outside my door. There must have been some mistake—I didn't buy anything. In fact, no one here could afford so many packages of anything at once.

A scarlet thread trailed from the top of the brown cloth, bright against the thick weave of the bag. I touched the silk, fine between my fingertips. I caught the whiff of damp earth. Had the Bean-Nighe given me something extra? She'd provided me with supplies as well as fixed my loom. My stomach contracted with hunger and worry. What would the price for this be?

It would be best to leave it all here, not to use it. That would be the smart thing to do. But as I gazed at all the supplies I'd have to be in debt forever to buy, I couldn't help myself. The Bean-Nighe only wanted a little blood, a prick of my finger when I used the loom. That wasn't such a high price. It didn't hurt very much. Perhaps that payment covered these supplies as well. I'd never find out if I didn't bring them in off the landing.

I hauled the sacks inside and shut the door quietly behind me. It was like getting presents on a birthday, and we'd never had money for that kind of thing. I wanted to extend the moment, delay the actual unveiling of whatever was inside. The bags were heavy, full to their twine-tied tops. I pulled them all up onto my bed and untied them one by one, letting the contents spill out.

It looked like I'd dropped a chieftain's ransom onto my threadbare quilt. Everything sparkled—spools of silk the colors of berries and strings of sequins glittering like gold. This was more than I'd ever be able to afford, more than anyone would sell me on advance. Ideas sprung to mind, visions of the beautiful designs, what colors to combine, the edgings and bright middles of flowers catching the sun. I could do waves crashing across the full length of a bolt. There could be jewels woven into the fabric, adorning my clients with all the glitter they could want.

I'd make bolts so special, so unique, everyone would want them. They'd whisper my name in the streets, wondering how to get my next design. I'd dress the Players, even, and they'd tell the Chieftain and his court how much they loved my wares and the nobles—royalty—would come buy from me. Papa's soul might see, from wherever it was, that I'd accomplished something great.

The Bean-Nighe had given me the silk, the fine wool, the sequins I needed to make it happen. I buried my face in the spool of raspberry silk. Yes, it had the same hint of wet dirt as the bolt of purple with the green flowers, but it didn't make me tremble anymore. Now it wasn't the smell of graves but the scent of fresh turned earth—ripe with possibilities.

I had everything I needed to sew my own success. I folded the purple silk and tied it off with a yellow ribbon. Odina would eat it up. I wanted to go to her with something else too, though—so she had options. I'd never been able to give anyone options like a real shop in the marketplace. She might buy both, or she might keep the purple and call her friend over right that very moment to buy the other bolt.

The raspberry silk would be perfect. It shimmered like a berry dipped in sugar. I loaded the spool onto the loom and held out one finger to the needle. This time I used my pinky, since that finger was probably the least useful in weaving. The needle pierced my skin and I held it there for a moment, letting the drop of blood well around the metal point, feeding the loom.

Beginning a new project sparked a fire in my belly. I always dreamed of what it would look like by the end, and that's what kept me going when my back and fingers grew sore. I never abandoned a pattern I'd started because I just *had* to see how it turned out.

This time I sent the shuttle through the threads faster than I ever had before. I didn't know if it was excitement or part of the Bean-Nighe's gift, but I didn't grow hungry or droop on the stool. I wove as the light from the window traveled across the floorboards, showing the spots of dirt and dust. It wasn't until the door opened with a squeak that I paused.

"What's this?" Mrs. Under said as she stepped into the room. "Where did you get all that, girl?"

I swung my legs over the stool and stood, but I had to bend over and catch myself because my knees were weak. There was something in my belly too, an emptiness that flowed into the rest of my body, making me quake. Black blots spread through my vision. I needed to eat.

"Ella!"

Mrs. Under grabbed my arm and helped me sit on the floor. "What have you done?"

I stared at her while the inky spots cleared from my vision. Her pale eyes shimmered with age. She didn't know all that I'd done, that I had more in front of me than I'd ever had before.

"I've bought my future."

## Chapter Eight

Mrs. Under grabbed me under the arms and hauled me up onto the bed with surprising strength for someone with such a frail body. She probably felt the wetness under my arms and on the back of my dress.

"I'm fine," I said and she let go of me.

"You look like you've been awake for days."

"I haven't . . . I just haven't slept well."

Mrs. Under's gaze slid over to the loom and the finished silk. The richness of its color stood out against the pale, old wood of my machine.

"You were finishing that?"

I nodded my head—a mistake I paid for with a deep throbbing behind my left ear. "I did the whole bolt last night. I just had to keep going and going and going."

Mrs. Under screwed up her mouth. "You can't weave a bolt in a day."

She was right; it was quick. The speed, the insatiable need to finish, must be part of the Bean-Nighe's magic.

"Well, I did somehow. But I'm certainly tired now. I think I'll sleep for a while."

"What about all the supplies? Did you buy them on credit? Getting so much at once . . . your father wouldn't have approved."

No, he wouldn't have. But he never got to see any of his dreams come true.

"Don't worry about my supplies, Mrs. Under. I know what I'm doing."

"Do you?"

When I didn't respond, the old woman nodded and drifted toward the loom. She laid a single bony finger on the silk and made a noise in her throat. Then she left, and I could finally crawl under my blanket and rest.

⁂

Presentation was important. Papa used to make me repeat it as I tied ribbons around the carefully folded bolts of his finest fabrics. He always scrubbed us both up before he delivered to a client. Soap and water from the ewer. A loose cravat falling over his shirt, a scrap of ribbon in my hair. I heard his voice in my ears as I picked away the river mud from under my fingernails and scrubbed a tiny sliver of soap into my hands. I washed my face first, then poured water over my head and into the bowl and scrubbed the remaining soap into my hair. With the lather from my hair, I washed down my body.

Drops of water splattered on the bare floorboards. Since I'd used peat last night, I didn't want to waste some for this bath. I shivered and stared at the cool, dead grate. Once I sold all these bolts, I'd never have to pick and choose when to use peat again. I could maybe even buy coal.

It took great effort to get up the courage to douse my head again, but I had to do it to get the suds out. Chilly water spilled over me and pooled in my ears. Thankfully, I'd had the foresight to set out a wrapping sheet before I started.

I owned exactly one presentable dress. Its light yellow wool was still bright and the sleeves were slashed with cream. No patterns or anything—that would have been a waste of time on my own cloth—but it was pretty enough and the colors made my red hair look even brighter in my hammered copper mirror. For luck, I slipped the purple paste gem the Player had given me all those years ago from the little clay bowl on the hearth where I kept it. I stitched it to the front my dress, just below the neckline. The purple shone against the yellow, bright and unexpected.

Unlike me, the silks barely needed presentation. I tied a yellow ribbon from one of the spools the Bean-Nighe had given me around the purple silk and chose a broad cream one for the raspberry. If I had to guess, I suspected Odina would want the purple most—because it was the color of the Players—but I knew the raspberry silk would appeal to her desire to stand out among the other merchants' daughters. I'd never seen a color quite like it before. I could ask much more for it than for my usual bolts.

I wrapped both bolts in the unbleached linen I used for deliveries and propped them up under my arms. The street came to life as I climbed the hill toward the marketplace. Merchants were setting up and performing the tasks they didn't want their customers to see. Farmers picked through yesterday's vegetables and tossed the molding ones into baskets for the pigs. Fishermen sliced through armored bellies to let the pink guts spill into buckets. A spice seller sniffed at his wares and pulled the most pungent to the front to attract passersby.

Papa had always admired the merchants. He'd said it was the next step for us. A stall and then a shop. You'd really made it if you had a shop of your own—a second roof over your head just for your creations. A place where people came to *you* because they wanted what you could provide. He'd never gotten there. Papa had never even had a stall along this street. You needed a boon to get there, something to help ease the strain of rent and food so you could afford enough supplies to get ahead, to make enough bolts for customers to browse through.

Instead, he said we were private weavers and that the finest clients would want us to come to them anyway. I nodded and smiled and did everything he needed me to, but I always knew it wasn't the whole truth. Yes, clients with real money liked to have things brought to them, but they also liked to spend their coin in shops where they could be surrounded by beautiful things and beautiful friends. I always felt like a servant coming to clients' houses, sneaking around to the kitchen door, trying not to be seen. In a shop, I could have held court like some fae queen.

I knocked at the kitchen door.

Odina's housekeeper opened the door and stared at me with her one good eye and tilted her chin toward the packages under my arm. "You're back again? What're those?"

I gave her a tight, tiny smile. "They're for Miss Odina. She asked me to bring her something pretty. Well, I have."

The cook made a noise in her throat and shook her head.

"If you say so. Hattie! Bring the weaver through to the parlor and call down Miss Odina."

Hattie, the maid, sat back on her heels. She'd been stoking the fire.

"She already has a guest."

"The weaver's not a *guest*, silly girl. Now get on with it," the cook said.

The maid shrugged and got to her feet. She wiped at her skirt. "Come on through, then."

I followed her as I'd done many times before, but I couldn't stop myself biting at the inside of my cheek. This was more important than all those other times. I wanted to sell the fabrics, yes, but I wanted something else too. An invitation.

"The weaver's here to see you, Miss," Hattie said by way of announcement at the door to the parlor.

Odina looked back over her shoulder and her eyebrows rose. "But I didn't call for you."

Hattie looked from Odina to me and opened and closed her mouth. I'd put her in a difficult situation, and I hoped she wouldn't get in trouble for it later.

I smiled and looked down at my shoes to show I wasn't trying to overstep. Too much.

"You didn't call for me, Miss Odina, but I have something I simply *must* show you."

She bent her head toward me and her dark hair slipped over her silk-clad shoulder. Watered blue. Pretty enough but not one of mine.

"I didn't want anyone else to have them before I gave you the chance."

This seemed to pique her curiosity just as I hoped it would. She stood from her chair and closed the space between us in two long steps. Yellow silk shoes peeped out from under her hem.

"Well, let's just lay them out on the tea table here," Odina said as she pulled one of the packages from my arms. It was the purple silk. Perfect.

She unwrapped the linen with reverence. The purple looked even richer in the soft yellow light of the big windows afforded by the parlor. The sequins in the green flowers caught the candle-light and glimmered. Odina gasped and buried her fingertips in the silk.

"This is, just . . . it's utterly perfect. This is exactly what I need for the party. Oh, Ella. You're incredible!"

I devoured her praise, ate it up, drank it in like cool, fresh water. It wasn't something I particularly liked about myself, but I couldn't deny it. I wanted Odina to like my work. To see me as someone special.

"Look, Callum!" she said, throwing her words behind her to a young man in a shadowed chair. "Isn't it perfect!"

He stretched his legs out in front of him and sighed as if Odina was asking him for an awful lot of work just to look at some fabric. I disliked him instantly. He was one of *those* people who didn't care about clothes or beauty. His own suit was sharply cut but plain, and his necktie needed a good bleaching.

"Well yes, it's purple," he said.

Odina tapped him lightly on the shoulder.

"Purple. *Really?* Callum, have you ever seen purple with this depth to it? And the intricacy of the flower pattern. Just look at it!"

Callum bent closer to the bolt and his hair fell forward to hide the side of his face. When he looked up again, his dark eyes found mine and something zipped between us. A niggle squirmed in my belly, and I almost thought I recognized him from somewhere . . . But no—it wasn't that. His face was just unsettling. Too pale, white, and sharp. I didn't like it. Was he challenging me? Was he going to say something to make Odina not want the purple silk?

He stared at me but I refused to drop my gaze. I'd risked a lot to get here, and I wasn't going to let some bored rich boy get in the way. *Stare all you like, Callum. I'm not going anywhere.*

"It's exquisite," he finally said.

"Oh, yes . . . yes, thank you."

I wasn't expecting that. He'd looked ready to throw me out of Odina's parlor, not compliment my work.

"And what's that one?" Odina took the second package from my arms and untied the twine around the linen. "Gods' fangs!"

"Odina!" But a little smile played at the corner of Callum's lips as he said it. He wasn't really reprehending Odina for her language—he thought it was funny.

"Well, I'm sorry but look! Have you ever seen silk this color before? And see how the pattern makes it shine?" She ran a hand reverently along the silk and then turned to me. "I want it all."

This was the tricky part. Odina had told me she didn't have any dress allowance left. If she had been lying to get me to accept that leaf necklace, that was completely awful of her, but at least she'd have money for these bolts. If she'd been telling the truth, she wouldn't have the money I needed to pay Gregory. I had a plan for that though—bargain with her for the purple bolt and convince her to show a friend the raspberry silk. Then I'd sell that to her friend.

I waited silently for a beat while Odina glanced at Callum, and he rolled his eyes.

"Fine, Odina. You know I'm a great supporter of artists."

*Artists.* He thought of me as an artist. Perhaps I'd judged him too harshly at first.

Odina smiled and her tongue darted out between her teeth. I wondered how she'd repay Callum—if it was the same kind of payment Gregory wanted from me. The thought sent a shiver up my spine.

"Thank you, Callum. It'll be worth it," Odina said.

Callum flicked his gaze toward me again, deep brown hair falling in his eyes. Something flashed there, a glimmer of mischief. Like a little boy about to run through a puddle his mother already told him to avoid. Something was going on here. He was playing a game.

"How much, Ella?"

I liked how his tongue caressed the *a* at the end of my name.

"Fifty silvers each . . . and there's something else."

"Oh?" he asked. Odina hung on his arm and gave me a smile. I wondered if I was about to wipe that smile from her face with my request. I balled my clammy hands into fists to avoid clutching the soft wool of my skirt. This was not a moment for weakness. Callum considered me an artist. I could do this.

"Those bolts will cost you fifty silvers each and an invitation to that party."

# Chapter Nine

Odina smiled but showed too much teeth for it to be real. "The party? What do you mean?"

I'd wondered if she was going to do this—try to make me seem silly for wanting to go. The party she was going to would be filled with potential clients. Odina had been my only steady, wealthy client for years, and I only met her because Mrs. Under introduced us. I needed more than one good client. If I could have more than one Player buying my silks, I'd be ten steps closer to getting my own shop.

"I've never been to a party like that, and I want to go."

She faltered, lips pinching together and eyes sparking with what looked like fury. Callum slipped his long fingers over her shoulder and squeezed.

"Stand down, Odina."

She twisted her neck to look at him. "What?"

"I think she should come."

Odina stepped out of Callum's grip and crossed her arms over her chest. "She wouldn't fit in."

I stared at her and bit the inside of my cheek. She was protecting her precious group of friends from the likes of me—happy to use me for my skill but unwilling to let me be anything more than that.

"I have something you want, don't I, Odina?"

She gaped at me, surprised, maybe, that I'd speak to her like that.

"There are other weavers in the city, Ella. Don't fool yourself into thinking you're that special."

Callum shifted toward the raspberry silk and ran the edge of the fabric through his fingers. "Oh, but she is. I can feel it in the silk. You'll glow when you wear this, Odina. What's the price of a party invitation, after all?"

Pink circles bloomed in Odina's cheeks, and her arms untwined a little. "You think so, Callum? Really?"

He shrugged and swept his dark bangs out of his eyes. "Yes."

His eyes were on Odina as he said it, but a little inflection in his tone made me suspect he meant the words for me too.

"So it's settled then? One hundred silver pieces and an invitation," I said. "I'll take the silver now."

Odina tapped a fingertip to her lips before opening a drawer in the carved side table beside her. She pulled out a velvet purse and loosened the string. So she wasn't going to make Callum pay after all and she'd been lying about the dress allowance. She'd made me take that necklace for my work even though she must have known it wouldn't have even bought me my dinner. And I'd let her do it. I'd let her do it because I couldn't risk the future work she might bring me. She had me dangling on a string like a fine-pointed needle.

But she was about to find out how sharp I could be.

I held open my palm and tried to ignore the sheen of sweat on my skin. So what if Odina knew I'd been nervous? That hadn't stopped me from getting what I wanted.

"Here," she said and set the bag of coins in my hand.

I tucked it away in my pocket. "And the party?"

Odina rolled her eyes but reached into the side table drawer again. Callum grinned—a flash of white teeth—and watched as Odina set a silver-edged invitation in my hand. The paper was thicker than any I'd ever held before. I pinched it between my finger and thumb, feeling the weight of it, the smoothness of it between my fingers. It was real. I had an invitation to a party in a big house.

"What will you wear to the party, Ella?" Callum asked.

His question caught me by surprise, and I instinctively pulled at my skirt with my left hand. This was the nicest dress I owned, so I'd have to wear it. I'd be able to dress it up a little, maybe, but I wouldn't have an impressive gown like Odina.

"I've not chosen yet," I told Callum and prayed my cheeks wouldn't burn red.

"You should wear blue," he said. "It would suit you."

"Blue?"

"Yes, a gray-blue, like the river at midday," he said and sank again into the armchair. He swung his legs over the side of it as if he was in his own house without any company to see.

*The river? Why would he say that?* I thought of the cold, black water rushing over my face. My throat tightened and burned, just like it had when I'd been holding my breath, waiting for the Bean-Nighe to release me. My eyes watered. *Was this really just a memory or was this happening right now? Was the cursed washer-woman reaching me here somehow?*

"Ella?"

Odina touched my arm. She must have been able to see it on my face—panic and fear. Still, I was surprised she even cared after what she'd said about me. I shook the image of the rolling water from my mind and opened my lips to suck in a breath. It was thick with the scent of the potpourri sitting on the side table and by the window frame.

Callum righted himself in the armchair and leaned over to pick up a polished stone from the table. He tossed it back and forth from hand to hand. There was something too casual about this movement—almost like a studied ease. He either hadn't noticed my reaction to his suggestion or he wanted me to think he hadn't. And Callum didn't seem like someone oblivious to what was happening right in front of him.

Perhaps he was taunting me. Maybe this was a game for him—something amusing to pass his many hours of free time. But he didn't realize I wasn't just a piece on the board; I was playing too.

"I'll see you both at the party," I said, meeting Callum's chestnut gaze. "I'll be the one in blue."

# Chapter Ten

I happily replaced the weight of the fabric bolts under my arm with the weight of coins in my pocket on the walk back through town. I loved the dull thud of the bag against my leg as I made my way through the busy streets. I could pay Gregory off, slip the shackle of debt from around my wrists. I pictured it, anticipated it, the first few delicious steps as I left Gregory's with my pockets a little emptier and my heart so much lighter.

A blacksmith's bellows huffed and puffed nearby, and a cow brayed for milking. I gave the sloped drain on the side of the cobbles a wide berth—there were too many unidentifiable bits floating in the sludgy, brown water.

Gregory was right at home on this street, with sourness hanging in the air like perfume. I rapped on the door with my knuckles and opened it. His wife looked up from a little table crammed into the back corner of the room. She couldn't have been much older than me. Her hair was free of gray and her face unlined. She had all her teeth as far as I could tell when she shot a trembling smile at me. The girl hadn't been married to Gregory long, and perhaps that was why her eyes still shone with a spark of health. I was sure she wouldn't be able to hold on to it. How could she in this dark room with this kind of man for a husband?

"Am I really seeing this?" Gregory stopped flipping beads on his abacus and stood from the little table in the corner. "Ella the Weaver? In my own shop?"

*Shop* was a pretty generous word for the front room of a tiny flat sharing a side street with blacksmiths and cow stables. He worked out of his front room and lived up a flight of narrow stairs. I was a bit surprised he'd never asked me for a nice bolt instead as part of my repayment, but maybe he didn't care whether his curtains were nice to look at or not.

Saying any of that right now wouldn't help my cause. I finally had the upper hand with Gregory. He couldn't argue with silver. I'd pay him back and be done with him, and I could go home without looking over my shoulder.

"I have something for you," I said.

He pushed his chair aside and came around the table. His eyes narrowed when I pulled the coin bag from my pocket.

"Is this a trick?"

So he saw me as a slippery fish, huh? I saw him as a river eel, so we were more than even.

"It's just coin. I'm here to repay my debt."

I grinned at him and it felt good to be the one with the words this time. I didn't have to just stand there and listen to what he decided about my future or let him bury his threats deep in my flesh. The money gave me something I very rarely had: power. A say.

Gregory stretched out his hand and it was larger than even I'd thought it would be. I counted out forty silver coins, and Gregory mouthed the numbers along with me. The weight that had lived so long in the pit of my stomach loosened.

"That covers my debt," I said.

I'd hidden the other sixty coins in my boot. He wasn't going to get more than he was owed, and I didn't want to go back to having nothing to my name.

Gregory chuckled, showing his brown teeth, and leaned against the bare wood boards of the wall. "This covers the principal. You still owe me the interest."

His wife stared at both of us from her seat, head turned toward her husband then me. My mouth fell open in a mirror of hers, but I quickly gritted my teeth and composed myself.

"What interest?"

"You didn't think I'd charge you interest on your little loan? You're late, Ella. I can't wait forever to be paid back. Not how business works, you know. I try to be kind, but the kindest thing is to treat you like any other customer so you can learn your place in the world. Someone has to teach you since your father can't."

Rage bloomed in my heart. This slimy ball of a man was cheating me. It wouldn't have mattered how many coins I brought him—he was always intending to snare me with interest.

"How much?"

Gregory splayed his hands and shrugged. I glanced toward his abacus and the ledger where he recorded debts with spiky numbers written across the page.

"I'll have to calculate."

He was playing with me. I glanced over at his wife, but she kept her head resolutely bent over her own figures.

I needed to get Gregory to give me a number, a solid number

he couldn't back out of later. If I didn't, he'd just keep adding to it as he "calculated" interest and I'd never be free of him.

"Tell me how much, Gregory. How else am I supposed to pay it?"

"You don't have any more money right now anyway, right? I'll have it calculated by the next time I see you."

He wanted me to writhe in his trap, tangle myself up in the little bit of string he gave me. I didn't want any string or any more time to pay him back. I wanted to be done with all of this right now. I didn't want to see Gregory again ever.

"There doesn't need to be a next time," I said. "Just tell me how much I owe you now and we'll be done with it."

Gregory's eyes slid from my face down over my chest and belly. I nearly tried to fold in on myself to keep him from looking, but I held my body still. He wouldn't see me wither in front of him.

"What? Do you have some extra coin stuffed down your bodice?"

Of course they weren't in my bodice—my breasts weren't big enough to stop the coins from falling through. My boot was a much more secure hiding place. I almost told him that, the words hot on the end of my tongue. I wanted to throw them at him. That I *did* have more. That not everything belonged to him. But I couldn't.

There weren't enough pieces of silver in the city to satiate Gregory's appetite. I'd given up those first forty for no reason at all. He'd still want more later.

His wife stopped writing in her ledger and sprinkled sand from a little pot over the inky paper. My gaze flicked over her. Her scalp was visible through her hair. She didn't look particularly happy.

He held us both in his palm. All he had to do was squeeze.

"How much do you think I owe?" I said.

Gregory smiled and my stomach squirmed. "Five hundred silvers."

An impossible amount. He might as well have said a thousand for the likelihood he'd ever get it from me.

"You know that's not a fair sum," I said, backing toward the door. I needed out of this small, close room.

"Who decides what's fair?" Gregory said.

I was going to a party with more potential clients than Gregory could even imagine. I'd have more orders and profits than I'd know what to do with soon. Even with them all, five hundred silvers still seemed unreachable. But maybe it wasn't. Surely Callum had seen that much money in his life. Odina too. If I thought bigger, maybe I could get to a place where Gregory wouldn't be a problem anymore.

"I don't have any coin in my bodice, as you say, but I do have an opportunity."

But Gregory laughed, and even his wife's lips quirked up in a half-hidden smile.

"Oh yeah? Gods' fangs, girl. I can't wait to see what that is . . . and I will. Soon. I won't wait long for my money, eh?"

My words slid off him like raindrops off an oiled coat. He didn't take me seriously or think he had any reason to be nervous. He still thought he had me exactly where he wanted me.

He didn't know I was about to slip through his fingers like my own best silk.

# Chapter Eleven

I'd stared at the spools of blue wool for three days before deciding not to waste it on a dress for myself. It was too valuable. Instead, I took a wide ribbon and tied it around the bodice of my yellow dress. It wasn't exactly wearing blue like the river as Callum had suggested, but it was enough to make a point.

The address on the invitation brought me all the way to the other side of town. It's the furthest I'd walked in a long time, and the muscles in my calves ached before I even reached halfway. As I got closer, carriages with gold crests stamped on their sides rolled by me, so I knew I was going the right way. I had to step into the gutter to avoid being run down by one of them, and I wiped my boot in the grass in front of the large, lit house. The hem of my dress was sodden, but there was nothing I could do about that now. I hoped it didn't stink. My arms tingled with goosebumps, and not just because of the cold. The house was the biggest I'd ever been this close to.

Someone had set candles all along the gravel drive leading up toward the house. They flickered in the breeze, waving in welcome. The wings of the house stretched out like arms, while the main building grinned down at me with yellow candlelight glowing through the windows running all along the bottom level and just two windows on the upper level—matching eyes. I wondered if the owner had done that on purpose, to make their guests feel a little trill of disquiet before stepping inside. Set them off-balance. I tried to shake off the small quake at the pit of my stomach, but I couldn't quite do it.

A man with a wolf mask guarded the door. I marveled at the intricacy of it as I climbed the stone steps to the entrance. It had real wolf hair woven into the linen, I was sure. Beneath the mask was a well-tied cravat and an embroidered silk suit entirely at odds with the wildness of the wolf. The man's dark eyes followed my movements. He reached out a hand and held it up, palm flat.

"What?" I asked.

He didn't speak. Another carriage crawled to a stop behind me, and more revelers stepped onto the gravel with their fine silk-heeled shoes. The wolf-man whistled, and I brought my attention back to his open hand. The invitation. Right.

I almost didn't want to give it up. The paper was so different from the thin sheets Papa had sometimes used to write letters to his sister in the mountains. The gilded edging added excitement too, like the party promised more of that kind of luxury—more beautiful things to look at and consume. But this was the party itself, right in front of me, and I wasn't just here for fun. I had work to do.

"Here you go." I dropped the invitation into the man's hand. He bowed and his silk waistcoat strained against the muscles of his back. What was his job beyond guarding the door for uninvited guests? I imagined he'd be quite good at getting rid of anyone his boss didn't want inside.

Stepping into the house was like walking into a waking dream. Odina's parlor was nothing compared to this. Wealth dripped from the ceiling in the form of cut crystal and glass chandeliers. Two staircases curved up and around and framed gilded double doors. I'd never seen so many candles in my life, and they were all lit. They'd burn down to nothing tonight and need to be replaced. The extravagance of it made me feel nauseous even though it wasn't me who'd be paying for them—I'd spent too many years with Papa insisting every bit of natural light be gone from our room before lighting a single tallow taper.

These candles smelled like lavender. They must have infused the wax somehow. Rich people could pay for things to smell good.

The double doors swung open and revealed a room filled with people, all a jumble of deep colors that almost rivaled the horde of silk spools the Bean-Nighe had given me. People in dresses with long trains tooled with gold thread. Others in suits of blue and green and yellow. Everyone bright. Everyone burning with laughter and a kind of glee I could only try to understand. Problems ceased to exist once you entered the ballroom—or so the host would have you think.

I slipped into the room and clung to the fringes of the crowd. A long buffet table skirted the back wall and I approached it just to give myself a direction, something to do with my feet. No one had noticed my entry, but their cut-glass laughter was too sharp for my ears—even if they weren't laughing about me. Their swirling dances overwhelmed me, and my palms grew damp before I even made it to the buffet.

Little bits of food sat perfectly arranged on silver trays. Tiny triangles of cheese and puffs of pastry. A bowl made of sweet bread held toasted nuts. Dandelion leaves adorned a silver-scaled sturgeon, and I wondered if it had been caught in our river. I was used to a hollow feeling in my stomach; I couldn't remember the last time I'd been uncomfortably full. Before coming here, I'd eaten two dry oatcakes. Now my mouth watered at the selection of foods I'd hardly ever seen before.

I took a walnut and placed it gently on my tongue, letting my lips fold around it. I wanted to savor it and give the flavor time to sink into my tongue. There was a spice, something I'd never had before, almost sweet but with a bite to it.

"Cinnamon."

Callum had come up behind me without my noticing. Damn it. I wasn't paying attention and I couldn't afford to make mistakes like that. I wasn't here for a party; I was here to get clients. There was no way as I was going to do that if I was so lost in all this opulence that I let Callum sneak up on me.

I crunched the nut between my teeth and swallowed down the gritty pieces.

"What?"

He smiled and pointed to the bowl of nuts. "The walnut you just ate was sprinkled with cinnamon. It's a spice. Do you like it?"

The question wasn't very personal, but I still wasn't sure I wanted to answer honestly. I didn't want to give Callum any real piece of myself, no matter how small. I needed him to see only what I showed him and nothing underneath that sheen.

"It's a bit too strong for me."

Callum tweaked the corner of his mouth up in a smirk. He reached for a silver cup from the table. "Have some wine to wash it down, then."

I took the cup and put my lips to the edge, but I didn't drink. I wasn't sure where I stood yet. He could still be toying with me. It seemed too blindly optimistic to think his reference to the river was a coincidence. The question was—how could he possibly know about my trip down to the Bean-Nighe?

His dark eyes sparkled in the hushed candlelight, and he chuckled. "It's from vineyards in the valley."

"How do you know?"

Callum tucked his hands behind him, which made his broad chest stretch his green silk waistcoat. He wasn't wearing anything made with my fabric, and that thought dropped a little pebble of sadness into my belly. I'd hoped he'd find the silks irresistible, even just for a collar.

"I ordered the wine myself. This is my house."

*His* house? I glanced around the wood-paneled ballroom with the expensive glass windows and gilded doors. When he'd been in Odina's parlor, I'd assumed he was from a merchant family like she was. Monied but to a point I could actually imagine—good clothes, food whenever you wanted it, frivolous things scattered through the house. This was very different. There was more money here in this room than my papa could have hoped to make in his entire life. People with money like this—people like Callum, apparently—had more than one house. They owned land that made them even more money. They were so far removed from people like me, I couldn't even close the gap in my imagination.

"It's a nice house," I said and then bit the inside of my cheek. *A nice house?* Gods' fangs, now he'd know for sure I'd never set foot in a ballroom before.

Callum shook his head. "It's only nice with people in it. When they're gone, it's too big. Too empty."

Was he lonely? I was alone in my one room most days of my life since Papa was gone. I didn't mind it most of the time, but there were days when the corners of the place seemed to echo with the solitary sound of my movements. Was it worse in a house as big as this? Or did the silk-lined walls and deep carpets dampen the sound entirely?

"You're not wearing blue."

I jerked my head back to him. "I am so."

Callum reached out and touched my sash with his fingertips. His fingers were long and spindly, like spider legs.

"Does this count, do you think?"

I stepped back, just enough to make the ribbon taut and he dropped it.

"It counts if I say it does."

He chuckled again, the sound soft in his throat. "What do you think, Odina?"

I hadn't even noticed her approach, but when I glanced up, I wasn't sure how I could have missed her. She wore the purple silk, and some skilled hands had transformed it into a gown with a pointed bodice, tight sleeves, and a little train flowing out behind her. Her dark hair had been plaited and twisted around her head. She glowed, radiant like she'd been lit from the inside. She'd never captured my attention like this before, never drawn my gaze so strongly that I couldn't, wouldn't drag my eyes away.

And that's how I knew there was something wrong with the purple silk.

# Chapter Twelve

Odina did a little twirl in front of me, holding out the skirt of her dress to show how the purple rippled in the candlelight. None of it was natural. The Bean-Nighe's magic had done something to the silk . . . made it *more*, somehow.

"Isn't it beautiful?"

I had to agree. It was the most beautiful fabric I'd ever seen. And it was mine—or, mostly mine. Even if the Bean-Nighe's magic had finished it off, I could still claim the work as my own to anyone who asked. The whole ballroom was full of potential clients. Clients with more money than they'd ever need.

"It looks lovely on you," I said. "The color brings out your eyes."

I was too practiced in flattery to miss a chance to make a client feel good about themselves in one of my creations. Papa always said we wanted people to feel like the best version of themselves while wearing our fabrics. It was clear Odina felt quite good—she beamed at us with a smile that made her brown eyes glitter like the sequins on her dress.

"I've already had five people ask me where I got the silk."

I smiled and my heart beat a little faster. "And? Did you give them my name?"

Odina's tongue darted out like a little snake, and she licked her lips.

"I told them it was a secret . . . I can't have everyone scrambling to you. Then my dresses wouldn't be the most special."

I shouldn't have been surprised, but hurt and anger coiled around each other in my chest, making it hard to breathe.

"That's my livelihood, Odina."

She grinned at me. "You played tricks with me yesterday; now I'll play tricks with you."

The barbed words were softened by the honey tones of her voice. She almost lulled my pulsing anger. That, and the way she shone in the purple silk, gave me an idea.

"Are you always this sweet-tongued, Odina? So persuasive?"

Callum laughed and handed Odina her own cup of wine. "Odina's never sweet. She might be sugared, but it's the kind that scrapes the inside of your cheeks if you eat too much."

Odina pulled on Callum's cravat, letting the knot unravel. "You like it that way, don't you? You never want anyone too comfortable."

It was an odd response, but as I looked around the room I got a startling sense of what Odina might mean. The tempo of the music was a touch too fast, causing the dancers to trip up or move their feet too quickly. More than one couple leaned against the wall, pink in their cheeks, taking gasping breaths. The food was also arranged just so, and no one had eaten any of it except for the little bowls of nuts and pieces of candied fruit. Perhaps people were too nervous to wreck the presentation to actually eat anything. All this laid out before us but too perfect to actually reach. It was too much to be a coincidence. Callum had done all this to intentionally throw his visitors—just like the illusion of the grinning house and the man in the wolf mask at the door.

Was this a test of some sort? Or was he simply playing a game only he found amusing?

Odina smirked at Callum again and picked a sugared nut out of the dish on the table beside us. She cracked the nut in two with her sharp front teeth. I wasn't going to get anywhere with either of them if I wasn't even willing to play the same game they were.

"What do you usually do at these parties?" I asked. "Why bring all these people here just to watch them trip over each other as they dance?"

Callum laughed and Odina caught my eye. I thought there might be resentment there, but that wasn't it. The glint in her eyes was more a glimmer of reassessment.

"You noticed?" Callum said. "Most people don't realize what's going on. They just get frustrated and give up."

"But why do it?" I asked.

He took a sip of his wine and glanced about the ballroom. The music twisted into a fever of thrumming and beats I felt all the way down to my toes. It vibrated through me like the music of the people who lived in the mountains. Raw and real. Like the wind and rocks and trees spinning out a melody together.

Callum took my sash in his fingers again and played with the ribbon. I wanted to back away, but I also wanted to hear what he was going to say. His lips parted, showing a hint of teeth.

"Because I like others to feel wrong-footed around us."

*Us.* The Players.

"I met some Players in the street once when I was young," I said, returning his grin. "Actually, the young man who spoke to me looked a little like you, now that I think of it. Except he had hazel eyes and black hair, not brown."

It was true. That was why Callum had struck me as familiar when I first saw him. The sharpness to his features reminded me of the young man who'd given me my paste jewel. He could be his brother. Maybe he was. Or his son. The Players changed with time, and I assumed the positions were passed through families like everything else worth having.

"Well, it sounds like you had an important encounter that day," Callum said.

"Did I?"

"Yes."

He was taunting me, a playful spark in his eyes. It was as if he wanted me to voice the question that hung on the tip of my tongue.

"How many of you are there?" I asked.

He twisted my sash in his hand, pulling me closer and bending toward my ear. His breath blew the little wisps of hair at the side of my head.

"We could be anyone here," Callum said. "Isn't that disconcerting?"

I pulled my sash free of his hands and took a step back. "Not for me."

"No. Of course not."

"How does it work? Joining. Do parents pass it to children?"

"Indeed. We turn over like the tide, you know? Young replaces old."

Another thing I could never have because I wasn't born to someone who already had it. They all, the rich and the Players alike, kept their circles tightly closed so no one else could break in.

But Callum was a Player. And he stood right there in front of me. Perhaps between him and Odina, I could get what I wanted.

He held my gaze and I moved toward him without willing my body to do it. I realized I wanted to be close to his heat, his fire, the passion that burned just beneath his skin and sparkled in his eyes.

Odina grabbed my arm.

"Dance with me," she said.

I didn't have a chance to answer before she pulled me away and into the middle of the room. She put one hand on my shoulder and kept her other hand in mine. I'd never danced like this before. I'd never even *seen* dances like this before. Everyone was making the same movements, replicating the same steps, even if they were slightly out of time with the too-fast music. I'd never seen anything like it. Back home, sometimes tired people would spill out of our gray wood buildings and trip over each other in the square, smiling too hard and laughing too loudly to truly be enjoying themselves. They tried, forced it, just for a chance to pretend to be carefree and happy.

That was the only kind of dancing I knew—the moving your feet to the music kind. The swirling around with your neighbor in your arms kind. I doubted very much Odina would like me to swirl her.

"Put your hand on my waist," she said.

I obeyed and let her move me around the room like a doll. My palms grew damp. Odina would notice. I fought the urge to let go.

"Why are we doing this?"

Her gaze snapped toward me. "The party?"

"No. Dancing."

She led me into a turn, squeezing my hands tighter, and I tried to relax and stop worrying about their dampness.

"I want to know what you want with the Players . . . and Callum," she said.

People stopped to watch us move across the floor. I couldn't imagine we made a very fine couple with me stepping on Odina's dainty velvet shoes every two steps with my leather boots. Yet, other couples stopped moving altogether and stared at us. No, not us. *Odina.* Their eyes shone, reflecting her light. Odina was charming, always had been, from the first time I'd entered her parlor after Mrs. Under sent me there. Odina's family were Mrs. Under's clients before mine—except I'd never made fabric for anyone else in the house. I'd never actually seen Odina's parents in the house either. They probably traveled. Perhaps they owned a mine near the coast that needed looking after or something. It was strange though, that Odina never asked me to bring wool or silk for them.

My stomach gave a little squirm at that thought. Odina stared at me as if she was trying to see through my eyes to my thoughts on the other side, and I very, very much hoped she couldn't.

"So?" she said.

"I already told you. I want people to admire my fabrics and buy more. I want clients."

She glanced over my shoulder, looking out at the crowd, and tightened her grip on me. "Like them, you mean?"

The dancers closed in all around us. Actually, they weren't dancing at all anymore—simply swaying a bit to the music as they clustered in on us.

"Odina, you look so beautiful tonight," a man with a green short jacket said.

"Odina, will you honor me with your presence outside?" A woman with a huge ruff reached for her.

"Odina, where *did* you get that purple silk?" Another woman leaned in and gripped her skirt.

I pulled my hand free from Odina's. No one's gaze followed me. They all remained focused on her. On the dress.

She was completely radiant, even as her lips pulled down and her eyes grew a bit wild, like a cornered cat.

"What's happening?" she whispered.

I didn't know, but I wanted to appear as though I did. Like it was just the beauty of the fabric doing its job.

"I said you'd get all the attention in that purple silk, didn't I?"

She turned me away from the crowd and we took tiny mincing steps to avoid tripping on anyone's feet. We found a space in the middle of the dance floor and Odina started to whirl me around again. The music grew louder, the drumbeats vibrating in my ears. I caught Odina's eye and didn't let go—I couldn't help it. The irises were strange, and as I looked closer, a bright blue ring flooded the brown. Odina bore into me with her suddenly icy stare.

"Ella, be careful," she said. "You'll step on my hem."

I blinked, slowly, the weight of my eyelids shocking. My head was full of something . . . smoke . . . a fog. I couldn't see properly, couldn't think.

"I'll be careful," I said.

A hand grasped my arm, pinching, pulling. I didn't want to go. I wanted to stay with Odina, continue looking into her blue, blue eyes. Callum yanked me away and shook my shoulders. The mist cleared from my head and the room came back into sharp focus.

"What was that?" he asked, eyes set on Odina.

She shook her head and rubbed her eyes. "I don't know. I had such a strange feeling of . . . control."

Callum laughed. "Your eyes! They glowed blue!"

"What?" Odina said. "Why?"

So she *did* have control over me. I'd felt it as clearly as if she'd been gripping my wrist with her fingers. In the low light of the candles, the prick on my little finger didn't stand out but I knew it was there. My drop of blood fed the loom. The Bean-Nighe's magic had repaired it, helped me weave faster than would have been possible before. It seemed like that magic had also done something else. It pulled me in to the beauty of the fabric, just as I'd wanted others to be drawn to what I'd created.

"You did something to me, Odina," I said, not wanting either of them to land on what I'd already figured out—that it was the silk instead of the girl. "I think you could have told me to do a head-stand in the middle of the dance floor and I would have done it."

"But . . . how?" Odina smoothed down her skirt. The green roses glimmered.

Callum laughed. "It's the silk, isn't it, Ella? It's special."

"I've never seen people react to silk like that before," I said. "I tried very hard to make it lovely, but it was Odina herself who held everyone's attention."

She stared at me. "Exactly. *I* must have been the one everyone wanted to stare at. Not some silk."

Callum smiled and shook his head. "You're lovely, there's no mistaking that. But lovely doesn't make people want to do headstands in the middle of the dance floor. Does it, Ella?"

What a foolish thing to say. Of course being beautiful, being alluring, didn't make admirers lose their senses completely. Well, most of the time it didn't.

"What did you do to make such a special silk, Ella?" Callum pressed.

Both Callum and Odina turned their bodies so they formed an angle around me. I couldn't slip away without pushing one of them aside. It was what I wanted, before—to be near them. They were interested in me, in my fabric. There might be a way to play this so neither of them would find out about the Bean-Nighe but they could still be lured into buying more of my special fabric.

"I said some extra prayers over my loom to make something extra lovely for Odina," I said. "I didn't expect this, but it looks like Nemain listened."

Callum's eyes flashed. "Let's see."

He grabbed hold of the arm of an old man and dragged him over to stand before us. Callum jerked the man too hard, and I raised my hand to reach out and touch Callum's sleeve in protest but dropped it again quickly. Who was I to tell this young man how to act in his own house? The older gentlemen was all right anyway. He fixed his jacket and glared at Callum.

"Can't even let me enjoy the party? That's supposed to be my right."

*Did anyone have a* right *to enjoy a party? What an odd thing to say.*

"You're here, enjoying, aren't you, old man?"

The man frowned. "What do you want?"

I flicked my gaze toward Odina, looking for her reaction to all this. She didn't seem surprised at all. Her foot tapped, just barely visible beneath the hem of her dress.

Callum grinned at me and slung his arm around the man's shoulder. "I'd like you to dance with Odina, here."

"Why?" the man said.

"For old time's sake. Shouldn't that be enough?"

The man shook him off. "I'm not one of you anymore, am I? Once my hair started turning gray, once my skin betrayed me with this infernal drooping"—he pointed to his jowls, which were, to be fair, quite impressive. "Once I didn't look young anymore, I was nothing. Just a guest, allowed to come to the parties and eat the food and drink the wine and maybe talk to a handsome man."

"I can apologize for whatever my predecessors did, I suppose, but there wouldn't be much meaning in it, would there, Brian?" Callum said.

Brian stared, jowls shivering.

"I've asked you for a favor," Callum went on. "And if you want to keep coming to these parties, you need to comply."

This man, Brian, was, at some point, part of the Players. He'd have been part of an older set, obviously, but it seemed like Callum still held some authority over him, because he nodded now and stretched out his arms for Odina. She shrugged and joined him, with one hand on his shoulder and one in his palm. The music swelled again, Callum somehow timing Brian's acceptance with the beginning of a new song.

Callum then grabbed my fingers and pulled me back a bit so we could watch. As soon as his grip loosened, I pulled my hand away and tucked it behind my back. I didn't like people touching me unexpectedly. It didn't give me any time to protect myself from their judgments—to wipe my palms on my skirts or take as many deep breaths as I could to try to force down my body's reaction to my nervousness.

"Let's see if this works, shall we?" Callum said.

I nodded, not sure if I wanted it to or not. But ultimately, I did want them to think my fabric was special. If this was why, it wouldn't be so bad.

"What are we watching for? Surely Odina isn't going to ask him to do a cartwheel or something."

"Shhh."

Callum pointed to the pair, drifting in a slow rotation. Brian's eyes glowed ice-blue.

"Look at that," Callum said. "It's working."

"He's under her spell now," I said. It seemed too unbelievable, even as I stared at Brian's unnatural eyes and remembered how Odina had made me feel only a few moments ago.

Odina's gaze slid over to us, and Callum gave a little nod. She leaned toward her dancing partner and whispered something in his ear. He broke off from her and went straight for the refreshment table, where he picked up a glass of wine, turned to his left, and dumped it over the head of an absolutely shocked-looking lady in buttercup yellow. My stomach squirmed with guilt. My silk had done that.

"That's what you chose to do?" Callum said when Odina joined us. "Pour a drink over someone's head?"

Odina's calm expression didn't falter. "Not *someone's*. Talisa's. She's been telling anyone who will listen that I could never be the best dressed in Eidyn Crag because I came here in a canoe. Which is a lie, of course. I came here on a very large ship."

Suddenly, I didn't feel as guilty about playing a part in Talisa's ruined dress.

"Well, if it worked for that, it can work for other things too," Callum said.

"Like what?"

I needed to know how he was planning to use my handiwork. I needed the money, and the recognition, but I didn't want to be part of doing bad things to people. Even if I could barely afford that much conscience.

Callum turned to me, brown eyes traveling over my face and landing somewhere near my lips. I pursed them and backed up a little, pressing into the wall. I'd never had a man look at me so plainly before. Usually, they met my eyes for a few moments and then dropped their gaze to their own shoes. Only Gregory looked at me full on, but that was different. He was taking what he could, because I couldn't stop him looking. With Callum, it didn't feel like that. His stare was softer, like the brush of fingertips.

"You're very curious, aren't you, Ella?" he finally said. "Do you think it would work again? If you weave something else and say the same prayer, will it give the wearer the same power?"

"Maybe. It worked once; why not again?"

Callum grinned. "Well, we're going to need another opportunity to find out."

# Chapter Thirteen

The streets were cold and dark after the golden warmth of Callum's house. I hurried through them carrying a piece of thick paper, a date scrawled in the center with a loose, carefree hand.

Five days. I had five days to wait—and to weave another bolt of silk. Well, really only three days for the bolt because it would need to be made into a dress. Callum said he'd send someone to collect it so I didn't have to make an extra trip in between parties.

The dancing hadn't even been over when I'd left, and he wanted to hold another fête in less than a week. I could only imagine what all that food had cost, plus the swaths of fabric hanging from the ceiling, the band, the wine. Actually, whatever number I imagined would probably be wrong—I had no idea how much good wine cost because I'd never been able to even entertain the idea of buying it.

To Callum, it all seemed like nothing, as extravagant as suggesting having pie for dinner twice in a row.

My room seemed to ache with quiet when I returned. It almost made my ears hurt when I stepped inside. At the party, I'd been able to feel Odina's body heat while we danced, smell the wine on Callum's breath. Now, it was only my own fingers that twined together, looking for some measure of comfort.

The loom sat in the corner, gilded with moonlight. I went to it and ran my hands along the smooth wood. This machine had been my companion since they took Papa away, but it wasn't mine alone anymore. The Bean-Nighe owned the loom now, in a way. I couldn't use it without my sacrifice to her. I wasn't just in debt with Gregory anymore. I was in debt with her too.

⁓❧

I decided on a blue thread this time, since Callum had been so insistent I wear the color. As I loaded the first spool into the loom, I imagined what the finished project would look like. There would be waves rippling across the silk—the kind of waves made by indulgent wind. They'd flow almost violently, crashing into one another in the tight weave of the fabric.

The metal needle seemed to stare at me like a hungry wasp. I pricked my finger and let the drop of blood well slowly. It was fed, and I was ready—for everything this all might mean. For the end of my worrying, and days picking which meals to skip, and nights curled into myself to protect against the frigid cold of my room. I could be more than all that. I knew it. And this was how it was going to happen.

Again, the magic made me faster. I wove all afternoon and had a good portion of silk by the end of it. Not a whole bolt, but I was sure I could finish it in the morning. I swung my legs around the stool and stretched my fingers. They ached and my knuckles cracked with the movement. I ladled out a bowl of cold water from the barrel and dipped my fingers in. Relief flowed through me, and I sank onto my bed. Everything was going to turn out just how I'd always wanted.

A young girl knocked at my door on the third day. She dipped a little curtsy and held out the sides of her fern-green dress. I tried to guess her age—she couldn't be more than eight, but her dark eyes seemed to hold more wisdom than her years suggested.

"Lord Callum sent me," she said.

I gathered up my words. "Yes, just a moment and I'll get the bolt."

The silk shone, even in the dusty light of my room. I'd tied a gray ribbon around it and the whole thing reminded me of the river during a storm. I handed it to the little girl with a tinge of regret. At least I'd get to see it again as a dress when Odina wore it.

"This is for you," the girl said and struggled to hand me a folded piece of paper. I took it from her and helped her position the bolt of fabric in her arms. Hopefully, she'd make it back all right.

"Thank you," I said. "Be careful walking back."

She grinned. "I'm stronger than I look."

I believed her.

When I closed the door, I examined the sheet of creamy paper she'd handed me.

*Come down to the garden. We'll have the party under the stars.*

Outside. A party outside. My best dress wasn't warm enough to stay outdoors for very long. I opened the chest at the foot of my bed and plunged in, pulling out my mother's old stays and a shift with a hole in the hem I'd been meaning to repair. There were wool socks that needed darning and an iron teapot with a rusted bottom. Nothing I could use to warm myself outside at night.

I sat on the dirty floorboards and leaned back against the chest. Callum probably thought nothing of the location change. What did it matter to him whether the party was in his cavernous dining room or in his glowing garden? He would have everything he needed—warm shoes and a cloak and gods knew what else. Odina, too. She'd have her dress made from my silk to suit the occasion. But I'd been relying on making my way quickly to Callum's house, and my movement keeping me warm enough until I was inside. Papa and I had only ever had one cloak to share between us, and he'd sold it before he'd been taken to prison. I'd never bothered to get another one because I'd figured out how to do without.

My shawl hung over a peg near the door. It wasn't lovely—not at all. It was a strip of plain, drab wool with no discernible color and certainly no pattern. I'd made it out of a cheap spool of wool I'd been able to buy with the supplies for another project. It wouldn't look good with my yellow dress. I'd stand out, obviously not someone who could afford multiple dresses and velvet cloaks.

I had to go anyway. Even with the shame heavy in my belly. It was the only path forward where I might be able to pull myself out of all this.

I stared at my ugly shawl for the next two days, or so it felt. On the afternoon of the party, I took my purple paste jewel from the neckline of my dress and stitched it to the underside of my shawl, where no one would see it but I would know it was there. A little tiny adornment to help cool the heat that rose into my cheeks whenever I imagined what I might look like next to everyone else. Then I peeled my brown dress off, scrubbed cold water under my arms, and stepped into the yellow dress. My reflection grinned at me from my copper mirror as I braided a cream-colored ribbon through my red hair. I thought I had freckles like my papa, but I'd never seen my reflection clearly enough to know for sure. Whatever I truly looked like, it would have to be good enough.

⚘

Three tables stood end to end at the crest of the hill in Callum's garden. Chairs with blue velvet cushions stood haphazard around it, as if guests had already sat and talked and drank and then abandoned their seats to dance to the music curling through the breeze. Bottles of wine and glasses and little trays of food littered the tables.

I grabbed a handful of nuts and pulled my shawl a little tighter around me as I took in ladies in midnight dresses and men in plum suits. Everyone had dressed to match the night, and I wore the color of the sun. At least this time I had a purpose. Instead of skulking around the edge of the party, I pulled in a crisp breath and went straight to Callum and Odina.

They sat on two wooden chairs that matched those along the table—deep brown wood and soft velvet cushions. There were a few of these scattered about in the grass so people could sit and rest between dancing. The music this time wasn't too fast. If anything, it was too slow for dancers to be able to keep a tempo. Most just swayed around the hilltop with their partners, trying and failing to let the sound of the fiddle and the pipes guide them.

"You're here." Callum stood as I approached and reached out his hands for mine as if we were old friends. I took them, just by the fingertips, and then quickly let go. He flustered me with this familiarity we hadn't earned. I turned around, the candlelight streaming before my eyes.

Odina stood too and I nearly gasped. Thankfully, I stopped myself because it would look a bit strange to be so enthralled by my own fabric. The dress was stunning. Odina had the neckline and sleeves trimmed with a bit of white fur, no doubt to keep her warm. The blue silk bodice ended in a slender point and the skirt opened full and lush like the petals of a morning glory. The waves I'd created in the fabric gave the whole thing a sense of movement even when Odina stood still. She didn't wear a cloak with it—perhaps her under layers were thick and warm.

"Your seamstresses did a wonderful job," I said.

Odina shrugged. "They're efficient, yes."

Of course, she couldn't give the craftswomen their due. Her gaze flicked from the empty table to the dancers to the dip of the hill and the river beyond. I wrapped my shawl tighter as a cool breeze from the water tangled around us, a bitter taste on my tongue. The Bean-Nighe might be able to travel down the river. Maybe she was watching, waiting to see how her magic played out. My stomach clenched and I needed a little more space between me and the dark slip of water. I stepped back, almost onto Callum's feet.

"Don't worry, the crest of the hill looks high, but the lawn doesn't slope down too sharply. You won't fall," he said, touching my elbow to stop me trampling him.

"No, of course I won't." My face burned. "I just stumbled."

Odina cocked her head, her long brown hair tumbling over her shoulder. "Aren't we here for something, Callum? Can't we get on with it?"

I stared at her. She'd say anything to anyone, it seemed. Her tone never concerned her. I watched mine all the time, shaping it, softening it as my clients—and anyone above me—expected.

Callum tapped a long, polished fingernail on his lips. "Oh yes, I want to try something."

"What?" I asked, the word stinging in my mouth. Was it too much, to ask him so frankly about his plans?

"There's something I've been trying to get, something that's been denied to me."

Odina snorted. "You mean Mrs. MacDonald? Good luck."

I followed her line of sight to an older woman sitting in one of the wooden chairs near the biggest oak tree in the garden. Its branches would have provided shade, but the sun had already abandoned us and left a pale gray light in its wake. The older woman tapped her foot to the winding music under the heavy skirt of her green wool dress.

"What about her?" I asked.

Odina clamped her lips shut, but Callum only tweaked my blue sash and smiled.

"She's going to give us a very lucrative trade deal."

So this was really what the Players did. More than dictating the fashions in the city, they got themselves in front of the right people—people who could make them even richer than they already were. This was the system that kept people like me where we were. Under normal circumstances, I'd never even be in the right rooms, or gardens. But now . . .

I dragged up all the courage I had stored in my heart, touched the paste jewel stitched into my shawl. This was my chance, an opportunity I might never get again. I ignored Odina's burning stare. The cold air played over the sheen of sweat dampening my skin, but I held myself firm, stopped my body from shivering.

"I want in," I said.

# Chapter Fourteen

The music shot up in a crescendo, the fiddlers angling their bows for a crisper sound. I liked how it pulsed through my veins.

Callum shot a look down his straight nose. "In?"

I nodded, swallowed too much air. Now wasn't the time to go around gulping like a fish. I had to carry this through. "On whatever it is you're doing here. I want to see how you do it. There's something I've been working toward, but I need money to get it."

Odina let an airy laugh slip through her lips. "There won't be any money exchanging hands tonight."

Why did she keep trying to make me feel foolish? I wasn't asking with empty hands. I had something special she wanted now—something Callum wanted. I was in the game instead of just a piece on the board.

"Are you thinking of a trade, Ella?" Callum asked.

Odina rounded on him with her hands out like claws. "You've let this go too far! First an invitation and now this?"

"I can't help it, Odina. She wants to."

Odina didn't want me in their circle of influence. Too bad. She wasn't going to stop me. Usually, I had to take what I could get—like her silver necklace as payment when it should have been coin. But this time I had something of value, something no one else in the city could make.

"You two want to use my fabric to get you what you want," I began. "This trade agreement . . . I want some of the profits too."

Odina clenched the silk of her skirt, and I winced at how she crushed the fabric.

"This isn't yours anymore. I paid for it. It's mine."

I thought she'd say that. Even so, the blow still stung.

"Yes, that *one* dress is yours, but are you going to wear it to the next party? And the next? You'll want me to weave you more, won't you? So you can do this again, beguile more people into giving you things?"

Her smile morphed into a grimace. "I have the raspberry silk too and the purple I wore last time. And do you really think the gods will bless your loom with magic over and over again? Just for praying?"

"They did twice," I lied. "And anyway, you've already worn the purple and now tonight, the blue. You only have the one bolt left unless you want people to see you repeating dresses."

I spoke to her like she spoke to others, leaving myself breathless in my brazenness.

Odina bristled, fists still full of silk. The music started up again, and a man with white hair who'd been lingering near a bowl of nuts on the long table sauntered off to take the hand of a young woman hovering nearby. *Her father or her husband*, I wondered. I'd never imagined dancing with a husband myself—that was always too far off into the future. The "now" was what I'd been trained to think about. Work, food, helping Papa. In stolen moments, I dreamed of Papa and I, not dancing but taking a whole afternoon off work and going for a walk along the riverbank.

It never came true. We'd never had that kind of time.

What did Odina dream of? I suspected it was exactly this—the promise of being the most alluring girl in the room, of being fawned over, of being in control of other people. So why was she taking so long to answer me? She was dragging it out, waiting for me to crumble under my own rash words. But I wouldn't. There was no letting this chance go.

"See?" I prodded. "You do still need me."

Callum brought his hands together and clapped. I glanced around, thinking the music had stopped, but it simmered on. Dancers wove together, following the slightly frayed thread of the melody.

"That was very good, Ella."

My neck burned and I imagined what he saw—the spreading of red like a wine stain across my white neck and chest. My body tattling on me, showing him my nervousness.

"It couldn't have been that good. Odina still hasn't said she wants more bolts."

Callum put a hand on her shoulder, and she stared at it but didn't go so far as to slap his hand away.

"She'll want more if it works again," he said. "Let's make a trial of a sort."

Another test. That was what we were here for, and the Bean-Nighe's magic wouldn't fail. Look at everything that had happened already.

"All right. What do you want me to do?"

"Actually, it's Odina who has to do all the work unfortunately. If she can convince that old hen to give us the trade agreement, you win the trial. I've been trying for two months, so if Odina can do it tonight, wearing your dress, I'll know your fabric is something special."

"And I just watch?"

That would be like torture, waiting, hoping something would happen.

He smiled, the skin beside his eyes crinkling in what might turn into crow's-feet one day. So he didn't mean to torture me after all. Not with that spark of light in his eyes. Its brightness spread to me, lifting me out of worry.

"No," he said. "You dance with me."

༄

He took my hand and pulled me out into the wide clearing that acted as a dance floor. I hadn't worried about it too much that first time with Odina, but now I urged my body not to let my palms grow all damp. I didn't want Callum to feel my nerves and think it was a weakness—it wasn't. The thicket of nerves was deep-rooted, but I knew how to break free of it when I really needed to.

I positioned my hand on his shoulder as Odina had done with me, and he gripped my waist, pulling our bodies together. He smelled of the cinnamon I'd tasted at the last party. Sweet and spicy at the same time. His hair tickled my ear and I almost swatted it away, but I didn't want him to think this whole thing was making me uncomfortable. Even if nerves buzzed up and down my body.

My fate was about to be decided by someone else. If the dress helped Odina convince the old lady to give her the trade agreement, Callum would think I was something special. They'd both want more fabric for suits and dresses. Maybe I'd get to dress all the Players and I'd have more than enough money for my shop.

"Who are the others?" I asked.

We twirled over the grass to the slow vibrations of the music. I followed Callum's steps but there wasn't much to it. Even so, I put my feet in the wrong place. He stepped on them, stumbling.

"Gods' blood, Ella!"

I slipped a smile into place. "Oh, I'm so sorry."

"You're not."

"No, I'm not."

His sharp brown eyes bore into mine. I searched for the glimmer I'd seen—the playfulness. There, just there in the corner of his left eye. A glint. A sparkle.

"Do gods bleed?" I asked. "I've never heard anyone say 'gods' blood' before."

Callum nipped at his bottom lip. "Of course they bleed . . . the ones with enough devotion just don't die from it."

None of the gods died in any of the stories the temples told. It was what separated them from us in the truest way. Death breathed down our necks from the moment we were born, waiting for just the right moment to swallow us up. Most gods had no such thing to worry about. With enough devotion from humans, they didn't have that weight around their necks. Perhaps that's why they could leave this world and cross the veil whenever they wanted.

Callum counted beats under his breath and stepped in time with the music. I followed obediently, because across the garden, Odina took a chair beside Mrs. MacDonald. I kept my eyes on them both, and I sensed Callum did too. Odina smiled and touched the old woman's knee. They both laughed, though I couldn't hear them over the music. Mrs. MacDonald leaned back in her chair and Odina pivoted her body so she took up too much of the old woman's space.

Odina wasn't a salesperson, not like I'd been trained to be by my papa. I'd learned just by watching him make himself a little bit smaller in front of customers, complimenting them, creating a little sense of urgency.

*"There won't be any more spools of the wool I used for that until next season, and just look at how the blue brings a spark to your eyes."*

As Mrs. MacDonald's smile dropped to reveal three remaining bottom teeth, my heart sank with it. Odina didn't know how to do this; she had to get Mrs. MacDonald to dance with her. I swiveled my eyes to Callum, who kept Odina in his own sights. I needed him to think this was working more than I wanted him to think me refined.

I stepped, hard, on his foot.

"Ugh, Ella! Again?"

"I'm not really made for dancing, I guess."

"Well, your hands must be much nimbler than your feet. You've tarnished my shoe."

My stuffy boots had left a print of dust on his shiny leather heeled shoes. If I'd stepped on them in the street, he could have cursed me and no one would have batted an eye. Here, though, his smile just grew strained.

I wrung my hands. "You can wipe it off."

He glanced over at Odina and Mrs. MacDonald, both sitting with their backs against their chairs and no longer smiling at each other, and back at me. "Stay here."

I breathed deeply again the minute he slipped through the crowd, then closed the space between the old woman and me. I stuck my foot out and caught it on one of her chair legs, falling forward in what I hoped would be a spectacular stumble.

"Oh dear!"

Her frail voice reminded me of the Bean-Nighe's and I was glad to have a second to catch myself. *None of that. No time to picture the wisps of her white hair or smell the rotting earth.*

Odina bent to pull me up by the elbow.

"What are you doing?" she whispered in my ear.

I gave a teeny, tiny shake of my head I hoped she'd interpret as *stop talking.*

"Are you all right, young one?" Mrs. MacDonald asked.

I clutched at my leather-clad ankle. "Ouch, I . . . just need to sit for a moment."

"Oh here." Mrs. MacDonald gestured to the chair on her other side, and I fell onto it.

"Thank you, that's better."

The old woman waved a hand in front of her face, and I noticed how smooth it was. Not at all what I'd expect from a woman her age. Her knuckles weren't swollen and her veins didn't stick out under her skin. Those were hands that had never known work.

"This music is strange," she said. "Too slow."

So, she'd noticed too. This woman was as sharp as Mrs. Under. No wonder Callum had been working on the trade agreement for months. I didn't even know what it entailed—was it for wool? Wine? Spiced nuts? How was I going to get what I wanted if I didn't even know what to ask for?

But Odina knew. I just had to help her to get it.

"That's such an unusual color, miss," I said across Mrs. Mac-Donald's lap.

Odina stared at me a beat. I gave her a stiff smile and she finally nodded. "Oh yes, my weaver is very good."

Mrs. MacDonald caught a fold of Odina's skirt in her fingers. "It *is* beautiful. You know, I've seen a lot of dresses, but never one that reminded me of waves."

*You've probably never seen fabric woven with magic before,* I thought.

"It's the best I could find. I wanted to wear something special tonight."

"Oh?" Mrs. MacDonald scooted toward the edge of her chair to look at Odina. "Well, you did. You look completely charming."

I wanted to kick Odina, but she was too far away. *Here's your opening. Take it!*

"That's so lovely of you to say, lady. And actually, I wanted to wear something special because I knew you'd be here."

The old woman grinned. "You don't think I know why Callum invited me here? He's been after me for weeks! I haven't decided who will get the coal agreement yet. He knows that. I've told him at least five times."

Coal. So, it was even more valuable than I thought. Everyone *wanted* coal instead of peat. The poorest people couldn't afford it, but to a lot of people, it was considered necessary unless you wanted to freeze to death over the dark months. The demand was constant. I needed to help them get this to prove what I—what my fabrics—could do.

I slipped from my chair and knelt in front of Mrs. MacDonald before grabbing hold of Odina's skirt and pulling her down with me. The old woman stared at us both.

"What's this?"

Odina's hands were limp at her side, but I picked them up and put them on top of Mrs. MacDonald's surprisingly smooth ones. A humming filled my ears, and it wasn't the music of the drummers or flutists. It was a wail after wail of sadness sewn into a song. The Bean-Nighe's song.

"Don't you want to dance with Mrs. MacDonald, Odina? The song demands to be danced to."

Odina flicked her eyes toward me. Her chest rose up and down with deep breaths, pushing her blushed cleavage against her blue bodice.

"Yes . . . please will you dance with me, lady?"

The woman laughed and I caught a hint of wine on her breath.

"I'm an old woman; my dancing's behind me. Why don't you two take to the music?"

"The fae are older, and they love to dance," I said.

Mrs. MacDonald spat, the glob gleaming in the grass, thanks to the clear moonlight. I tried not to grimace.

"Don't compare me to the fae; we're nothing alike," she said. "Fine, I'll come if we can step slowly."

Odina took Mrs. MacDonald's hand and led her to the clearing. I followed behind, trying to spot Callum. He waited for me in the middle of the throng. His eyebrows shot up into his hairline when he saw Odina and Mrs. MacDonald clasp hands and count themselves into the dance.

"So?" he whispered in my ear as he took my hand. His skin was hot to the touch and I let my hand lie limply in his grip this time. Maybe it was nothing to him, this casual touch. Perhaps I should be more like that too.

"Just wait," I said.

We stepped into the dance and kept close to Odina and Mrs. MacDonald. Odina stared into the old woman's suddenly ice-blue eyes. Her cheeks were slack, accenting her jowls.

"Give us the trade agreement," Odina told her. "We'll do something good with it."

"You'll do something good with it," Mrs. MacDonald repeated.

"It's ours."

"It's yours."

Callum and I looped around, determined not to lose our spot beside the pair of dancers we cared most about.

"So you'll give it to us?" Odina asked.

"I will." Mrs. MacDonald nodded.

Callum broke his hold on me and took her arm instead. "Come, Mrs. MacDonald. Write a note and sign your name. I'll bring it to the Chieftain tomorrow and it'll all be done. Simple. I wouldn't want to inconvenience you."

He laid it on thick, like honey, but the old woman seemed to be lapping it up with relish. Her eyes were unfocused, landing on nothing in particular. She leaned into Callum's arm.

He snapped his fingers and a tall, willowy man in a dark cotton suit appeared from behind a tree.

"Paper and pen," Callum said.

The servant left toward the house and came back rather quickly with a piece of white paper rolled in his hand.

This had all come together so easily for Callum. One stroke of the pen and he'd be awarded the trade agreement for the city's coal. So much power from a bit of ink on paper.

Mrs. MacDonald shook her head and rubbed her powdery cheek. The beguilement was wearing off.

What if she realized what had just happened? I swallowed the hot lick of panic in my throat and took her elbow.

"Now, come here, lady, let's get you some more wine."

# Chapter Fifteen

After Mrs. MacDonald had been plied with wine and settled back comfortably in her chair, Odina took my hand and steered us through the crowd. She stopped so abruptly near the long tables, I stepped on the train of her dress.

"So you got what you wanted," she said.

I squared my body with hers and rolled my shoulders back. She wasn't going to make me shrink inside myself.

"So did you. You and Callum wanted the trade agreement . . . well, now you have it."

Her eyes flashed as cold as the river on a winter's morning.

"And what do *you* have exactly? You've passed Callum's test. Now what?"

Though her words were sharp with spite, there was a genuine question there too. Odina might want to know if I'd show up in her parlor more often than once a month to sell her fabric—if I was about to become a more permanent, and frequent, fixture in her life. The truth was I didn't know what would happen next. I wanted the money that went along with their world. The fortunes bestowed at the nod of an old woman's head.

"I want to make you fabric and help you and Callum and the other Players get what you want," I said. "And in return I want to be paid. Well."

Odina glanced over my shoulder, and I turned to find Callum hovering behind me. He reached out for my blue sash and reeled himself in, closer to me. His brown eyes fixed on mine and a shiver of excitement traveled from my heart to my fingertips and toes. This was it. I'd passed his test and now he was going to order more bolts. He wanted the magic in the fabric I wove—magic he'd recognized. I didn't even care if he suspected I'd been to see the Bean-Nighe. What did it matter if he taunted me by telling me to wear blue like the river? My wish had been granted and all it cost me was a drop of blood each time I used the loom. It was nothing. That part was already done.

"What color should I do next, Callum? A deep green would bring out your eyes."

He tilted his head and his eyes roamed over me, like he was sizing me up. I stood as tall as I could. I didn't want him to see someone who owed Gregory money and who depended on debt to keep her business running and who went from glittering parties to a bare room in a crooked building. I wanted him to see everything I could be if given a chance. The maker of irresistible things.

"I want to be your patron," he said.

The words took a minute to go from my ears to my brain. Patron? As in, he'd pay for my housing and food and materials? That was much more than I'd expected. The thought of

Callum being my patron hadn't even crossed my mind. Artists had patrons—not weavers.

"What?"

He nodded and his hair fell into his eyes. "You have something special here. Something I need. I want you and your fabrics for myself. No selling them to anyone else."

His words spun around me, making me dizzy.

Odina huffed out a breath and rolled her cold eyes. "Really, Callum."

"Do you love how you feel in that dress, Odina?" he asked.

She gripped the silk skirt and then ran her fingers over the rippling blue threads. "Yes."

Callum put a finger under her chin and lifted her gaze to his. Her chest rose and fell behind the hard neckline of her bodice, red splotches spreading across her skin.

"And you got the trade agreement out of Mrs. MacDonald," Callum said.

She nodded and shot a glance at me. "I could have done it on my own though."

"I'm sure you could have, eventually. But a dress that beguiles can come in so very handy."

My heart pulsed with nerves. Callum wanted to be my patron; he wanted me to stop selling to anyone else. I'd hoped to see lots of people in my designs, have my own shop. I couldn't do that making fabric for just one person. But if it was enough money, it might not matter. It could be more than worth it.

"What do you mean when you say you want to be my patron? What does that entail?" I asked.

Callum let go of Odina's chin and took a wine glass from the row placed out on the table. He handed it to me and took another for himself. I sipped, hoping the wine might steady my breathing.

"I want you and what you can make. You'll live here, with your loom, and you'll weave me fabrics. The Players will wear those fabrics, and we'll get everything we want. Sound good?"

It was too quick, too tightly bound. Live here? Be Callum's personal weaver? The idea coiled around me, making it hard to breath.

"For how long?" I asked.

Odina clicked her tongue, but Callum held my stare.

"You'll stay here for three months and get a purse of coin if we succeed."

"Why three months?"

"We will have a party for the winter solstice. That will be the apex of our deal."

There was nothing to hold on to except one of the metal candle stakes. I gripped it and the cold seeped into my palm.

"What do I get?"

Callum smiled and I tweaked my lips to match his. *Mirror them*, Papa used to say.

"You'll get a purse of coin if we succeed."

"How large a purse?"

Now he laughed. "Larger than you've ever seen, I'm sure."

Odina huffed and turned her back on us, staring out over the river. How could he know how much coin I'd seen? How could either of them think they knew what my life was like? I stood straighter, let go of the stake, and faced Callum.

He probably wanted all his Players to have fabrics for this party, a party where everyone with influence would likely even be in attendance. How many of them were there? I didn't know. So far, I knew only Callum and Odina, and that old man from the last party—Brian—but he wasn't even a Player anymore. I wanted to ask how many bolts I'd have to make, but I was scared to open my mouth. If I said the wrong thing, Callum might take the offer away. Three months was long enough to weave lots of bolts with the Bean-Nighe's magic. I could do it. There was really only one important question to ask.

"How much coin?"

"Eight hundred pieces of silver." He sipped his wine.

So, there it was. My worth. My fabrics imbued with the Bean-Nighe's magic, with my own blood, in exchange for eight hundred silver coins. My gut soured, even though eight hundred silver coins would be enough to buy a lease on a small place in the market street. I wanted more, wanted to be worth more. But eight hundred coins was the most anyone had ever offered me for anything.

I glanced around the garden, candlelight twinkling like fallen stars. The garden resembled what I imagined magic would look like if it were visible—glittering and ethereal. The food, though probably not considered a full meal for someone used to groaning tables, was in greater supply than at the last party. I thought of the spicy sweetness of cinnamon on my tongue and wondered when I'd tasted something that had no other job but to be savored.

Not thick, cheap bread made of oats to sit in the belly like a stone to stop hunger. Not charred old meat nearly burned over the cookhouse's fire to make sure it didn't come back up as soon as we'd swallowed it down.

I could live here, and I could do it knowing exactly what Callum wanted out of me—my loom and my weaving. I was closer than I'd ever been to wealth. The exchange—the money—was worth it. When the patronage was over, I'd have the means to set myself up. My chest swelled with all the possibilities.

"I accept."

He smiled, and the glint in his eye was back. It sparkled out at me, full of mischief.

"Good. Isn't that great news, Odina?"

She ran a hand over the patches of red on her chest. I wondered how long they'd take to fade. For me, it was often damp palms as well as a blush, and Odina had at least one of those physical markers of her emotions too. She knew what it was like to not be able to hide it. I couldn't help but feel a little thread of similarity with her, linking us, pulling me just a tiny bit closer to her.

"I won't take anything from you, Odina," I said.

Was that what she was afraid of? That I'd take Callum's attention away from her or fill a spot she thought was hers?

"You're stepping into something you have no place in, Ella."

I took another sip of wine and let it sit on my tongue while I watched Odina. There was poison laced in her words, but I wasn't sure if it was meant for me or Callum.

"This is a party, Odina," Callum said and handed her a glass. "No need to be so serious."

Odina pushed aside Callum's offering.

"I've had enough for tonight, and that music is too slow this time. It's unnerving," she said before clopping off in her heeled shoes.

We both watched her disappear into the darkness, toward the house and the road beyond. Callum finished the rest of his wine in one swig and took a sip from the cup he'd offered Odina.

"Do you want to see your room?" he asked.

"What, now?"

Callum nodded. "I don't like waiting for things."

He must have been used to having his demands given into immediately; after all, it seemed he could afford to pay anyone for anything. But I wasn't just anyone. I had something he wanted, something no one else could give to him, and I couldn't forget it.

"Are you saying you want me to sleep here tonight?"

His eyes swept over my face, and I fought back the chill climbing up my spine.

"Yes."

"That's absurd. My loom isn't exactly hidden in my skirts, you know. It's at home. I have to go home."

Callum turned away from me and took in what was left of the party. Perhaps Odina leaving had given others the opportunity to do the same. A lone couple spun each other around in the middle of the clearing, much too quickly for the sigh of music from the flute.

"I'll have some men bring it tomorrow."

My loom was delicate. It was old and brittle before it broke, and now magic swirled in the wood grain. The loom and supplies were everything I had and my only chance at anything more.

"Only if I can oversee them."

Callum flashed me a smile full of very white teeth. "You're staying?"

I realized I'd already decided. The loom was just a detail to figure out. My future was here, in that house full of everything Callum had to offer. I knew what he wanted, and I knew what I wanted. He might think he was using me for his own ends, but he didn't seem to realize my eyes were exactly as open as his.

# Chapter Sixteen

Callum left the lonely dancing couple to themselves and led me up to the house. We stepped in through a very tall window that opened right into a parlor. Nighttime's shadows turned every-thing into indistinguishable shapes, so I followed Callum out and through the hall to the ornamental staircase that led to the gallery. The bright light from many lit candles illuminated the carvings on the railing. Faces stared out at me from the wood pillars, caught by the chisel in moments of abandon. Thick, wide smiles took up too much of most of their faces. Only one figure didn't laugh. His mouth stretched wide, but there was some-thing about his eyes that suggested speech instead of laughter. I brushed away the shivers in my arms, the touch of the tendrils of fear. It was just wood.

"Who's this?" I asked, running my finger along the smooth planes of the carved god's face.

"Lugh."

The craftsmen god. He was a maker too, but he worked with wood and metals.

"Where's his hammer?"

Callum's fingers joined mine on the wood. I let my fingertips linger near his, just touching the skin of our hands together. I liked his warmth, and now that I'd be staying here—well, it was a good idea to have him fully on my side.

"He's dressed as a human," he said. "They say he likes to watch other people laugh."

I stared at the faces again, the gods and humans twisting beneath Lugh's carved throne.

"They don't look happy."

"Do you need to be happy to laugh?"

I thought of all the times I'd forced a smile in a client's parlor or even made myself laugh when Gregory's hand squeezed my shoulder too hard. It was all for show; none if it ever reached my heart.

"It's not a very nice carving," I said, and then bit my own tongue. *Why did I just say that?* I was trying to make sure he liked me, and criticizing his massive house's decor was not the way to do that.

I chanced a look at Callum's face, not very far from mine. His eyelashes sat on his cheeks, and he vibrated with something—fury? I stepped back to the bannister and felt behind me for the silk-hung wall. Callum put his hands on his knees and rocked, but I saw now it was with laughter.

He finally straightened himself and crossed his arms over his chest. "You're right, it's not. I wish I could say I inherited it from the previous owner, but I commissioned this one myself."

Previous owner? Normally these kinds of houses passed from generation to generation, not by a sale and coins. Where had Callum been before, then?

"You commissioned it? What about your parents?"

He couldn't have been more than a couple of years older than me, and I'd seen only seventeen winters.

"It's just me, no parents here."

"I'm sorry."

They must have been dead, and I'd just reminded him of them. Foolish.

"Well," I said, to fill the silence between us. "It's good of you to commission Lugh; I've never seen any other carvings of him in the city. I'm sure he's pleased. Why'd you choose him?"

Callum's eyes flicked up and down the carving. "Everyone's obsessed with Nemain in this place, but it's Lugh who loves chaos . . . spirit."

"And good craftsmanship. He likes that too."

"Yes, and have you ever met a creator who made anything worth looking at without a little abandon?" Callum's eyes shone as he grinned at me.

Abandon. Most craftspeople worked because they needed to pay for the day-to-day of their lives. They'd learned a craft as an apprentice or were lucky enough to have some natural talent in their fingers. It wasn't about abandon, joy, fun. Though I couldn't deny the flare of passion in my chest every time I picked up the shuttle.

"Do you think that's why Lugh is the craftspeople's god?" I asked.

Callum nodded. "But here, everyone worships Nemain whether they're craftspeople or not."

"You say that like you don't belong to Eidyn Crag."

"I don't. I like to move from house to house."

I couldn't imagine having more than one house to go to. There must have been a great level of freedom in that.

"Well, the carving is good but something about it makes me uneasy . . . all those twisted faces."

The wind had picked up outside, but its hissing only just met my ears here. I leaned against the back wall of the landing, away from the carved faces, where it felt as though we were alone. Callum copied me, grinning. A tiny butterfly fluttered in my belly.

"What are you smiling about, then?" I asked after a moment.

"You. I've never met such an honest salesperson."

"Oh, well I'm not really a salesperson. I'm a weaver." I crossed my own arms over my chest, mirroring him. My sash was coming loose and apparently so was I. This night needed to end now. A lot had happened, and I needed to lie by myself and straighten it all out in my head like the tight weave of winter wool. "I didn't mean anything by it. Everyone has different tastes."

He moved forward and leaned against the railing, and my breath hitched in my chest. Suppose the wood gave out? It was a long way down to the floor below. It didn't seem like Callum was afraid of taking risks. I'd have to keep that in mind. Even if he was my patron, I had no doubts that he would be perfectly happy to risk *me* to get what he wanted.

"Is that how it is with your fabrics?" he asked. "Some people like them and some people don't?"

I thought of all the times Papa and I had been turned away, bolts sagging under our arms. It rarely had to do with what the fabric looked like. Everyone had colors and patterns they preferred, yes, but beauty was beauty. It always came down to the price.

"The shine of a coin is sometimes more alluring than the prettiest length of cloth."

"Money," Callum said. "How disappointing."

I shrugged. "Not everyone can afford to buy beauty."

"And yet, it's everywhere. Free for the taking." He spread his arms wide, and I took in the ceiling painted with tiny silver stars, the clear glass window, the evenness of the floorboards beneath my feet.

"Nothing in here was free."

Callum waved a long finger at me. "That's not what I'm talking about. Do you go down to the river?"

I hugged myself tighter. I was fairly certain he knew I had and had somehow guessed something about the Bean-Nighe and my wish. His comment about wearing blue like the river had been too accurate to be a guess as a way to unnerve me. He seemed to enjoy digging around for heightened emotions.

"I love the river," I said, honestly. The rush of it drowned out the thoughts I couldn't unknot.

"So you've likely sat there by the water in the afternoon, listened to the birds, felt the sun on your skin."

"Of course."

"And was it not beautiful?"

"It was. But none of that does anyone any good—not unless we teach the birds to hunt for us. Or eat them."

Callum closed the gap between us with two long strides. His finger touched the skin under my chin, and he tilted my face up to look at him, just as he'd done earlier with Odina.

"Your world is very small, Ella."

I stared into his meltingly dark eyes and tried to ignore the squeezing of the muscles in my stomach, the sudden dampening of my palms. He wasn't wrong. I'd hardly ever left the city, and my life consisted of my tiny room, the marketplace, and other people's parlors. The river was my escape, but even it was only a quarter hour's walk from my front door. And what about Callum? What did he know of the world? He wasn't born in this house like I'd expected. What had he seen? Enough to be part of the Players.

I stepped away from his touch.

"You may know more of the world than I do, Callum, but I know the people of this city. See them as they move through the day. Have you and your Players never thought that having someone who sees the scraps under the tables of your great banquets might be beneficial?"

He clasped his hands behind his back.

"I don't think you've ever scrounged around under tables, Ella."

I couldn't help a smile. "You're right; I would never ruin my skirts like that. Anyway, with a shop, I might have a seat at those tables."

"Is that what you want to do with the money?" Callum tilted his head. "Perhaps you will have a seat, but sometimes those chairs are rather slippery."

I checked the swell of anger rising through my chest. In time, Callum would find out that I could hang on tight. But sparring with him right now wouldn't do any good.

The music trailing from the garden finally fell away. I wondered how many servants were still awake, sitting on the cold top steps on the kitchen staircase, waiting to be allowed to do their jobs. It wouldn't matter how tired they were—they'd need to keep their eyes open and their hands ready to work until the very last guest tumbled down the front steps into their carriage.

I knew what it was like to bend your own needs to the whims of others—my clients, my debtor. Tonight, though, I didn't have to. There was a bed somewhere here for me, and all I had to do was ask for it.

"Will you show me where I'll be staying? My feet are tired from my boots."

Callum glanced down as I pushed the toe of my black leather boot out from under my yellow hem.

"Those look good for walking. I'm glad you have them because I want to take you somewhere tomorrow, after your loom has been delivered."

"All right, but like I told you . . . I'm supervising its transportation."

He nodded and held out a hand toward the left side of the gallery. "Just down here."

Callum led me along the gallery and down a simpler hallway of white stucco walls. Blue stars had been painted where the wall joined the ceiling, and they twinkled in the light thrown by the candles in evenly placed sconces.

He turned the handle of the first door to appear. I glanced down the rest of the hallway—there were four other doors. Was one of them Callum's room? I thought not. It seemed like this was the part of the house for guests. It felt lonely, temporary. Callum seemed like he was a person who would leave his mark on his space. His bedroom was probably off a hallway hung with red and gold tapestries, not stark white walls.

I followed him into the space, trying not to have any expectations about what it might look like. Really, anything would be better than my claustrophobic home.

The room stretched wider than I would have thought. A bed sat on the left-hand side, hung with delicate linen curtains the color of moss after rain. A fire had already been lit in the grate and it illuminated wide floorboards and a carpet of knotted wool. Two carved chairs sat ready for their users to receive heat from the hearth. Opposite the bed, a large window let in the pale glow of the moon. There was a space beneath it.

"I want my loom to go there," I said, pointing to the empty spot under the window.

Callum nodded. "That's what I was thinking too."

"And this wardrobe for my supplies?"

I stepped toward the hulking thing and ran my hand down one of the smooth doors. The grain was beautiful—like trickles of water flowing down the wood.

"If you want," Callum said.

It would fit everything perfectly, almost as if Callum had planned all this out. Like he'd been expecting me.

"I want to talk tomorrow . . . about what you want from me. Exactly what fabrics, how many bolts, for whom."

"Haven't you guessed what I want from you?"

He closed in on me again, the spicy-sweet scent of him flavoring every breath I inhaled. He took my hand, and I stopped myself from slipping out of his grip. A small tingle of nerves, and they'd grow cold and damp. I saw people's faces when they shook my hand or gripped it in farewell. A frown followed by the not-so-surreptitious wiping of their own palms on their skirts or trousers.

I held myself still, waiting for Callum's face to change. It didn't. No grimace, no disappointed frown pulling at his lips. He brought my hand to his mouth and kissed my knuckles.

"Goodnight, Ella," he said before he slipped out of the room.

Again, the muscles in my stomach tightened and a tiny ache throbbed in my chest. He did this to me—there was no sense trying to pretend that wasn't true. Callum was handsome and the touch of his skin made mine burn. Even if he wanted me for my loom, and even if I wanted him for who he knew, there might still be some fun to be had here.

I'd given up any thoughts of marriage when Papa was taken away. No one would marry a daughter whose father had died in debtor's prison—not even the value of my loom could overcome something like that. I was tarnished silk, rotten wool. Something that might have looked good once but was past saving now.

Without the prospect of a husband's expectations, there was no reason not to kiss a boy here and there. The only boy I'd kissed had smelled like metal from all the blood soaked into his shoes. He'd tasted salty though, like he'd dipped his fingers into the crystals and sucked it all off when he was supposed to be salting beef at the butcher's shop.

Callum wouldn't smell like blood or taste like salt. He'd be fresh, crisp, sweet. The way he'd cupped my chin and raised my hand to his lips made me think he might wonder how I tasted too, but what did I know? This wasn't at all the same as being pulled into a red-tinged puddle in the alley behind the meat man's place. I didn't know if his desire for my fabrics extended into a desire for me.

It didn't really matter yet anyway. Maybe it wouldn't matter at all. I was here to earn money for my shop—not to kiss Callum.

I pulled the knot of my sash free and let it fall to the floor like a cool, blue snake. My dress slipped easily from my shoulders. I folded it and set it on the edge of the bed. There was a little table near the fire and a fine mirror of glass hung over it. I hadn't looked at myself in anything other than hammered copper or the shifting surface of the river for a long time.

My white shift seemed to suck all the color from my skin. Usually there was at least some pink from what I could tell, but now there was nothing. A few freckles stood out like pinpricks on my cheeks—so I *did* have them. I shook my auburn hair around my face, and there was one strand different from the others. A gray hair, slyly tucked away with the red. I didn't know anyone else my age with gray hair. What was wrong with me? Was something leeching the color from my body?

*Stop it. Not everything is a reason to think something bad has happened to you.*

It could be anything. A fluke. Or maybe my mother had gone gray young—I'd never thought to ask Papa. This wasn't anything to worry about.

Even so, I ran from the mirror and jumped into bed, pushing my feet under the blanket and closing the green curtains around me as if I could escape what I'd just seen.

# Chapter Seventeen

The coal fire in the grate died sometime during the night. I wrapped myself tightly in my blanket and peeked out of the drawn curtains. The window panels were bigger here than in my flat, square instead of diamond shaped. It was easier to see out of them and look across the stretch of closely cropped grass studded here and there with oak trees. We'd been out there just last night, but there were no remnants of the party. No forgotten chairs or candleholders. Someone must have worked into the small hours of the morning to clean it all up.

This room was still, cold, as if no one had been in here in a long time. Who had slept here before me? Did Callum have any other family? It didn't seem like it last night. He'd claimed the house as his, so perhaps he didn't have any siblings, like me. Or maybe he did and they just lived somewhere else. I flexed my fingers and toes, trying to shake away my prickle of unease. I didn't know this house or the person in it. What if I'd made a mistake?

The thick emptiness of the bedroom filled my ears. Not even the sound of a mouse scurrying across the floorboards or a fly buzzing against the windowpanes. Nothing was ever this quiet at home. The walls of my flat were made of chips of wood plastered together, and their thinness gave me a clear idea of how many children my neighbors had *and* if we should expect another one in nine months' time. Mrs. Under's footsteps always sounded over my head, heavy and slow through the ceiling. It was also easy to hear when she boiled a pot of water on her fire, so I knew when to climb the steps and knock on her door in hopes of a cooked egg or softened turnip.

When I sometimes stayed late in my own bed in the morning, it was to listen to the sounds of everyone else getting on with their morning. Children playing outside my window. Women and men dumping their night pots onto the streets with a splash. Friends hollering from the top of the hill. A rat skittering and pausing, skittering and pausing as it performed a fruitless search for food in my room.

It was usually the rats that got me out of bed. I couldn't let them stay—they'd ruin my spools of wool and silk and they chewed easily through linen. I caught them by their silky pink tails and forced my sash window up, tossing them to the cobbles below. They never died, either. I always watched as they shook off the fall and slipped into the bushes leading down to the river. I envied their resilience.

A rap at the door broke the unsettling silence in the room I was in now. Another three forceful raps made me jump out of bed and tiptoe across the floor. It was too cold to put my whole foot down on the boards.

Callum's face filled the crack of the door when I opened it. "Good morning."

I let him push the door the rest of the way open but folded my arms around me. The only thing between him and my modesty was a thin linen shift, and I wasn't going to give him any reason to look harder. He wore a full suit—shirt, jacket, breeches, and white stockings. We were totally imbalanced. He was armored. I was exposed.

"You're cold," he said.

My arms hid my breasts from view, and I wound them tighter over myself. Could he see? I glanced down at my chest.

"Gooseflesh." He reached a finger out and touched my collarbone. I jerked back as if he'd put ice to my skin.

"The fire went out and I haven't started it yet."

"Don't bother. I came to bring you down to breakfast so you could go with my carters to fetch your loom."

His carters. He paid their wages and so he commanded them. He could do that because without him, they'd starve and their children would shiver with cold on the streets. Callum's money had probably come from his parents or was otherwise given to him because of his blood. He'd started at the top and now his purse grew fat off what else he could take. Like the trade agreement last night. Callum could count on more coin in his pocket, but wouldn't have lost anything if he didn't get it. If his carters didn't help me get my loom this morning—or gods forbid they broke it—what would happen to them? How far away were they from ruin?

How far away was I?

That loom was all that sheltered me from that existence—an empty belly full of fear and worries.

"They'll be careful with it? You trust them?"

Callum flashed his eyes toward mine, and I almost missed the sparkle in the low light of the morning.

"Do you think I would go to such trouble . . . ask you to stay here in my own house so I can be your patron and then risk your very special loom with clumsy hands?"

His eyes seemed to dare me to look away. I didn't.

"Why did you ask me to wear blue to the party? Blue like the river?"

He grinned and leaned toward me, taking a long breath in through his nose. "You smell like the water and the reeds and the rocks."

I went cold. Had the Bean-Nighe's magic left a mark somehow that Callum could detect?

"Why did you want me to come to the first party in blue, Callum?"

He stepped back. "I thought you'd look nice in blue."

He might have suspected something about the Bean-Nighe. It wasn't a secret that she could grant a wish if you were willing to pay the price, but the magic could have come from elsewhere too. Nemain, for one. It could have been just as I'd said—that I prayed to Nemain over the loom and was sincere enough for her to grant me my wish. It was incredibly unlikely that she'd pay any attention to someone like me, but not impossible. I liked that version better, wanted Callum to believe it. He didn't need to know I'd gone down to the river and almost drowned for the privilege of weaving fabric with a dusting of magic.

"Maybe I'll weave myself something new once my loom gets here. Something blue," I said. "I'm growing tired of this yellow dress and blue sash."

*Growing tired?* What a thing to say. I didn't have the luxury to grow tired of anything.

"Maybe you should, but first can you put that dress back on so we can go down to breakfast?"

Prickles of embarrassment erupted all over my skin. While talking, I'd forgotten to keep my arms crossed over myself.

"Go out, please," I managed to say.

He smiled and his eyes twinkled. Damn him.

I tiptoed over to the bed where I'd flung my dress and sash the night before. I'd never owned anything complicated enough to require a second person to help me into it, so I slipped the dress over my head and forced it into shape by tying the blue ribbon tight around my waist.

"Ready," I said, sweeping into the hallway and bowing at the waist. "Though I'm a bit overdressed for breakfast."

Callum released a little chuckle at the joke and my stomach flipped. Why had I said that? I wasn't someone who wore different dresses at different times of the day. I'd made the joke because I thought *he* might find it funny. Well, no more of that. I could admit to myself that Callum was handsome, and that I might like some fun with him—but I wouldn't start telling disingenuous jokes to make that happen.

"What do you normally eat for breakfast?" he asked as we went down the corridor back to the main gallery. The sight was no less impressive in the morning. Light drifted in, hazy yellow from the tinted glass in the windows beside the front door. I checked the bannister carving as we walked by. Lugh and his deranged court. It still made me uncomfortable in the daylight.

"Well?" Callum prompted.

I dragged my eyes away from the carving and settled them on Callum's.

"If anything at all, porridge."

It was cheap and fast and could be made in my own hearth. Sometimes I had an egg if I was lucky.

Callum's white teeth shone when he smiled. He didn't look like he'd lost any of them. They weren't even yellowing at the top. I ran my tongue over my own teeth—it felt like they'd molded in the night with a thin layer of fuzz. Hopefully Callum wasn't looking at my teeth as closely as I was looking at his. I missed my brushing sponge.

"That's what I like for breakfast too."

"Really?" I asked. "When you could have anything?"

He led the way down the wide staircase and past the ballroom. A smaller dining room opened up off another pair of double doors. The long, dark wood table took up most of the room, but a silver bowl filled with fluffy white porridge stood on a matching sideboard. Beside the bowl sat two tiny silver pitchers—I hoped they were filled with cream and honey.

"What could be better than this?" Callum said and filled a porcelain bowl to the brim with porridge. He took one of the pitchers and poured thick cream on top. "Don't you know even the gods eat porridge?"

I hadn't had cream on my porridge since before Papa had been taken. Saliva gathered on my tongue as I took the honey and poured it on my breakfast.

"Do they? It must be a habit."

Callum laughed and pulled out a chair beside me. "This stuff does go back a long way. All those who came before us on these lands ate it."

"That's a bit poetic for porridge."

He took the pitcher of honey from my hands and drizzled the amber liquid into his bowl. "Ah, but this *is* poetic."

I couldn't argue as I mixed my honey in with the cream, creating golden swirls I wanted to lick up straight from the bowl.

The first mouthful was perfect—warm and sticky sweet. I made it through half my bowl before I wondered where the servant was who'd brought out our breakfast. Everything had been laid out on the sideboard and it had been hot. How had they managed that when they couldn't have known how long we'd take to come downstairs? The questions brewed as I took another bite of porridge.

"Your staff is very efficient," I said.

Callum licked some honey off his spoon and nodded. "I keep only the best in this house."

"Does that include me?"

I didn't want to tiptoe around things the way I'd tiptoed over the cold floorboards upstairs. We'd said we'd talk about what we wanted, why he'd asked to be my patron and why I'd accepted. I meant to do exactly that.

"Are you the best weaver in the city?"

It wasn't a claim I would have made a few days ago. Good, yes. Quite good in fact. But the best? If that were true, I wouldn't have owed Gregory any money. I'd have sold and sold and sold to many clients and they would have told their friends about me, and I'd have sold some more.

But now, with the Bean-Nighe's magic in my loom I could be the best.

"I am," I said.

He raised his brows. "Then yes, that includes you. I like to collect beautiful things, objects I can look at when I feel sad. And I mean your fabrics, by the way, not you. You *are* lovely, but you're not an object."

Heat burned my cheeks. He was right—I wasn't an object. But I was the means to one. The supplier of beautiful things. That was where my value lay.

But even so, he'd called me lovely. I couldn't pretend that wasn't nice to hear.

"So you want my fabrics to get you more money, more power."

Callum pushed his heavy chair back from the table with a scrape against the floorboards and turned in his seat to angle himself toward me.

"Don't you want to be part of something, Ella? Something great?"

I dropped my own spoon back into my empty bowl and leaned toward him, elbows on the table, chin propped in my hands. I did want to be part of something, but not for him. I wanted it for me. Eight hundred coins was a good start—enough to be comfortable, but not this kind of wealth. Not Callum's kind of wealth. That could be reached only by being one of *them*, the people who made decisions and agreements and traded influence behind doors closed to the likes of me. I loved the process of weaving, the creation of something beautiful, but there was always something that could go wrong. Silk prices rising, disinterested clients, too much competition. Having my own shop would help, but it wasn't enough on its own. Working a trade would never be as secure as pulling the strings. I had to think of that.

"What is your plan, Callum?"

He let his spoon fall from his hand and it clattered in the bowl.

"I want to wrap my influence around this city like a scarlet ribbon and squeeze."

# Chapter Eighteen

Cinching the city with his influence sounded ambitious armed with nothing but suits and dresses, even if they were imbued with the Bean-Nighe's magic.

"Are you some kind of military strategist?" I asked.

Callum laughed and shook his head. "I think you know better than most people that swords and cannons aren't the only way to exert influence."

I didn't know what he was talking about, but I didn't want to say that outright. It would be better to play along, let him reveal more of his plans. I wanted to learn how I could fit into them.

"Force isn't the only way, but it's usually the fastest, right?" I asked.

A shadow fell over the dining room, descending on us as a cloud cloaked the sun beyond the windows. What had been a cheerful room of white linens, honey, and cream was now a faded chamber of dark corners. An ember burned in the deep fireplace, glowing like a mythical dragon's heart among the ash.

"Do you want me to tell you more?" Callum asked.

"Yes."

I wanted to know everything, all the things he knew about taking everything life could offer.

"One string at a time, Ella. Before you know it, you'll see the whole pattern."

"So you won't tell me what the Players' next moves are?"

He leaned in even closer. Our shoulders touched, and I stopped myself from jumping back. Instead, I pressed harder against him, showing him he couldn't make me uncomfortable. He reached out for a piece of my red hair and coiled the curl around his finger. I enjoyed the sensation zipping through my body—a little exciting, a bit scary. His lips glistened where he'd licked them; I wondered if they'd taste like honey from the porridge.

"Ella," he said, letting his tongue curl around the *l*s in my name.

"Yes?"

"The carters are here. You want to go with them to collect your loom, don't you?"

I pulled back and my hair fell free from his finger. It didn't seem like he'd been thinking about my lips *at all*.

"Y-yes, I want to go, but I also want to know what I'm in for."

Callum stood from his chair and brought his bowl over to the sideboard. He placed it just next to the serving bowl and arranged his spoon carefully beside it. He didn't need to do that—I was certain his servants, the best of servants as he said, would collect his leavings from the table itself. Did he do it to make their job easier? That was unexpected.

"No one knows what tomorrow will bring except the gods," he said. "Why should you be any different?"

I stood as well and gathered up my bowl and spoon, copying him by setting them on the sideboard.

"You're twisting words. I don't want to know *exactly* what will happen tomorrow, but I do want to know what you expect of me. How will I help you take over the city with my fabrics? What exactly does that mean?"

He clasped his hands behind his back. I counted three breaths while I waited for him to answer, and every one of them cost me. My belly twisting, whirling, and spinning with all the thoughts of what he might say. What if he wanted me to do something I really couldn't? Manipulating people with the Bean-Nighe's magic wasn't exactly hurting anyone. But if he wanted more?

"You weave, Ella. Just that. Make me beautiful things."

Callum left me standing in the dining room, staring at the back of his gray wool coat. I was more than happy to make beautiful things, but I suspected it wasn't going to be as simple as that.

⟡

Three carters waited outside in the semicircular drive. My boots crunched the gravel underneath them as I approached the two men and one woman. They all wore strictly utilitarian clothing—baggy trousers with room for bending, linen shirts already so stained around the edges no one would care if they got any dirtier. Only two of them wore thin wool coats. One man shivered in the morning chill.

I pulled my brown shawl around my shoulders, but I was completely aware of how ridiculous I probably looked. A wide piece of wool wrapped around my shoulders and a dress better suited to a party than manual labor, finished off with a bright blue ribbon.

"It's your house we're going to?" the woman asked. Her brown hair sat in a knot on top of her head and her ears were pink from the unforgiving breeze.

"It's a room, a flat in an old building . . . not a house."

She shrugged. "Where?"

The others perked up, listening intently. They wanted to know how hard a job this was going to be, how far they were going to have to pull the handcart.

"Down the hill from the market, near the river."

The woman sighed and waved a hand at one of the men. He grasped the handles of the cart.

"We split it," he said. "We all do one-third of the trip."

"On the way there *and* back. You're not pulling it empty all the way there and getting me to pull it full and heavy back here," the second man said.

"Ugh, let's just go," the woman said. "Show us the way, girl."

The cart wheels rolled along the cobbles with a clatter. It wouldn't fit down the main market road with all the people meandering along, so I led them through side streets. We almost got stuck twice where the road seemed to disappear and the buildings leaned too close to each other. When we emerged into the courtyard in front of my building, the woman dropped the cart and rubbed her hands together.

"Blisters," she said.

I nodded because I knew her pain. Blisters and callouses and sore fingers had been part of my life for as long as I could remember. Even now, my hands hurt if I flexed my fingers. One of my knuckles caught my eye as I did so. Swollen. It was strange because that usually only happened right after I put the shuttle down and slid off the stool in front of my loom—not a day later. This knuckle looked like one of Mrs. Under's, and her swelling never went away.

My kind of life had consequences. Even though I loved the act of it, and the things I could make, weaving left its mark on me. Eventually I wouldn't be able to do it anymore because I'd done so much of it. It was a strange thought, but it was exactly what had happened to Mrs. Under. She worked herself into an old woman before her time.

I didn't want to let that happen to me. If I had it my way, I'd weave for pleasure—because I could and because I was good at it. I'd do it to make something beautiful. For no other reason but that. Not to sell, not to make something to suit a client's taste. I'd weave pieces just because I wanted to.

But to make that future happen, I needed money from somewhere else. Finding myself someone rich to marry wasn't likely, and the idea of tying myself to another human being just for their coin turned my stomach sour. An arrangement like that was bound to have consequences for the person with less.

Building my own fortune was the less obvious answer, but it was the one I liked most. If I could fit myself into the Players' world, I could have access to the very thing that made them *them*: money.

The carters leaned against the faded plaster building, waiting for me to produce a key. Another man leaned with them and passed them a smoking pipe. The cracked wood door to the stairway of the building was never locked, but they didn't know that. Whoever owned this place—and I'd never actually met them because Mrs. Under collected my rent on their behalf—didn't care enough about anything inside to worry about it getting damaged or stolen. Including us.

I led the carters up the stairs and pulled an iron key from my pocket. The door to my room swung open with a little push. It had been only a night, but the distance made me see the room anew. The bed was the only piece of proper furniture, and the loom was the only impressive thing in the entire room. Everything else was the dregs, the things other people hadn't wanted anymore. A chipped ewer and bowl painted with ugly swirls of brown and orange. A thrice-mended pot someone had given up for good. A hairbrush with missing bristles that Mrs. Under had given to me, taking pity on me and combing out the mats at the back of my head.

What did these men see? The woman? Did they wonder how on earth I'd come to be in a house like Callum's?

"What's all this?" the woman asked.

"I'm a weaver. That's my loom, those are my supplies."

She raked her eyes over every spool of thread, every glittering string of sequins. I tried to imagine how she saw them, the flash of something shiny and the deep blue color of expensive wool thread. She probably thought I owned these things, that they were mine to enjoy and not tools for work. And because these supplies had come from the Bean-Nighe's magic, they *were* mine, but I still needed them to do a job for me.

The woman picked a square of silk off a nail sticking out of the wall over the loom. It showed a pattern of irises against a background the color of fresh churned butter. A sampler. Papa insisted we make them to show our clients what could be done. *"Entice them,"* he'd say. *"Show them what we're worth."* It often worked, and the client of the day would order a patterned bolt instead of plain broadcloth. Papa always loved those moments. He'd step lightly away from the house and tweak my ear.

*"See, Ella? The thread that went into this sampler was worth it."*

I'd always held my tongue. I never spat back at him that now he'd have to sit at the loom for twice as long to make the new bolt with a pretty pattern and earn only one and a half as much as he would for a solid color. He didn't like to hear it, and when I was little, I didn't understand why. All I knew was that Papa's attention would be elsewhere longer. Now I knew he was lost in a lovely world of his own making when he wove flowers or birds or waves into his creations. I understood because it was the same for me. I got lost in it.

The woman held the square of silk between two fingers, stretching it wide to see the shape of the flowers.

"You made this?"

I nodded. "It's a sampler. I use it to show my work to the people who want to buy."

She turned her whole head toward me and her eyes sparked with some kind of energy. Excitement?

"Could I buy this piece?" she asked.

"What? It's just for show."

"C'mon, Leesa. Let's get this job done," one of the men said from near the door. He and the second man squatted on the floorboards since I hadn't been able to offer them a chair.

"Hang on, Joe. Think of it . . . we could give this to Mam. Cover her *Tales of the Gods* with it."

"Mam's never had something like that," said the other man.

I suspected now they were all siblings, and they did all share the same chestnut hair. It would be bright with the dirt and grease washed away.

"So how much?" the woman, Leesa, asked.

No one had ever wanted to buy a sampler before, but it was a clever idea. These little pieces of fabric could be used for something beyond luring clients in. Once they'd done that job, they could be sold to the people who could never afford the full bolt.

"Four bronzes," I said.

Leesa narrowed her eyes at me but nodded. "You've got talent here, girl. This silk is something special."

Despite myself, my heart glowed with satisfaction.

"Here, I'll wrap it for you in some linen. But you get started with the loom while I do, all right?"

Leesa waved a hand at her brothers, and they started to disassemble the loom with my instructions. I helped them with the shafts and the warp beam. Carefully, because I watched every movement, they carried the separate pieces down to the waiting cart. I stuffed in the bags of thread to help cushion the loom pieces.

When the last spool of sequins had been loaded, I stared up at the window above my own. Mrs. Under stood there and held up a finger. I waited for her at the bottom of the stairs, and she made her slow, careful descent.

"Do you want help?" I asked.

"I can manage." She braced herself against the wall for the last step. "There, that's my outing for the day."

I glanced down into her lined face. It was getting harder for her to move around, and she didn't have any family I'd ever seen. Who would fetch her food, ale? All the little things needed to sustain a life?

"Get the worry out of your eyes, Ella. I've money to pay someone to take care of me."

She'd read the thoughts behind my furrowed brow. "I'll be back, I will. But I couldn't not do this."

"And what is *this*, exactly?"

The words tumbled out in a heap. "A rich man, well a *young* man, said he'd be my patron."

One of Mrs. Under's gray eyebrows shot up and my cheeks flamed.

"It's not like that!" I said quickly. "Not at all! I'm just weaving silk for him. And like I said, I'll be back."

She shrugged. "Maybe you will, maybe you won't. Don't waste concern over me, Ella. Worry about yourself."

The heat fled my cheeks, replaced by a coolness that spread through the rest of my body. "What do you mean? Do you think it's dangerous?"

Mrs. Under steadied herself by clinging to my arm. I braced it against her weight, not wanting her to fall as she shuffled around to face the stairs again.

"I don't know what will happen, Ella. I just want you to be careful."

I met her wet eyes. "I will."

She retreated slowly up the stairs back to her room and watched from the window as the carters argued over whose turn it was to pull the handcart.

The pipe man still leaned against the wall, watching us pack up. I didn't recognize him and that was strange. Most people didn't visit our courtyard by accident.

"Where you off to?" He spat a piece of tobacco to the ground.

"Why do you want to know?"

He smirked and straightened, pocketing the pipe in his vest.

"It's not me who wants to know, Ella. But don't worry. I already got the whole story from these two."

He nodded toward Joe and his brother. Joe waved.

The pipe man knew my name. He'd come here to watch me, and I'd given him quite a show. He knew where we were bringing the loom thanks to Joe, and I was sure he'd report every detail to his boss. To Gregory.

# Chapter Nineteen

I followed the carters out of the courtyard and onto the street the magistrates had once dragged my father down. Gregory's man didn't follow—he didn't need to. He already knew where I was going. I let that thought settle in my stomach, souring it, and followed the carts back to the big house on the hill.

My loom fit perfectly under the window in the room Callum had given me—just like I thought it would.

Callum watched me set it up, his eyes following my arms and hands as I slipped each piece of wood into place and tightened the strings. I tried to pretend he wasn't there and just get on with it, but I couldn't help the prickles running down the back of my neck.

"It looks so easy when you do it," he said.

"I've done it before, many times."

"Why?"

"Before we came to the room I live in now, Papa and I moved around a bit. We left whenever the rent got too high. The loom had to be taken apart and put back together each time we moved."

Callum watched me from where he sat at the end of the bed, and I twisted my body away from him so he couldn't see the gap between my dress and shift as I bent over to pull a string through.

"So you don't belong to a place, then. A house or a room?" he asked.

I stood and shook my head. "I belong to the city, I guess. It's the only home I know, though we come from the mountains, and I have a few memories of our time there."

*And I belong to the river.* It was where my mind quieted.

"I envy you that," Callum said. "To know your home."

"Haven't you been here long? You have quite the house to show for your time here."

He swept his hand out, a gesture to encompass the whole of the room. "Wood and stone. Moveable, breakable. It's the heart of this place, this city, you feel like you belong to. I've never had that."

He wasn't wrong. Even though I was like a thread trailing from an unhemmed edge, I was part of the fabric of the city. I knew the side streets stretching out from the marketplace like spider legs. I could climb down the riverbank without slipping because I knew exactly where to put my feet. There were never any questions about which shop to go to for bread when I had enough coin because I knew McTavish's bakery sold the freshest, sweetest loaves.

"You really feel no tie here and yet you want to influence all of us, help us decide what we like and don't like," I said.

The loom was finished now, and I swept my skirt under me to sink down into the well-worn grooves of the bench.

"Maybe that way, the city will let me into its heart."

"What do you mean? The people have more than let you in! They've embraced you. Look at your guest list from the last two parties. Most of those people wouldn't even let me brush against their shoulders if they knew I was just a weaver."

Callum stood from the bed with a creak of the ropes and dropped to his knees in front of me. I wondered if he was going to touch me, put his hands on my legs or take my fingers in his own. He didn't, and I was surprised at the little sliver of hurt stuck in my throat.

"You're looking at it all wrong, Ella. They come to my parties because those parties take place in this house. They eat my food and dance to my music and smile their performer's smiles. But they don't give themselves over to me. Not really. I never get to see abandonment. Never what's underneath the stiff fabrics and paints."

So he wanted to see the raw city? The people stripped bare of their societal armor? He only needed to spend a little time in my courtyard or any of the other streets with jumbles of buildings and people pulling themselves along by sheer will into the next day.

"You're just seeing the wrong people, Callum."

He nodded and finally slipped his fingers into mine on my lap. I gazed at him, wondering what I was supposed to do next. Was I meant to close my hands around his or keep my fingers limp as though his touch wasn't heating my body?

In the end, I landed on closing my fingers over his. He smiled.

"I want you to help me with that, Ella," he said. "Your fabrics can let me see into people, into how far they'll go, what they'll really do . . . and if I can see into them, I can be a part of them."

"But why do you want to? You have everything already."

He pulled his fingers away and a wave of loss swept over me.

"No, I don't. I want people to see me. Love me."

I swung my legs back around the bench to face my loom. The long needle, the Bean-Nighe's needle, shone in the streams of sunlight coming in through the window. I didn't know if the loom could do what he wanted. If *I* could do what he wanted. Last night, the blue silk had beguiled Mrs. MacDonald, but it had worn off quickly when she walked away. And people wouldn't love Callum for holding the trade agreement for coal in his hands—most would resent him.

Callum stood and went to the mirror over the little vanity against the wall on the other side of the fireplace. He leaned over the small table and rested on his hands. What did he see when he looked in the glass? I'd been too scared to look again this morning. I didn't want to see any more gray hairs or even the sight of my swollen knuckles reflected back at me. It was unnerving. Callum probably saw himself exactly as he expected, since he likely had a pure glass mirror in his own room too. Nothing in his reflection would have been transformed by the dents in a circle of copper or the ripples of a bug skittering across the river's surface.

He expected my fabrics to act like this perfect mirror, to show him the true reflection of people, and I was sure they couldn't do that. I wouldn't tell him that though. It would undermine exactly why I'd agreed to his patronage in the first place. I had to give something he wanted to get something I wanted, so it was best to keep him thinking I could provide that very thing.

"Are you going to elaborate on why you want people to love you?" I asked.

Callum turned and leaned against the little table. "Not yet."

I hadn't expected him to, not after knowing me for less than two weeks. In fact, he'd already told me quite a lot for a near stranger. It was probably everything he needed me to know to play my part.

"So, I'm here . . . my loom is here. What do you want me to do, Callum?"

He swept over the spools of thread I'd emptied on top of the bed. Some rolled toward him when he sunk his knee into the mattress as he climbed up. He picked up a silk the color of starlight.

"Make me something luminous."

"For you yourself? For a suit?"

Callum nodded and picked up a spool of silk as bright as daffodils. "And this for Odina."

"It will take some time," I said. The gleam in his eye didn't remind me of patience, and I wouldn't be scolded later for weaving too slowly for his liking.

"It takes how long it takes. I understand. I also want you to do two more silks . . . you can choose the colors . . . to outfit the other members of the Players."

"There are only four of you?"

I'd always imagined more, at least a dozen highborn people pulling sway on the city and guiding the Chieftain toward his decisions. Four people didn't seem like enough.

"I didn't say that . . . I've just asked you to make enough fabric to clothe us four."

No truth was going to be easily won with Callum. He liked the shadows he cast, the dark unknowns he brought with him into every room. I wondered if anyone else knew where he was from or how long he'd been in this house. Odina, maybe?

In the end, I supposed it shouldn't matter much to me. I wasn't concerned about his past—I was interested in my place in his future. The Players' future.

"I'll start on them today," I said and took the spool of starlight thread from his hand. Our fingers brushed and he bit his lip. A little bolt of invisible lightning zipped through my body. I leaned in a little closer, pretending to get a tighter grip on the spool but really wanting to smell the spicy sweetness clinging to his skin.

"Ella," he whispered.

"Yes?"

I watched how his lips moved, how they smiled after forming my name. Was he leaning closer or was I falling into the soft mattress?

"I want to show you something," he said.

I shifted backward, pulling the spool of silk thread with me. There had to be some space between us or I might bury my nose in his neck. Better to sit back on my heels and hope Callum couldn't hear the *thump-thump-thump* of my heartbeat.

"Now?"

"No. Get started on this and come downstairs after lunch. I'll have a tray brought up for you so you don't have to disturb your work."

"How thoughtful."

Or it was a very nice way to keep me confined to this room until he wanted to see me. I ran my finger along the smooth thread on the spool. I was okay with that. I wanted to get lost in my work for a bit so I could calm the questions dancing through my mind.

Callum stood and stretched his arms above his head. The movement revealed a small gap between his loose linen shirt and wool trousers, a strip of flesh with dark hair running from his belly button and disappearing down his waistband. Beside that was a tiny swirl inked into his skin.

Embarrassment and something else, something fiery, hissed inside me. I'd never seen any man's body before, nothing of what was hidden beneath swaths of fabric. Even Papa had been careful to ask me to turn my back when he undressed.

Should I pretend I hadn't seen or should I ask him about the swirl? I'd only ever met a handful of people with ink marks.

"Do you have everything you need?" he asked. "I've asked for some day dresses to be delivered to your room."

I almost did it, almost asked him who'd hammered the ink into his skin, but the words hung on the end of my tongue. In the end, I closed my lips around them and smiled. "Then I have everything."

And it was true—I did have everything. The Bean-Nighe had granted my wishes and given me everything I needed to create the life I yearned for. It was all here, in my hands, to weave together just how I wanted it. The purse of money coming, the agreement. I just had to be careful not to let the fine threads get hopelessly tangled.

# Chapter Twenty

I pricked the exact same spot on my smallest finger, and that was a mistake. It hurt more this time, but I made myself squeeze two drops of blood onto the long silver needle. Now fed, my loom seemed to tremble with energy. I laid my hands on the wood and let the vibrations tickle my skin as my ability, my talent, the thing that made me *me*, came flooding in.

Papa always used to say weaving was jolly work, and I knew he was right. It was something very special to enjoy doing the thing that made you money. I always thought about that when I saw the butcher's girl catching blood in a bowl for puddings or sweeping up foaming red messes. I had a trade, and that was something I thanked the gods and Papa for. Even better, it was a trade I enjoyed.

I liked picking the colors and deciding what picture to paint with the thread. Callum had told me what spools to use for him and Odina, but he hadn't said anything about the patterns. He'd asked for something luminous, and I could certainly deliver that. The silk thread itself glittered, a delicate silver that would catch the light. There was another spool of silver thread, so dark it was almost gray, and I plucked it from the bed. I'd use it to form the shape of stars.

It was easy for me to imagine the finished product before I even sent the shuttle through the thread the first time. That was part of the thrill—picturing something beautiful in my mind and challenging my hands to make it. Sometimes it worked, sometimes it didn't quite. But trying was the good part.

I strung up one spool of silver thread and loaded my shuttle. Each pass was the same at first—over and under, over and under. Rhythmic and familiar. Like a lullaby. The edge of the fabric formed under my movements, and pride glowed in my chest. I made that. It was just the beginning, the promise of something lovely, but the potential of it was the most exciting part.

The star pattern would need to be woven in after I left enough room for a sewing edge. Callum's seamstress, whoever she was, would need room to hem and there was hardly any point extending the pattern that far. I strung in the first thread of dark gray and hoped Callum would like it. I wanted it to be unlike anything he'd ever seen. I wanted to be the only one in the whole world who could give him something like this.

I'd imagined the pattern being easier to achieve than it was. My fingers weren't as agile as usual—perhaps from nerves, from everything that had happened in the last two days. The stars weren't shaping up as crisply as Papa would have liked, but it was still pretty.

Light moved within the room. The sun reached its high point in the sky outside my window and began its daily descent into darkness. Did the sun mind sharing the sky with the moon? Did they ever spar over who could shine brighter? Or maybe both the sun and the moon worried about the stars outdazzling them. The ones on this bolt of cloth certainly would.

When my legs began to ache and I had to arch my spine to stretch the muscles in my lower back, a knock echoed through the door. It was a welcome excuse to stand from my bench. I opened the door swiftly, hurrying to catch the servant who'd brought my lunch, but there was no one. Just a tray sitting a little off-balance on the edge of the woven rug running down the white-plastered hallway. The candles were lifeless; whoever had built the house thought to include small, narrow windows on the wall at the front of the house every few feet to light the corridor during the day.

Where were the servants? Could they really be so efficient that they were almost invisible? It seemed unlikely. And yet, I'd seen only one yesterday at the party and none today—except the carters, and I wasn't sure they counted. They probably didn't just work for Callum alone. I bent to pick up the tray of oatcakes and tiny bowls of whipped yellow butter and amber honey.

The crockery trembled on the platter, just a little, but enough to make a noise. Someone was running, shaking the floorboards. Just around the corner maybe?

"Hello?" My voice came out as little more than a whisper. I'd meant to shout, but the tiny seed of fear in my belly had grown enough to strangle me.

Bells. Tiny, tickling bells rung somewhere in the distance. No, not bells. Laughter. The giggling of a high-pitched voice.

"Hello?" I tried again, and this time I managed to throw my voice down toward the gallery.

I strained my ears, filling them with the silence. Nothing else, no bell-like laughter. No steps. The crockery stood still on the tray.

I brought my lunch into my room. My skin prickled all over and I realized *I* was the one making the bowls and plate rattle now. Those oatcakes would just get stuck in my throat, no matter how much butter or honey I slathered on. My mouth was dry, tongue sticking behind my teeth. It was a big, old house with a history of its own before Callum even came to it, and what I heard could have been anything. I wasn't familiar with the noise of this place yet, not like I knew the sounds of my room. There was likely a very simple explanation I hadn't discovered yet.

Either way, lunch was a lost cause and my fingers were too slick with nerves to work the shuttle. Callum had told me to find him after lunch, and I wanted to know why. I put on one of the navy day dresses that had been delivered that morning and went down.

❦

Callum had been vague when he'd asked me to come downstairs after lunch, and I'd kind of assumed he'd magically appear as soon as I descended the stairs. Well, he didn't. The grand stairway spilled out onto the gleaming floorboards of the foyer, but Callum didn't block any of the light from the windows on either side of the double doors. The place was missing all the warm bodies of the night before, and I shivered in my plain wool dress.

Completely unsure what to do, I followed a corridor off the foyer and realized it probably mirrored the one upstairs where my room was located. It, too, benefited from small windows set into the wall every few steps. I should have paid more attention when Callum had led me to the dining room earlier, but I'd been too busy talking to him about that damn creepy carving of Lugh.

I peeked in through a door off the hallway. It looked like a parlor but lacked the prettiness of Odina's or the dainty detail of the others I'd been in. This room was darker, with thick wood columns running from floor to ceiling and walls covered in deep blue silk. The place was empty, so I stepped over the threshold and walked on my toes over to the back wall, as if by not fully connecting my feet with the floor, I could claim I hadn't really been snooping around in here.

The silk drew me in, begging to be touched. There were panels of it, but still—this would have been a big project. A huge task for any weaver. White flowers popped against the deep shimmer of the blue. The pattern was masterful. I ran my fingers along the thread and tried to guess how the weaver had done it.

"What does your professional eye think?"

I didn't jump or yelp or pull my hand away from the wall because that was likely what he expected. Instead, I went on feeling the pattern of white flowers with my fingers.

"It would have been complicated to do."

I heard Callum step into the room and the rustle of his day jacket as he got closer. How had he approached the room without me hearing? Maybe I'd been too absorbed in this incredible silk.

"That's it? It's complicated?"

I turned then and met his eyes. Warm with a hint of their sparkle.

"It's beautiful, of course." *Masterful,* I thought again but didn't want to say. Callum didn't need any reminders of other weavers' mastery right now. I wanted to keep him enticed by *my* fabrics.

"I wish I'd known who the weaver was," he said.

I shrugged even though I wondered the same thing myself. Could it be Mrs. Under's work? She'd once shown me a sampler with a very similar pattern. Or maybe the wall panels were even older than that. Perhaps it had been someone famous, renowned in the city for their fabric arts, with their own shop in the market.

"Why did you want me to come down here?" I asked, turning away from the silk.

Callum sat on the green velvet arm of one of the sofas and rubbed his hand through the faint stubble dusting his cheeks and jawline.

"There's something I want to show you."

"Oh?"

Maybe there was a particular design he wanted me to use for one of the bolts and it was inspired by something in the house. I glanced around the sitting room and took in the carved columns with their roses formed of swirls, the facets of the cut glass bottle holding amber liquid on a table under the window. Just as he'd said, he surrounded himself with the best, most beautiful things.

"It's not in here," he said.

Callum had watched me take a tour of the room with my gaze. My cheeks threatened to burn, but I took one long, deep breath and the feeling subsided. I hadn't done anything wrong by looking around. I was his beneficiary, not his servant.

"Well, where is it then?"

He smiled and gestured toward the door. "Come and see."

∞

The expanse of grass studded with heather and tiny pink wildflowers sprawled from the back door. It stretched until it dipped down toward the river. It had been lively and beautiful last night and was peaceful now. Callum led the way, catching a long yellow piece of grass in his fingers and tugging it free. I kept just a little behind him.

"Is this all yours?" I asked.

"The grounds are as impressive as the house."

He said this as if he was a bit detached from them, and I guessed he was since he hadn't designed the house or the lands around it. Neither had his parents or grandparents. He was tied to this place only by a chain of coin. His heart didn't live here.

"Well, it's all beautiful," I said. There was no denying that as the sun gilded the pale green leaves of the birch trees.

"Where do your ideas come from, Ella? The colors you use, the patterns you create?"

No one had ever asked me a question like that before. I suspected my clients generally didn't care how I came up with my ideas—as long as the end product made them shine.

"I suppose I hoard memories. The way a snail's shell curls over its body, the color of a rose petal seen through a raindrop, even the feeling I get when I hear the chimes from the temple."

"So it could be anything, then? Nature or human-made?"

"Anything that catches my eye ... or my heart."

Callum seemed to chew on this. I'd probably said too much. Why had I told him how I actually felt about it? He was a client in the end—different from any I'd had before, but still. I had to keep that line between us. Wanting to kiss him was innocent enough, simple fun, but telling him a truth of my heart? That could be dangerous. The better he knew me, the more likely he was to forge that knowledge into a weapon he could use against me.

We were on the same level as we tramped across the lawn. We both had something the other wanted, and that was enough.

"Nothing can replicate how sweet the air tastes or how bright the first sunny day is after a week of rain, but I enjoy seeing artists try," he finally said.

"Because you can buy the results?"

I fell into step with him as we crested the hill. The land dipped down toward the strip of water I'd seen last night— narrower here than back in town. This section of the river tumbled into itself, the water frothing and bubbling in delight as it played. I stared at it, envious of the water's lightness, its abandon.

Callum's fingers slipped into mine and I stumbled, my foot slipping on a wet patch of grass. He acted like he didn't notice. His eyes never left the river even as he let go of my hand.

"It's more than buying the results, Ella. I like to watch people try to re-create something they can't. They try and try and some people give up and others embrace the frenzy that comes with dedicating your life to the impossible."

I put my fingers to my throat and felt the hot skin of my neck with my cold hands. *Frenzy.* I'd never felt that way when working on a piece. My loom made me calm; weaving didn't wind me up like a spool of thread.

"You speak of everyone as if they're the same . . . all the people who try to make beautiful things."

Callum laughed and the wind whipped the sound away, probably carrying it down toward the water. "They are, in fact, a chaotic bunch, artists. I enjoy them."

I kept an eye on the roiling surface of the only river we had—the one that snaked around these outskirts and then right into town. The air smelled of the grass and the leaves, their tips starting to turn yellow and orange. No cloying scent of dirt. The Bean-Nighe wasn't here. She had no reason to be here.

I reached out this time and took Callum's fingers then, just as he had done mine a few minutes earlier. I let the fissures of excitement crackle through me, feasting on them as I rubbed my thumb against his. I couldn't help it; this was better than the sweetest honey. His gaze met mine and I studied him—the sharp contours of his cheekbones, the smooth line of his nose. He looked sharp, but I already knew he could be kind.

What I didn't know was how far that kindness extended.

"Why are we down by the river, Callum?"

# Chapter Twenty-One

He didn't answer my question. Instead, he let my hand go and trailed down the hill to the water's edge. I followed close behind.

"Are you just going to ignore me?" I asked.

He picked up a rock and ran his thumb over the flat surface of it. "I'm not ignoring *you* at all. I'm not addressing your question because I don't have an answer for it. I know nothing more than you, I think. Your loom is special somehow, and it helps you weave fabrics with a drop of magic to them. More than Nemain would give."

It didn't matter much if he did or didn't know where the magic came from. He knew about it, and that was why he'd offered to be my patron. All of that was fine. I'd already decided to be all right with it and use the chance to my advantage. He couldn't hold anything more over me even if he did know where the magic in my loom came from. The old washerwoman had already granted my wish—what else was there?

Callum crouched and skipped his rock across the surface of the river, like a dragonfly just touching its legs to the water and taking off again. Touch, take off, touch, take off. Sink.

I knew from watching them that if a dragonfly's wings got wet, they weren't able to fly anymore. One slipup and the river would keep the insect as its own. I remembered the weight of water on top of me, the crushing realization that the one thing I needed more than anything was out of reach—air, breath, life.

I pulled a crisp breath in now through my nose. This time of year was my favorite. Air like the first bite of an apple. Leaves painted rich hues of yellows and reds. I'd always wanted to capture those colors in a bolt of cloth. Maybe I would after I was done with all this. If my shop was a success, I'd have the money to pick and choose any spools, any color of silk thread I wanted. And I'd make the fabric for myself, no one else. To wear to remember harvesttime.

"What does it matter whether it was Nemain or not? You're getting what you want," I said.

"Are you going to tell me which fae is responsible for the magic?"

"There are only a few who grant wishes."

Callum's smile twisted into a frown. "Always at a cost."

"Not one you have to worry about."

He reached up and squeezed my hand. "But I do worry."

No one had worried about me since Papa had been taken away. Mrs. Under did a good approximation sometimes, when the mood struck her, but she'd go on just the same as always if I never came back to the room below hers. Callum didn't know me enough to worry about me though. Just because he held my hand didn't mean he cared for me like that. Heat crept into my cheeks, and I pulled my fingers from his before they grew damp.

"Why'd you want to come down here with me?" I asked.

"Didn't you tell me you like being near the water?" he said as he squatted where the river met the sand.

He was right, I did like it here. At the part of the river near my building's courtyard, there was always the possibility of being interrupted by loose dogs or playing children. Here, though, there was stillness. Birds called and flies buzzed over the water, and the long grass rippled in the breeze, but there weren't any other people around to get in the way. Whether Callum wanted to know more about the magic to weigh his risks or not, this was a nice place to be for a few minutes. I squatted beside him, ignoring the fact that my hem trailed in the damp sand, and dipped my aching fingers into the cool water. The current pulled the river around my knuckles, and it was almost as good as a massage.

"What's your plan, Callum? Where will you wear the fabric I'm making you?"

He turned his head toward me and squinted into the sun. Two lines appeared at the corners of both eyes that told stories of laughter. I wondered who he'd done that laughing with. Perhaps his mother and father before they died. Or maybe Odina and the other Players, and whoever the Players were when he joined their ranks. How many people had been part of that exclusive group over the years? Used up for what they were worth while they were young and then cast out—allowed only, for what it was worth, to still attend the parties. Like Brian that first night in Callum's dining room. He'd said he had a right to be there. Who made that rule? Who led the Players before Callum? All of these thoughts passed through my mind before he even opened his mouth to answer my question.

"I'll be wearing my silver suit to a party, and it will help me get one step closer to what I want."

"Which is?"

"I already told you . . . influence."

"I want to know exactly how you intend to do it. And what role my fabrics will play."

He glanced sidelong at me. The river flowed past our feet. Could the Bean-Nighe hear us? Even if she was somewhere else along the water? The idea of her being near had unnerved me at first, but there was something else underneath that feeling—an odd sense of comfort. She'd helped me, granted me my wish. I wasn't a stranger to her anymore, and perhaps that counted for something. Maybe not her protection, exactly, but at least her interest.

"Tell me how you would do it, Ella," he said. "How would you influence the city?"

I stumbled back on my heels, my ankles cracking in protest against my weight. I wasn't planning to take over the city or the people in it—I was only planning to take over my own life. To pull the control of it free from the hands of my clients and people like Gregory.

Callum's brown eyes shone, so similar in color to the wet sand at our feet. I wanted to play this game with him, for the fun of it and because he was probably more likely to let things slip if he was amused.

"I wouldn't start at the top with the Chieftain," I said. "I'd begin at the roots, dig deep and change the way things are done to my benefit. Then my influence would spread naturally, unstoppably, like a weed in a rose garden."

Callum chuckled and brought his thumb to his bottom lip to wipe away a fleck of spittle. A smile forced its way onto my lips. His face was so different now than the first time I saw him in Odina's parlor. Then it had been cast in shadow. Now the sun lit up every inch and contentment softened the angles. I liked it.

He dug his fingers into the wet earth at our feet, making a little hole.

"I want to plant a seed too. We're going to another party, Ella, where most things are done and decided. The Chieftain's party. There we'll convince him to give us control over the rents on Market Street."

"The whole market?"

I knew you had to get permission from the Chieftain's office to open a shop on Market Street, or even to set up a stall. It cost a hefty fee too.

"People will still be able to sell their vegetables on little tables lining the roads," Callum said.

"And the shops?"

"I'll pick what they are, who can sell what."

I didn't need to ask why. If Callum and the Players got to pick and choose what was sold at the marketplace, they'd have control over more than just coin. They could shape the market. They could create shortages if they wanted—reduce supply to increase demand. It could be chaos, all orchestrated by them.

My dream of having my own shop, of people longingly running their fingers over my fabrics, *my* creations, was either completely out of reach or the closest it'd ever been.

"You know I want one," I said.

"One what?"

"One of the rents. A shop to sell my fabrics."

Callum smiled again, but this time a cloud swept over the sun and the sharpness of his cheekbones and nose stood out in relief.

"And with your purse, you might be able to buy one."

"If we get the rents from the Chieftain, I want one of them for free. I'd have helped get them, after all."

"It can't be as easy as that, Ella."

He stood so he towered over me where I still crouched on the edge of the river. I sprang up, shaking the sand and dirt from my skirts, so we were nearly eye to eye.

"You need me. You can't do this on your own or you wouldn't have offered to become my patron in the first place."

"I have natural qualities, just like you do, you know," Callum said. "You may have learned your skill from your father, but there's talent in there too. My talent is to get people to do what I want."

"That's any rich person's talent."

Callum raised his brows and made a *tsk* noise in his mouth. "Maybe, but people follow me, and what I say, because they want to. Because they like it. Not because I pay them."

If he was talking about the other Players, about Odina, he was probably telling the truth. Something had compelled them to follow Callum, to let him be their leader. It had to be a natural flair for manipulation and control. I'd have to watch myself even more closely, make sure the balance between us never tipped in his favor.

"You earned their loyalty then, or they follow you because they have to?" I asked.

"Loyalty."

"And do you think you have mine?"

His eyes roamed over my face, and I bit my cheek to keep myself steady. I didn't want him to know my underarms grew damp under his stare.

"I think I do, as long as our goals take us in the same direction."

"You're right. And I want the purse of coin *and* one of the rents in Market Street. Don't you want to keep me happy, Callum? So you can get what you want?"

He looked out over the river for a few moments. I took a deep breath and tried not to count as the seconds slipped by. This was it. With a few simple words, he could give me everything I wanted: a future. Something secure, a chance to make more of myself. I hoped I made a strong enough case for why keeping me happy would benefit him too.

He sighed. "Fine, Ella. *If* we succeed and I get the rents in hand, you can have one."

Relief washed over me like warm summer rain. I could do this, beguile the Chieftain with my fabrics and get Callum the rents. We'd done it so easily with Brian and Mrs. MacDonald, and I had no doubt this time would be even better because there would be more of us wearing the magic silk. And then I'd have my purse of coins and my shop. I'd have control over my life and could be the best weaver this city had ever seen. People would come to me. Those who never would have looked at me before would seek me out. Everything was falling into place.

"We should get back to the house," Callum said, already turning from me.

Was that disappointment on his face? Did he think he had the worse end of the bargain?

Well, too bad for him. He was getting everything he wanted—maybe he was just not used to other people getting what they wanted too.

"You're right, I should get to work. You've ordered four bolts from me, and we have the Chieftain's party to prepare for."

# Chapter Twenty-Two

After two weeks, the Bean-Nighe's supplies were running out. I had to go into town and get more blue silk thread, with money in my pocket from Callum. I'd never bought a single spool of thread with money that I wouldn't have to pay back. I batted away the nervousness I was accustomed to, the guilt that chased me like one of the horseflies from the riverbank. Every time I'd bought what I needed to weave, I'd already felt sour about owning back the coin paying for it.

This dyer knew me, and she smiled at me as if I was any other paying customer, because she didn't know I'd always used borrowed money for her wares before. She let me dig through a small basket of different blue spools until I found the one I wanted. The woman waited on a little stool behind a piece of wood set up across two barrels. Nemain was painted on the front of both, wearing a flowing yellow gown. Those paintings were the only decoration in here. This place wasn't for wealthy customers, so there was no need to impress. It was for us—those who would make beautiful things for rich people.

After I paid, there was one more errand I wanted to run.

Gregory's shop wasn't far. The buildings on his street were old wood, sun-bleached, and pocked with rot. Signs hung above the shops, letting would-be patrons know whether they'd find a locksmith or a bookseller. It wasn't likely he'd be in at this hour of the morning—far more likely he'd be at the ordinary for his breakfast with the other brutish men he spends his time with. Still, I approached the shop carefully, pressing myself against the planks of his neighbor's establishment.

There was one window with grimy glass, and I had a hard time peering through it. I narrowed my eyes to see better and picked out the figure of Gregory's wife bent over her account book at the little desk in the corner. No sign of Gregory himself, but that didn't mean he wasn't there.

If he was in, up in their little apartment over the shop or out back or somewhere else I couldn't see, he'd ask me again for the money he'd determined I owed him. His never-ending interest. I was sure it had been his man leaning against my building and watching the carters load up my loom. He was keeping his eye on me. I should have just melted away, into Callum's house where someone like Gregory couldn't reach me. Instead, I was here, outside his shop, because I wanted to speak with his wife.

But I had to hurry. Callum would look for me if I was gone too long, and he didn't need to know anything about this.

The door stuck as I pushed it open. I shoved and it scraped over wet stone. Gregory's wife must have emptied a bucket of water over them to wash away the smell of the street.

"Hello?" I said.

The young woman stared at me, surprised perhaps to have someone in her shop in the early morning. Her blonde hair was tied back tight from a round face. Spots of pink stained her cheeks, and she looked like one of those people who was always a little flushed.

"Hello."

"Is your husband in?"

I wanted to be sure.

"He'll be back shortly. I can help you for now, I'm sure."

She stood from the table and wiped her ink-stained hands on an apron that had once been white. It seemed she wanted me to think she wouldn't be alone for long—or maybe it was true and Gregory would come through the door any minute. I didn't have long.

"You *can* help, actually. It was you I came to see," I said.

Her pale eyebrows lifted. "Me?"

"Yes. Do you recognize me? I was here a while ago."

She searched my face with her eyes. She likely saw so many clients she didn't memorize each of them. Lots of people needed coin.

"Oh, yes I think I remember you. You owe, don't you?"

I looked around the dim shop, the one candle burning in front of a cracked mirror and the stack of leather-bound ledgers on the small table in the corner.

"Doesn't everyone who comes in here?"

She shrugged. "Most."

"I have an idea I wanted to share with you."

She backed away from me a step, put a hand on the top of her chair. "Me? Why?"

"Because you have something valuable: knowledge. You help your husband run this business, don't you? Keep his accounts."

"Yes."

"Well, I have something too, or I will soon. A purse. And some of it could be put to good use here."

"So you'll be paying Gregory back, then?"

"That's not what I mean."

"No?"

"No. I don't owe him anything. I paid my debt and he decided I owe more interest. He can't just make up the rules."

Her eyes flitted to the door, for the husband who would probably give her trouble for talking to me.

"He makes the rules because it's his coin in your pocket, isn't it?" she said.

I studied her face to see if she believed what she said, if they were her own thoughts or if she was just repeating what Gregory told her. I couldn't tell. I didn't know this woman well enough to be that familiar with her tells.

It was clear though, from this little room robbed of light, from the bent way she stood and the stains on her fingers— he worked her. She'd want to get away from that. What person wouldn't?

"Look, I think we can start something, you and me," I said. "With my coin and your knowledge. We can build a shop like no one's ever seen before."

"What? My husband would never allow me to work with you."

"So don't tell him. And once it's all set up, we can get people with deeper pockets to invest in the shop. That's how we'll make our money even in lean months. You'd be able to leave Gregory."

Her eyes snapped with something—hope? Daydreams?

"Leave Gregory?" she said.

"Yes."

"This is so much to consider. I . . . I just don't know."

I stepped closer, hoping she wouldn't move away. She didn't.

"We can make our lives better. Think about it."

She trembled, her quaking causing the chair she held to quiver. "But Gregory . . ."

"Don't tell him. Not until we're ready," I smiled and hoped it was reassuring. "I'll come back when I have the money and I'll help you get away. Then we can begin. What's your name?"

"Bryn."

"Think about it, Bryn. You could live your dreams instead of Gregory's."

She shook her head. "How could you possibly know what my dreams are?"

Bryn was right. I didn't know her dreams, but I guessed they didn't include being married to a cruel man and working in a dark shop until she lost her eyesight trying to record all the money changing hands that was never hers.

"Is this what you dreamed of as I child?" I gestured around the room. "A business that sucks people in and crushes them like a waterwheel?"

She dropped her eyes. Her expressive face went slack. "No. It's not."

"See? Use what you have, Bryn. Do something about it."

"Why'd you come to me? You don't know me at all."

Honesty would be best. She was right: I didn't know her from any other clerk or shopkeeper. Bryn had something I needed to make a second plan. The purse from Callum would be a start but not enough to build a lifetime on.

"You have a skill I don't: keeping books. And you know other lenders. I need that skill and those connections to make my plan work."

She seemed to roll this thought around in her head, her cheeks pulling in as she considered.

"You say you don't have this money yet?"

"Not yet, but soon."

"Come back when you have it, and we'll talk."

She wasn't saying yes, but she smiled at me. Her first one since I'd entered her shop. It lit up her entire face.

I nodded. "I'll be back soon, Bryn."

"I do hope so."

# Chapter Twenty-Three

Callum and I skirted around each other, like a thread flirting with the eye of a needle. I wasn't his guest exactly, but I wasn't a servant either. Sometimes we ate together, but often Callum was nowhere to be found at dinnertime. There were days when I didn't see another soul. A breakfast of porridge was laid out on a tray and placed carefully in the hall so I didn't knock it when I opened the door. I'd leave out the tray with my bowl wiped clean, and it would be replaced later in the day with a slice of leek and sturgeon pie or an herbed loaf and piece of blue-veined cheese.

When the trays didn't appear, I'd make my way down the gallery and the grand staircase to the dining room. After a morning spent alone with my loom, I admit my heart leapt a little to find Callum staring into the fire at dinnertime, one arm draped across the mantel. He always leaned right in toward the flames, too close for my liking. It was easy to imagine a spark jumping and catching his deep green silk vest on fire.

"Is that a habit of yours?" I asked on the seventh day of my stay. I'd just finished hemming Callum's starlight fabric and my fingers hurt from all the work. It was harder than before somehow, as if I'd lost that spark of excitement that used to carry me through. It was probably because, even though my tiny flat wasn't as comfortable as my room here, I was more at ease there. Red bloomed on my knuckles, sore and cracking from the constant washing with my bowl and ewer. Silk was a delicate material—I had to keep my hands clean to work with the fabric.

"I get so cold here," Callum said.

"It's colder up in the mountains."

He shifted to look at me. "Have you ever been there?"

I nodded. "I was born there, but I only remember a little."

Callum left his spot by the fireplace and picked up a plate from the sideboard. Slices of meat were fanned out on a tray—some kind of bird, it looked like—drizzled with a brown sauce smelling of spices I couldn't place. Before coming here, my food had been something to fill my belly with. Taste barely mattered. The sweetest treat I could come by was a softening apple sold at half-price.

My stomach wasn't as pleased as my tongue with all the food served here. I nibbled the cheeses and slurped down the rich stews, but they sat heavy in my gut.

It seemed like a ridiculous problem to have, to spend my life a few coins away from hunger and now to be wary of the plate in front of me because of the stomachache I knew would come later. Callum didn't seem to suffer from the same predicament. He'd probably eaten rich food all his life. He speared a piece of meat with his two-pronged fork and brought it to his lips. I was still getting used to the forks, too.

"Where's your family from? Your parents?" I asked.

He shrugged. "Everywhere. We've never been good at planting roots."

"How long have your parents been gone?"

"A long time."

"My mother died a long time ago too."

I think because I didn't remember her, she'd never been very real to me. Papa was the real loss, the hole in my heart that sometimes festered.

"How long have you been on your own?" Callum said.

Papa had died three years before, but he'd gone to prison two years before that. It wasn't something I liked to share though, that my father had spent his final days in debtor's prison.

"My papa died of fever a few years ago."

Callum stabbed another piece of meat and dragged it through the sauce on his plate. I dipped my meat timidly, just a tiny bit of the brown sauce for taste.

The richness of it hit my tongue and made my cheeks hurt, but after that initial burst of pain, I relished the complexity of the spices.

"Do you miss him?" Callum said.

"Of course."

It was too simple an answer for the grating pain I often felt, like someone was dragging my insides over a laundry stone, scraping everything away to make me clean and numb.

"There's nothing for me to miss," Callum said. "I didn't know them enough . . . I don't have anything to hold on to."

Like me with my mother. How unmoored Callum must feel without the memory of someone loving him to keep him steady.

"Is that why you want to tie yourself to this house, to the city?"

He stared down at his plate and pushed a piece of roasted turnip around. Without thinking too much about it and because the sound of the knife scraping against the plate made my skin crawl, I reached out and cupped my fingers over his. His hand stopped moving. My stomach tightened with nerves, but I kept my hand where it was. The warmth of his fingers bled into mine. He wasn't cold after all.

"I'm tired of drifting," he said. "They've made it like that, almost impossible to stay in one place."

"Who's made it like that?"

His pinky finger tickled my palm. "Those who decide what my kind of life looks like. Different houses, too big to ever be properly warm, different cities and clan lands. Never in one place long enough to grow roots."

"Or power."

I suspected the Chieftain liked it that way—all his important branches and families moving around without ever creating strong enough ties to muster their own support. The clan lands have always been precarious. Papa said he'd seen three different chieftains for this city in his life alone. Taking over a city and a few villages wasn't so hard, and the rival chieftains did it from time to time. It wasn't often fighting that made it happen but promises of trade and even marriages. As long as none of us working people were called to an army, we didn't really care which shadowy figure sat in a fancy chair up at the big house.

"You're right, power is out of reach unless I dedicate myself to one place," Callum said.

"And you've chosen Eidyn Crag?"

He slipped his hand from under mine. A stab of disappointment tore through my chest, but he soothed it by grabbing my upper arm and pulling me closer.

"I like the people here. The feeling in the streets . . . there's life here. Lots of noise."

"Noise?"

He nodded. "Don't you find that noise warms the blood in your veins? Reminds you there are others out there, and that they might be a little like you. It's turbulent. Don't you enjoy that too?"

I wasn't at all sure about that. In fact, no, I didn't like that at all. I hated anything that threw off the balance, that pushed me toward hunger. Papa and I had always worked with the goal of a solid routine—buy supplies, weave, sell, eat. Over and over. When things slipped, when they got turbulent, it was always a bad thing. No money for supplies. No food. Debt.

"I like steadiness," I said.

Callum leaned in closer. I realized it was odd that we were sitting beside each other and not across from each other at the table. Had I sat down beside him, or had he sat down beside me? I couldn't remember now. His brown eyes bore into mine and their spark lit a fire in my belly. He ran a finger down my arm, and it was like a moth fluttering its wings against my skin.

"Don't underestimate the power of the unexpected, Ella."

I let myself drink him in, absorb the energy in the air around us.

"What are you going to do next?" I asked.

Part of me hoped he'd lean a little bit more forward and brush his bottom lip against mine. The other part of me knew I probably wouldn't be able to stop at kissing. Not with Callum. I wanted to touch him, explore him, find out if the skin of his back was as hot as his fingers.

"What do you want me to do, Ella?"

I hesitated. I'd only ever kissed one person before.

"I want you to come and see your fabric," I said. "I finished it and I'd like to show you how it sparkles."

I led Callum from the dining room and up the yawning staircase. We swept through the gallery, my skirts swishing with every step and hitting Callum's legs. As close as I could get to him.

I'd laid the length of cloth out on my bed, and the way the golden evening light fell across it from the window made the silver thread shimmer like the sun touching the surface of the river on a clear morning. Callum took a handful of fabric and turned it this way and that to catch the light. Papa might not have approved of the workmanship of the stars, but I'd tried my best. Callum likely wouldn't know the difference—the fabric still looked lovely.

"What do you think?" I asked, and then wished I hadn't. I really wanted him to like my creation, but I didn't want him to *know* how much I wanted him to like it.

He dropped the silk back on the bed and reached out to me. I wasn't sure what to do, so I just stayed still and let him sweep my hair back with his fingers. He didn't tuck it behind my ear. Instead, he bent to look closer at the strands.

"Your hair is turning the same color as the silver thread."

"What?"

I pushed him away and grabbed at my own hair to look. The sun from the window hit a few threads of silver-gray. What was happening to me? There wasn't this much silver the last time I looked. And my hands—they were red, raw, knobbly. Much worse than that morning. I needed to soak them in milk. Weaving Callum's silk had been harder than normal. My hands had begun to hurt right away, cramp up. That normally only happened after I'd been weaving for hours. I flexed them now, testing the level of pain. High.

"Don't worry," Callum said. "The strands of silver look good on you."

I threw him a glare. This was *not* normal. Something had to be wrong in my body. My hands and hair were starting to look way too much like Mrs. Under's.

"I didn't have them before. Not even a week ago."

Callum shrugged and took my shuttle in his hand. He turned it over, playing with it. Then he spotted the long pin that only my loom had. He reached out a fingertip.

"Don't!"

"What?" he asked, finger hovering over the pin.

I wasn't sure exactly what would happen if he pricked his finger, but it felt wrong to me. Only *my* blood should feed my loom.

"Be careful, that's sharp."

He dropped his hand.

"Did you pick a color for yourself?" he asked.

"Not yet."

"Pick something that will look nice next to mine."

I swallowed. It was like having ten of the silk butterflies from Odina's parlor fluttering around in my belly.

"So you like it then? The star silk?"

Callum smiled. "Star silk?"

"Doesn't it look like starlight?"

He reached out and swept my hair away from my face, but this time he didn't examine it for silvers or grays. He cupped his hand around the back of my head and pulled me in. His breath plumed over my face, hot and scented like the spices from dinner.

"It's the most beautiful fabric I've ever seen. It sparkles, just like the weaver who made it."

His top lip brushed my bottom one as he spoke. All the muscles in my body clenched, waiting for the next moment. I leaned into him, trying to catch his lips to mine, but he pulled away.

"What is the pin on your loom for?"

It took me a few breaths to figure out what he was talking about. I leaned on the side of the bed, not caring if I creased the silk splayed across it. It was as though my eyes decided Callum was the only thing worth seeing, my heart knowing he was the only thing worth caring about.

"It's nothing," I said.

"I've never seen anything like it."

"It's a rare design. An old loom."

"Ella?"

I glanced up at him, drawn in by the way his tongue caressed my name. "Yes?"

"Be careful," he said. His eyes locked on mine. "It looks really dangerous."

# Chapter Twenty-Four

The yellow silk, as bright as daffodils, brought out the little brown freckles in Odina's cheeks. She stood in Callum's dining room while he held the cloth up to her so I could see the affect, heart in my throat. It took me longer to finish than usual, another week after my trip into town. My fingers were slower, stiff.

"It suits you," I said with relief. She looked beautiful.

She nodded and gave me a tight smile. "It's quite pretty."

"Oh?"

It wasn't exactly a glowing compliment, but I suspected it was hard for her to say anything after the way she'd left Callum's party. She still didn't seem pleased with me or how I'd helped her get the trade agreement from that stodgy old woman.

"What do you want me to say, Ella? You know it's gorgeous."

"Then say that." Heat burned in my cheeks. I shouldn't have prodded her. How needy, how vain.

Her smiled drooped. "Fine. It's gorgeous."

The compliment ricocheted off me. There was no way to know if it was true or she was appeasing me.

Callum gathered the fabric and placed it on the long wooden table in front of us. The fire snapped in the hearth, and I was afraid the silk would smell like smoke after this.

"It has a job, just like the two of you," Callum said.

I flushed again. Whether or not they liked the fabrics didn't matter. Only the magic in them did.

"Who else will be there?" Odina asked as she pulled out a chair with practiced familiarity. She'd been around this dining table many times before.

Callum put a finger to the side of his nose and Odina's mouth tightened into a firmer line.

"You won't tell me who the other Players are?" I asked.

"It's not a secret if everyone knows," Callum said.

Shame pooled in my belly. Still, after everything, I was on the outside.

"I'm not 'everyone.' I'm helping you."

Callum pulled out his own chair and dropped into it. I remained standing, leaning my hands on the tabletop. When I lifted them, I'd leave behind marks from the dampness of my palms. I'd have to do it when Odina wasn't looking.

"You're supplying the clothes," Callum said.

That stung, and it hurt even more because I couldn't be sure if he'd meant it to. It was like we'd been dancing with each other these past few weeks. We moved close, then out of reach. Spinning around one other without ever really touching. Sometimes I thought there was something pulling me toward him, a delicate thread tying us together, but then he wouldn't show up for breakfast or I'd hear the dinner tray being set outside my door and I'd wonder if I'd been imagining it.

I tried not to think too much about the almost-kiss. If I did let my mind wander to it, it was usually when I was weaving.

I turned the episode over and over in my mind until it was so worn out it might as well have been an old dress that had been worked over till there wasn't even enough left to make a hair ribbon. I had to let it go. If I wanted to make something happen, I could try. Otherwise, it was best to just forget all about nearly kissing Callum.

I pushed the thought of it away and glanced toward Odina. Her long, straight hair was swept back over her shoulders, offering me a glimpse of red in the apple of her cheeks. Was this whole thing making her nervous as well? Was the pressure of it, of beguiling, seeping under her skin as it was mine? My fingers itched to reach for hers, to wait for her eyes to snap up and meet mine. I'd smile at her, try to tell her it was all going to be all right. We'd be all right. But she didn't want that from me, so I kept my hands on the table.

Odina took a handful of the yellow silk and pulled it toward her.

"So, this will do the same as the other dresses? It will transfix, or whatever we're calling it, someone if I dance with them?"

Callum nodded. "Yes, just like with Brian and Mrs. Mac-Donald."

Except he—we—wanted more this time. My stomach twisted and I gripped the table harder.

"Tell me how it's going to work . . . where you want me that night," I said, needing to know what to do, where to stand, what to say.

I was sure the Chieftain's party would be bigger and more luxurious than even Callum's parties, beyond anything I could even conjure up in my mind. I wouldn't know anyone except Callum and Odina, which was a good thing because that meant no one would know me either, but I couldn't help the writhing in my belly. We had a big thing to accomplish, and so much of it depended on the magic in my fabric working the way we thought it did.

Callum took a walnut from the bowl in front of him and set in on the table. He spun it with one long finger. The shape of the nut disappeared into a blur of brown.

"We want him like this."

Odina and I both looked from the spinning walnut to Callum's face.

"The Chieftain?" Odina asked.

"We want him dizzy?" I asked.

The nut wobbled to a stop and Callum snatched it back up. I took a breath of relief; watching the nut gave me a wave of nausea.

"Yes, dizzy and overwhelmed by us. Unable to see past the fun we're creating for him. We want him to want us, so he'll give us the thing that will keep us happy just to make sure we remain at his fingertips."

That was a lot to pin on my bolts of cloth. And what would happen to me if it didn't work? I'd have no money and no shop. The room spun around me, and I stared at Odina and Callum. I was here, with them, and they needed this to work just like I did.

Then Odina leaned her head on Callum's shoulder, and a little flame of jealousy licked at my heart, pulling me from my fear. But it shouldn't have. So what if Callum and I almost kissed once? It didn't mean anything beyond the fact that maybe we'd both just wondered how soft each other's lips were in that moment. There wasn't anything heavy behind it. No weight of feelings. I liked things crisp and focused—the future I wanted in my sights, clear as the river on a quiet day. No one was going to splash into the shallows and kick up the dirt and mud. I'd breathe out all my nerves, all my fear, and focus.

"You want us to dazzle the Chieftain?" Odina said, glancing up at Callum from under her eyelashes. "I know *I* can do that."

Callum shrugged her off and gripped the mantle, the flickering light from the fire illuminating his wool trousers.

"It won't be so easy, Odina. Even with Ella's fabrics. The Chieftain's eyes are always wide open. They have to be because of people like us."

I walked over and stood in front of the fireplace, just close enough to feel the heat and smell Callum's spicy, sweet scent.

"We'll just have to show him all the fun he'd be missing if he didn't dance with us," I said, dipping into confidence I wasn't sure I could sustain.

"And you know all about fun, do you?" Callum said, a little smile flirting with his lips.

Surviving didn't leave a lot of room for fun, but he'd never know that. Not when he'd grown up in houses like this one.

"I know a lot about pretending," I said, my chest heavy. "I can pretend to be however you want—charming and lively, somber and serious. Papa taught me to watch a client's mood and be to them what they needed most. Sometimes that's a voice to tell them how exquisite they are, sometimes it's an ear to listen to troubles."

I glanced at Odina. She watched our exchange, but she didn't look angry or jealous like I'd expected. Her hands gripped the arms of her chair, her nails digging in so hard the varnish peeled off the wood. It wasn't anger or jealousy in her eyes. No. It was fear. She knew all these situations better than I did. She'd likely met the Chieftain before. She would know if he was someone to be scared of.

Fear was contagious, so I dragged my gaze away from her as it began to sizzle inside me. I couldn't let myself question what I was about to do. I needed to be a part of this so I could get my shop and, eventually, a life where I wasn't reliant on how much one person liked what I made.

Callum touched a finger to my chin, tilting my head up toward his. "Are you as slippery as your silks?"

He asked it with a smile in his voice and a crinkle of his eyes that cooled the heat rising up my neck. He didn't mean it in a bad way. I could play along.

"Isn't that what you want, Callum?"

He nodded. "We all need to be able to twist and turn when necessary. It's a talent I look for in all the Players."

"But she's not a Player," Odina said. She pushed back her chair with a scrape of wood against wood and gripped the edge of the table. "Right?"

"Right. She isn't a Player," Callum said, glancing back to Odina.

She needn't have worried. Callum might play with me and smile and touch my chin, but I wasn't one of them. Not really. I needed to remember that when I quipped back and let a drop of confidence run away with me.

I stepped away from Callum's touch. "Who will make the suits and dresses?" I asked.

My fabrics were the base of the creations, but someone's skill with a needle and thread was needed to make them come to life. I'd thought many times about apprenticing myself to a seamstress. It would be smart to be able to turn my own bolts of cloth into garments to be sold. Papa had always said no whenever I mentioned it. He said one trade was enough for anyone, and I wouldn't be able to master weaving if I was always trying to learn to make patterns too.

"My seamstresses," Odina said. "They're quick and brilliant at tailoring to the body."

Callum nodded. "They have four days."

Odina waved a hand. "They'll get it done."

I sat down in Callum's vacated chair. It was still warm. For someone always complaining of being cold, his body seemed to exude heat. Maybe that's why he always needed to warm himself up—his own warmth leaked out of him.

"So we go to the party, surround the Chieftain, and swirl around him in our pretty garments until he's drunk on the very sight of us? Transfixed? And then he gives you control of the market street rents?" I asked.

"Exactly," Callum said.

"And if that doesn't work?"

His eyes flashed gold from the reflection of the fire. "If it doesn't work, our bargain is broken."

At that reminder, the wave of nausea rolled over me again. None of what I wanted was guaranteed.

"What have you promised her, Callum?" Odina said.

"Nothing that isn't in my power to give."

She shook her head. "Sometimes you overestimate that."

He shrugged and stepped back from the fire. He wasn't concerned by what Odina said, so I tried not to be either. She was in a bad mood—that was it. Swatting at everything Callum said to her. Though he wasn't promising me the rent of my shop without strings attached, he *would* be able to give it to me when the Chieftain granted him control of Market Street.

The sun had slipped below the horizon while we talked, and shadows spawned in the corners of the room. Callum's face was thrown into relief, and I marveled at how very sharp his features became. It instantly changed his face into something more menacing. Fear even flickered in my chest for a breath. No wonder people listened to him easily.

"I've only promised money and such, Odina," he said. "But Ella really is too talented to let go."

It was what I wanted, to be called talented, to be recognized for things my hands could do with a loom and thread. I unwound tangled spools and turned them into something beautiful. It was the only thing I was really good at. My skills were why Papa had died as happy as he could be—because he knew I'd be able to support myself. He told me so in his last letter.

My weaving was *me*. My heart glowed with Callum's words; he *did* want me here, needed me here. I shifted my body toward him, let the hem of my skirt sweep over the tops of his boots just to be closer to him.

"Don't worry, Odina, I won't tread on your toes again," I said.

She shook her head, eyes on the tabletop instead of me. "You don't know how to do what we do."

"Odina." Callum threw her own name at her like a dagger. I moved away from him, surprised his voice could be so cold.

She smirked and her upper lip caught on her eye teeth. Her chest flushed a burnished red, bright against the frothy white lace at her neckline and her light brown skin.

"Nothing comes easily, Ella," she said. "You should know that."

"Stop," Callum said. He put himself more firmly between us and rested his hands on the back of the chair in front of him. "You know the rules, Odina."

I wanted to know the rules too, to know exactly why Odina's eyes had lost their usual gleam, her brown irises turning almost black. She probably just didn't think the price, whatever it was, was worth it because she'd never experienced anything less than a warm home and a full belly. So what if we had to manipulate the Chieftain at a fancy party? That wasn't exactly trying work.

Odina swished away from both of us in her silk skirt. Silk during the day. How many dresses did she own that were made out of other weavers' fabric? She'd gone wherever her taste had taken her, wrapping herself in whatever lovely things she wanted without considering the gnarled fingers or the blisters that had likely popped over her precious bolts. My hands were stiff from the work of the last few days, and my back ached in an entirely new way. My shoulders were tight and pulled forward and curved my back unpleasantly. If I wasn't careful, I'd end up like one of those women who look like they can't straighten out.

"Have this delivered with the others, Callum," she said, pointing to the yellow silk in the middle of the table. "My seamstresses are quick, but they'll need to start tonight."

She stuffed her hands in her pockets—clever seamstresses indeed to add those—and rounded the corner out of our sight. Disappointment settled over me. I'd never know what was bothering her so much now.

"I guess she'll show herself out," Callum said.

I wondered again at the servants. Surely there was a housekeeper somewhere to open the door for people like Odina.

"I never see anyone here."

Callum went to the fireplace again and turned around to warm his back. "What do you mean? You see me."

"But never the servants. The food appears and disappears. No matter how hard I try, I can never catch anyone when they leave me my tray. Whoever does it is already gone by the time I get the door open. The only time I've seen anyone was at your parties."

Callum shrugged. "They're efficient."

An ugly thought niggled at me, like the little flies I'd found digging into a piece of bread I'd left on my tray overnight.

"You do let them out though, right?"

His eyes flicked toward the ceiling, and he sighed. "The servants go wherever they want, whenever they want. If you ever need them, just call and they'll come. You can ask them for anything you want and they'll bring it to you."

"Anything?" I said it with a smile, to show I was joking. Callum didn't change his expression. It remained as stoic as before.

"Anything."

Maybe he meant it as a comfort, but it unsettled me. I didn't need other people to get me what I wanted. Callum turned his back to me and faced the fire again. He didn't need to be so hot and cold.

"Callum?"

"What?"

"Look at me."

He did, pinning me to the spot with a searing stare as hot as the flames behind him. He might have thought he'd scare me or stop me from challenging him. But he was so very misguided. All that look did was harden the resolve in the pit of my stomach, like a ball of iron cooling after the forge.

"What do you want to see, Ella?" he asked.

"I wanted you to see me, that's all. I have a request and I didn't want to make it to your back."

He blinked and all the fire in his eyes went out. "What do you want?"

I needed to start on the same level as him and Odina the night of the party. They'd had a lifetime of learning how to act the part. I was good at pretending, as I'd already told him, but I needed the script. I rolled my shoulders back and lifted my chin.

"Teach me how to be intoxicating."

# Chapter Twenty-Five

We sat with our knees touching. I'd pulled one chair out from the dining table and Callum had taken another. When I'd left a reasonable space between us, he pushed his chair closer to mine. His trousers pulled at the thin wool of my dress every time he shifted his knees, and little zips of excitement flashed through me. His foot jiggled, and butterflies flapped their wings in my belly to the same beat.

"Am I making you nervous?" I asked. "You're fidgeting."

He'd never seemed nervous around me before. Angry, curious, totally wrapped up in a tangle of emotion—yes. Nervous—no. Did he think I wanted more from this, something . . . something intimate? He knew so much more than I did about being someone people want to be near. That's all I needed, though—a bit of his knowledge.

"I want to do a good job," he said with a slow smile. "Showing you."

My breath caught in my throat. It was always me who was trying to prove myself to Callum. *I* was the one who came from a used up flat with barely more than an old loom to my name. He didn't need to prove anything.

"I just want to know what you've known all your life," I said.

"Tell me how to bow so I drag the Chieftain's eyes down with me. Teach me to laugh so he hears only my voice."

"Your dress will help you with that."

"The beguiling fabric."

Callum nodded. "Exactly. That's what happens when someone's wearing it and they dance with another, beguilement. It's Nemain you pray to, isn't it? She's the one who's made the fabric special."

My mouth went dry. "Nemain, of course. Our city's patron."

"She must be very powerful with the whole city's devotions, don't you think? Immortal by now."

"I suppose."

She was always powerful though. Immortal or not, she was still much more powerful than either of us could ever hope to be. It didn't matter whether she'd reached that echelon—she wouldn't have needed to be immortal to gift my loom with magic.

Callum turned his head left and right like he was trying to shed a thought. "So yes, 'beguiles' is a good word for what your fabric does."

"Well, I need to know how to get to that point . . . how to be enticing to begin with." My cheeks burned now. I didn't mean "enticing" to him, necessarily. Just in general. Oh gods. Our eyes met and I shifted my legs away from him, the blush spreading into my chest.

"Knowing how to be enticing and *being* enticing are not the same thing," Callum said.

My breath stumbled in my lungs.

"Just like going to a Player's party doesn't make me a Player?"

The corner of Callum's lips quirked into a smile and he slid his eyes away from me, studying the flames in the hearth. "Right," he said quietly. "But Ella, you already have that pull."

The mass of butterflies woke up, flapping their wings in my belly again. I swallowed, trying to make my mouth work. He couldn't possibly mean that I was enticing to him. That's not at all what he meant. My palms dampened and my underarms prickled. Callum still looked away, and I couldn't read his expression.

"What pull?" I finally asked.

He flushed, a pink stain spreading over his ears and cheeks, and slowly brought his gaze back to mine. We locked eyes and I pushed down my urge to look away.

"This pull." Callum leaned forward and put his hands on my knees, bringing them back between his. He framed his legs around mine, and I kept mine very still. His warm breath hit my cheeks, and I shuddered, my skirt grazing his trouser legs.

I flushed, a new kind of heat all tangled up inside me. He stared back and took a shallow breath. Was he was waiting for me to do something? To show him how to be enticing? I didn't care about that anymore, not really. All I could think of was him, his warm brown eyes and his sharp cheekbones and the tiny, infuriating smile turning up the corner of his lips.

I couldn't let it go this time.

With a deep breath to push away the butterflies, I took his linen cravat in my fingers. It was fine lawn, soft against my skin. Callum's Adam's apple bobbed up and down as he swallowed. Fire burned through my limbs, right to my fingers and toes. The feeling was new, fresh, addictive. I reeled him in like he'd done to me with my sash at the party. My body tingled, waiting for what would happen next. Then I pressed my lips to his and he moved them under mine, opening, welcoming. So unlike my first, sloppy kiss. *This* was why people wanted to do it. Callum's mouth burned with heat and the taste of spices. His fingers wrapped themselves in my hair. Every inch of my body came alive. My skin prickled and I shivered when he ran one hand along my arm.

"See?" he said when we finally broke apart.

I licked my lips, tasting him on them.

"That's not quite what I want to accomplish at the Chieftain's party," I said.

He smiled and cupped my cheek. "No, but the principle is the same. It's you. Be yourself. You've swirled up my thoughts, Ella. And even when they stop spinning, they come back to you. Always you and the beautiful things you make."

I wanted to capture his words as if they were flowers, to dry and keep in an old box and look at whenever I was sad. He understood that my fabrics were a part of me, that creating them *was me.* And he liked it.

I sighed, satisfaction easing through my body, unraveling every knot in my muscles, every nerve wound tight. I was worth something to Callum, and I wanted to hang on to that feeling forever.

I spent the next morning down by the river, at the spot Callum had taken me. My fingers still hurt even though I'd finished the last bolt of fabric the day before. I dipped them in the clear, cool water of the shallows. The swelling wasn't going down, and when I hung my head over the water, I saw even more strands of gray. Nothing about this was normal—but neither was weaving fabrics with magic in them. My knobby knuckles and silver strands were connected to the Bean-Nighe's magic. They had to be. It was like each session was draining me. The loom took my blood, but the magic took more.

I had to find a way to fix it though. There was often an out in the stories about creatures touched by magic—a price that could be paid. The Bean-Nighe had said it would just be my blood, but she hadn't mentioned what losing my blood to the loom would do to me.

The water moved over my hands, numbing my sore fingers. Did the Bean-Nighe know I was here? Was she slapping her old, dirty shirt against a rock just beyond where I could see? I sniffed but there was no smell of wet dirt—just the cold clip of early morning air and the gentle hint of heather in the breeze.

My hair blew out of its leather string and flew around my face. I pulled it back behind my head and jumped when another pair of hands cupped themselves over mine.

"Oh, Callum, you scared me," I said. Before all the words had even left my mouth, I realized it wasn't Callum behind me. The smell wasn't right. Briny instead of spicy.

"Hello, Ella."

Gregory cinched my wrists together and yank my arms down. They burned with pain.

"Let go of me!" I screamed.

"Nah, I don't think so. Look at you, staying here in this grand house when you still owe me the interest on your debt. And then you came back for my wife."

Bryn. Gregory had found out about my visit to Bryn. I kicked out, but he only tightened his hold on me. My throat burned with my ragged breathing. I glanced back up toward the house, but there was no one. The wind had swallowed my scream.

"He doesn't pay me; it's not like that. I don't have any money. And I don't know your wife," I said.

"No? You think you're so smart, don't you? But she told me about your visit and your little plan. 'A shop like no one's ever seen before.' You really think you can pull that off?"

"She told you?"

I couldn't believe it. I'd thought Bryn was suffering under Gregory's cruel reign—that she'd want something different. I was so sure of that. And she betrayed me instead. Bet on her husband instead of freedom. Or instead of me.

My stomach roiled and I spat sour saliva onto the ground. Gregory thought he'd won. Maybe he had.

"Where's Bryn now?"

"At home, nursing a bad bruise. She tripped, hit her head against the doorframe."

"You hurt her."

Anger fought the fear in my belly and it all twisted into something red hot. This disgusting man did something to his wife. She'd never escape now, and my safety net had been slashed through.

I gathered the saliva in my mouth and spat in Gregory's face.

His grip on me slipped, and I twisted my arms again, pulling my skin against his fingers until my arms burned. Gregory yanked my wrists, pushing me into the shallows. The cold shocked me and water filled my leather shoes up to my stockinged ankles.

"You think she was rash like you?" he hissed. "That she'd take that big a risk just because you would? She's safe with me. She'd never give that up."

The wind blew stronger, sharper. It rippled along the surface of the river, agitating that once-calm water. Bryn had chosen the monster she knew. I stared into the blue-gray and clenched my teeth together, trying not to show Gregory the water was making me cold. I didn't want him to see me shiver.

"She's not safe with you. You're a horrible man."

"She's not on the streets, is she? I plucked her out of a doorway one night, you know that? Taught her everything I needed her to know."

"You're chaining her with her own fear," I said.

Gregory advanced again, both of us standing in the water now.

"Those chains are really strong, Ella. You should learn that for yourself."

Gregory took what he could and twisted every situation to benefit him. He lent money to people knowing they wouldn't be able to pay it back easily, because that gave him something to hold over them. He'd done exactly that to Papa and now he was doing it to me. I guess I should have known better than to take any coin from his dirty hand, but there wasn't really any other choice. I needed to buy materials to weave. I needed to weave to make money to live. Gregory was the rickety bridge between those two truths. I walked across because I needed to, but I never knew when that bridge would break under my feet.

But I knew it was broken now.

Gregory treated himself to a tour of my body, running his eyes over my face and breasts, my waist and hips. I shivered but didn't shrink under his gaze. He didn't own anything here.

The water rushed by my legs, quick and angry. Gregory reached for me, and I stumbled back, further into the water. He fell with a splash, water droplets speckling my face.

I smelled her before I saw her. Damp earth. My heart leapt.

"What's that?" Gregory righted himself, soaked and dripping.

The light seemed to crack, split, on the opposite bank. A sliver of shadow against the gray light of day.

Gregory stared at the spot on the bank across the river where the woman with spiderweb hair slapped an old, bloodied shirt against a flat rock. She shimmered, just like she had before, her outlines insubstantial. Her torn skirts soaked up water and grew deeper black at the hem. Her white hands, threaded with thick blue veins, scrunched the shirt and released the water from it. Then she slapped it on the rock again. It didn't grow any cleaner for all her efforts. Prickling unease crawled up the backs of my legs. Why had she come?

Her humming drifted across the water, like woodsmoke floating on the breeze. The melody wound around me, but I didn't go further into the water this time. I knew better now.

Gregory didn't though.

Maybe he'd heard the same stories I had and decided to try his luck with his own wishes. Maybe he was just lured to her like a fish on a hook. He splashed in, leading with his hands outstretched in front of him. He lost his footing as the riverbed gave way beneath him to the deepest section of the water. The Bean-Nighe never looked up or acknowledged him in any way. She didn't speak to him like she'd spoken to me—or if she did, I couldn't hear it.

Then the water closed over Gregory's head without a sound. He just slipped under as if he were never here at all. The old woman went on washing, slapping and wringing and soaking the shirt. A job without end.

Her head snapped up. She looked a little different, like someone had smoothed some of her wrinkles away with the backs of her hands. Strange. I stared.

"Ella." She stretched my name in her mouth. Her voice scraped against her throat. "Is it worth it?"

Did she mean her wishes? They were bringing me everything I wanted. Of course it was worth it.

"Yes!" I shouted across the water.

She shook her head and stared at her gnarled hands, ruined with work. The Bean-Nighe opened her mouth and revealed a hole of pitch black, as dark as a night without a moon, and screamed. The pitch of it tore through my ears. I put my hands to them, trying to block out the sound, but my ears were full of the Bean-Nighe's scream and the sound of my own whooshing blood.

I stumbled up the hill, hands clasped to either side of my head. When the house came into view, I turned and looked back. The Bean-Nighe was gone, and there was no sign of Gregory. She'd taken him.

The ground came up too quickly beneath my feet and I sprawled into the grass. I let out a shuddering breath. My whole body throbbed with energy. Gregory was gone, drowned by the Bean-Nighe. I hadn't done it to him; she'd lured him in herself and he'd gone willingly enough, but I couldn't stop the strange spasms of guilt in my chest. Guilt and anger.

What would happen to Bryn now? I wasn't going to see her and find out, not after what she'd done. She'd betrayed me to keep Gregory's protection and now that was gone. She'd never have it again. Gregory was gone, gone, gone.

He'd never come and find me again, never threaten me.

The relief bubbled up inside and escaped through my lips in a peel of giddy laughter. I didn't owe anyone anything anymore. I was *free*. I wanted to find Callum, to kiss him and run my hands through his hair.

The Bean-Nighe's shriek had faded to the mewl of a kitten in my mind. Everything stretched out in front of me. Opportunities. No one could claim I owed them anything anymore, and I intended to enjoy that.

# Chapter Twenty-Six

Callum and I sat under the window in his library, letting the sun warm our backs. I hadn't told him about Gregory, because he'd never known about my debt, and I didn't want him to think of me like that. But I'd still sought him out soon after I returned.

"What's your favorite thing in your house?" he asked.

We'd spent the morning asking each other our favorite things—colors, food. Callum preferred blue and, of course, porridge. I told him I loved purple and the chicken with the gravy his cook made, and he grinned. But this question, it was harder to answer.

"Well, my loom, I suppose . . . but I also have this little paste jewel, and I always liked to look at it when I was sad. It reminded me of what was possible."

"What do you mean?" He propped himself up on his elbow to look at me.

"Sometimes, I'd do the same thing every day for a week or two weeks or even a month. On those days, when the only thing I looked forward to was a pie from the ordinary on Sunday, everything felt stale like an old piece of bread. But when I rubbed that paste jewel between my fingers, I'd remember that other people had different lives, and if those lives were possible for them, they might be possible for me too."

I stared out the window so I wouldn't have to look in Callum's eyes and see any pity there. It wasn't what I wanted. But he took my wrist and helped me lean against him and trailed his fingers through my hair.

"I like that you wanted more. And now you have it, don't you?"

Clasped in the warmth of his arms, looking out the window at the stretch of lawn and the glittering river beyond and the prospect of the party and my own shop, it seemed like I was close.

Callum pressed his lips to mine and lowered me down onto the thick rug. I pulled him to me by the neck of his shirt. Our lips met and it was different this time, less hesitant. He let his weight fall on me and I welcomed it, wrapping my arms around his back. I wanted him closer, wanted him to touch me. His fingers flitted over my cheeks, my chin. It wasn't enough, and I gripped him harder and kissed deeper.

After a few minutes, he pulled away and I raised my head, trying to reach his lips again. He smiled and kissed my nose.

"It's getting late. I have a few things I must do before I lose the light, and I suspect you do too."

He was right, I did, but I didn't want to leave this perfectly warm moment.

"See you for dinner." Callum dipped his head for one more brush of a kiss and left me in the library with the afterimage of his touch burned into my skin.

∽✆∾

The library became our refuge from work, and we spent as much time there as we could before the party, wrapping ourselves around each other and talking until we couldn't ignore the rumble of our stomachs anymore.

This time, we'd been smart enough to bring a plate of oatcakes and honey into the library with us. We ate, careful to suck the honey from our fingers so it wouldn't get on the book we took turns reading to each other. It was a compilation of tales most temples had in their libraries, about the gods and the creatures who lived in their world. With every turn of the page, I'd been bracing myself to see the Bean-Nighe depicted in scratchy ink, but she wasn't there.

"That tickles," I said as Callum's lips crawled across my neck.

"I wasn't going for 'tickles.'"

"No?"

"Shivers would have been better. Delicious shivers."

"Well," I leaned my back against his chest and tilted my head up to look at him. "Keep going and we'll see if we get there."

He grinned and kissed me full on the lips. I turned in his arms to face him and open my mouth for his kiss. He ran his tongue along my lower lip and pressed hard against me.

"Is this okay?"

"Yes."

I wanted the taste of him back in my mouth and I covered his smile with another deep kiss. We eased down to the thick carpet and wrapped our arms around each other, twined our legs together so there was scarcely any space between us at all. It was as close as I'd ever been with another person, and I was beginning to crave this—the thrill in the pit of my belly, the ache somewhere a bit lower. When we were apart, I tried to remember his breath in my ear and the brown hairs curling against his pale skin where his shirt gaped.

We hadn't done everything yet, and I was happy with that. I didn't want to risk what I'd built here with the appearance of another person to take care of. That was how it happened—babies. The very thought made my stomach turn. I didn't want to be responsible for a small human. Not now, with the Chieftain's party just one more sleep away and all the security I'd ever desired so close. Gregory gone, my gorgeous silks imbued with magic being made into dresses and suits even now. And then there was Callum, who was the unexpected sparkle, the glitter of sequins in the sun. He wasn't something I'd been looking for, but now that we'd found this way to be together, I didn't want it to stop. The warmth I felt in my stomach when someone told me my fabrics were beautiful? Callum gave me that feeling every time he looked at me. I wanted it all the time, became gluttonous for it. I took what he gave me, even though I wasn't at all sure what I gave him in return. Did I stir something in the pit of his stomach too?

∽

Odina brought the dresses and suit back the morning of the party. I'd never risen to this kind of feeling before. We had something to prepare for, something to look forward to. Even the house seemed to have been scrubbed and waxed. The carvings along the gallery shone deep brown with hints of amber. I stooped down to look at the laughing faces and Lugh standing above them, and my stomach didn't twist like usual. Callum had said they were wild and not all laughing came from happiness. He was right, but I didn't want to think about that right now. At that moment, with success within reach, I wanted to look at the smiling faces and imagine they were celebrating.

I almost skipped into the dining room, grabbing the thick doorframe and launching myself in. Callum sat in the chair closest to the fire and Odina fussed with the dress of daffodil silk spread out on the table. She moved a little stiffly, not swinging the dress out to make the hem swish and catch our eye, and she looked paler than usual—like she'd been the one to sew these dresses in four days by herself.

"The dresses are ready!" I said.

She glanced up and pinched her lips together in a false smile. "Yes, and they're lovely—especially considering they were made with just measurements and no fittings."

Callum shrugged. "No time for fittings."

"No, well, anyway, they're done. Here's yours, Ella."

Odina lifted a package wrapped in thin linen and a black ribbon from a chair and passed it to me. I'd made myself a bolt of watery blue silk, like Callum had requested for the first party. It had been an easy fabric to weave after the challenge of the star pattern, and that was a good thing because I'd had such a hard time with it. I'd actually taken a rod and tied it to my back with a couple of ribbons so it would force me to sit up straight. I wondered how the seamstress had given the dress shape.

"Try it for us," Callum said.

"Show me the others first."

Odina handed another package to Callum, and he pulled on the black ribbon. The linen fell away to reveal the silver silk patterned with almost iridescent stars. He brought out the jacket first, cut sharply in the current fashion. Even men who lived around my courtyard were trying to copy it by cutting off the bottom third of their old wool jackets. It never had quite the same effect.

The breeches were cut short, just past the knee, and Callum would wear white stockings over his calves. He brought the jacket over to the window and let the sunlight flash against the pattern of stars.

"Mesmerizing," he said.

I'd never heard anything I'd made described with that word before. I tucked it away in my mind so I'd always remember it. It almost made all the aches in my body worth it.

"Can I see yours?" I asked Odina.

She took the yellow dress from the table and held it against herself. The color lit up her eyes, but she still looked like she was on just the other side of an illness. As fragile as the flower I'd named the color of the silk for. Pull too hard and the petals came away in your fingertips. This party and the job we had to do were dragging at Odina, loosening her, breaking her apart. But why? I didn't know how long she'd been a Player, but I was sure she'd been to these kinds of parties before. She'd had no trouble with us tricking Mrs. MacDonald. The greed of the whole thing shouldn't bother her now.

I didn't know her well enough to ask, and I especially wasn't going to say anything in front of Callum. He was sure of what he wanted out of tonight's party and so was I. For the first time in my life, I wasn't scrambling up the side of a muddy hill and slipping down—I had boots with grip. I had a chance of getting to the top.

"Have you tried it on?" I asked.

"It'll fit. My seamstresses made it, after all," Odina said and dumped the dress back on the table.

"How do you know if you haven't put it on?" Callum asked and pushed the mound of fabric back toward her.

Odina sighed and reached behind her back to pull at her own laces. I suspected she usually had a maid to do it for her, but she shrugged out of her bodice quite quickly. Next, she untied the skirt and let it fall to her feet. She stood before us in a crisp white shift, the lines of her body faint shadows underneath. I watched this whole performance with a knot forming in my belly. I couldn't believe she'd let Callum see her like that. He'd never even seen *me* like that, and we were . . . something. We were getting familiar with each other's bodies and we'd never come close to actually taking our clothes off. Perhaps Odina did this because Callum had already seen the shift, maybe even what was underneath.

I prodded my feelings like poking a stick into a smoldering fire. I wasn't supposed to care. I'd kissed Callum because I wanted to and because I liked the light-headed thrill of it. That was all it was ever meant to be, but I had to admit to myself I'd let it become more. I loved talking to him. The only people I'd ever really had to talk to before were Papa and sometimes Mrs. Under. Papa and I had mostly been too busy with the business of survival to talk about much beyond where we'd get our next box of thread or how we might dry and preserve meat by hanging it from our rafters without attracting too many rats. Mrs. Under told me tales and stories about the gods and their creatures, and on occasion she told me off for wanting too many things.

Callum just let me be, let me explore my thoughts out loud. He did the same. I gave and he took, and he gave and I took. It was fair and satisfying.

Odina finally finished slipping the dress on and tying the back of her bodice, though it hung looser than it should because no one had tightened the laces for her. Callum swept his gaze over her and offered a curt nod. He didn't seem enthralled by what he'd seen.

"Good."

Odina rolled her eyes to the ceiling—painted with the illusion of being carved—and grabbed her discarded dress from the ground.

"I'll see you at the party," she said.

"We'll be there in the carriage at seven."

Odina's gaze drifted across the table to me, and the sadness in those brown eyes unnerved me. I dropped my eyes to the chair back I held.

"You'll help Ella get ready, won't you, Callum?" she said.

"Of course I will."

"You'll prepare her?"

"There's no preparation needed. Not now that we've decided our plan of attack. Be enticing, intoxicating, dancing with the Chieftain."

She turned to him and tightened her grip around the bodice and skirt in her arms. "Are you sure about that, Callum? Or is it more that there's no amount of preparation that could help?"

Something was going on between them, but it only seemed to bother Odina. Callum was completely cool. He leaned closer to the fire and let the flames light up his face.

"You're dampening my mood, Odina."

"Gods forbid," she said and trailed out of the door. A few seconds later, the heavy front door creaked open and then slammed.

"Why is she so mad?" I asked.

"Maybe she doesn't like the dress."

That stung, even though Callum smiled to show he was joking. Why wouldn't she like the dress? The silk glowed like sunshine.

"We should get dressed," Callum said. "I want to see you in that blue."

I leaned in to him and walked my fingers up his chest.

"What did Odina think you needed to prepare me for? We've already talked about the plan," I said, planting a soft kiss on his chin.

"She probably just thinks you won't know how to behave at a party like that, since you didn't grow up going to them."

Shame flushed through me, burning my cheeks. I could handle myself just fine, and Callum had already said I drew people in. He'd said that would be enough.

We walked up the stairs hand in hand and parted ways at the top of the gallery. I watched as Callum was swallowed up by the shadows down the hallway before I turned for my room.

Night was falling already, and the candles should have been lit by now, I realized something as I deposited my own dress on top of my bed—Callum always came to my room but I'd never seen his. I didn't know what coverlet he'd chosen for his bed or what trinkets sat on his dressing table. I didn't know if he took advantage of the light from the window or kept his bed out of the line of sunlight. He knew all those things about me, and it suddenly seemed wrong I didn't know them about him.

I turned on my heel and slipped down to the gallery. He'd disappeared into the hall, so I didn't know which door to open to find his room. I tiptoed, wanting to surprise him even though I wasn't sure it would be a happy surprise. He might think I was prying, and maybe I was, but I wanted to know more about him. Each time we were together, I felt one of the hard layers I'd formed around myself slough away. He held on to his, letting them wear thin much more slowly.

Voices met my ear when I pressed it against the fourth closed door. Callum had people in there. The invisible servants at last? I rapped my knuckle lightly against the wood so I could claim knocking if he got angry, then pushed my way inside.

# Chapter Twenty-Seven

Callum stood in the window in his dazzling star silk suit. A man and a woman sat on his bed dressed in clothes made out of the other two bolts of cloth Callum had requested. They were the other Players.

I didn't recognize them from Callum's party. The woman's long black hair fell around her arms like a shawl and clashed brilliantly with her purple dress. Her nose flipped up a little at the end, a gentle slope, and her dark eyes flicked over me in a quick appraisal, but it was impossible to discern her conclusion from the steady expression on her tawny face. The man slipped an arm around her waist. His skin was so pale I wouldn't have been surprised if even five minutes in the sun turned it pink.

Callum reached out a hand to me and I couldn't tell whether or not he was annoyed at my intrusion.

"Ella."

I moved toward him, muscles tight, waiting for the retribution for interrupting. The room was as cold and plain as Callum's eyes at that moment. No color or decoration of any kind. Simple furniture, plain wool blanket thrown over the bed. No curtains hanging from the four posters. It looked a lot like my room before I came here, but that didn't make any sense. It was odd that Callum, who lived in a house built for beauty, choose to keep his own bedroom so austere.

He caught my outstretched hand and reeled me into his side. Relief relaxed my muscles. He wasn't angry.

"Friends, this is Ella. She's responsible for the gorgeous clothes you wear tonight."

Both the woman and the man smiled without showing any teeth.

"Well, I only wove the silk," I said. The seamstress also had something to do with how nicely the suit and dress had turned out, and taking the credit for someone else's work just tasted wrong in my mouth.

"How talented you are," the woman said. "I'm Serene."

"That's a pretty name."

"She knows," the man chimed in. "I'm Andrew."

I nodded and smiled at both of them, hoping my face had settled into a mask of confidence.

"We were just discussing the plan for tonight," Serene said. "Callum tells us Odina is already informed."

"Yes, we talked about it," I said.

"Callum is getting liberal with his definition of a secret, isn't he?" Andrew said and shot a look at Callum. He shrugged, his shoulder moving against mine.

"We need her."

So he hadn't told them about me? Did they even know what my fabrics could do? He was keeping secrets from other Players. Odina knew, but it didn't look like these two did. I couldn't help the happiness bubbling up inside me. I knew something someone else didn't, was on the inside of the plan with Callum. I stood in a room with the Players, about to put on a silk dress and go to the Chieftain's party.

"Where's your dress?" Serene asked.

My hands went to my moss-green wool skirt. I'd hoped to spend a minute in here with Callum, discover a little something more about him. I hadn't accounted for a conversation with two new people. I had to get dressed so we could leave.

"It won't take me long to put it on."

Callum brought my fingers to his lips and kissed them, slipping my pinky into his mouth and nipping it.

"Go quick."

Full of far too much giddiness and nerves, I ran back to my room to slip the blue silk skirt around my waist and tie the bodice on. The laces were, luckily, in the front so I could do them up myself. I wondered if Odina had asked for them to be that way because she knew I didn't have a servant or because she didn't want Callum to help me? Something lingered between them that hinted at more than friendship. Their conversations sparked, like a flash of far-off lightning bringing a faint glow to an otherwise calm night.

I pushed away those thoughts as I checked myself in the mirror. Maybe Callum and Odina had been something at some time. But it didn't matter anymore. I liked the way his lips felt on mine, and I was pretty sure he enjoyed the way my mouth tasted. We talked about things I'd never even thought to say out loud to anyone else. I was just going to enjoy that for now.

When I looked in the mirror, I found more gray wound

through my red hair, but in the candlelight it looked almost silver. I'd soaked my hands in milk and honey to take the redness away and make the skin soft. Even my knuckles didn't look so bad tonight. I'd slept with them above my head, hoping to coax the extra blood making my fingers knobbly down my arms. Mrs. Under had told me she did that herself sometimes to ease the swelling. It had worked, to a point, but my hands still looked decidedly worse than they had even a week ago. It wasn't just swelling; little brown spots had sprung up on the back of them like mushrooms in the grass, and I hadn't even spent much time in the sun lately. My back still hurt too, shoulders still tight, but I could ignore it for a while—as long as the pain didn't creep up my neck into my head. I'd never been good at handling headaches, and now wasn't the time to lie on my bed with a hand over my eyes and the blanket up around my ears.

I tied a blue ribbon around my head and let it trail under my hair. It was a scrap I'd saved from the bolt that made my dress. I looked like a river fairy now, the silk shifting shades of blue as I moved from side to side in the low, glittering light. I hoped Callum would find *me* beautiful as well as the dress.

⤬

We gathered on the large stone steps of Callum's house and waited for the carriage to be brought around. I'd never been in a carriage before, and I didn't want it to show. I clung to Callum's arm so I could step forward when he stepped forward, bow when he bowed.

Serene and Andrew stood beside us, and Serene ran a finger along the neckline of my dress. I shivered. Candles flickered low on the steps, so only her chin and the underside of her nose were illuminated. I supposed I looked the same.

"Did you combine two colors to make this? It has such a sheen to it."

I stepped back and hoped her hand would naturally fall away.

"Yes, two different silk threads. A true blue and a gray. I wanted it to look like a flowing river."

Again, it had been harder to make than I suspected. As if enjoying myself meant letting bits of my talent drop away. I couldn't let that happen. I was tired, and that's all it likely really was. I'd never woven so many bolts so quickly before.

"And it does look like a river! Oh yes, it certainly does." Serene clasped her hands together and bent her head. Now that the candlelight lit her eyes more, I was shocked to see a few tears clinging to her lashes.

"Are you okay?" I asked.

"Me? Oh, don't mind me. I just get so flustered sometimes. Everything's so solid here, so *unmoving* and it just makes me so homesick."

"What do you mean—you weren't born here?"

Her looks suggested her family, at least, had come from different shores, but her accent sounded like she'd been in the city for a long time.

Andrew took Serene's elbow and sighed. "It's the dress, isn't it? Callum said the silk, ah, enhances certain virtues. Intoxicates, enraptures. Serene's always a bit wobbly when we go to parties."

"You're both indulging yourselves," Callum said. "Parties are for fun, not wallowing. And don't forget we have a job to do."

Both Serene and Andrew bent at the waist, very subtly bowing to Callum. It was strange to see him as the leader of the Players when he'd just been Callum for the last few weeks. There was etiquette to these things. I knew to bow to the Chieftain every time we saw him and to do it the first time we met anyone new at the party. I wished I'd stitched these rules on a sampler or something that I could have stuffed down the front of my bodice and looked at it when I forgot them.

Serene bent her head into Andrew's shoulder, and he whispered something I couldn't hear into her smooth hair. Callum snatched my fingers and pulled me closer.

"It's beautiful, you know."

"The dress?"

He nodded and bent his head to kiss my earlobe. "It's spectacular . . . your talent is spectacular."

My heart fell a little. Yes, I wanted him to think the silk I wove was extraordinary, but tonight I also wanted him to see *me* in the dress, not just the dress itself. I'd never had the chance to wear any of the good silks I'd created before.

I hated myself for asking it, but I let two tiny words fall from my lips. "And me?"

Callum smiled and worked his lips from my ear to my mouth. "You." *Kiss.* "Are." *Kiss.* "Lovely."

I breathed out a little in shallow relief. He'd said I was lovely. I just wished I hadn't prompted it so I could believe him.

Two horses, white with black manes, pulled a black carriage. It rolled to a stop in front of us. I'd expected to see a crest on the side, to learn a little more about Callum's family and history, but the door was solid black, shiny and smooth. Callum stepped forward and held out a hand to Serene.

"Are you ready?" he said.

She sucked a breath in through her teeth and nodded. "I can do this."

Why was everyone acting like tonight would be so hard? Odina and now Serene? We had magic in the fabric of our clothes, and we were only trying to convince the Chieftain to give Callum ownership of the leases on Market Street. We weren't staging a takeover of the principality. Was I supposed to be more nervous? Like them? Perhaps they knew something I didn't. I swallowed on a suddenly dry throat and coughed. Callum gave me a questioning look and helped me into the carriage. He held my hand tight, but I let mine go a bit limp.

"Ella," he said and tightened his grip even more. "You are going to glitter like a jewel tonight."

I squeezed his hand back as I stepped up, but his words didn't mean as much now he was trying to lighten all of our moods. I hoped I'd shine enough for people to want to be near me, for the Chieftain to want to get closer so I could play my part. If we succeeded, I'd have my purse of coins and the lease on a shop. I would show everyone a smooth, glimmering surface—free from the scratches life had etched into me.

We sat close together in the carriage. I pressed up against the side, yet Serene's knee still pushed against mine. I gathered a handful of blue silk from my skirt and squeezed, not caring for once about the marks my damp palms might leave. I needed the magic from the fabric to help me. If I had any charming qualities, the magic could go ahead and make them stronger now. I also wished it could strip away my nerves, make me more confident. The trouble was, confidence wasn't a natural quality I possessed. It was all put on for show while standing in a client's parlor, and it cost me a lot.

Callum put his hands on my knees, eased the silk of my skirt out of my grip.

"We can do this."

I nodded. What else was there to say? I wasn't about to leak my worries into the carriage like poison. Callum's eyes shone with what looked like excitement. He watched Andrew and Serene giggling, heads together, and shifted his gaze back to me.

"If we get what we want tonight, you'll honor everything we agreed to?" I asked.

I wanted to hear him say it so the nerves bubbling in my stomach would settle. He took my hand from my lap and squeezed so hard my fingers slipped under each other.

"Ella, if we get what we want tonight, your life will never look the same."

I sat back against the padded carriage seat and watched the glow of the street lanterns flick by. Back in my courtyard, we had only the moon to light our way. I'd spent my life watching out for shadows and who they might be hiding—men like Gregory, debtor police. This part of the world was different. There were fewer shadows to hide in. I wondered if that meant bad things really didn't happen here or if everyone just ignored them, fluttering like moths to bright and beautiful things in their world and ignoring the dull and dirty.

A stray thread sprang up from the hem of my sleeve. My fault or the seamstress's? I examined the line of small stitches. The thread poked up from the fabric itself. I'd missed something here, failed to secure the ends properly. I sucked in a breath and Callum shot a look at me. I avoided meeting his eye. I didn't make mistakes on my cloth. Papa had taught me to be very careful, very caring of every bolt I worked on. This was a slip. I was getting wrapped up in this world, in Callum, and I had to watch myself or I'd start to unravel just like this watery blue silk.

# Chapter Twenty-Eight

We rushed through a thick, deep forest. The tree branches stretched into the road like arms, brushing against the carriage in fleeting greetings. The house looked as though it had carved itself a place in the woods, nestling in the foliage. I'd expected a wide lawn swooping away from the estate like Callum had—with paths picked out in gravel for tame strolls. Here, wildness won. The trees and brush fought back against the house. They leaned and climbed and consumed. The ivy even covered the windows, as if the gardener hadn't been able to cut it back.

The carriage rolled to a stop outside the wide front doors. It looked as though they were made of iron, not wood, and I guessed a chieftain needed more protection than Callum did. But those doors weren't keeping all the threats out—we were about to sweep in with an invitation in our hands.

I was the first to step out, being crushed against one of the carriage doors. I almost fell to the ground when the driver opened it. He offered a hand, and I took it to avoid sprawling in the packed-dirt drive.

Serene and Andrew came next, eyes seeming to gobble up the beautiful and strange house in front of them. I wanted to look too, but Callum slipped from the carriage next and took my hand.

"Do you like it?"

He asked the question as though my answer mattered, as if we were looking at a cottage we might buy. I took in the stone, just the same color of gray as the rock ledges near the river. The house was natural here, an extension of the woods. A rounded tower on the left side mimicked the shape of the thick tree trunks beside it. The rest of the building stretched out from the tower, two stories with diamond-paned leaded windows across both the bottom and the top floors.

"It's alluring."

Callum quirked an eyebrow. "I've never heard a house described like that before."

I shrugged. "Well, it is, and I want to go inside."

Really, it was hard to tell if the house itself pulled me in or if it was simply all the possibilities it contained. I placed a hand on my bodice and breathed in. Lightness floated through me, a feeling I'd begun to associate with the cups of deep burgundy wine Callum always set out with our suppers. My nerves calmed, worries melting away. This was it.

Andrew helped Serene up the stairs and bowed to the attendant. At Callum's party, the man guarding the door had worn a wolf mask. This man hid behind a fox's face. The burnt orange fur flared out from a shiny black nose and white snout. Through the cut eyeholes, I watched the man's bright blue eyes. He nodded to us and ushered us through the doors with an elegant extension of his arm. Another figure stood waiting, this one wearing a long, dark cloak and a headpiece crusted with black sequins. She held out a basket of silver masks. Callum took one, so I copied him.

"Thank you," I said to the woman, but her attention was already focused on the next guests.

"Do you need help?" Callum said.

"Yes, please."

I handed him the mask and he placed it over my eyes. The world grew smaller, outlined in the silver rim of the eyeholes. Unease prickled down my spine—I could barely see beside me without turning my head. The mask tightened around my face as Callum tied the ribbons behind my head.

"It goes nicely with your dress," he said.

I wished there was a mirror so I could see how the gray-blue of my bodice set off the silver of the mask. It probably matched my strands of gray hair too.

"Put yours on. It will go with your stars."

Callum obliged, tying his own mask with his long fingers. I pulled it down a bit so it sat better on his nose.

"There, now you're ready."

"Are you?"

I knew he was asking more than if my mask was straight.

I nodded. "Let's go."

❧

The ballroom looked like a sea of wildflowers moving in the breeze. People swirled, dressed in every color, long skirts sweeping the floor and coattails trailing to the back of men's knees. The very air was perfumed—huge bundles of heather hung from the ceiling on thick gold ribbons. I touched the toe of my soft leather shoe to the intricate floor. Thousands and thousands of what looked like tiny shells had been pressed together to form an iridescent pattern.

"Have you ever seen anything like it?" Callum asked.

I shook my head.

"He embraces every whim, the Chieftain."

"Every whim? That sounds dangerous."

Callum's eyes twinkled. "Sometimes it is."

Serene and Andrew came into view, sidestepping a tall woman in a draped dress. Now we just needed Odina.

"Which one is he?" I asked.

I'd never seen this chieftain before. The old one was his brother, or maybe a cousin, and I'd only seen him once, though not close enough to see the features of his face. There were no kings here, no princes even. A jumble of families controlled all the pieces of land on this island between them—each branch of the family had a leader, who called themselves the chieftain. Borders changed sometimes, but Eidyn Crag's had remained the same for a long time.

Callum pointed through the crowd toward a big man dressed in cream silk and frothy lace. He threw back his head and laughed at some joke one of the others told, his Adam's apple bobbing. So this was the person who made all the rules? It was hard to imagine one word from his mouth could change everything, but it was true. He held sway over all of us—even Callum.

"How do we get him by himself?" I asked.

"I'll introduce you."

"Me?"

Callum nodded. "It gives us all a reason to speak to him, and that gives us the opportunity to start to let the magic work. Then we'll lure him outside into the woods to talk."

Odina pushed through the crowd to join us, her bright yellow dress like a lit torch. People turned to look at her, stared at her back as she moved past them. One of the men grabbed her arm

"Where did you get that dress? The color is . . . stunning."

Odina pulled her arm back and looped it around mine. I almost tore free from her grasp, but there was no reason not to be civil, especially in front of a potential client.

"This is the weaver, sir. Isn't she clever?"

"The weaver! Right here in the ballroom! Well, that's one way to get people to know your name."

If it were so easy, Papa would have started going to parties well before he was carted off to prison. The only reason I'd been allowed entry to this place was because I'd entered on Callum's arm. Odina probably wouldn't have even given my name to the man if I wasn't standing right beside her.

But I've never been one to waste an opportunity.

"Yes, sir, the silk is my work. If you like bold colors, I can make you something too."

He grinned and a red gemstone flashed on his left front tooth. "Where do I find you?"

"You can call at my patron's house. Callum . . ." I broke off, realizing I didn't know his family name. "Well, it's the house with the green shutters, on the hill overlooking the river on the other side of town."

"Ah, I know it."

"Good," I said. "But watch for me in Market Street. I plan to open a shop there."

Callum gripped my other arm and squeezed a little too hard. I kept my smile in place, but I shifted so my skirt hung over his foot and stepped down on it. He didn't let go. Yes, he didn't want me selling my magic fabrics *now*, but I'd obviously have to once I opened my shop. I was only thinking ahead.

The man nodded and moved off. Odina and Callum both dropped my arms.

"What were you thinking?" he said.

"What? He doesn't know *why* I'll have a shop."

"What if it gets back to the Chieftain somehow? We want to surprise him with our request, not give him time to decide against it before we even ask."

Anger flared in my belly. I wasn't stupid. I knew what we were trying to do here and wasn't going to put that at risk. I had more at stake here than any of the others. If we failed, Odina could still go back to her pretty parlor and Callum to his grand, empty house. Serene and Andrew would presumably go back to their own big, beautiful houses. I was facing a tiny room with rats for company.

"Don't talk to me like I'm a silly girl who isn't smart enough to think things through! I just secured a customer."

Odina's fingers pinched the flesh of my arm, and I almost threw her off, but I realized when I looked at her that she was using me for balance. All the color had been swept from her cheeks. She stood there with wide, watery eyes and chalky brown skin. I was used to seeing a blush creep across her chest, but even the tops of her breasts were pale over the severe cut of her bodice.

Callum glanced around us before focusing on Odina. He put a finger under her chin and pushed her face up toward his, just like he'd done at his party that first night.

"I told you to stop this, this questioning," Callum said.

"I know."

"I'm not sure what your problem is, Odina, but I want this," I said. "I want to help so I can own one of the rents in the marketplace for my shop."

She flicked her fiery gaze over my face. "You don't know what you've asked for."

Odina was wrong. I knew exactly what I wanted and what I'd asked for. A shop to display my creations, people to dream about stepping through the door just to run their hands over *my* bolts of silk.

"You don't get it, Odina. You don't need to do anything special; you don't need to prove yourself over and over again. You have your place in life just because your mother became rich."

Tears welled on the rim of her eyes. One broke free and trailed down her cheek, leaving a path like a snail's slime on a soft leaf.

She turned to Callum. "What are we waiting for?"

Music swelled from the delicate pianoforte and the man playing a handsome violin dipped and swayed with the melody. People rose and joined hands to drift over to a cleared space of mosaic floor, but the Chieftain didn't join them. He leaned against the wall in a corner just out of the candlelight's reach, the long stem of a pipe between his lips.

"Now?" I asked.

Callum crooked his fingers to Serene and Andrew, who

both stood near a table stacked with silver platters of crawfish. Serene dropped the red shell she'd been sucking onto a platter filled with empty bodies and beady black eyes.

"It's time?" Andrew asked.

Odina's attention seemed fractured—her gaze flew all around Andrew and Serene but never landed on either of them. Like she wouldn't even bother looking at them or saying hello. This wasn't how I'd heard the Players described. They were supposed to be a group, as close as the threads tightly woven in a dress. That was how they kept their secrets from falling through, like sand through a sieve.

Serene stood up on her toes and did a little spin. Her blue silk shoes peeked out from beneath her skirt, and I noticed something odd. It looked like she had too many bones—four knobs on her ankles instead of one on either side. The angle of it struck me as unnatural too, like her foot had been smushed into a shoe that didn't fit its shape.

Before I could get a better look, Serene stopped twirling and her skirts fell over her white-stockinged ankles again. I'd probably just seen wrong—the candlelight flickered with the movement of all the people in the room or her stockings were lumpy.

Standing here doing nothing was making me uneasy. Waiting for something to happen, to start, was the worst part of being nervous, and I was done with feeling as though my stomach was caught in a rough current. I wanted to be on the other side of this.

I slipped my fingers between Callum's and took Odina's with my other hand. Serene and Andrew could follow behind. It was time for us to put on a show for the Chieftain.

# Chapter Twenty-Nine

He let out a puff of smoke that swirled around his head like raw wool. Thick and scented with something a bit stronger than the heather strung from the ceiling. He didn't wear a mask, and Callum and the others pulled off theirs too. A sign of respect? I copied them, setting the mask down on a little table with a bowl filled with the broken skeletons of langoustines.

"Chieftain," Callum said as we approached.

The man pushed off the wall and stood straight to greet us. He nodded to Callum and gave Odina a familiar smile.

"Miss Odina, I'd hoped you'd come back to one of my parties."

Red splotches sprawled across Odina's chest like spilled ink. "And why wouldn't I, sir?"

He took another drag on his pipe and blew out a perfect circle this time, letting the smoke leak out of comically rounded lips.

"You left in such a hurry last time, I thought I must have scared you off."

Callum barked a laugh, hard and sharp. "Not our Odina."

"No? Well, my mistake," the Chieftain said. "I barely remember that night to be honest."

So this wasn't their first party with the Chieftain. What had they been after last time? By the sounds of how quickly Odina left, they hadn't gotten it.

I wondered how long I'd have to stand here until Callum introduced me and decided not to wait to find out. If he was mad at me later, so be it. I was sure none of it would matter anyway as long as we got what we wanted out of tonight.

"Chieftain," I said. "Can I ask the name of the craftsperson of your mosaic? I've never seen a floor made of shells."

He waved a hand. "They break. All the time. Always need to be fixed. It's almost not worth it, but the fixers seem to like doing it. Tiny hands, you know."

Callum grinned at the Chieftain, baring his sharp eye-teeth. I placed a hand on his arm, and it was so warm, the heat seeped through the silk of his sleeve.

A current seemed to pass between them, and I wished I knew what the meaning of it was. Why did Callum care about the Chieftain's mosaic floor?

"I'd like to see how it feels to dance on it. Will someone indulge me?" I asked.

Andrew and Serene both nodded and continued nodding so much I thought they must be making themselves dizzy, but I found the Chieftain's gaze and locked my eyes to his. I'd never tried to make someone dance with me before, but whatever I was doing seemed to be working. The Chieftain put his pipe in his embroidered pocket and moved toward me.

Up close, he looked like any other man. Pleasing to the eyes—well, *my* eyes—yes. But a man just the same. Two eyes, a nose with a small bump at the bridge. Lips with a tiny bit of flaking skin that looked like they could use a little grease smeared over them. Dark brown hair somewhere between wavy and curly. He was the same as any of us and yet he held so much power in the hands that now reached out for mine. He crafted the rules of our city, and he owned most of the farms and fields beyond, leasing them out to tenants who had to pay to work the land. The Chieftain approved the stories the temples could tell us about the gods, and he chose to keep Nemain as our patron god when he ascended to power. He let the debtor prisons run and let my papa be hauled off to his death in a cold, dark room.

And yet his hands, his powerful hands, were calloused and dry. He held my fingers lightly and led me toward the swarm of people in the center of the room. Music swelled and everyone melted away from the middle of the dance floor, making way for the single person who could make or ruin their lives with a flick of his fingers. I exhaled a hot breath full of all my anger and frustration and lost myself in the giddiness of the dress. It was right there, had been since we arrived at the party, that chance for release. I just needed to let myself feel it, give in to it, let it pour over me like cool river water on an unusually blistering day.

This was *my* chance to have some control over the Chieftain, over my own life. I had a job to do, and I'd always been good at working. I glanced up over the Chieftain's shoulder to meet Callum's eyes. He gave a tiny, almost imperceptible, nod.

The Chieftain offered his arm, and I laid my fingers against his sleeve, careful not to apply too much pressure, not to overstep. But I needn't have worried, because as soon as we reached the middle of the floor, he took my hand and gripped my fingers tight.

"What's your name?"

I swallowed, groped around in my mind for it. "Ella," I finally said.

The Chieftain smiled. "Your dress," he said, pulling me in close. "It's one of the most beautiful I've ever seen. The silk ripples like the river on a breezy day."

I smiled, even though my nerves ate at my voice and my words came out in a squeak. "I used two spools of silk thread."

"You?" The Chieftain pulled back and stared at me. "You wove the silk yourself?"

I nodded. "I'm a weaver."

"Have I heard of you before?"

"Likely not. I don't have my own shop yet."

He made a clicking sound in his mouth. "It's a crime on the city then, to not have your talents widely accessible."

We were getting to the point already, which was good, but I knew from my experience with Mrs. MacDonald that I needed to pace myself. It wouldn't help my cause to jump in with a request too quickly. Create the problem and let the Chieftain conjure up the solution all on his own.

"There's no room for a new shop in the marketplace, and that's really the only place worth being," I said.

He nodded, bit his bottom lip. He stared at me with glassy eyes and tightened his grip on my fingers. His other hand found my waist and all of a sudden, we were swept along with the tide of dancers. I followed the Chieftain's feet, trying to disguise the fact I didn't know any of the steps. Luckily, it seemed to be a simple dance of two steps forward, one step back. I managed to get through an entire circle of the dance floor without stepping on the Chieftain's feet or the hem of anyone's skirt. His eyes remained a stubborn hazel. The beguilement wasn't working yet.

I tried to let myself roll into the dance. My shoulders were tight, and I held them up around my ears—as Papa always told me I did when I was stressed. It wasn't usually easy to make an effort to keep my body relaxed, but there was no resistance this time. My muscles relaxed as soon as I thought about it, and I concentrated on the Chieftain's grinning face. He was enjoying the dance, leading me in quick, practiced steps across the shiny mosaic floor. I couldn't help but feel sorry for whoever's job it would be to repair the intricate work—already cracks snaked through a number of rounded shells.

People swirled around me, and I wondered if any of them minded that they crushed such beauty under their heels. No one seemed to notice. A few of the guests wore masks with long hooked noses or sequins stitched around the eyes, but there was something that made me stare at them longer than I should. It was as if the masks were hiding something more than an identity. I whipped my head around as the Chieftain turned me across the floor so I could keep an eye on one man in a bronze mask who seemed to have a blue beard stuffed under the faux bronze chin.

The magic must be playing tricks on me, making me feel as though I'd had too much wine, making me see things. The Chieftain threw back his head and closed his eyes. He hummed in perfect tune to the trilling music from the pipes. The tang of sweat built on the dance floor. Bodies pushed too close together, swaddled tightly in layers of fabric, writhing, panting. A woman next to me rolled her head around so hard in laughter, it looked to me like it might just fall off.

I brought the Chieftain in even closer, locking eyes with him again. His pupils ate up all the green-brown color around them.

"Do you like it?" he asked.

"Like what?"

"The party."

I wasn't sure *like* was the right word. It was exhilarating, and I could get used to the burning fire of success in my belly. This was going to work. I had his attention; the beguilement would begin any moment. Then I just had to get him outside.

"Of course I like it. It's like drifting into a story about the fae and the gods." I said.

The Chieftain smiled and twirled me so the room spun around and around. He pulled me back in and our eyes connected again.

"You could get lost here. That's the best part, letting go of everything that was behind you. Moving ahead even though you can't see what's in front of you."

I wasn't sure what he meant, but Callum crooked a finger at me from the shadowy corner near the open doors to the terrace. I stretched to see over the Chieftain's shoulder. Odina swayed on the spot to the music, and Serene and Andrew were just visible through the open doors. We were ready, but the Chieftain's eyes weren't blue yet. He was still aware, not yet pliable. Why wasn't the magic working? Panic swelled like acid in my belly. It had to work. I had everything at stake. Maybe if I got him outside and danced with him again there, away from all these people, the beguilement would take hold.

"Come with me for a breath of air," I said, pulling us to a stop on the edge of the dancers.

The Chieftain pulled the pipe he'd been smoking earlier from his pocket and grinned. "I have something better we can breathe."

There was no way I was going to smoke whatever herb was in that pipe, but I could play along. After all, we had the Chieftain's attention—now it was time for us all to coil ourselves around him like beautiful silk snakes and squeeze.

# Chapter Thirty

The terrace spilled out into the trees. Thick trunks, wide with age, circled us like spectators watching a dance. The music drifting out from the open terrace doors mingled with the *shhhh* sounds of the breeze playing in the leaves. Serene and Andrew almost tumbled from the terrace, catching each other in a fit of giggles. Odina trailed behind the Chieftain and me, with Callum behind her.

I let the Chieftain lead us further into the trees. The moon lit the night with a soft light that almost made the dark seem blue instead of black. I was grateful for it, because it meant I could see everyone's faces. Their thoughts flitting across their features. Their reactions to words. I suspected we all needed to be able to read the Chieftain properly to steer him toward our own wants and plans.

He let go of my arm and scratched a match into life before dropping the flame into the mouth of his pipe. Smoke billowed around his face, obscuring his features. When it cleared, he smiled.

"Who's next?" he said.

Serene took the pipe from the Chieftain's hands and stuck the end between her lips. She sucked, her cheeks caving in on themselves, and blew out a curl of smoke.

"Don't hog it, Serene!" Andrew said.

The Chieftain chuckled and sat himself on the only tall stump in sight. Even here, he had a chair around which we could gather.

"You're all quite tantalizing tonight," he said. "Is it because of your new friend?"

He nodded in my direction and Callum smiled.

"She's brought artistry to our little group," he said.

"Your group is smaller than it used to be, isn't it? Did you lose some followers, Callum?"

I'd assumed there were more Players somewhere that I just hadn't met yet. If this was really it—just the four of them—the group was *much* smaller than I'd always thought. Just four. How could they be so powerful with just four people? I glanced around at all of them. Each was more than the average person—more beautiful, more charismatic. But it was easy to be polished to a lovely sheen when you didn't have to scrape the most out of each day just to survive. I knew that now. If everyone else realized that too, the Players might lose their edge.

"These are just my most trusted Players," Callum said to answer the Chieftain's question. I didn't believe him, and by the look of the smirk on his face, the Chieftain didn't either.

"And you're all wearing the lovely Ella's silks?"

"We wouldn't wear any others, now that we know hers exist," Callum said.

Odina drifted over to the Chieftain and leaned against the stump. She must know him quite well to do that. I wondered how many of these parties they'd all been to—this whole sparkling life going on while I nursed my sore fingers in my near-empty room.

"I knew her, actually," Odina cut in. "She's made the fabric for many of my dresses, but I've never had one quite like this before."

She flashed her gaze on me and I stared back. Even without the Bean-Nighe's magic, my fabrics had always been well-made and people liked them. Was she trying to say that wasn't true?

"They *are* special tonight," Callum said. "Imagine if we brought more goods like this to the city."

The Chieftain waved his hands. "Traders . . . and goods . . . come and go."

"And yet, most of the city's people go to the marketplace for everything they're looking for."

Serene passed the pipe to Andrew and dropped down onto the dirt and the moss. I flinched—her dress would be dirty when she stood up again.

"So what?" the Chieftain asked. "They need one place to go. Not everyone can afford to have the goods come to them, Callum."

"Exactly. Which is why we need to curate."

Odina lept on to this, gripping the edge of the stump and titling her face up to the Chieftain so it caught the moonlight. "Oh yes, imagine if all the *best* things were in one place. We could go to the market without jostling for space with the same people buying pig cheeks for their dinner."

I'd never even been able to afford pig cheeks. They were something Papa would have bought for a special occasion when he was still around—my birthday, maybe. Shame burned my own cheeks, but I knew what Odina was doing. She was trying to make the Chieftain see the marketplace as the domain of the rich, instead of the mixing ground of our city. It was a strategy they were using on purpose. I pressed the back of my hands to my face to cool it, hoping everyone else was in too much of a fog to notice.

"Odina, you *are* clever," the Chieftain said. "But there are all sorts crammed into that street."

Callum took the pipe Andrew offered and sucked in a mouthful of scented smoke. The sweetness of it filled my nostrils and I wondered if he would taste like it later—and if I would get the chance to find out. The feeling of giddiness that had enveloped me on our arrival at the party was turning on me. Now, the lines of the forest seemed blurred, dizzying. I wanted to drop my head on Callum's shoulder and feel the softness of his lips under mine. I wanted to steady myself on him.

"What do you think, Ella? Could you sell your dazzling silks in your very own shop in the market?" he asked.

He wanted to bring me into the conversation, and he was right. I had to be part of it. If I wanted my prize, I had to play their games.

"I want to be where everyone can touch my silks," I said, kneeling beside Odina. She pushed into me, drooping against me, and I almost pulled away in surprise. But there was no malice to it, none that I could feel. Instead, it was as if she leaned against me for comfort, to help hold her up to this task.

With Odina's arm against mine, I looked up at the Chieftain. His eyes were round and bright, the slivers of color around his pupils still hazel. The whole forest seemed to bend and sway in the breeze. The Chieftain loved pretty things; I only had to look at the crushed shells on the mosaic floor in the ballroom to know

243

that. He seemed to find joy in it, in its beauty—but in the very act of enjoying it, he destroyed it.

We were offering something more permanent.

"Imagine all the best things the city has to offer in one place, Chieftain," I said. "To touch and feel, smell and taste."

His tongue darted out like the head of a snail and wet his lips. "Yes."

"All that beauty, all that loveliness to wrap yourself up in."

"Yes," he said again.

"Isn't it an irresistible thought, Chieftain?" Odina asked.

"It's delicious."

Callum laughed and passed the Chieftain back his pipe. Odina and I were the only ones who hadn't smoked—even so, the magic in my silk dress twined itself around me, pulling against my limbs so they were heavy and hard to move.

"And why shouldn't you do it? You're the Chieftain, after all," Callum said.

"Or better yet, get someone else to do it for you," I said, planting my knees in the pine needle–strewn dirt of the forest floor. I had to hold on—keep focus.

Odina giggled, but the laughter didn't reach her eyes. There was something sharp there instead. Pain. Fear. It reminded me of how she'd looked in Callum's dining room that day when she challenged Callum. I'd expected jealousy, but I couldn't find a trace of it in her face.

*Why was she scared?*

"Odina," I whispered and touched her arm. She leaned against my shoulder but wouldn't meet my eyes. I wanted to show her some comfort, even though I wasn't sure she'd ever try to give me any. The fear in her eyes was too harsh, like a sliver under my skin. I couldn't let it go.

"Odina, everything's all right," I went on. "It's all working. Don't worry."

She didn't react to my words, just let her head fall a little more heavily into my shoulder. I shifted so I could take her weight.

Serene took Andrew in her arms, and they began to dance around the wide tree trunks, singing a tune as they went. The air smelled ripe, like rain, and a few people we could see in the distance fled the terrace as the first drops began to fall. We were protected under a thick canopy of ancient branches and fall leaves.

While the Chieftain took another long drag on his pipe, Callum gripped my hands and pulled me up. Odina found her own strength and stood as well, though she stared into the trees instead of looking at me and Callum. I wanted to slip my fingers into hers, to show her I cared, but Callum drew me in, running his eyes over my face and my dress.

"A river goddess."

"If I were a goddess, I could have anything I wanted."

"And don't you?"

I almost had what I wanted, but the thought didn't settle me. I'd imagined there'd be a sense of calm to come with security, but maybe all this good fortune was just too fresh and new. It hadn't settled in yet.

Odina took the pipe from the Chieftain's hands. Serene and Andrew continued their off-key song and swayed around the clearing and wove between the trees. That left Callum and me.

We gripped each other harder, pulled each other closer. Our bodies moved in tandem, and it wasn't enough. I wanted to be enmeshed with him. His scent filled me up, but it only made me hungrier for more.

"What else do you want, Ella?"

I leaned my cheek against his chest and felt the rise and fall of his breathing. This. I wanted *this*. I'd been alone for a long time, and that loneliness crashed down around me. It swallowed me up like a wave. I hadn't even realized how bad it was until now. All alone in that tiny room with my loom. After Papa was taken away, there was no one left to touch me. No pat on the head in the morning or quick tap on the arm when I dropped a stitch. No arms to envelop me before bed. Callum filled a void I'd barely even known I had. His eyes glowed faintly blue. My dress and the dancing was beguiling him. His was likely doing the same to me. It didn't matter—I wasn't scared of him.

"I want you," I said.

He released me a little, just a tiny lessening of pressure on my hands, but it was enough to make my stomach squirm. Did he not want me too?

"You came to me out of nowhere, Ella, and I thank whichever god made that happen."

My muscles relaxed and I pulled in a steadying breath. He was happy I was here, with him, at the Chieftain's party.

Funny though, because *I* didn't come out of nowhere—*he* did. I'd been coming to Odina's parlor for at least a year with my bolts of wools and silks. I'd never seen him there before that first day after the Bean-Nighe granted my wish for the loom and supplies. It was as if her magic called him there too, an extra wish granted.

Serene and Andrew ended their song just as the musicians inside struck up a new tune. Callum let go of me, and a little stone of loss settled in my chest.

"So, Chieftain," said Callum, moving to take his hands. "I can build you what you want . . . a market full of only beautiful things."

He leaned in close to the Chieftain's face and I wondered if the Chieftain could smell cinnamon.

"It will be so simple, so easy," Callum went on. "Give me the leases, and I'll give you exactly what you want."

"Tell me what it is I want, Callum."

Blue skirted the Chieftain's irises and his eyes slid over Callum.

Callum leaned in and pressed his lips against the Chieftain's. My breath caught, heart contracting. His kisses were supposed to be for me. I started to move toward them but Odina caught my arm and shook her head. She held my hand in hers and stroked the back of it with a finger. Calming. Soothing. I had to stay on track.

The Chieftain grabbed the back of Callum's head and pulled him in closer. I didn't want to watch, but I couldn't look away. I knew what Callum's lips tasted like. This was all an act, a show—he might have kissed the Chieftain and meant it before, but he didn't mean it now. Now *I* was the one he kissed. He only slipped his tongue into the Chieftain's mouth because he wanted something from him. I knew that, but the fact didn't stop my heart from splintering. We'd exchanged more than kisses, Callum and I. He knew things about me, and I thought I knew things about him. We'd traded pieces of ourselves, and I suppose I'd thought we'd each keep them safe. But maybe it had all meant less to Callum.

They let go of each other and the Chieftain smiled. Serene and Andrew swirled near, humming their own raucous song again. The broken notes and the patter of rain filled my ears, and nothing seemed clear, like I was underwater.

"Dance with me," Callum said.

My stomach dropped as the Chieftain took Callum's hand and stepped among the pine needles and raised roots of the trees. I wanted to be the one to beguile the Chieftain; it would have felt more like earning my reward. I glanced around at the group—Odina, Serene, and Andrew. Why waste the magic in all our fabrics? We'd be stronger together.

I gestured to them. "A circle dance."

Odina grinned and nodded. She took one of Callum's hands and gave a quick nod when Callum looked at her in surprise. Serene and Andrew followed. I closed the circle by taking Andrew and the Chieftain's hand.

We moved, feet in sync. The music thrummed through me, drums and fiddles and windpipes. I abandoned myself to it, closing my eyes and letting the magic in the silk flow. My head was light, muscles relaxed in a way I might have expected if I'd smoked the pipe. The music built on itself, louder and louder, faster and faster. We held our arms up and moved our feet to the tempo of the melody.

Breath held tight in my chest, I looked over to the Chieftain. His eyes glowed icy blue. It was working. I breathed, light again as a playful breeze.

Callum slowed and the rest of us followed. He broke from the circle and took the Chieftain's hands in his.

"Give us the leases," he said.

The Chieftain nodded.

Odina and I closed in over Callum's shoulders.

"We can make you feel this way again," I said.

"Give in to it," Odina said.

"Yes," the Chieftain said, letting the s play on his lips.

I tilted my head back, soaking it all in. We'd done what we came here to do. I'd have my own shop and people would buy my cloth and wear it and the city would be full of this feeling of titillation, this sweet intoxication I was drowning in.

The gold in my pockets would only help me sink deeper, deeper into satisfaction.

It was all here, right in front of me. I reached for it, taking it, letting it envelop me, feeling the success settle over me like a sparkling mantle until a scream sheared through it, and it fell to pieces around me.

# Chapter Thirty-One

A flash of red splattered against Serene's purple sleeve, but it wasn't her blood. It was Andrew's.

The blood seeped from his shoulder, pulsing like a heartbeat. Serene held a long, thin knife in her hand. Where would she have concealed it—up her sleeve? Strapped to her calf? In any case, she'd brought a knife to the Chieftain's party and killed her companion. Because Andrew was undoubtedly dying. His skin paled, leeched of color. His features grew lax like he didn't even have enough strength to hold his mouth closed anymore. Odina stepped back from the blood and the mess with a hand to her mouth. The Chieftain pressed the back of his hands into his eyes and shook his head as if freeing it from cobwebs.

Callum grabbed my hand and tensed. I returned the pressure, happy he was there to hold me in place. If not, I might have run screaming out of the woods. The blood flowed as freely as the ale and wine inside. I'd never seen so much, and it was a deeper red than I'd imagined. In contrast, Andrew's face paled to the color of cheap paper. His eyes looked different, the spark draining from them. I flexed my hands, wanting to feel my own muscles move. They were stiff with a cold I hadn't felt before.

Serene laughed. A deep-throated laugh, one that would make her stomach muscles hurt tomorrow. A chill broke over me like a sudden cold rain.

"He stepped on my hem and said my dress was shoddy," she said, eyes flicking to each of us as we stood there, like that was a completely acceptable reason to stab someone. A shudder crept through my body, from the top of my head down to my toes.

Andrew grabbed at his shoulder. His fingers came away covered in thick blood at the knuckles, stained pink at the fingertips. No one sprang forward to help him.

I moved, not because I could help him but because I couldn't stand the thought that his life would fade from his body without anyone even touching him, holding him. In my darkest thoughts, that was how Papa had died. Alone in his cell with no one to even offer him the comfort of a hand on his arm. I prayed to all the gods that someone had been there, had offered him a little bit of kindness as he left the world. I could at least do that for Andrew.

Callum grabbed for me, but I slipped from his grip and dropped to my knees beside Andrew. He'd fallen to the ground and then sprawled on his back in the dirt. I took his bloodied hand in mine and tried to catch his gaze.

"Andrew, it's going to be all right."

It wasn't, but how do you tell someone they're dying? He would know anyway. And wherever he went after—wherever it was the gods took our souls—the temple made it sound rather nice. I'd pictured Papa there sometimes. Sitting back against a riverbank, a fishing rod in his hand. He told me once he thought he'd like fishing if he ever got to do it.

Andrew rasped and coughed blood. I squeezed his hand harder since that's all I could do.

Someone placed a hand on my shoulder. I turned my head to find Odina kneeling beside me.

"Ella—"

"No," I cut her off. "He shouldn't die alone. Why are you all acting like you don't care? Why has no one grabbed her?"

I stared around the group, from face to slack face. Serene's was the only one still smiling. Sick.

Nothing made sense. No one was reacting properly. Was I the only one here who wasn't numbed by whatever was in the Chieftain's pipe?

Andrew shook beneath my hands. A garbled breath erupted from his mouth.

"Look what you've done!" I yelled at Serene.

She didn't flinch. She just giggled in a way that made me wonder if she hadn't realized what had happened. That Andrew was losing his life in front of us.

I expected his skin to cool with the loss of blood, but when I touched his cheek, it was extraordinarily warm. Hot like he'd just spent an hour sitting too close to the fire. He vibrated under my hands. I sat back on my heels, shock zipping through me.

Then Andrew sat up.

I jumped back, fear squeezing the breath from my lungs. This couldn't be happening. Time didn't move backward, and dying people didn't get better just like that.

"Serene!" Andrew said and looked down at his blood-spattered shoulder. "You've ruined my suit! And you went pretty deep this time."

Callum reached for me, and I wound my arms around his waist. Calm. I needed calm. I buried my nose in his chest and sucked in the scent of him before I fixed my eyes on Andrew.

"How did you do that? What are you?"

I looked up at Callum as realization dawned on me. No one reacted because they all knew he'd come back. They knew Andrew wasn't dying—that he'd heal.

The Chieftain leaned back on his stump and let out another fluffy cloud of smoke. His eyes glowed bright hazel again, the beguilement over.

"What have you all done to me?" he asked.

I'd been cold before, but now I was freezing. I shook with nerves and the chill. The magic had abandoned us, and the Chieftain knew his own mind again.

I stared around the group. Odina buried her face in her hands. Callum released me and let me step away from him.

"What do you mean, Chieftain? We were discussing how to make your city even better," he said.

The Chieftain closed his eyes for a long moment. When he opened them again, they were clearer than I'd seen them all night.

"No, I don't think so. You want something for you, Callum. You always do. I heard about the trade agreement you managed to get out of the Lady MacDonald, and I left it because it doesn't matter to me which of you holds the agreement over coal as long as someone pays taxes. This is different. You always want more, don't you? And sometimes I let myself lose enough of my senses to give it to you."

He flung the pipe from his hand into the trees. Maybe he thought that was why he'd almost given into us.

"Chieftain—" Callum started, but the Chieftain held out a hand to stop him.

"I'm going back to the party. Clean up this mess, won't you?" he gestured to Andrew and the blood staining the leaves strewn around him.

I bit my cheek to try and settle the sourness in my stomach. I had everything in my grasp, everything I wanted in my hand, and now it was being ripped from me again. I wasn't going to get my money or the lease for my shop, because we hadn't succeeded.

The Chieftain walked away from us, back to his party, and took all my dreams with him.

"Someone better explain what just happened here," I said.

"Ella," Odina said. Not Callum—not the man I'd let kiss me and touch me. Not the person who'd made this deal with me to begin with. Odina stood and took my hand in her icy one. "Serene and Andrew aren't who you think they are."

"Yes, I've realized that now."

She shook her head. "They're only playing in our world."

"What do you mean?"

The only other world was the realm of the gods—the place where magic lived. Where the Bean-Nighe lived.

"Are you saying they're gods?" I asked.

Serene snorted with laughter, and Odina glared at her. She turned back to me and squeezed my hand, as if telling me to hold on.

"They're faeries."

# Chapter Thirty-Two

Serene and Andrew didn't look how I imagined faeries would, but all I'd ever seen were paintings in the temple. In those, the artist had shown the fae to be small, winged, translucent creatures. Perhaps the artist had never seen a real faerie. They were said to hide from us, only showing up in our world when a person was alone and unprotected. They liked to play games, and the rules were different for them because they weren't as vulnerable as us. They *could* die, if the wound was so terrible their bodies couldn't possibly heal it. If Serene had taken Andrew's head off, he would have actually died. But they were entirely safe from fevers and bad teeth and pox. And, apparently, stabbings.

Andrew's body had rejected the possibility of death, brushed it off like a bit of dirt on a sleeve. It didn't seem like the experience had stained him in any way. He got to his feet.

"Gods' fangs, Serene. You've ruined Ella's lovely silk."

Serene shrugged, but a little pink bloomed in her tawny cheeks. "I don't know what happened. I just . . . couldn't help myself. I was compelled."

"By what? Your temper?" Andrew said.

"What does it matter anyway, you're perfectly fine."

"My suit isn't."

He was right, but I could weave more silk. I'd be spending a lot of time at my loom. My fingers ached at the thought, and I rubbed at my knuckles. My skin was soft from the grease I'd rubbed into it earlier, but it seemed thinner somehow, as if I was rubbing too hard and sloughing too many layers away. I examined my hands in the moonlight. There were two dark round spots near my left index finger that most certainly weren't there before.

Age spots. Papery skin. Lines I hadn't yet earned. The small of my back throbbed hard enough to get my attention. Now all the excitement was gone, my body remembered all its hurts.

"Ella, can you fix this?" Andrew asked. "Do you have some concoction to get the blood out?"

I tucked my hands behind my back so he couldn't see they were the hands of an old woman.

"I'm a weaver, not a laundress."

The image of the Bean-Nighe flashed in my mind. Her determination to scrub the blood from that white shirt, even though it would never be clean again. Would she be able to slap Andrew's silk jacket against her flat rock and coax the blood out? It didn't matter, because I wasn't going back to her. I'd given drops of my own blood to my loom and thought that was enough payment for the magic, but it seemed it wasn't. The silver hair, the aching back, the thin skin and lumpy fingers. I was growing old before my time, paying for the magic with my own life, and I knew I wouldn't come back like Andrew after it had all drained away from me.

"See, Serene! You've ruined it, just ruined it all."

"Oh come off it, I didn't go nearly deep enough to kill you," Serene said.

"Calm down, Andrew. We'll make you another suit," Callum said. "We have a bigger problem. The Chieftain thinks we tried to manipulate him!"

"We did try to manipulate him," Odina said.

Callum whipped around, a finger in Odina's face. "He wasn't supposed to realize that!"

I swallowed my shock and looked beyond Odina and Callum, toward the open terrace doors. People in dresses that caught the moonlight, others in suits that bled into the shadows—they still stepped and twirled to the tinkling music, still opened their mouths for the juicy flesh of crawfish, still sucked down the contents of their silver mugs. The party wasn't over for them yet, but it certainly was for me. There were faeries here, on this side of the veil, in our midst. That was dangerous. The fae had magic. Humans didn't—only what the fae decided to bestow on us, and it always came with a price, a steep one. What were Andrew and Serene doing here, and what price might *they* exact for being part of the Players? Everything was falling apart. Disappointment and exhaustion weighed down my limbs. We hadn't accomplished what we'd come here to do, and I wasn't leaving with anything I wanted.

⌒⌒

Callum held my cold hand while Serene and Andrew bickered all the way back to the carriage. I kept staring at Andrew, trying to see the pulse in his neck, the blue veins running under his pale skin. He was alive, when just minutes ago he'd been lying drained of blood on a forest floor. He poked Serene in the ribs, and she squealed. It didn't seem like enough retribution for stabbing him.

"Ella."

Odina caught at my sleeve, and Callum and I stopped.

"You've seen something now only Players are meant to see."

This was the moment she'd decided to make it clear to me I wasn't welcome in their group? Really?

"Well, it's too late to do anything about that. I'm not a Player and, as you said, I've seen."

Callum gripped my hand harder and I wondered if this meant anything. Maybe he going to give me my prize even though I hadn't won the bargain. He'd touched me, taken the kisses I'd given and pressed his own back on my lips. Maybe that would count for something. "Leave it, Odina."

Odina's eyes flashed with what could only be fury. Her body trembled with it and her hands curled into fists at her side. She seemed to be pushing her fingernails into her palms, her knuckles moving up and down.

"I'm trying to protect her!"

Callum scoffed and held my hand even harder. "Protect her from what?"

"From everything!"

I gripped Callum's hand. I didn't need that kind of protection anymore. Callum had taken me in, become my patron, given me the opportunity to be here tonight. Plus, he listened to me when I talked. Actually listened. His eyes didn't gloss over and he didn't nod absently until I left, like Mrs. Under sometimes did. He listened to me like Papa used to, and like no one had done since.

Odina had been jealous since the minute I asked for a party invitation in her parlor. She didn't want me here, so she was trying to scare me away now. Well, it wouldn't work. What happened with Andrew made my skin crawl, but I could live with it. If neither he nor Serene could die, what she did to him was no different than a punch on the arm. But it lost us the leases; it still hurt us.

"You know what, Odina?" I said, rolling my shoulders back. "You're wrong. The only person here I might need protection from is you . . . because you can't stomach me close to you or Callum or the Players."

Odina's copper skin flushed rose at her neck. She was uncomfortable. Good. She'd spent enough time trying to make me squirm.

"You're the one who's wrong, Ella. You have everything completely backward."

I didn't want to hear any more. She was trying to take this from me, this little bit of happiness I'd found. Callum thought I was wonderful because my fabrics were wonderful. I wasn't going to give any of that away.

"You shouldn't come back with us," I said. "If we're so backward."

"Exactly. No need to come to the house. Ella still has use, Odina," Callum said. "Just wait and see."

His words should have eased the jumble of nerves in my chest, but they didn't. He wasn't going to give me the money. Why not? He had it in his power—that much was obvious. But he was going to make me prove myself again. Fine. I could do that. He knew I could. Just look what I'd made for the Chieftain's party. Magnificent silks. I turned away from Odina, still holding Callum's hand, and pulled him with me.

I'd weave whatever he asked me to, and they would be the best bolts of cloth he'd ever seen.

# Chapter Thirty-Three

I curled my sore hands in my lap and tried to hide them with my skirt. I didn't want Callum to see the thin skin or the dark spots and wrinkles that shouldn't be there, but I wasn't sure the darkness in the carriage would be enough to hide them. My loom may be draining my youth along with my blood, but I had lots left to work with. My hands being a bit worn out before their time wasn't the worst that could happen. As long as I could still weave and work for my future, everything would be fine.

Callum put his arm around me, and I leaned into his shoulder. Nothing about tonight was what I'd expected—or hoped for. But it wasn't over yet. I glanced at Callum's profile. Straight nose, harsh cheekbones. He didn't look as soft as I knew he could be once his shell was cracked. He was a little older than me, more well versed in life, so it was likely someone else had seen under the veneer before I came along. At least I was one of the few he'd chosen to show.

I wanted to ask him if we could try again, if I could still earn a rent in Market Street, but I couldn't do that with Serene and Andrew slumped against each other on the opposite bench. Their arguing, and Andrew's brief encounter with death, seemed to have taken a lot out of them, because now they both snored softly.

"Where did you find them?" I asked.

"I've known Andrew and Serene a long time."

"But they're faeries . . . they're not supposed to live in this world," I said, picking at a thread in the carriage's upholstery.

"They don't. Not always."

"Why aren't you giving me a straight answer?"

Callum brought a finger to his lips and shushed me.

"What?"

"They're right there!" he said.

"They're asleep!"

He rubbed his eyes with his index finger and thumb. "I've known them since I was young, all right? Faeries visit this world all the time. They just don't always show themselves to humans."

"They pretend they don't have magic?"

His shoulder rose and fell next to mine. "There are all types of different faeries with different kinds of magic."

"That's how you guessed about my loom, isn't it? Because you'd seen things like it before. Magic things."

Callum nodded. "I saw something special in that raspberry silk right away. It simply shone with a hint of . . . more."

We rolled on out of the woods and onto the cobbled streets of the city. Towering black shapes lurked outside my window—moldering buildings squashed so full of people that their detritus overflowed into the streets. I smelled it, the tang of urine and the sour scent of rotting turnip peelings.

Callum didn't react to the stench. He leaned against my shoulder, a light pressure, and stared straight ahead at the sleeping

Andrew and Serene. Would they stay at Callum's house tonight or disappear back into whatever faerie circle they'd come from?

I'd never seen Callum entertain visitors beyond those at the parties, never noticed the invisible servants tending to anyone else. The servants—what if that was why I never saw them? Perhaps they were faeries too. But that couldn't be true. I doubted there were many faeries for hire.

We pulled up into his circular drive and the horses slowed to a stop. I hadn't looked at them properly before, but they were enormous, with thick legs and big hooves. Their coats were mostly white and their manes shone a lustrous black. Callum must have hired them, because there were no stables on the ground. Perhaps the driver, a tall man with a felt cap, had come from the same place as the horses and the carters who helped me move my loom. Callum borrowed the things he needed to give the appearance of who he wanted to be.

I got out of the carriage on my own, refusing the driver's offer of his large, calloused hand. Callum came behind me, but Serene and Andrew didn't emerge.

"Aren't you going to wake them?"

Callum shook his head and peered back inside. "They can sleep it off in there."

"Wait!"

Andrew's arm emerged and he gripped Callum's wrist. I jumped.

"Let go, Andrew," Callum said.

Andrew dropped Callum's wrist like it burned him.

"Sorry, sorry, I just . . . you know we came here because, well . . ."

"Spit it out," Callum said.

Serene swooped down out of the carriage, her skirt swirling around her ankles.

"We have to tell you something," she said.

"Oh?" Callum said. "Perhaps Ella should go inside."

I planted my feet more firmly in the gravel. "What secret will the faeries tell you?"

"Secret," Andrew snorted. "'Tis no secret."

"Well then," I said. "Go on."

Callum stared at Serene, and I wondered if he flashed her a warning glance, but I couldn't see from where I stood. If they were going to talk about the next chance to get the Chieftain to hand over the rents, I wanted to be there. There was no point hiding any of that from me now.

"Nemain is angry," Serene said.

"What?" I asked. "The god?"

Andrew nodded. "It's no secret on the other side of the veil that people in this city aren't praying to her as they once did. Rumor is that she's close to losing her immortality."

This had nothing to do with us. Gossip about beings who we'd never meet, who lived a world apart.

"We're going in," Callum said. "I'm not in the mood for any of this. Get the driver to take you two back to wherever you came through this time."

He turned toward the steps and took them at a run before pushing open one of the big wooden doors. I followed. Silence filled the hall. I'd expected to come back here with Callum, Odina, Serene, and Andrew to celebrate our success. I'd hoped for the clinking of glasses as we toasted ourselves and the leases we held in our hands. I'd imagined Callum would brandish the papers over his head and we'd all clap at our cleverness and then he might say how they couldn't have done it without my silks—without me.

None of that would happen now. Instead, Callum and I wandered into the dining room, where embers glowed red in the grate. Callum threw in a couple pieces of wood and prodded at them with an iron poker. The fire caught and crackled to life. I was glad for the sound, because I couldn't stand the disappointed silence any longer.

I stepped forward and wrapped my arms tentatively around his waist, holding my breath. I hoped it would soften him, loosen the anger from his muscles. It seemed to work. He bent his head and rested his chin on my hair.

"We can still get the rents," I said.

"You don't know the Chieftain. He'll be on guard now that he knows I want them."

"We painted him a pretty enough picture. And then Serene ruined it."

"They both did. Next time they will behave better or they won't be allowed to come to any more parties."

Now, while we were alone, I couldn't stop myself asking the question that had been lingering in the back of my head.

"Why did you kiss the Chieftain?"

Callum extricated himself from my arms and went to the sideboard to pour a measure of amber liquid into a flawless glass cup. I wrapped my arms around my body instead and bit the inside of my cheek. I wanted my stomach to settle, my heart to slow its beating, but I couldn't comfort myself.

"You know why I kissed him," he said after a moment. "It was just part of everything, part of the aesthetic of the night."

"Have you kissed him before?"

I hoped he'd say no, that he didn't have—and had never had—any feelings for the Chieftain.

But Callum shrugged. "A few times."

I unfolded my arms and folded them again, foolishness flooding through me and making sweat prick at my underarms and the backs of my legs. Of course, he'd had other people in his life, people he'd kissed and touched. I knew that. And yet, it hurt. It wasn't the same for me. I didn't have any girls and only one boy I'd kissed. Plus Callum. He filled that space in my heart.

"But tonight didn't mean anything, right?"

"Of course it didn't," Callum said and swallowed the contents of his glass.

"He seemed a bit wary of you."

"Because he doesn't want me to have too much."

"He thinks you're a threat?"

Callum smiled and poured more whiskey. "He knows I am."

I hadn't thought about it like that. I just thought Callum wanted more wealth for him and the Players. More power, sure, but not anything that could threaten the Chieftain. How could Callum threaten him really? The Chieftain could change the way we lived in our city with a snap of his fingers. Callum couldn't.

"I want to talk about something," I said. I'd already asked one hard thing tonight, and I could do it again. He'd lost out on something tonight, but I'd lost more. And he had the power to help me get to a place where I wouldn't have to stake everything on the decision of someone else. Where I would have more than one spool in my basket to use.

He lifted his gaze to me. Purple bruises seemed to have bloomed underneath his eyes in the last few minutes. The party, and its outcome, had exhausted him. Well, fine. Good, even. He'd be more vulnerable this way, and even though I wanted to hold him up on my shoulder so he could rest, I wasn't going to forget what had brought me here in the first place: the chance at a life that's more than survival.

"I want to be a Player."

Callum spread his arms wide. "Why? I already promised you money. Why do you want more?"

Because I didn't have the purse yet, and now we didn't have the leases. I didn't have Bryn and her bookkeeping to help me find people with deep pockets who would be interested in investing in my future. I had nothing. Except Callum's ear.

"Even money isn't a guarantee."

"And you think being a Player is the answer to all your problems?"

"The Players are like the well—no, the river that feeds the well. Why take a bucket of water when I could have access to the source?"

He considered me with his dark eyes. "You're not wrong, but we didn't even succeed this time."

"So you think this is my fault? That my silks weren't good enough?"

"They didn't get the job done. I thought there was magic in them, but perhaps not. Perhaps the weaving wasn't quite good enough."

If he'd taken a knife from the sideboard and slid it between my ribs, he couldn't have hurt me more. We both knew it wasn't my silks—it was Serene and Andrew and their bloody games. Red-hot pain shot from my heart through my veins, reaching every inch of my body. The thing he'd wanted me for, maybe even loved me for, wasn't good enough. *I* wasn't good enough. And if I wasn't a weaver of wonderful, *magical,* cloth, what was I? A girl from a single room in a crooked building with absolutely no one to call her own.

"What can I do?" I took his hand. "Please. Let me fix this."

I wanted to prove myself. I could and would be the person he wanted me to be—his partner, who could help him achieve all his desires. I'd weave more bolts of silk, bolts of wool and linen. Anything to make me one of them, to be valued and have my future secured. I didn't even care anymore if my patronage came with Callum's soft kisses or his rough, dry hand in mine. When I stripped that all back, all that mattered was my own life.

Callum leaned against the edge of the big wooden table. Firelight flickered over his face, giving it the illusion of shifting from lovely to something terrifying. I wondered if that's what Serene and Andrew really looked like—razor sharp features and eyes full of menace. Did they slip on human skins like I'd stepped into this elaborate dress earlier tonight? Was Callum wearing any disguises?

"There's something else I want from the Chieftain," he said. "But we're running out of time. If there's any . . . disturbance because of this anger, this jealousy of Nemain's, the Chieftain won't want to be distracted by anything else."

So that was why Serene and Andrew had thought it necessary to tell Callum. What happened with the city's patron god affected the Chieftain and therefore affected how well the Players could sway him.

"Why is Nemain angry?" I asked.

Callum shrugged. "Perhaps because the Chieftain's planning to commission a couple new statues of Lugh for his garden, even though he's supposed to be loyal to Nemain as the city's patron."

"The one you have carved in the gallery railing? A few statues is enough to make her jealous? She can't possibly be at risk of losing our people's prayers . . . There are temples dedicated to her all over the city."

Callum nodded. "I know."

I lowered myself into a chair facing the fireplace and let the heat soak through my silk sleeves. Nemain, the Chieftain . . . it was all so far removed from what my life had been, it barely seemed real.

"Do you think that Nemain feels threatened because of it?" I asked.

Callum stood up straighter, and the glow from the fire no longer reached his face. I caught the glimmer in his eye again and kindled the little spark it lit in my chest. He was still the same person I'd known yesterday. Truly, he was.

"What statue stands in the marketplace?" he said.

I'd walked by it so many times it had become part of the road itself, and I needed to think for a moment before I could remember the statue's face, her full lips and waving hair.

"Nemain."

Callum nodded. "Her statue is in all the temples too."

I hadn't gone into the temples very much after Papa was taken to prison. Nemain hadn't stopped that from happening no matter how hard I'd begged. All the gods seemed too far above us to notice what we wanted or even the gifts some people left for them on altars. What did they need a couple sprigs of wheat for? They had both worlds, ours and theirs, at hand. The lower faeries and creatures like the Bean-Nighe were different. They were more likely to answer prayers and grant wishes.

"So what if Nemain's statue is in the temple? As you said, the Chieftain has a deal with her. We worship her, so she'll protect us."

Callum's eyes flashed. "Oh yes? From what?"

"Well . . . war, right? She's a war god and protects us from uprisings and strife."

"Perhaps it's time there's a different patron god," Callum said with a slow smile.

"Why?"

What did it matter who people left out bowls of honey for? For now, we had a war god as a patron, and if she ever did lose her hold on the city, perhaps we'd have a god of the forest or harvest who'd offer us something else. There was always a patron god, and only the Chieftain got to decide who it was.

Callum swept forward and grabbed my wrists. I nearly yanked

my arms away, but I knew that wouldn't compel him to give me anything. Anger bubbled in my belly and up into my throat, but I swallowed it back down. He was cruel tonight, cruel with my failure, but I let him hold me and dip his face close because that was how I might get what I wanted. His lips brushed mine, and a shiver ran down my spine. Dammit, I still wanted him. I shouldn't have been in his grip at all, shouldn't have let him touch me after making it all out to be my fault, but he was like a fire I couldn't turn away from.

"Think how much better it would be if Lugh was the city's patron god," he said, and settled a kiss on my cheekbone.

My knees trembled, and I had to search for words. "What?"

The art still made me uncomfortable, with all the smiling faces who looked as though they might actually be screaming.

"He's growing weak without prayers."

"How can a god become weak?"

Callum barked a laugh. "We think gods, and even the fae, are infinitely powerful because humans are not. Their magic makes them seem invincible. But they're not. Without prayers, they wither, their magic crumbles."

Our eyes met, his with a faint suggestion of tears. Gods might not all be immortal, but they still didn't need my sympathy. None of them had ever gone hungry or cold on the other side of the veil.

"Lugh was my family's god of choice, because he brings happiness. Don't you want happiness for everyone, Ella?"

I didn't think making Lugh the patron god of the city would necessarily bring everyone happiness, even if he loved craftspeople and beautiful things. Not being plagued by war was probably already making quite a few people happy, and that was Nemain's doing as a war goddess.

"I don't have any affinity for one god or another. If you want to make Lugh the patron god of Eidyn Crag, I'll help you," I said. What did it matter anyway? We were nothing to the fae and the gods, little more than spiders. We existed, and we performed something useful to them by praying, but they didn't care about us. So I couldn't make myself care about them either.

Callum leaned forward, still holding my arms, brushing the stubble on his cheeks against my skin. A wave of longing spilled over me. His tongue darted out and touched my bottom lip. I drew him in, taking the kiss because I wanted it, not because I was giving it to him.

"What do you need me to do?" I asked when we pulled away. It was for him, for myself, not for any god.

"Weave me enough silks to dress the three of us—you, me, and Odina. If we succeed in getting the Chieftain to change the city's patron god, I'll not only make you one of the Players—you'll be their leader, with me."

Images flashed through my mind like paintings. Me choosing which key to power we go after next. Me with enough money that I wouldn't have to rely on other people thinking my fabrics were beautiful to make a living. Me, at the center of it all, no longer alone without anyone to catch me if I fell. I'd be Callum's equal, no longer looking up at him. We'd be eye to eye.

I let those ideas flood me, fill me up, as Callum and I met in a kiss. With our lips pressed together, tasting each other, we tangled our bodies and sank down to the ground in front of the blazing fire.

# Chapter Thirty-Four

The carpet in front of the hearth was soft, thick, expensive—exactly what I'd come to expect from Callum's house. The pain of the evening pulsed through me, and I wanted to forget the loss of the leases, of the strangeness of Andrew's non-death, the work ahead of me. I needed to be wanted, to be filled up with someone else's desire.

"Do you want to do this?" Callum asked.

The heat of his chest pulsed into mine, and the feel of his weight on me made all of the reasons I'd hesitated before—the fear of what might happen—disintegrate like a castle made out of sand.

"Yes," I said.

His lips brushed mine again, teasing. Then he fluttered them against my eyelids and my neck, nuzzling the square neckline of my dress. My skirt got in the way, so I stood and untied it. The great heap of fabric fell around my legs. As I stepped out, Callum freed himself from the silver suit. The star pattern twinkled in the firelight as he discarded it on the polished wood-plank floor. The swirl tattoo stood out against the skin of his hip, and his eyes sparkled with the same fire he'd had that night of the first party.

Callum pulled the bows of my stays free, and I let the bodice fall on top of the skirt. My shift wasn't nearly as fancy as the dress—plain linen, free of the silken bows I imagined adorned Odina's. I stood in front of Callum in my near-nakedness, but this time I didn't want to cover myself up. I wanted him to see even more of me.

No one had before. I didn't know if my body would look strange to him or if there was something about it that was utterly wrong that I wasn't aware of. But I took a breath and I pulled the shift over my head. My hands fell to my side. I was all right with this, with showing him.

His eyes explored my body, lingering on my breasts, my legs. Then he rushed to me and caught me up, finally crushing his lips to mine and letting me taste him. His drawers came off with an easy tug. I tried not to stare, but I'd never seen a man's body before. I'd felt his excitement and knew there was something there, but this was different than I thought. My cheeks flamed but Callum only smiled.

"Can we do this safely?" I asked.

"When did you last bleed?"

My breath stuck in my chest. Papa had ignored my moon's blood altogether except to hand me a cloth when it first stained our bed. I'd never discussed it with anyone. I didn't even know why Callum was asking now. I brimmed with embarrassment, but I wanted to do this properly.

"Last week," I said. "It stopped a couple days ago."

"We should be safe then."

"How do you know?"

He smiled again. "I've been around women before. Midwives too. People who know these things."

Midwives seemed like people who would know how to make sure no baby latched onto my womb.

"All right."

"Are you sure, Ella?"

I nodded. "Yes."

He moved toward me slowly, our chests pressing against each other, skin to skin. It warmed me, and I melted entirely when his tongue flicked my bottom lip. We sank back down in front of the fire and let ourselves explore.

It was everything I expected and yet completely new. It seemed natural somehow, like our bodies fit knowingly together. I gasped at each unexpected touch, each new sensation. Callum kissed me with a hunger I'd never tasted before, and I returned it, losing myself in the fever of it.

⤜⤛

When it was over, we lied fused together before the fire. I didn't want to lose the closeness of being together like this, so I rested my head on his damp chest. Even while my body had pulsed with longing, I'd thought I might regret it after it was done. But I didn't. Whatever happened now, that brief moment of respite had been worth it.

His hand played in my hair.

"You'll help me, won't you, Ella?"

I pulled my head up and rested my chin on his chest.

"You think I can help you make the Chieftain change the city's patron god?"

Callum grinned, eyes soft. "I think your fabrics can."

My fabrics. Not me. Suddenly the fire seemed to lose its warmth and a draft washed over us. I shivered and pulled my shift on. I'd just let him get as close to me as anyone had ever been, but he still saw me for what I could do for him. I bit my cheek until it hurt. It was silly to expect anything else when he'd been clear from the beginning why he wanted to be my patron. It was the loom full of the Bean-Nighe's magic, the silks threaded through with it.

"I'll help you, Callum," I said, swallowing down the hurt. "I'll make enough silk to drape all of us in magic so strong, the Chieftain won't be able to shake the beguilement this time."

Callum nipped at my ear and pulled me back against his chest. "You're going to be wonderful standing at my side. The two of us, leading the Players."

He promised me something bigger this time, but he asked for something bigger too. The Chieftain hadn't even given us the leases to the marketplace; establishing a new patron god for the entire city would be much more difficult. I wanted to know why it was so important to Callum. I'd understood why he'd wanted the leases. Control over what was available to people made sense as a starting place for Callum to build up his own power. But the patron god? Most people didn't care who the patron god was. As in any city, there were pockets of the devout, but people prayed to Nemain and carved statues of her simply because the temple told them to.

"What do you think you can do with this, Callum? Why Lugh?"

I tilted my head up to look at him and he stared down at me. "You don't see it, do you?"

I wanted to—that was why I'd asked. He didn't need to narrow his eyes at me like that, like there was something very important I was missing.

"You understood why the marketplace could be used as a cornerstone to power. I thought you'd get this right away," he said.

Shame leaked into my heart. I pushed myself up and made some space between us, so he wasn't looking down at me anymore.

"You don't have to make me feel stupid."

He chuckled. "I'm not making you feel anything, Ella. Feelings, your own anyway, are all your choice."

The shame turned molten, shifting into anger.

"But you're trying to make me question myself, aren't you?"

"Why would I do that? Come here, Ella." He grabbed my wrist and pulled me down into his lap.

I nearly stood right back up, but the comfort of his closeness won me over. He tucked my hair behind my ear, and the brush of his finger against my earlobe softened me a little. Heat still throbbed in my chest, but not as strongly as before.

"I certainly don't think you're stupid," he said. "And I'm not trying to make you doubt yourself. I just wanted to see if you would get it."

The last bits of my anger dissipated like crumbling leaves blown away in the wind. I leaned against Callum's shoulder. So much had happened tonight, and I just wanted to be still for a moment.

"I *do* get it," I said. "You think if the city worships Lugh, god of craftspeople and chaos, they'll be more even willing to accept whatever you have coming next. But it must be more than the latest dish or trend. It can't be something like a trade tax agreement."

Callum grinned. "Why do you think I have something more in mind?"

"Because making Lugh the patron god gives *him* more power, not you. You'd only do that if it were part of a bigger plan . . . but you won't tell me what that is, will you?"

He smiled. "Not yet."

"When I'm your partner? Leading the Players?"

He stood up, forcing me to stand too. Callum took my shoulders in his hands and squared me to him. His brown eyes shone almost black without the flicker of the fire to light them. He hung on to his secrets like they were a fish he'd caught in the river—wriggling and slippery and likely to jump out of his grip—but he didn't need to. We wanted the same things. If Callum saw the way to power over the city through changing the patron god, then so did I. I'd do anything for my spot, to secure my future.

"Just help me succeed this time, Ella. I know you can do better; I see it in your fabrics. The magic is there . . . maybe you just need to give more of yourself to the weaving."

More of myself? I glanced down at my wizened fingers. Callum hadn't said a thing about them, but there was no way he hadn't noticed. Not when they were roaming over his body a few minutes ago.

He caught my hands up in his and my breath hitched. He'd seen me looking.

"Don't worry about this," he said.

I pulled my hands back and cradled them in my lap, not wanting him to really see how wrinkled they'd become. "What's 'this'? Do you know something about what's happening to me?"

He sat back, put his own hands flat against his knees. "What are you talking about? So your hands are a bit raw from all your work? That's to be expected when you just wove bolt after bolt for the party."

He wasn't wrong. I had woven all those bolts of silk faster than I'd ever woven anything else in my life. Of course my hands suffered. No wonder they were sore. My back too, bent as it was over my loom for days. I brought my hands closer to the dying embers of the fire, trying to see the wrinkles and age spots. Maybe I'd just been concerned for no reason.

"Ella, stop," Callum said and pulled me close again. He settled back down on the plush carpet and eased my head onto his chest. I let him because my mind was full of wool and my eyes burned with exhaustion. Nothing was making sense anymore, and I suspected that was because I was absolutely done with the day. Done with the failure at the party and Serene and Andrew's gruesome display and Nemain's supposed anger and the new deal with Callum. I just wanted all of that to go away.

I let my head rise up and down with Callum's breathing and focused on an ember in the fire grate. It glowed, red and orange against shadowed gray. It burned its way to its own decimation, slowly turning itself into cold, dead ash.

By agreeing to help Callum with the patron god, by telling him I'd weave more fabrics, give more and more and more of my blood to my loom, was I agreeing to burn myself out?

I couldn't let that happen. I'd have to protect my strength and myself so I could do what Callum wanted. I had another chance at the life I dreamed of, and I wasn't going to mess it up this time.

Callum's breathing steadied. I held his body and closed my stinging eyes, because being with him was better than being alone.

∽ℯ∾

Something pinched my leg. I startled and my eyes flew open. Callum didn't move, his sleep uninterrupted.

I rubbed at a red splotch on my calf. A spider, maybe.

The fire had burned itself out completely now, and the dark outside the windows was as deep and steady as when I'd closed my eyes. I had no way of knowing how much time had passed. I could go back to my room, leave Callum to wake up alone in the morning. He wouldn't take it personally if I did. He'd probably think I'd just gone to get a head start on the day's weaving. Actually, that was probably a smart idea.

The dark leached all the color from the oak table and the scarlet runner topping the sideboard. Every item in the room looked to be the same hue, even though I knew they weren't. Funny how perception can shift with the circumstances. Without the light to show me different, the beautiful table and ladder-back chairs, the sideboard with its spindle legs—every piece of lovely expensive furniture looked just like a dull hulking shape.

Maybe I hadn't shone enough light on my silks for the people wearing them. I had to do better this time, and I needed to make a plan. What would truly make all of us shine?

Something fell to the floor. Metal, by the sounds of it. It rolled and stopped abruptly. I jumped to my feet and thought about kicking Callum awake, but I wanted to see if this was finally one of the elusive servants come to collect the pewter cups left over from dinner the night before.

"Hello?" I whispered.

"Heeell . . ." a voice whispered back a broken word.

There *was* someone there. I stared into the black and tried to pick them out of the shadows. A little pang of fear pierced my belly, but there was nothing to be afraid of. I'd been lying here sleeping—if whoever this was wanted to harm me, they could have done it already. Plus, I wanted to know who'd been bringing me trays of food and taking my dresses away to be laundered while I was out of my room.

"Who's there?" I asked. "I want to meet you."

A shape, low to the ground, crept closer. I knelt and tried to make out the features. A bulbous nose and the outlines of bushy eyebrows. The tiny bit of light coming in through the window threw his features into silhouette, and the air left my lungs. They squeezed too tight, as if I was drowning—the same way I thought *he'd* died.

It was Gregory.

# Chapter Thirty-Five

Gregory stood in front of me, scaled down like a miniature in a doll's house—or a very large rat. How? I'd fed him to the river, to the Bean-Nighe. How could he be here in Callum's house? Who shrank him down to this?

A faint whisper escaped my lips. "How can you be here?"

A tear welled in the corner of Gregory's eye and caught the blue-toned light from the window. I shouldn't have cared at all about his tears, but I did. I wanted to know what could possibly make this horrible, greedy man cry.

"How?" I asked again.

He shot a glance at Callum, still firmly in the world of dreams, and backed away from both of us. I thought I saw fear there, playing in the shadows of his face. Just like I'd seen fear in Odina's eyes. What were they so afraid of? It couldn't be Callum. Odina was his friend—she was the only reason I'd met him in the first place. He'd never done anything to hurt her.

Had the Bean-Nighe done this to Gregory, and he'd decided to come back up to the house on the hill for help? He wasn't going to find it from me.

I stepped back over Callum's outstretched arm. Gregory

reached out a hand to me and opened his mouth. Whatever he had to say to me, he could save his words. I didn't want to hear them; they wouldn't change anything. He'd held me at the end of his leash for too many years. He'd threatened me—didn't he remember that? He knew I feared the debtors' prison where Papa died, and he'd used that knowledge like a knife at my throat to try to get what he wanted. How could he ever think I'd help him now?

Gregory's mouth opened and I waited for the pleading, waited to bat it away, but nothing came. He stepped forward, almost falling over Callum. Callum stirred and Gregory jumped, skittering to the side like a beetle trying to run away from the smack of a broom. When Callum didn't wake up, Gregory stepped forward. As he got closer, he stretched his mouth open again. This time he was near enough that I could see his tongue stretched up—well, what was left of it anyway. The raw edge hadn't healed fully and though I couldn't tell what color it was, the dark glisten of it suggested blood.

My stomach turned. Someone had cut out Gregory's tongue. The stump of it made my skin crawl. I'd never heard of the Bean-Nighe doing anything like this before.

He advanced on me, and I moved backward, shuffling my bare feet against the polished floorboards.

"Get away," I said.

Gregory pointed to his mouth and then back at Callum. "He . . . he . . . himmm."

He smacked his lips together to pronounce the *m*. My whole body went colder than it already was. Callum did this? Did he find Gregory intruding in the house and cut out his tongue? That still didn't explain why Gregory was the size of a doll.

"You're blaming Callum? Well, you deserve it, you horrible man."

He shook his head and wiped at his cheek—perhaps the tear in his eye had fallen. "R . . . ru . . . ruuu . . . runnn."

Spittle landed on my hand, and I wiped it away. I didn't want any part of Gregory to touch my skin.

Callum sucked in a loud breath and flopped his arm over his chest. Gregory jumped and scurried away, back into the shadows of the dining table. My heart beat hard and quick in my chest, and fear prickled its way down my body. I didn't understand what had just happened, but I didn't need to know exactly what was going on to know it was bad. Unsettling.

I tiptoed toward the door at the back of the room, leaving my bulky skirt and bodice. It would be impossible to lie back down with Callum now. I'd startle him with my clammy skin and shivering. He'd know something was wrong, that I'd seen something I shouldn't have. Maybe it had nothing to do with him at all. Perhaps the Bean-Nighe *had* shrunk Gregory and cut out his tongue and he'd wandered out of the river and up the hill, looking for help in the house. But his wet whisper was a warning. *Run.* From what? I used to be running from *him.*

I wanted my room, wanted space to think. Darkness hung thick and heavy in the hallway but was punctured by a blue-gray light from the windows surrounding the door in the entrance hall. I took the stairs at a run and tried not to even look at the carved panel of the gallery. I didn't want to see Lugh and his followers' twisted smiles. There was already enough going on to make my stomach writhe like river reeds during a storm.

My room was the same as I'd left it. No servants had come to tidy up yesterday, it seemed. My day dress lay draped over the end of my bed where I'd flung it in excitement before slipping into my silk gown. Hair pins were scattered on the top of the little vanity table under the mirror. I didn't look in the glass, didn't want to see if I had more gray hair or new wrinkles that shouldn't be there.

Instead, I went to my loom. The bench squeaked under my weight, but I fit into the grooves made by hours of seated work. I placed my hands on the frame and squeezed, trying to leech some comfort from the wood. This was mine, all mine, and no one could take it away from me. As long as I had my loom, I had a chance at the life I dreamed of. I could create bolts of cloth people yearned for. Their praise would fill me up like rich ruby wine in a glass cup. I'd be worth something.

Dried blood tipped the needle. Why hadn't that been enough, why did the Bean-Nighe need to slowly suck my life away too?

A floorboard in the hallway squeaked and I startled, imagining the small figure of Gregory padding around outside my door. I should have paid more attention to where he'd gone. I'd just lock the door now, so no one could come in uninvited.

My fingers wrapped around the cool metal key in the keyhole and turned. The mechanism clicked.

"Ella?"

It wasn't Gregory outside my door. It was Callum.

Heat bloomed in my cheeks and where my shift sat over my chest. He'd seen *all* of me now and I couldn't ever take that back. I'd been more daring last night by the glowing fire than I was right now as the pink light of dawn softly filtered into the room.

"Ella, please open the door."

I had no real reason not to. Any number of things could have happened to Gregory, and I was just so sure Callum wouldn't have cut out his tongue. That wasn't the kind of thing people did. It was a punishment fit for the gods. Even the temple wouldn't use it for criminals.

The metal key grew warm in my hand. I turned it back over and pulled the door open.

"Good morning."

Callum stood there in his silver-starred breeches and no shirt. A fine dusting of dark hair stood out on the white skin of his chest, and a thicker trail of darker hair disappeared into his pants. The muscles between my legs clenched and I realized how sore I was. But it was a good sore, a satisfactory pain.

"Good morning," I said.

"You ran away."

"I didn't run. I just needed to come back to my room to change."

He cocked an eyebrow and gave me a wry smile. "You're still wearing the shift from last night."

I looked down and noticed a few telling spots of blood where the fabric covered my thighs.

"I must have fallen back asleep," I said.

He glanced over at the made bed but shrugged.

"Do you want breakfast?"

I thought of the huge dining table waiting for us and who had been scurrying between its legs not long ago. I wanted to hear from Callum's lips that he had nothing to do with Gregory's lack of a tongue, but how did I even bring something like that up? Plunge right in, I guessed.

"I saw something strange this morning," I said.

"Do you want me to stay in the doorway while you tell me?"

I backed up so Callum could step into the room. Normally we sat on the bed while we talked, but he went over to the bench in front of the loom and sat. It was probably still warm from my body.

"Come here and tell me," he said, holding out his arms.

His lap was warm too. I wrapped my arms around his shoulders and tried to see if the closeness felt any different—because of all that happened last night, the failed mission, the way our bodies joined in front of the fire. I wanted there to be a little shimmer of something between us, something stronger or different, but it was the same. Not more than usual, but I still melted into him, and the closeness settled my nerves.

"Like I said, I saw something . . . strange early this morning. In the dining room."

He leaned his head on my shoulder. "While I was asleep?"

I nodded. "It was a man, a man I knew actually, but he was the size of a doll."

Callum lifted his head and met my eyes. I tried to read his, but they were blank.

"Go on," he said.

My tongue dragged against the roof of my mouth, and I wished there was water in the pitcher in my room. More evidence the servants hadn't been here while we were gone, but why? That's who I'd thought Gregory was at first—one of the servants collecting the pewter cups on the table.

"He talked to me, or he tried to. His tongue was cut out."

I thought he might be repelled or at least shocked by this news. Instead, he drew in a steady breath, much steadier than I was managing at the moment.

"Did you hear what I said, Callum? His tongue was gone! And I knew this man from before I came here. He thought I owed him money."

"He thought or you did?"

I slipped from his lap, hurt and shame burning through my limbs. How could he say something like that after everything I'd told him about my life, about Papa?

"He wasn't playing fair. I paid him back and he decided I owed him interest." I crossed my arms over my chest.

Callum slapped his hands on his silk-covered knees. "That's how things work though, isn't it, Ella? Lenders charge interest, everything costs something . . . even money."

"I'd already paid him back fair."

Why were we even talking about this? It didn't matter anymore. Gregory had been shrunk and maimed! He wasn't exactly in the best shape to come after me for interest.

"How did he get into your house, Callum? Who cut out his tongue?"

Callum stood from the bench and took the tinder box from the mantle. A fire had been laid at some point in the last couple days, so he lit a curling piece of birch bark and threw it into the heart of the wood pile. I didn't want a fire. I already burned under my shift. He'd turned this conversation around on me somehow—questioning *me* when I was the one who'd seen something that couldn't have been real.

"Do you often go down to the river, Ella?" he asked.

"Sometimes. Why?"

"I went down there the other day and there was this peculiar smell. Rotten, actually. I had to pinch my nose shut it was so bad."

I froze, ice replacing fire in my veins.

He knew what happened to Gregory.

# Chapter Thirty~Six

Callum and I stood square to each other. I bit the inside of my cheek, tried to play out where he might be going with this in my head. He couldn't possibly be upset for Gregory being lured to his death by the Bean-Nighe—why would he care? He didn't know the slimy man.

"How did you get him in the river, Ella? He was so much bigger than you," Callum said.

"I didn't get him in the river." There. A truth.

"No? Who did then?"

I didn't want to tell him about the Bean-Nighe. He didn't need to know about her or what she'd done for me.

"He went in himself. He was hot and wanted to cool off. He slipped and I didn't try to save him."

Callum grabbed my upper arm, stuck his face down into mine. "You didn't help him? You would have let him drown? Well, I guess you can be glad I came. I saved him."

I wrenched my arm away. It stung where his fingers had pressed in.

"Saved him? He's the size of a doll and his tongue was cut out! Did you get Andrew and Serene to do that? To use their faerie magic to punish him . . . for what? For being on your property?"

"No! Not that! I punished him for what he did to you."

I froze. Callum didn't know what Gregory had done to me, not unless somehow one of his carters had spoken with Gregory's man as they hauled my loom out of my flat. A few minutes ago, Callum had been telling me I wasn't living in the real world because I wouldn't pay Gregory his made up interest. Callum was playing a game with me. It hurt, stung my heart like the needle on my loom had been pushed through the middle of it. Last night, I'd given him more of myself than I'd ever given to anyone before and this morning he did this.

Well, I could play too. I was close, *so close*, to getting everything I needed. As a leader of the Players, I'd have access to enough money and power to open my shop. I'd have a steady stream of people admiring my work, telling me I was enough. I wouldn't be lonely. I'd be filled up. I wasn't going to let Callum ruin that by dragging me into this twisted charade. I'd join on my own terms.

"You punished him . . . for me?" I asked, eyes open wide and chin tilted down—as innocent as I imagined I could look.

Callum nodded and opened his arms. I went to him, but a shiver crawled down my spine. Last night he'd warmed me, comforted me. Today his touch was cold.

"You had Andrew and Serene shrink him down?" I asked.

"I wanted him to know what it felt like to be small . . . like you'd felt. He's my servant now and I can tell him what to do, like he once thought he could control you."

In fact, it was Callum's words that reduced me. To have him try to solve this problem for me without even telling me. All of it over my head.

"What about his tongue? Did you do that?"

Callum squeezed me tighter against him, the scent of cinnamon cloying in the back of my throat.

"He threatened you, didn't he? Back at his shop. And then there was that man of his there when you picked up your loom. I wanted to make sure he never bothered you again."

I nodded against his chest because I knew my anger would make my voice shake.

"How did you even know who he was?" I asked.

How was Callum able to bring Gregory from the river? I'd have thought the Bean-Nighe would hold on tightly once Gregory was in her grip.

"Everyone knows who he is, Ella. He's the biggest moneylender in town. And I realized what you'd tried to do when I found him in the river. Unfortunately, you came close but didn't finish the job. Like last night at the party . . ."

I bit my cheek harder and willed myself not to pull away. It wasn't all my fault we hadn't convinced the Chieftain to give us the leases; none of us had managed to get him to say the words to grant them to us. He'd been mystified by us, and that was because of my silks. And I'd do even better next time. I'd weave bolts of cloth in patterns no one had ever seen. The colors would be intoxicating. We'd get the Chieftain to change the patron saint of the city to Lugh and then I wouldn't ever be beholden to Callum—or anyone—again. I'd have so many customers in my shop, no single one's shopping whims would hold any power over me.

"I'll make sure we get what you want this time," I said. "You won't believe how beautiful the silks will be."

He smiled and let me go, ran a hand along the smooth frame of the loom.

"I'm sure that's true, but I think I need to have a little more say this time."

"What do you mean?"

"I want you to make certain patterns—"

"But I already have ideas!" I cut in.

Callum shook his head. "We tried your ideas last time. Now I think it's safer if you do as I say. I know the Chieftain better than you do."

Shame burned my cheeks. It was true, even though I didn't want to admit he could be right about anything. He *did* know the Chieftain much better than I did, and presumably he understood his tastes.

"Fine, I said, wrapping my arms around my body. "What patterns do you want me to weave?"

"I want waves and stones, leaves, and the rays of the sun."

"I can do that."

At least, I hoped I could. I'd been planning to do something simple that *looked* complicated since the star pattern had been so difficult for me last time. Now I'd actually have to weave to Callum's specifications. My chest tightened and I took three measured breaths to help release it.

He grabbed my wrists and unfolded my arms. I flinched.

"Good," he said. "You don't have long, two weeks."

"Well, I need these to weave," I said, flexing my fingers.

He didn't let go and my skin burned in his grip. I tried to pull away, but he yanked harder, dragging my hand under his lips for a kiss. My breath caught and my stomach flipped, but not in a delightful, butterfly way. Panic swelled in my belly.

"Make me something beautiful, Ella," he said with a smile that didn't match his commanding tone. "I'll invite the Chieftain here for a small party. Weave enough silk for you, me, and Odina. Andrew and Serene won't be wearing your fabric this time, not after their last performance."

I nodded. I would certainly make myself something beautiful—a life where I never had to feel this used up again.

⁊

Callum picked the colors and laid the spools of silk thread for my first bolt out on my bed. Once he left, I loaded the loom and pricked my finger. I tried to use a different finger each time to let my skin heal between weaving sessions, but I'd used all of them by now and couldn't avoid poking an already-tender spot. Blood beaded on my skin, and I let the needle absorb it. The metal glowed. My hand hurt—not just the finger I'd just pricked but the muscles in my hand, as if I'd been weaving for hours already. My back muscles ached so badly I could barely sit on the bench without squirming, and now the pain traveled up into my shoulder, my neck, my head.

But it didn't matter. I had to keep going. The Chieftain would be here in two weeks, and I had three bolts to finish. Callum had selected a coppery thread for my dress. I didn't like it, and the color would look awful on me with my red hair, but perhaps it would all be gray by then. I hadn't bothered saying anything when he'd handed me the spool. He'd already decided, and his mouth had been set in a firm line.

"*The Chieftain will like this color. Make a pattern like stones . . . the stones at the bottom of the riverbed,*" he'd said.

What did it matter if I didn't like the color and didn't want to wear a dress made of stones?

For Odina, he'd chosen a bright green and asked me to thread it through with a darker moss color to make the impression of leaves. His own suit would be made of a buttery yellow shot through with golden thread. Callum would be the sun.

And he was, wasn't he? We were all drawn to him, turning our faces toward him in hopes of warmth. I'd certainly hoped for it—and felt it for a time too. Now, I was left with nothing but a startling coolness.

I didn't want to care, but I did. He'd been someone to talk to, to touch. And he still could be, perhaps, if all this went well. I slumped against the loom. The weaving had drained so much out of me before the Chieftain's party. It wasn't entirely Callum's fault; it was mine too. I'd never told him what happened with Gregory down by the river, and I should have. Then he wouldn't have kept the secret of what happened to the man. We'd been honest with each other from the beginning, clear about what we both wanted. Now wasn't the time to start keeping secrets. Not when we were so close to succeeding.

I sat back up on the bench and tried to imagine Papa was there beside me. He'd wouldn't have let himself get as far into this as I had. He never wanted to be beholden to anyone, which is why he ignored his debts. He seemed to believe they'd simply vanish if he stopped acknowledging them. He was wrong, of course; his debts didn't disappear—they became mine after he died.

Pretending things aren't real doesn't do any good. I held my hands up in front of my face and examined the papery skin, the thick, raised veins. How long did I have before the rest of me started to look like this? Would it affect my insides too? My heart and other organs—would they simply stop one day long before they should have because I'd given all my years to my loom?

I picked up the shuttle and started working, pulling the thread through, tightening it, pulling, tightening. Every few minutes I had to pause and flex my fingers. My knuckles swelled as the light faded. I lit a candle and kept going, closing my sore eyes, and relying on touch. This was all I was good for, so there was no point stopping. I'd weave until my body gave up and then I'd crawl into bed and try not to think about what might happen if I failed to hold up my end of the bargain.

# Chapter Thirty-Seven

The morning cold assaulted me, little puffs of white hanging in front of my mouth with every breath. I wrapped the blanket around my shoulders and padded to the door. Pangs of hunger crisscrossed my stomach, and I hoped there would be a tray of breakfast waiting outside. Callum and I hadn't eaten together in days.

I was in luck. A bowl of porridge with a yellow swirl of honey sat on a wooden tray. I hoped Gregory hadn't been the one to deliver it, but I was hungry enough not to let the thought stop me from eating.

Mist clouded the air outside my window, low and thick. I imagined it licking the surface of the river too, just touching the water and floating away. Did the Bean-Nighe see the same morning I did? I didn't know how much she lived in our world and how much she resided in the plane of the gods. Did she wash her shirt over there too? A continual cycle of drudgery that she could never be free of? A shiver ran through me at the thought. That would be the worst punishment—to use your hands every day and accomplish nothing, to never feel that spark of inspiration when you know you can create something, bring it out from your mind and make it into a solid thing.

After a week, I'd only half finished my bolt of coppery brown silk. It waited for me on the loom, and I wasn't excited to work on it. Usually, I got a little thrill from the prospect of finishing a project, but I just wanted this one over with. There was no guarantee it would be good enough or what Callum wanted.

I finished my porridge and put the tray back outside my door. The house was silent. A bit of light came in from the hallway windows, but mostly it was shadow everywhere I looked. My tired eyes played tricks on me, and I imagined Gregory scurrying down the hall like a rat looking for crumbs. Who were the rest of the servants, then? I'd seen a couple at the parties, and they hadn't been shrunken down into doll size, so there had to be people here of their own free will.

The loom beckoned me, and I took a seat on the bench, shimmying into the right position. I gave the loom another drop of my blood and the needle shone even without any sunlight to reflect off it. The fabric wasn't very beautiful. I knew that, could look at it objectively. I wasn't as good as I used to be, and my hands hurt so much. My hair was half silver now, but Callum hadn't seen me enough since he'd told me about Gregory to remark on it. I minded now though. It was slow enough at first, like a dream I could see but not understand, but now, it was unavoidable. I thought I could just get on with it all and deal with my life being sucked away when it became a real issue, but now fear snaked through me like shadows, choking out the light.

My fingers twinged when I wrapped them around the shuttle. I dropped it.

"Gods' fangs!"

My knuckles had cracked open when I'd bent them over the top of the shuttle. Blood welled in the small breaks of skin, not quite oozing to the surface. I rubbed my hands and tried to work out some of the cramping in my muscles. I'd worked too long last night, and this was my reward.

I tried again, bracing myself against the sting of my cracked skin. My hand should have fit around the shuttle like a glove. I'd been using the same one since I'd learned to weave, and I knew exactly how it curved and where to place my fingers.

But I couldn't do it.

Panic flared in my chest. I'd given the loom my blood, so why wasn't I able to hold the shuttle properly? I placed it in my lap and stared at my swollen, bleeding knuckles. The loom had taken too much last night, and now I couldn't do the only thing that made me worth something.

I needed to be able to weave. I had no choice but to find out why the Bean-Nighe's needle was draining my life away along with the blood.

⟡

The wind picked up, blowing bits of gritty sand into my eyes. I rubbed at them, making things worse. Tiny droplets of water blew from the river onto my cheeks.

The first time I'd seen the Bean-Nighe, I'd barely thought of her as a person at all. She was some other kind of creature from a different world. But once I'd gotten a better look at her, I saw hints of humanity. Pain in her eyes, the whiff of hope in the fresh earth smell of her. Maybe she'd been a human once; maybe she'd understand my desperation, why I needed answers.

"Bean-Nighe!" I called out to her, but the wind whipped my voice away.

She might not come to me this time. She wasn't mine to call on and control. I didn't even really know why she'd appeared last time when Gregory had surprised me. I'd just accepted it at the time because it was what I'd wanted, but she must have wanted it too. If not, she could have just stayed behind the veil in the realm of the fae.

"Bean-Nighe! Please!"

The cold wind made my fingers ache. I tucked them under my arms, rubbing them against my wool sleeves. What I realized I had to do next would be awful, but I needed to get the Bean-Nighe's attention somehow.

I gritted my teeth and untied my gown. My laces came free easily since I'd only been able to tie them loosely. I folded up the dress and left it pinned to the bank under a large rock. The cold water bit my ankles as I waded in. My shift grew heavy and stuck to my legs. The stones under my feet were slippery with algae and grime. I tried not to think too hard about what else might be down there that I couldn't see.

The water reached up to my belly button and I couldn't stop my teeth from chattering. I held my hands out of the river to spare them the numbing pain my toes were subjected to. This had all better be worth it.

"Washerwoman! I know you're there!"

The wind blew my hair around my face, and I closed my eyes while I pushed it away. When I opened them, the Bean-Nighe unraveled herself from the mist on the far bank. Her hair first, then her face and the rotting linen of her dress. I launched myself into the water and kicked toward her. Each wave against my arms was like a thousand tiny needles pricking my skin. I kept on, pushing and pulling my body through the river to reach the Bean-Nighe.

She was so much different this time.

Her hair didn't hang in limp patches from her scalp anymore. It fell thickly over her shoulders in rich brown waves. Her wrinkled face had been smoothed out and her rheumy eyes were clear. She wasn't an old washerwoman now. The only things that were the same were her decaying dress and her gnarled hands.

The cold of the river numbed the shock, but my heart still sputtered in my chest. There was nothing to grip, to hold on to, except slimy weeds the current dragged past. I treaded water and tried to keep my head up.

While my life, my youth, had been draining from me, hers had returned.

# Chapter Thirty-Eight

I dragged myself up onto the rocky bank. The Bean-Nighe dipped her bloody shirt in the water and swished it around. The blood stain was bigger this time, I was sure of it.

My teeth chattered together, but I forced my mouth open, the muscles of my jaw aching. "What is the blood stain? A debt?"

The fae woman opened her mouth and the now-familiar smell of damp, freshly turned earth wafted over me.

"You have it wrong," she whispered.

"Then tell me what's going on. You're around me, obviously! You came for Gregory and now when I called. Why do you care to stay here?"

She tilted her head to the side and raised the linen shirt out of the water. "This is your blood, Ella."

"What?"

My muscles clenched and stopped the shivering for a moment, but I couldn't appreciate the sudden calm. *My* blood? This is what she'd been doing with my blood. This was where it went after the needle sucked it up—to spread over the Bean-Nighe's dirty shirt. A burden for her to clean.

"But you're taking something else from me too, aren't you? Look at my hands, my hair, my posture!" I cried.

I held my hands up in front of her face so she couldn't avoid them.

"My talent, the raw part that was just mine, is dwindling," I went on. "And yet as I seem to grow older and less apt, you seem to be getting younger."

The Bean-Nighe looked down at the water lapping at her skirt. "The river doesn't offer a very good reflection. I wish I could see it."

"See what?"

She stared at me, searching my eyes like she might find a better reflection there.

"The change. I kept track of everything, of every wrinkle, every fading hair before. It had all happened so quickly. I was young and then I wasn't, and the right number of years hadn't passed. Now I wish I could see the reverse. It would be nice to see my face again as I remember it."

Her voice wasn't the silken thread of a whisper anymore either. Now, it had weight to it. She almost sounded like me.

I sank down to the cold stones of the riverbank as her words flowed through me. What was happening to me had happened to the Bean-Nighe too. She was taking my life, slowly, in drips and drags, but someone had done this to her once. It seemed we were spinning in a circle, like dancers who couldn't let go of each other's hands.

"What happens when my blood fills your shirt?"

She grinned, but there was no happiness or humor in it. "Once the shirt is filled, I will give it to you, and then you will spend your days trying to scrub out the stain. Once it's clean, he'll give you another girl's life, and you'll be the one who collects blood to grow young again. You'll get your turn, as long as you earn it."

This was all an endless cycle of torture. The Bean-Nighe drained my life from me just so she could get her own back. How long had she been stuck like this? Who had she been before? I stared at her in her rotten dress—at my own future—and my stomach soured. I didn't want to be a Bean-Nighe. I had plans for my life, and becoming a cursed old woman wasn't one of them.

"Who did this to you?" I asked. "Who's 'he'?"

"Lugh."

My stomach sank. A high faerie, a god. How could I ever win against a god?

"Why does he do it?" I asked. "Why bother with the likes of you or me?"

The woman lifted an eyebrow. "Because no one else does, do they? How easy it is to make us vessels, to use us as the makers, the creators, and then let us bleed ourselves dry. There's always someone to take our place. But with each one of us, Lugh gets one step closer to showing the Chieftain he can't live without the loveliness we create. He can't live without Lugh."

"But you granted my wish!"

The woman grinned without any happiness. "I was told to."

"By who? Lugh?"

That wasn't possible. No god would know about me, have anything to do with me.

"Lugh's not been the one watching you. He wasn't the one who broke your loom and forced you down here. He's too important for all that."

I pressed my cold palms to my forehead. "You helped me."

The Bean-Nighe laughed, her smile pulling out the little lines around her eyes. "The magic he gave me has firm rules. I can't leave, can't help myself. But there's enough of it to help people like you, if I want."

"Why?"

"Lugh's love of chaos has spread to me, I suppose. I just direct the chaos at him instead of anyone else." Her words clipped through the air, hard as skipping stones.

I thought of the carving of Lugh in the gallery of Callum's house, of our new deal to push Nemain down as the city's patron god and put Lugh in her place.

"Does Lugh visit you?" I asked. "To make sure you're filling the shirt?"

She pointed toward the house on the hill, the shirt stained with my blood clutched in her hand, dripping pink water back into the river. "He comes from there sometimes."

The world tilted. It couldn't be. Callum was human; I'd felt the blood pulsing through the veins beneath his skin. He wasn't a god, wasn't fae like Andrew and Serene.

I sank down to the shore, the sharp edges of rocks pushing against my skin. Bile rose in my throat, the sharp, sour taste of it coating the back of my tongue. Everything I'd done to get the life I wanted was worth nothing now. Callum had never cared for me. I was a toy, a game to be played to his will. I'd shared pieces of myself with him, and he'd only been collecting them to rearrange in a way that suited himself.

I didn't have a life in front of me—it was being sucked out of me and handed over to the creature on this riverbank. People would never come into my shop and praise my work. I wouldn't be able to collect their words and store them away to warm my heart. I wasn't going to be one of the Leaders of the Players. And the sharpest pain of all—I never was going to be who I wanted to be. Callum had known that the entire time and he'd stoked the flames of my dreams anyway, knowing they'd never flare. He was happy to watch them smolder out. I'd thought we'd shared something, but it had all been lies used to get me to do what he wanted.

And now I could see, as if a thin veil of linen had been lifted from my eyes. The little comments about how I wasn't enough, his insistence on dictating the patterns for the new silks. He wasn't trying to fill me up. He was scraping me out, emptying me so I could be a vessel just for him and his plans.

Callum was Lugh.

I'd let him hold me and touch me and take me and he'd been playing with my life all along. The leases had probably meant nothing to him—he just wanted to be the city's patron god to feast on people's devotion, on their chaos, to make him truly immortal. He'd strung me along with the promise of a place in the Players and the deals he'd made me because he knew I'd give more of my blood to my loom that way, and he was desperate. The Chieftain had said the group of Players had grown small. Odina, Andrew, and Serene were probably all he had left. Three people. That wasn't enough to feed his power. That's why he wanted to be the city's patron god.

The Bean-Nighe sat quietly beside me, working a stone over the shirt with my blood. That's what I was worth now, what I'd become. A stain to be cleaned out. A body to be used. I didn't matter to anyone anymore. Mrs. Under might notice if I never came back to my room, but she wouldn't go looking for me. She'd shrug and boil an egg for herself. The people who were supposed to miss me were already gone. I let the cool wind blow my wet dress against me, let it break over me again and again. This is what was left for me—numbness. An absence of feelings. If there was no one to care about me, no one to think I was worth anything at all, then what point was there in caring about myself? I was only ever a maker to everyone else—someone who provided things. Worthless without my skill.

I dragged my body along the rocks and immersed my legs in the frigid water. I had to swim back. I wasn't a Bean-Nighe yet and I wouldn't stay here on the riverbank with her. She caught my eye and shrugged as if to say it didn't matter if I left now, that I would be back so I could take her place, clean the shirt, do the task. Known for nothing more than that. I glanced at her, at the life she'd stolen from me brightening her from the inside. A nugget of strength lodged itself in my belly and I dragged my hands through the freezing rocks on the bottom of the river. Little stones stuck under my fingernails, but I welcomed the pain.

I wouldn't do it. Not after everything. My hands still belonged to me, my heart, my strength, my determination. Callum had bled me dry, but. But. But.

I plunged fully in and the cold broke over me, over my sore back and my cramped legs. My graying hair fanned out behind me on top of the water.

*I* was still in here.

No matter what Callum had done to my body. I was still me.

I didn't need him to tell me I was worth something. I'd prove that myself.

If Callum was Lugh, his strength was dependent on other people, on their devotions, their gifts, their carvings and statues. That's why he wanted to be Eidyn Crag's patron god—so he could grow his power to the point where he didn't need constant prayers, where he was strong enough to effortlessly play between the world of the fae beyond the veil and the human world.

The carving of Lugh in the gallery—most of Callum's strength must have come from it, since it was one of the few carvings of Lugh in Eidyn Crag. But gods couldn't commission their own effigies. They wouldn't be effective that way; the worship needed to come from humans. So, someone was helping Callum.

I stopped swimming and looked back to the bank. The Bean-Nighe spread the shirt full of my blood out over her lap. The blood was deep red, as if it had just drained from my body. She knew what was happening here because it had happened to her too.

"How do we get out of this cycle? We need to stop this," I yelled over the wind and the rush of the current.

The Bean-Nighe slapped the shirt against her rock, the sound sharp in my ears.

"I don't want to stop it. I'm nearly free."

"And what if I never use my loom again? I won't give it any more of my blood."

She shrugged. "You will. Because weaving is the thing that makes you *you*, isn't it? You won't be able to stay away."

"You don't think I can stop weaving even to save my own life?"

The woman fixed me with a stare. Even from my place in the water I could see her pale eyes were leeched of color, as gray as the clouds in the sky and the river below them.

"It's already being siphoned from you," she said. "You can't stop it no matter what you do. You might as well enjoy what you have left, because I can tell you there won't be any comfort afterward."

My chest tightened, a cold fist around my lungs.

"I want one more thing from you," I said.

"You've already had your wish."

"You're taking my life! I'm only asking for a small thing in exchange."

She cocked an eyebrow. "What?"

"A spool of unbreakable thread."

The idea was only mist yet, but that kind of thread could make it work.

The old woman grinned, and her teeth weren't as brown anymore—just a bit yellow now.

Something bobbed out of the water, as if suddenly released from the depths. I grabbed for it, spinning in the water, until my fingers folded around the spool. It was thick, white silk thread. Unbreakable. I clutched it to my heart.

The Bean-Nighe began to fade, disappearing into the steely day. A drop of rain fell on my forehead and slid down my nose. More followed, pounding into the surface of the river. I floated, the rain hitting my face. It stung, but I didn't care. The sting of it was better than the pain eating away at my heart.

# Chapter Thirty-Nine

Water filled my ears. The rolling thunder and the *ping, ping, ping* of the rain on the river all sounded very far away. The Bean-Nighe had left me. Callum waited for me in the house, knowing I'd fallen exactly into the trap he laid for me. I couldn't go back yet.

I ran home, back to the messy, busy square and the crooked building with the crisscross beams and Mrs. Under's thin door. She answered after two knocks, and my heart calmed a little.

"Ella?"

I took a breath to dispel the nerves in my belly. "Can we have a cup of ale?"

Mrs. Under nodded and ushered me inside, as she had so many other times. She poured ale from a small barrel in two earthenware cups and handed me one before taking up residence on the one chair in the room. I sank down to sit on the floor beside her. The ale was bitter and warm, but I took a second sip anyway.

"What's wrong, Ella?" she said.

*The Bean-Nighe tricked me. Callum used me. I'm aging too soon. I'm alone again and have only the whisper of an idea of how to keep going.*

"Something happened."

"With that boy? At his house?"

"Sort of."

"Spit it out, Ella. I don't have many years left and I don't like waiting."

I looked up at this woman who'd been so kind to me since my papa had been taken. It didn't sit right to burden her with all this now, but I had no one else. The weight of it all was too heavy to carry alone.

"It's . . . I made a deal. And I'm only now realizing the cost is more than I thought."

Mrs. Under put her cup on the chair's armrest, reached out a hand, and stroked my hair.

"What have you promised?" she said.

I could barely squeeze the words through the thickness in my throat. Tears burned in my eyes. "My life."

Mrs. Under made a *tsk* sound like she might to an errant cat prowling the courtyard below. "It's not your life, Ella. You've not given that away. It'll only be for a little while and then you'll have your life, many lifetimes actually, in front of you."

My limbs went numb. I dropped my cup of ale and the liquid splashed up onto my face. I didn't wipe it away.

"What?"

"It's not a loss, I promise you child."

She knew. Mrs. Under *knew*. It wasn't Lugh, or Callum, watching me at all—it was her. I scrabbled back, batting away her hand and stumbling to my feet.

"What are you?" I asked.

The old woman shrugged. "Does it matter?"

"Were you a Bean-Nighe too?"

She laughed, more strongly and sharply than I'd ever heard before. Her voice had lost the wobble of age. "No, I was never a Bean-Nighe. I don't need to be. I was born beyond the veil. Like him."

Him—Callum. Lugh. She knew him. She'd been the one who told me of the Bean-Nighe in the first place, about her granting wishes. It had only been to get me interested, to lay a path for me to follow. Shock rippled through me, like a strong wind over the surface of the river. She probably broke my loom too.

"Why did you do this to me?"

Mrs. Under shook her head, sadness pulling on her features. "I didn't do this *to* you, Ella. I did this *for* you. He wanted girls who needed more in life . . . who could *be* more! He saw you the day your father was taken away and knew you might be special. He sent me to you."

The Player I saw in the street that day, the one who had given me my paste jewel. It had been Callum, or Lugh. That truth sunk through me like a stone. But I remembered the faces from that group and they hadn't looked like Callum or Andrew or Serene . . . or even Odina. I didn't think so anyway. The only one I remembered clearly was the young man who spoke to me, and he'd had blue eyes. Callum had brown.

But Lugh was a god. He could probably make himself look however he wanted to. And he'd picked me, selected me then to entrap in his scheme to become patron god. Maybe I should have felt special, but I didn't. This isn't the kind of attention I wanted. Hot anger licked at my ribs.

"You've cast me into the river and left me there to drown, Mrs. Under," I said and pulled open her door. Pieces of my heart chipped away as I fled the room that had once been a comfort and the woman who had once fed me little bits of cheese when I was hungry. None of that had ever been for my sake. She'd just been trying to trick me. She'd made me think she didn't want me to go call on the old washerwoman, but she'd known exactly what she was doing by telling me those stories in the first place. She knew I'd follow the thread where it led, that the promise of wishes would lure in a girl who thought a boiled egg was a treat.

I didn't go back to the room underneath hers but to the river. I ran over the rain-slick cobbles in the courtyard and slipped down the muddy embankment, pulling at the long grass to steady myself. The trees soared up above my head, green leaves against gray clouds. Beneath my feet, mud gave way to pebbles and I skidded toward the water. I didn't care if the Bean-Nighe could see me, if she was here. I just wanted to be in the place that had once offered me calm, that might cool the anger in my chest.

The water sluiced over the rocks, the river full from the rain. I dipped my hands in and wiggled my fingers to cool the burning in my joints and dampen the pain. I cupped my hands and pulled up enough water to dip my face in. It stung, cold and unforgiving, but as the air hit my wet cheeks, my mind was clearer.

Mrs. Under was fae. It made sense now—I'd never seen anyone visit her. No one had known her before she came to live in our building. Usually there was some sort of connection to our courtyard for the people who moved there—a cousin's cousin, an uncle's wife. Mrs. Under had been entirely alone. It's why I hadn't been so afraid to let her see my loneliness. I thought she'd understood.

But she didn't, because she wasn't alone at all. She was Callum's servant and she'd picked me out as the next Bean-Nighe. She'd played me. They both had.

The cold water numbed my skin, my muscles, but not my heart. That burned with hurt. No one had ever seen that there was more to me than what I could make with my hands. I'd always been a tool for someone else. Even Papa. He loved me, as fathers often love their daughters, but he'd taught me to weave as soon as I was able to help him make more bolts of cloth, more chances at coin and prestige.

To Callum, I was the same: a thing to produce goods for him, which he could use to get what he wanted. I'd never weave him one more thing, but that wouldn't be enough. All of this flowed from him—Callum, Lugh. He threaded me through his game, and I wouldn't be able to pull myself free without unraveling the whole thing. But maybe that was exactly what needed to happen. If the game was over, if there were no more Players, maybe this horrible circle of using up young women until they were washed-up old crones would end.

I needed to turn the magic on him, use what he'd given the Bean-Nighe, and she in turn had given me, against him. Determination settled in my bones. I would need some help, and there was only one other person I could think of who might have just as much reason as me to want to stop Callum. I was pretty sure I knew who'd been helping Callum, who'd commissioned the carving of Lugh in the gallery. Someone with fear in her eyes.

I just had to hope she'd be willing.

༄

Odina's house sat back from the road, and I trudged through puddles of mud to get there. The rain started up again, determined to make the day as gray as possible. The housekeeper opened the door when I knocked. I'd seen her before—a woman with a face that told the story of long hours and hard work—but now I wondered if she was even human. Her skirt covered her ankles completely and I couldn't see whether or not they looked different than I would expect, like Serene's had.

She showed me into the same parlor I'd been in many times before, but the shine had rubbed off. I didn't look at all these sparkling trinkets and velvet-cushioned chairs with longing anymore. If I was right, Odina had paid highly for them—much more than I was willing to.

"Ella?"

Odina wore a plain dress of mustard wool. The color suited her and brought out the beautiful brown tones of her skin. Her dark hair fell loose around her shoulders, but she'd plaited part of it back from her face. I tried to picture what she would have looked like before, when she was wizened beyond her years, when her hair was as thin as dandelion fluff. I didn't like imagining her that way. It made my heart beat too fast. I tucked my wrinkled, swollen hands behind my back.

315

"I need to talk to you," I said.

Odina perched at the end of one of the dainty chairs, so I did too, my wet skirt dampening the fabric. I listened for noise deeper in the house—parents walking up and down the stairs, siblings running down the hallway. But only stillness met my ears. There was either no one here but Odina and the housekeeper, or everyone was playing a game to see who could be the quietest.

"I didn't think I'd see you again until the party," Odina said.

She stretched her hands out to me and I took them in mine. I remembered the heat of them when we'd danced at Callum's first party. They were warm now too, even though there was a chill in the room, and the feel of them helped still the storm raging in my belly. My own hands were icy from the walk in the rain. She rubbed a finger over one of my swollen knuckles.

"You're still all right, aren't you?"

I shook my head, heart a little lighter because she'd cared to ask. No use lying or pretending. Not when I wanted her to tell me the truth.

"I can't weave anymore. My fingers are too swollen and warped to hold the shuttle."

"Oh." She dropped my hands and wrapped her arms around herself. "I didn't think . . . I mean I suspected you'd last until the party at least."

Her words fell on me like the dull pounding of the rain on the windows. I thought she knew, but the confirmation still hit me in the chest, made it hard to breathe.

"You knew what was happening to me all along?" I asked, all lightness gone.

Odina stood. Her skirt dragged across the carpet as she walked to the window and stared out into the rain.

"I know what's happening to you intimately."

"Because it happened to you too?"

She nodded her head but kept her back turned to me. "How did you find out? Did Callum taunt you with it? I knew he'd break soon."

My tongue was thick in my mouth. Taunting. Playing. I shook my head. "It wasn't him. He doesn't know I know. I went to the Bean-Nighe."

"Ah." Odina's cheeks colored, and I wondered if it was with shame.

"How did you get free?" I asked.

"I earned my way back here, scrubbed my stain out of the shirt and then collected another girl's blood," she said. "But I didn't enjoy it."

I imagined slapping the Bean-Nighe's shirt against the rocks, scrubbing my own blood out of the threads. The taste of sour bile hung in my mouth, hid between my gums and cheeks. I tried to swallow it away and almost gagged.

"But you had magic for a time, didn't you? You were fae while you were the Bean-Nighe! Why couldn't you escape?" I asked.

Odina closed her eyes and pressed her fingers to her cheeks. "It's all up to him," she said. "He gave me that magic and I could only use it how he told me to. It was never really mine—there were ends to it, hard ends. So many things I couldn't do. Time stretched into a piece of ribbon while I was there, beyond the veil. It wasn't possible to leave the riverbanks. It seemed like a decade and also a day. There was no way to tell until a girl came along and wished for her spices to taste better than anyone else's. Cinnamon was her specialty."

My stomach turned and I pressed a hand to it, trying to hold all the hurt in. The cinnamon. Callum's taste, his smell. All because he'd trapped a girl into doing his bidding.

The rules Odina described were so similar to what the Bean-Nighe had said, the one who used to be a girl with spices. Callum—Lugh had wrapped them up so tightly. And he would have done the same to me. I seethed, feeling the brush of his lips on mine, seeing his soft stare. He'd tricked me so completely.

Odina turned finally and tear tracks glistened on her cheeks. She swiped at her nose with the back of her hand. It came away shiny. Her eyes were heavy, weighed down with sorrow. Even with everything she'd just told me, I still wanted to wipe her tears away.

"The one who made the wish to me is the one filling the shirt up with your blood now," she said, voice quiet. "Then she'll get to come back, and it'll be you lost between the worlds, wandering the riverbank looking for the perfect washing stone."

My stomach churned. Not me. I wouldn't be stuck there.

"So, your punishment is over?"

She laughed but her mirth bordered on madness. "You think it's over? It's never over. I'm one of his now and I always will be. He tells me what to do and I do it. He told me to live here in this big empty house and pretend to be a normal young city girl with a rich mother and indulgent father, so I did. I hate it here."

Her pain leeched into my heart, like she shared it on purpose. I took it, hoping it might lessen it for her. I'd never seen Odina's parents. It had always just been me and her in the parlor when I'd shown her the fabrics I made. She'd talked about her mother and her dress allowance and there'd never been any reason to doubt it. But now I knew the truth.

"Why do you do what he says? How is he making you?" I asked.

Odina's eyes grew wet with the tears she tried to hold on to. She blinked and they fell.

"I'll be put back in the rotation if I don't. Once the Bean-Nighe collects your blood and you dry up into a husk of yourself, Callum is the only one who can make you *you* again. If he wanted, he could just stop that magic that keeps me as I am. I'd turn back into an old washerwoman who doesn't belong in this world. I'd be fae again and not able to stay here."

So he'd have a hold on me forever—that's what he wanted. His. For all time.

"Why? Why does he need us? He's a god!"

Odina laughed but it was bitter. "He likes to play here, where he has more control. He's been tweaking the city to his taste for years, working with whatever chieftain is in power. He's been trying to create a city of splendor with himself as the patron god so he can be immortal. But he can't just use his own magic directly on the Chieftain of the city . . . Nemain protects the ruler from that. Callum has to do it in a roundabout way, so he created a granter of wishes with very specific magic of her own. He can't control exactly what the Bean-Nighe gives, but he drives girls toward her who have a talent for creation and not much else."

"He picks girls who don't have what they need and gives it to them just so he can use their gifts to shape the city into one that would relish Lugh as its patron god. A city that loves beautiful things," I said.

He'd patched up the holes inside me not because he cared for me but because he wanted me to need him. He bet on me needing to go back for more, again and again, to feel like I could be in one piece. And it had worked. For a while. Now I'd rather poison fill me up than Callum's words.

"How long have you been alone?" I asked.

Odina sat back deeply in the upholstered chair. "A long time. My Kiju disappeared at sea, left on a trading trip and never came back. I was too scared of the water to try to get back to my country. I stayed, but I had no one."

"And that's why Callum picked you? But you and me . . . we aren't the only orphans in Eidyn Crag. Why us?"

"We both had a talent he wanted to harness, something he could use. It's how he entices people into doing his bidding . . . People get addicted to owning and tasting beautiful things. He's been working toward getting the Chieftain to choose Lugh as the patron god for a long time. I've noticed he's been weakening for the last five years or so. He's becoming desperate."

Callum's urgency around beguiling the Chieftain made sense. He'd slowly been trying to influence the choice of patron god, but it hadn't worked. Now, he wanted to coerce the Chieftain . . .

with my magic. A hard rock sank to the bottom of my stomach, a weight I hadn't thought I'd carry.

"How did it happen for you?" I said.

Odina frowned. "He picked me a few months after my Kiju died. We'd lay out my wares in his dining room. Then wine would be served, and Callum would roll smoothly into a conversation about beauty and desire and how wonderful it would be to have just one statue to Lugh in the city. Then one more and one more. People would be enthralled, nearly hypnotized by my beadwork. He'd tell them they could have more of this feeling if they built statues of Lugh."

My tongue lay thick and dry in my mouth. All of this for himself, all of this because he thought no one would stop him. My chest filled with vitriol I wished I could spit at him. We dolls to be dressed and posed, made to do whatever the Player wanted. Odina and I were more than that. The girl the Bean-Nighe had been was more than that. Everything hardened inside me—disgust and fear and anger.

Callum was in a years-long game, but what did time matter to him? He'd never die of illness or age—and if he got his wish and became patron god, he'd have enough devotion to be truly immortal. Living forever to create both beauty and chaos as he saw fit. He didn't need anything else, not like us. He'd never been cold or hungry or poor. But it wasn't enough. He just took and took.

And Odina—he'd hurt her too. I didn't want to imagine what the other world would be like if you weren't fae. That long stretch of time tied to the riverbank and the shirt full of her own blood.

I wasn't going to do that. Callum wouldn't force me there. He'd built his lies around me like a prison, but there was still some strength inside me. I'd break free from this—from him. He could take his kisses, and that sweet taste of cinnamon, and his orders about how *I* should weave *my* bolts, and jam it all down his own throat. Or I would. Fury burned everything away. Made it all clear.

"We're going to stop his horrible game," I said. "But I need your help to do it."

Odina stared out the window a moment before moving over to a chair and perching on the edge. "I can't. It's too dangerous. Risky. Callum is a god, the most powerful of the fae. I'm just a human who lost everything."

"What did you make with your beadwork?" I wanted to know what Odina was capable of, what her fingers could create.

"Trinkets. Those beaded butterflies in the window? I made them a long time ago."

I didn't expect that. Those butterflies were a wonderful work of craftsmanship, and Odina put on such a good performance as someone who never had to use her hands for anything other than lifting clear glasses of ruby-red wine to her lips. It was a good thing though, helpful for what I had in mind.

"I want you to help me stop Callum," I said.

Odina spread her hands wide, her perfect, long fingers splayed. "What can I do?"

"You can weave for me."

"What? I don't know how."

"I'll teach you, and I'll stand over your shoulder the entire time. I'll show you what patterns to weave. We're going to weave enough silk for two dresses that Callum will think we've made to beguile the Chieftain."

"But it's Callum you want to beguile?"

I knelt in front of her chair and took her warm fingers in mine. "Yes. I want him so enamored with us he'll follow us away from the party. And . . . there's one more thing I want you to weave. We'll stitch it together with a spool of thread the Bean-Nighe gave me."

"What?"

"His shroud."

# Chapter Forty

Odina moved quickly, throwing an extra shift and a pair of silk heels into a bag.

"I'll just say I'm coming to prepare for the party. Callum wants us all to look our best, so he'll be happy I'm putting the work in. A milk bath, I'll tell him. Cool river air to lash color into my cheeks."

I held the strings of the velvet bag in my damp fingers while Odina laced up her black leather boots.

"Do you ever go back there, to the river?" I asked. "Do you ever see the girl you . . . well, you know."

"The girl I used to buy my life back?"

I nodded, my stomach squirming again. This was Callum's fault, all of it. He'd given Odina an impossible choice, and I knew I'd have made the same decision in her place. I'd let someone else's blood soak into the shirt if it meant I'd get my life back. I didn't like that I'd sacrifice some another girl to escape being a Bean-Nighe, but it was true. That was something about myself I'd have to wrestle with eventually, but for now I wanted to stop Callum from making anyone choose their own life over another's ever again.

"I don't go to the river, and I've never seen her," Odina said. "I just . . . can't. I spend my days trying not to think about my time on the other side of the veil, because when I do, I can't breathe."

"You're scared?"

She shook her head. "It's not just that. I don't ever want to go back, that's true. But I don't want to be reminded of it either. It makes me sick to my stomach, to think about how it felt to stand with my feet in the freezing river water and scrub and scrub while life went on without me just beyond the veil. If I let myself *feel* it, I'm just crushed under the weight of it. It's usually days before I can get back out."

"What magic did you trade yourself for?"

What had Odina wanted so much she'd been willing to use the Bean-Nighe's wishes to get it? Someone with a family and a comfortable home wouldn't make that kind of deal. A trade like that was done out of desperation, just like mine had been.

Odina went to the bay window at the front of the parlor and cupped her hand around one of the beautiful sequined butterflies hanging there. I wanted to touch one too. They were simply so lovely they drew me in.

"I made so many of these. Butterflies and bees and foxes. Sometimes I stitched deer with a crown of green sequins on their heads. My nookomis, my mother's mother, taught me back home before I sailed here with my mother. After my djoodjo was lost to the sea, I sold them at the market on a little table and sometimes I made enough to buy a few eggs or a dried fish with my loaf of bread."

I knew exactly what that was like. Picking and choosing. Eggs or lard to make a greasy soup. Fish or a sticky bun. The guilt that came with buying a treat even though there was so little else to look forward to.

"So you went to the Bean-Nighe and made your wish?"

Odina dropped her hand and took the bag of her things from me. I followed her out the front door and waited as she turned a pewter key in the lock. She dropped the key in her pocket and started off down the lane toward the street that would bring us back to Callum's house. I let her walk in silence for a bit, guessing that she needed time to gather her words, though I kept close to her. She helped settle the writhing in my belly.

Our boots tapped on the cobbles of the big street before she spoke again.

"I wanted to sell enough of my creations to buy a little cottage outside of the city. I thought if I could get away from the smell and the filth and the people scrambling for scraps, I could get away from the fact that I was fighting for scraps too. I wanted to plant a garden so I'd never go hungry again. I know how to tend a garden from Nookomis. I even thought I could teach myself to hunt . . . small things like rabbits maybe. I just wanted to escape."

"But you didn't."

"No. I wished for the little animals I sewed to be irresistible," Odina said while we walked. "And they were . . . after my deal with the Bean-Nighe, it was like the creatures were breathing. People scooped them up and I made more money than I'd ever imagined. Enough to get my cottage. But by then I knew something was wrong. Callum had offered to be my patron and supply me with housing and materials . . . just like he did with you. And I turned gray and wrinkled and then my hands stopped being able to sew sequins on my butterflies. After that, Callum took me down to the river and led me through the veil and told me what I had to do to get back to normal. The real trick of it was, I never really belonged to myself again. There was no going back."

My heart hurt for her, for all she'd lost. I wanted to help her get some of it back. To make sure Callum didn't take from anyone else, including me.

We slipped through the streets as Odina talked. People went on with their business around us—a customer debating the cut of a lamb hock and a father scooping a small girl with a grazed knee off the ground. None of them knew what danger lurked in plain sight. Callum could choose any one of these young girls as his next victim after me, and they didn't even know he was a threat. Everyone knew the story of the Bean-Nighe as a single cursed washerwoman—but not as a series of stolen girls. Callum had probably controlled the myth just as he controlled the creature at the center of it.

He didn't have the upper hand anymore though. He might be a god, but he wasn't immortal yet.

"All this time, I thought you were jealous of me," I said. "Of how close I'd gotten to Callum, but that wasn't it. You didn't want me in the Players because you knew what would happen to me."

We stopped outside the gates to Callum's lane. The house stretched out in front of us with the same wide-eyed stare I'd noticed when I'd first come. How many more fae were in there, cooking for him and dusting and polishing the carving of Lugh on the gallery stairs? It was quite bold of him, actually, to show me a carving of his true self that first night. He must have felt sure I wouldn't work it out. But he was wrong.

Odina reached out for my hand and squeezed. "I don't know who it was before me or what Callum's done with her now. I don't know what will happen to the girl currently tied to the riverbank. Callum promised me he was finished after her, but I should have known better. He has no reason to stop."

I returned her pressure, gripping her hand, hanging on to her as hard as I could. "We're about to give him one."

◌◦◌

The door opened silently, as if the hinges had recently been oiled. Had it been Gregory to rub the grease into the metal? I glanced around the entrance hall and tried to see into the dark corners behind the stairs. Nothing.

"Is he home?" Odina said.

"Of course I am."

Callum stood at the top of the stairs, dark and elegant in a suit the color of deepest summer leaves. My whole body tightened, and I tried very hard to keep my breathing steady so he wouldn't see. He needed to think everything was normal. I wanted him to believe he still had me between his fingers.

"I wouldn't leave right before a party. We need to prepare," Callum went on. "What are you doing here anyway?"

Odina stepped further into the hall and set her velvet bag beside a glass vase of bluebells. She put on a very good show—she was practiced from her time with Callum and she knew how to wield that against him. Odina exuded confidence,

328

like she had every right in the entire world to be in his house right now.

"Same as you. I wanted to prepare for the party. It's important, isn't it . . . more important than the leases?"

I pushed the door closed and the light from outside vanished.

"Ella! Where did you go when there's so much work to do?" Callum took the stairs two at a time and came to a stop in front of me. He took my cold, stiff hands in his. "Your hands are so cold. Be careful or you won't be able to weave."

I smiled even though bile filled my mouth. "I just went for a walk. Don't worry, Callum. The silks will be ready just like I promised."

"Good."

He raised my fingers to his lips and kissed the ends of them. I tried not to shudder.

Odina went around to take a taper from a sconce on the wall and relit one of the candles that had gone out.

"It's so dark in here, Callum. I do hope you'll have better light for the party. What good will Ella's lovely silks be if no one can see them?"

Callum licked his thumb and finger and pinched the flame that Odina had just coaxed to life.

"Don't worry. Everyone will see just as much as they need to."

"Oh, I'm sure they will," she said with a smile. "I'll stay in my regular room, all right? And I just need to get these muddy boots off."

We both watched as Odina climbed the stairs. I was impressed with the facade she'd drawn over herself as soon as we'd stepped into the house. If I didn't know better, I would never have guessed that she'd recently agreed to help me take down the god who'd stolen her life.

"I saw your work in progress on the loom," Callum said.

"I had to take a break, rest my hands."

Callum played with the bluebells in their vase. "Rest is good. Important. But you'll get back at it now, won't you? You don't have long to finish the rest."

I nodded and started toward the stairs, eager to get away from him before I said something that would ruin my whole plan. *Screw him and his demands.*

He grabbed my arm and pulled back my hair, tucked it behind my ear.

"And Ella?" he whispered. "Promise me you'll work hard? I really want everything to work this time."

I grinned because he didn't realize how committed I was to doing my best. Odina and I would weave the most beautiful piece of fabric he'd ever seen—and once we sewed him up in it, he'd be staring at that pattern for a very long time.

# Chapter Forty-One

I found Odina in my room. She sat on the bench in front of the loom, the shuttle already in her hand. The silk I'd started was meant for me, with a round, stonelike pattern dictated by Callum.

"Have you ever used a loom before?" I asked.

Odina shook her head.

"You're good with a needle though. That'll help."

"At home I'd decorate the little animals and stitch pouches with glass beads. Nookomis, my grandmother, could do whole dresses, but I never learned the patterns before my mother brought me over here on the ship. Mother was a sailor, an adventurer. I was the opposite. I wanted roots."

I sat down on the bench with her and she slid over so we weren't touching. I leaned away, trying to keep the distance she obviously wanted, even though that hurt a little. We were allies now.

"Do you still think you can plant those roots, if Callum is gone?"

Odina shrugged. "It's been a long time since I wanted anything other than not to go back to being the Bean-Nighe."

Callum thought he'd made Odina his creature, but she was so much more than that. She might have tucked away her dreams in favor of survival, but that didn't mean they were gone for good. He'd underestimated us, both of us, by assuming his patronage was the only path forward.

"Are you ready?" I asked.

Odina gripped the shuttle and she finally leaned toward me, some of her ice melting away. Her shoulder pressed against mine. I placed my fingers on top of hers, lightly, gentle so my knuckles didn't scream at me. With my other hand, I reached out to the pin and pricked the tip of my smallest finger. The steel needle drank the bead of blood and glowed.

"It was the same for me," Odina said. "I thought my blood was giving my little stitched animals life of some kind and that was why they were so irresistible. It wasn't until I started to fade that I realized the true payment for the Bean-Nighe's wish."

"*Callum's* wish. The Bean-Nighe you went to was just another player forced into Callum's game."

"That's true." Odina nodded, a soft look in her eyes. "I used to live in a tiny room in those low buildings near the edge of the city. There was this old woman who took pity on me, brought me hard-boiled eggs sometimes. I'd heard about the Bean-Nighe before, from other traders, but she told me more. She talked a lot about the wish I could be granted."

Hearing that she'd done this to Odina too made another fissure crack through my heart. There'd been moments when I'd thought the old woman cared for me, in her way. But that was never true.

"Was her name Mrs. Under?" I asked.

Odina turned her head to stare into my eyes. "No, it was Mrs. Overton."

Over and under, around and around. A game. Just another game.

"A fae," I said. "Callum's servant."

Odina's eyes filled again, tears shimmering along her lower lashes.

"Don't let him take that from you," I said. "If you remember her kindness, hold on to that."

"Kindness? She tricked me, didn't she?"

"Yes, but did she make you feel less alone sometimes too?"

Odina seemed to think about this, squeezing her lips into a thin line.

"Let's just get on with this. I want it over, all of it," she said.

I wanted to be on the other side of the plan too, with Callum taken care of, but I also wanted to revel in every movement I made that was contrary to what he wanted me to do. Each pass of the shuttle would be like a rebellion, and I wanted to taste my steely resolve in the back of my throat.

I pricked my finger again just to make sure it would work and let the blood pool on the tip of the needle. It didn't even hurt this time.

"Okay, follow my movements, Odina. See how we lift the wrap to make space for the shuttle? Pull it tight. We're going to use these different threads to mimic a fishing net."

"A net?"

"We want to catch Callum, don't we?"

Odina grinned. "Show me how."

We barely slept the next two nights. Odina made appearances in the dining room so Callum wouldn't wonder why she was suddenly spending so much time in my room. He never asked about me. Trays of food appeared outside my door, just as before. I didn't miss him, not now that I knew who he was and what he was trying to do, but his absence unnerved me. I thought he'd be watching me, making sure I made the silks exactly to his specifications. He only asked to see the progress once and his mouth twisted into a little frown when he saw the patterned gray silk.

"I thought I said green with leaves," he said.

I held the shuttle loosely in my hands. My knuckles were still so swollen that my fingers couldn't close around it. When we'd heard Callum's footsteps in the hallway, Odina and I had swapped places. Now I was on the bench, and she lounged on the bed, looking up at Callum from under her eyelashes. My heart beat fast against my ribs. Odina and I had agreed leaves were too soft, flexible. We wanted unstoppable waves in her dress.

"This one is for me, isn't it? she said.

Callum shifted his glance toward her. "Yes."

"Well, I wanted something different. Darker and more . . . tumultuous."

"I've planned this, Odina, every color, ever pattern, to trap the Chieftain."

She slid off the bed and came to stand in front of him. I admired how she didn't even flinch, but then, she'd known who Callum really was for a lot longer than I had. The thought of being that close to him now made my skin crawl.

"You must allow for creativity, Callum. Don't worry, this silk will work very well for beguiling . . . won't it, Ella?"

I smiled, a glow in my belly replacing the fear. It wasn't just me trying to do this alone. It was us. Odina and me.

"It'll be perfect," I said.

But not to trap the Chieftain. We wanted Callum knocked off-balance from the beginning, so it would easier to make him so dizzy he'd follow us anywhere.

◦◦◦

I didn't need to teach Odina to hem the edges of the bolts—she already knew how to do that beautifully. We spread all four of them across the bed. The coppery orange with the pebble pattern for me. Silvery waves woven into the gray for Odina. Rays created with dark and light gold thread shone from Callum's fabric. And his shroud was white with a shimmering net pattern woven in with silver thread. I hid that one in a basket that was tucked into a corner of the dining room.

"We did it, Odina. Look what you made," I said with awe in my heart.

She took my hand and squeezed. "We both made the silks. I couldn't have done it without you."

"I wouldn't want to do any of this alone," I said. "I'm happy you're here."

I was tired of being alone, thinking everything through myself, every plan, every meal even. There was a moment when I hoped Callum might fill that empty space for me, but he never could.

Warmth surged through my chest as Odina smiled. It had been a long time since I'd had a friend.

A knock sounded at the door and Callum strode in. We dropped each other's hands. My breath caught in my throat. He stood in front of the bed, legs spread wide and hands on his hips, and eyed the silks.

"I'm not sure I like the waves." His arm shot to the side, and he gripped my wrist so hard it hurt. He bent down, so I was forced to buckle at the knees and look up at him. My heart beat hard against my ribs and a sour taste coated the back of my throat.

"It's better than leaves, I promise."

"Don't snap her wrist, Callum. Then you won't get any more silks out of her," Odina said and flicked her gaze toward me. Her bright eyes betrayed her fear to me, but she was so very good at pretending for Callum.

Callum released me and smoothed his hair at the sides where it had come undone from his leather tie. I scrambled to my feet, swallowing hard to get the taste of fear out of my mouth.

"I have a lot riding on this one, and so does Ella." He stared at me. "You still want what we talked about, don't you?"

A little flame of ambition licked at my heart, but one look at my gnarled hands was enough to douse it out. Callum's words were nothing but empty promises. He never intended for me to be anything but the next Bean-Nighe.

"You know I want that. It's the thing I want most, so why wouldn't I do my best not to screw it up?" I asked.

Callum scanned my face, as if looking for a lie. I froze my features, determined to show him nothing. He'd never asked why my tiny wrinkles had spun out from my eyes or why the number of silver hairs among the red had grown so quickly. Now I knew why. He didn't need to ask. He'd known the reason, had watched as my life slowly dripped from my body like he let the honey fall from the wand into my porridge.

"I have something to show you," he said. "But first, the seamstresses are here."

This time, he didn't bother to try to pretend Odina knew an astonishingly quick human seamstress. Two spindly creatures, with bodies that looked to be made of sticks and hair that jittered like leaves in the wind, tiptoed into the room. More fae. Their beady, black eyes swiveled in my direction, staring as if they might say something, but I didn't flinch. They didn't scare me, not after what I'd seen, what I'd learned.

The fae creatures gathered up the silks in their long, double-knuckled fingers and took them away.

"We'll have outfits before the party starts!" Callum said and clapped his hands together under a stiff smile.

"Wonderful," Odina said far too brightly to be believable.

"It is. Don't you think, Ella? Andrew and Serene sent these little helpers." Callum grinned and held it a beat too long, waiting for my reaction. I took a breath, let it fill my lungs, let it expel my trembling.

"How convenient to be friends with the fae," I finally said, calm, steadily.

Callum laughed, his eyes sparking. "You're shrewd. Yes, I quite like the little extras I get."

"And will Andrew and Serene be joining us, Callum?" Odina asked, her eyes on the floor.

Panic flared in my chest. If they were, they might get in our way.

Callum nodded. Damn.

"But I didn't make any silks for them," I said. "You didn't tell me too."

"I'm not letting them near the Chieftain this time, not after their performance at his house. But they won't be kept away from a Players party, so." He shrugged. "Oh, don't frown, you two; you'll give yourselves wrinkles. Come and let me show you what we've done to the ballroom."

I flinched at the word *wrinkles* and he laughed. Laughing at me, at us. Amused as he watched us flail in his web. Or so he thought. We weren't prey anymore.

Odina and I followed Callum out into the hall. I averted my eyes as we passed the carving of Lugh and his grinning followers in the gallery. I didn't want to see the mania that had somehow been carved into their blank eyes.

The ballroom doors flew open as we approached—more fae, presumably, waiting for our footsteps. Stepping inside was like slipping into a clear night. Gauzy fabric of the darkest blue was strung across the ceiling to form the sky, and it had been picked out with tiny silver sequins. They flashed like stars in the candlelight. Potted trees clustered in the shadowed corners, and the scent of heather drifted toward me from the bundles strewn around the edges of the room. A long table was pushed against the back wall, and glass pitchers full of wine the color of blackberries stood at attention on the dark blue velvet tablecloth. It was too lovely. Too perfect.

"Beautiful, isn't it?" Callum said, sweeping his arm out.

Odina nodded and closed her open mouth.

"I've never seen anything like it," I said.

The beauty of the room unnerved me. He'd taken other people's—other fae's—things, their talent, and strung it up to enthrall the Chieftain. Who had made the twilight gauze? Who had dragged those trees around to form the illusion of a forest? The creators remained in the shadows while Callum swept out his arms and smiled as if he'd projected this image from his mind and simply willed it into reality.

"This is going to work," he said. "And once the city has Lugh as its patron god, things will be better. Everyone will be happier."

"Especially you?" I asked.

He grabbed my hand and I instinctively recoiled. His eyes crackled with fire.

"You're looking a little tired, Ella. Worn out. Go rest before your dress is ready."

His gaze roamed over my body and fixated on my hands, my wrists, my hair. I held back a shudder so he wouldn't see, gave a quick nod, and turned my back on both Callum and Odina, hurrying back upstairs.

The light in my room wasn't strong enough, so I lit a candle and carried it over to the mirror. The skin of my neck sagged a little under my chin.

I put a hand to my chest, my lungs burning. The stairs had left me winded, which had never happened before. I walked all the time. I was strong and healthy. But now, I wheezed like Mrs. Under had when she'd climbed up to her room. It wasn't just my hands and skin and hair anymore. I was starting to wear out on the inside too—the price of all the silks I'd made. My chest tightened, my panic like a vice. I'd weakened, and I truly didn't know how close I was to being a Bean-Nighe myself. The thought of that trickled down my spine like a cold drop of rain. I closed my eyes and prayed to whichever gods would listen that it would all be worth it.

# Chapter Forty-Two

Odina brought my dress to my door and helped me into it. She was encased in her own gray confection with the wash of waves down her overdress. The fae seamstresses were good. Odina's bodice dove down from her neckline to a sharp point over her voluminous skirt. The lace cuffs of a lovely shift spilled out of her sleeves. The silk shimmered in the candlelight, and I was proud of what Odina and I had done together. This fabric was as lovely as any I'd ever made. My own talent had faded with each prick of my finger, but Odina had done well. The rolling waves faded in and out of sight as she twisted and turned to show me the cascading skirt.

I tied my own skirt around my waist and Odina helped me lace up the bodice. I didn't want to glance in the mirror and see how I looked. I knew the copper would suck all the life from my skin, and I had no desire whatsoever to stare at those tiny wrinkles near my eyes again. I needed confidence tonight. We'd made it this far. We could do this. I dug deep into that space in my heart, gathered up the wisps of confidence there, and tied them together. It would be enough.

Callum wasn't going to make me into the next Bean-Nighe that easily. I held on to that like a talisman, like I'd once held on to my purple paste jewel.

The hum of noise filled my ears as soon as we opened my door. Guests arriving and exchanging empty words with each other, the click of shoes on the floorboards, and the swoosh of a fan opening. Odina held my hand as we descended the stairs and found ourselves swept away with the tide of merrymakers.

The ballroom glittered. The silver sequins studding the deep blue gauze strung across the ceiling sparkled, and the guests below twinkled with the gems at their throats, in their hair, on their wrists. Part of me wondered if we'd already crossed the veil—if this was the world of the fae and the gods.

"Ella," Callum gripped my elbow and steered me away from the front door. Odina followed. We stopped in front of the food table, where Andrew stood slurping clams. He tossed the shells to the floor and ground one under his heeled shoe until it splintered and cracked and turned to dust.

I tried not to stare at the odd way his ankle bulged out where a bone was but shouldn't be. I'd been right about that—his and Serene's non-human-looking legs and feet. I repressed a shiver.

"Where's Serene?" Odina asked him.

"She's dancing somewhere," he said and waved a hand glistening with clam juice toward the crowd in the middle of the room.

"It doesn't matter," Callum said. "Neither of you are going near the Chieftain this time."

Andrew sucked his fingers. "We're not even dressed in the *special* fabric this time. We're just here because *he* wanted another report on Nemain."

Callum forced his arm under Andrew's chin and pushed him up against the wall. I sucked in a sharp breath that caught in my throat. I'd never seen Callum put his hands on anyone like that before. He was big, bigger than me and Odina, and he was definitely physically stronger too. If we didn't get him where *and how* we wanted him, he'd have all the power he needed to punish us—physical power, god magic. We had to get this right. There would be no second chances.

"Tonight has to go perfectly," Callum whispered to Andrew. "The Chieftain *must* say yes this time. You're the one who said we don't have any time left before Nemain throws a fit and his attention is distracted from us entirely."

Andrew wriggled out from under Callum's arm and adjusted his necktie, flicked his curling brown hair over his shoulder.

"Your worries are dragging you down like . . ." Andrew trailed off and glanced at Callum.

"Like what?" Callum said.

*Like humans.*

"Like toilers. Like people with problems. You, my friend, have no problems you can't solve," Andrew said.

"You're right," Callum said, smoothing his hair. "And I'm going to solve this one by getting what I want out of the Chieftain tonight. By the time the sun comes up, Lugh will be the city's new patron god."

"And where is he, the Chieftain?" Andrew said.

"Are you sure he's coming?" I asked, just to trip Callum up. I wanted him as unbalanced as possible.

"My goodness, if he's not, that would leave us between the bark and the tree," said Andrew.

Odina tapped his arm with hers. "Don't say things like that, Andrew. We can't jump to conclusions."

Callum's cool expression grew more and more icy.

"Enough."

He didn't need to yell for the word to have impact. A frisson passed through me. Everyone stilled and quieted. We'd gotten under his skin.

I slipped my hand into the crook of his elbow and marveled at how familiar he felt. Even though I didn't want him, even though I knew he'd been wringing everything he could from me, touching him gave me a fleeting moment of comfort. Whatever part of my heart was responsible for that needed to get over it. Callum would never, ever give me any real comfort again.

I stroked his arm. "Perhaps his carriage has a broken wheel or sheep are blocking the road. He'll be here. Don't spend your time worrying. Dance with me instead."

Callum didn't know I knew who he really was. As far as he was concerned, I'd done everything he'd told me to do. Maybe I hadn't followed the patterns he described as closely as he'd have liked, but that was my biggest transgression. He had no reason not to take my offered hand and follow me onto the dance floor. But still I held my breath and my palm grew clammy waiting for his answer. His gaze swept over Odina and Andrew.

"Watch the doors," he said and took my hand. I released a trapped breath.

We melted into the dancers, joining the throng. I wrapped my arm around his waist, and he took my other hand and held it high in his. My eyes found his and we stared at each other. I tried to find Lugh, the god, in his eyes but saw only the second person I'd ever kissed. My heart insisted he was familiar, he was comfort, even though my head knew otherwise.

This wasn't going to be as easy, no matter how many tough things I'd told myself. I knew him as Callum, not Lugh. Even knowing what he planned to do to me—what he *had* done to Odina—I couldn't totally excise the good memories from my mind.

A slow hum buzzed in my ears, dragging my attention toward it. The magic in Callum's sun ray suit and in my copper dress was awake. Nerves wriggled in my belly like worms, but I kept my eyes on his as we moved, spun, dipped. His hand flailed in mine and his other arm squirmed against my waist. He was beginning to get tangled in me, as I'd been tangled in him. It was working, but unease still hummed in my chest. We weren't done yet.

"Do you remember our first dance, Callum? I do. I was taken with you, couldn't drag my eyes away from you."

I hardened my heart, tried not to remember how light I'd felt in his arms.

He shook his head like he was trying to get rid of the memory. "Let go of me, Ella. I'm stuck to you."

I squeezed him tighter. "No, I don't think I will. I didn't weave a pattern of stones like you asked. I wove drops of honey."

His head snapped back toward where we'd left Odina and Andrew, who'd been joined by Serene. Fear bubbled in my chest, but I held it there, stopping it from spreading.

"Honey? That won't do us any good," he said.

"No?" I asked. "It's keeping you here, isn't it? Sticky."

Callum's eyes grew wide. He grimaced. "Let go now, Ella! The Chieftain might be here. I have to go see."

I turned my fear into stone, let it weigh me down, keep my feet on the ground and my eyes on Callum.

"No, Callum, not yet."

"What?" he tried to stop moving but I dragged him along. The magic grew thicker, like tulle, and wrapped itself around us. My breath came faster. Callum's brown eyes began to pale, and a circle of bright, icy blue formed around his pupils. Elation rose through me, making me so much lighter than even the first time I'd danced with him. It was working, really, truly.

"I need the Chieftain," he said but his words slurred as if he'd been smoking the Chieftain's pipe. "Patron god . . . Lugh . . ."

"You're not looking well, Callum. Come with me, all right? I'll find you somewhere to rest."

I searched over the shoulders and heads of the other dancers but didn't see Odina anywhere. Perfect.

"Come, Callum, follow me."

The frosty blue circle took up all the brown space in his eyes. He'd sunk under the magic now, while I still floated above it. I turned but held one of his hands, even though my own was so cold and stiff, leading him back to the food table and through the door behind it.

The wall between the dining room and the ballroom muffled the sound of the party.

Odina stood in front of the cold fireplace, the shroud laid out on the floor before her.

"Come, Callum," I pulled him closer, closer to the stretch of silk.

He came willingly. Odina wrung her hands as she waited for us. I caught her eye and smiled, but she gave a tight shake of her head. Nerves spilled through my body; a bottomless cup poured over me. It was nearly done. We had him. We were going to be free. Just a few more moments . . .

"Ella," Odina's voice sliced through the air, through my reverie.

"What?"

"I think she's trying to warn you."

I jumped and dropped Callum's hand at the sound of his voice, but he caught mine again and gripped it so my fingers bunched painfully together.

"Callum!"

His eyes glimmered.

Gooseflesh puckered my skin and my throat tightened, making it hard to suck in air. The magic was broken, and now Odina and I were alone in the dining room and had no way of overpowering Callum.

"What were you trying to do, Ella? What is that silk for?"

I ripped my hand away and put myself between Callum and Odina. My underarms pricked with sweat. Callum was a god; he had more power than I could dream of. His very being was laced with magic, and I was just a human with a body that could fail so easily. A rotten tooth, a cut that turns green, skin that wrinkled too early, knuckles that could swell into uselessness.

I had to do this. Had to face him. I balled my hands into fists at my side, even though my joints screamed with pain.

"I thought you wanted tonight to go perfectly, Ella, so you could run the Players with me. Isn't that what you want? Money, prestige, power, people falling over themselves to get your bolts of cloth?"

That was exactly what I'd wanted, but now I knew why. I assigned myself value based on how beautiful, masterful, people found my wools and silks to be. The scales were always tipping in opposite directions. Some days I was worth a lot because I'd soaked in enough compliments; other days, I was hollow because no one's words had filled me up. But I didn't want that anymore. Callum didn't have the power to decide what I was worth. No one did. I loved weaving, but the fabrics I made weren't my only measure of worth. I was more than a bolt of silk.

"I did want those things, Callum. You knew it from the start. That's why you sent Mrs. Under to persuade me to ask the Bean-Nighe for a wish, right?"

Callum's smiled twisted into a sneer. "You noticed right away something was wrong, with your hands . . . your hair. I'm surprised it took you so long to say anything. You don't usually hold back, Ella."

I backed away from his sharp teeth and flinty eyes, whatever was left of him in my heart shattering. Odina grabbed my arm and pulled me to her side.

"You beguiled me," I said to Callum.

He laughed. "Like your silks?"

"I thought we'd shared enough with each other to mean something, but everything that came out of your mouth—about your childhood, growing up—were lies, weren't they?"

Callum shrugged. "Some were. Others weren't."

I glanced around the room while he talked. The long wooden table was bare, polished for the party in case anyone came in here from the ballroom. The shroud, bright white against the dark wood floors, lay waiting to receive Callum. A little box sat beside it with a needle and the spool of unbreakable thread. Shears. I held them in my vision, a whiff of hope.

The door to the dining room whined open on hinges in need of oil. I jumped but it was just Gregory, as shrunken as before, scurrying into the room. Odina whimpered and I squeezed her hand. The stick seamstresses came next, wearing Andrew and Serene's clothes. I froze, heart beating in my ears. Andrew and Serene were Callum's seamstresses. There wasn't any time to stare at them, trying to find their faces in the bark. Two more tall creatures entered the room, dripping what looked like moss and lichen from their leatherlike skin. Callum didn't look back, but he smiled. We were cornered and outnumbered. I needed to reach the shears. I pushed gently against Odina's leg, urging her to move sideways toward the sewing basket. She returned my pressure but didn't budge. Panic swelled in my chest and my vision darkened around the edges.

Callum arched his shoulders back and shook his head, his hair flowing out around his ears. His shadow, cast against the wall by the moonlight streaming in through the two windows framing the fireplace, elongated. He stretched, his legs growing taller and his feet bursting from his silk shoes, hardening into something more like a horse's hoof. Horns curled from his thick brown hair. All the fear I'd been trying to keep down burst through, crawling up my throat. I trembled, clutching Odina. Knowing who Callum really was wasn't the same as seeing it. Now it was inescapable, trapping me like the net we wanted to use on him.

Here he was. Not Callum at all, not anymore.

Lugh.

# Chapter Forty-Three

Lugh stood in front of us with his sharp eyes and long, pointed chin. I bit my cheek, sucked in a raggedy breath. Odina let go of my arm and pushed herself back against the empty fireplace. Lugh's fae servants flanked him, Gregory hiding behind Serene's leg.

The only magic I had was in the dress, the magic I'd bled for. Panic tightened my lungs. The fae, Lugh—they could do things I wouldn't even be able to imagine. Odina and I weren't going to be able to overpower them, but there was something else I could try. Lugh fed on worship, and we could try to starve him.

The stick seamstresses clicked their needle-sharp fingers together and advanced on us.

Odina whispered behind me, "*I don't want to go back, I don't want to go back.*"

Her words scraped against me like the sharp end of a needle. Neither one of us was going to be trapped as a Bean-Nighe. I wasn't going to let that happen.

"Andrew! Serene!" I said.

They kept moving, sliding their long feet closer and closer. I edged away from them, back, closer to Odina.

"He's worked you, hasn't he?" I said to the two fae. "Demanded, made you stay up all night and sew dresses?"

Lugh laughed and I heard Callum behind his deepened voice. "You won't trick them into turning against me, Ella. They're rewarded handsomely."

My shallow breaths made me dizzy, and my heart hammered in my ears. It didn't look like my words had any effect on the beady eyes glaring at me. Andrew and Serene, with their leather-like skin and moss dripping from their heads and noses, put their hands to the floor. The wood cracked, a thin fissure running from them to us. I jumped back, body tight and coiled. Odina seemed to snap out of her fear then because she bent down and covered the crack with her hands.

"Move, Ella!"

I flew to the side as a thin tree trunk burst from the crack, splintering the floorboards in front on the hearth. People of the other side of the door, in the ballroom, screamed at the noise. Their footsteps clattered over the dance floor as I imagined they fled from a party that was no longer fun. I fixed my eyes on the tree, not able to stop it, unable to look away. The trunk grew thick and wide and tall and the leaves pushed up, abutting the ceiling. A long branch shot out like an arm and grabbed me around the waist, knocking the breath out of me. I wriggled and scraped my fingernails against the bark. My fingernails burned where the splinters went in. Odina screamed from where a branch held her above me. The sound of her anguish pierced my ears and stoked the fires of my own fear.

None of this was supposed to happen. Callum was supposed to be beguiled by the magic in the fabric and lie down in his shroud because I asked him to. The magic hadn't worked, hadn't been enough to hold him. The silk wasn't good enough. Disappointment crashed over me, threatening to drown me. I fought back, slicing through it, pulling myself up to the surface. If I could get Callum to the gallery, to the carving of Lugh . . .

"Gregory!" I yelled.

He snapped his head up to look at me.

"What about you?" I asked. "You were a man and now you're a creature of the fae. Do you like what you've become?"

He covered his face with his hands but stood in front of the tree.

"Look, faeries! Look what Lugh did to this man."

Tears slid down Gregory's cheek. He didn't look back at Lugh, and I imagined he was scared. Scared like I'd been when he tried to touch me. I was using him now, yes, but it was only fair.

Gregory stuck out the stump of his tongue.

"I didn't do this," Lugh said. "I found him like this and took him in, gave him a place to stay in return for his service. You can't trick them, Ella."

"I don't need to trick them, *Lugh*. Anyone can see how you use people—faeries—suck them dry, just to make sure you get what you want. But you're never going to be the patron god of this city. You won't get the worship, the power."

He flashed his teeth, and the tip of his horns grew red, as if burning with rage.

"Andrew, Serene," I went on. "Didn't Lugh use you? He made you sew dresses through the night until your fingers bled and then ridiculed you at parties."

Andrew and Serene clicked their fingers together and snarled, but not at me.

"Don't forget what I've promised you," Lugh said. "Time in the human world."

"You never let us leave this house," Serene said, her voice like the creak of an old tree in the wind.

Andrew pushed his stringy green hair out of his eyes. "Will you ever let us go? We want to play."

I didn't want to know what they would consider "playing" in the human world, but I grabbed onto those words like they were a rope that could pull me free of the tree's grip.

"He'll never let you play!" I said. "He wants all the fun for himself."

"Everyone is just a toy for Lugh," Odina shouted from her branch.

"Enough!" Lugh put his hands together and slowly pulled them out to the side again, as if there were spiderwebs between them he was delicately pulling apart. A shimmer—a darkness and a shimmer, like the sparkled tulle hanging from the ceiling in the ballroom. Except this was right in front of me, a sheer black wall studded with stars. Lugh reached out one large hand like a knife and sliced the veil open. Wind from the land of the fae filled the dining room, blowing the pins free from my hair and rustling the leaves of the tree holding me in its grasp. The gusts whipped the seamstresses' shrill screams away and amplified them, until the noise filled the room, and my ears were much too full of the wind and the cries. My arms were weak against the rough branch holding me. Shock rippled under my skin. This was magic I didn't have, didn't understand, couldn't fight against.

Lugh smiled, and it was that twisted, too-big smile of the Lugh in the carving. Fear crept over me as if a thousand spiders had burst out from this evil tree's leaves and crawled up and down my arms, into my stays, under my petticoat. I twisted in the branch's grasp but it only held on tighter.

"If you're not having fun here, go home," Lugh said, voice echoing through the wind.

Andrew and Serene shrieked and tried to wrap their long fingers around the tree trunk. Gregory pumped his legs, trying to run, but the strong wind wouldn't let him. All of a sudden, the gusts turned inward, sucking everything into the veil. A silver candelabra flew from the sideboard and disappeared into the sheer black wall. I tried to look through it, but there was nothing but indistinguishable figures moving beyond. The faeries couldn't hold on. They flew, screaming, into the shadows. Gregory followed, his mouth open, the stump of his tongue gleaming with saliva.

Then Lugh turned toward me. I couldn't find even a hint of Callum in his eyes. My heart squeezed, terror wrapping its long limbs around me, and I breathed out the last of my feelings for the man, my hesitancy.

He offered a hand to me. "So, you want to dance?"

# Chapter Forty-Four

The wind calmed and the magicked branches unwrapped their hold on us. There was no moment of relief. We weren't there yet, it wasn't earned. I slid down the bark, holding on to the knots in the trunk. Odina fell with a quiet thump on to the thick carpet in front of the fireplace and I flew to her. She looked up at me with watery eyes, and I examined her for cuts, bruises. I breathed a shaky breath. She was all right.

Callum stood in front of us again, his normal size and recognizable features, but he still had his curling horns. He opened his arms to us, but I reached for Odina and we closed in together instead.

"I'm a god. You're humans. What did you really think you'd be able to do?"

"You're done playing with us, Callum," I said. "We don't exist for your amusement."

"No? My game has been incredibly successful so far. Wouldn't you agree, Odina?"

Her hands shook in mine, and I squeezed.

"Find someone else to torment," Odina said.

Callum raised his brows. "Sacrificing someone else? That's not very noble of you, Odina."

"Nothing we've ever done has been noble. The Players are manipulators."

He leaned against the tree trunk in the middle of the dining room. "And are the chieftains not manipulators and thieves? They make rules to benefit themselves, don't they?"

"Maybe," I said. "But they also risk war, a takeover from another clan if they go too far. You risk nothing."

He smirked. "Nothing? I risk *everything*. The Players are barely more than a scraggly group of nobodies now, and they're all I've got left. Everyone else pulled away, and my chance at immortality drifted away with them."

"You started with so much more than everyone else. We aren't immortal either, and we never can be. You have more than even the Chieftain could dream of."

"And you wouldn't say the Chieftain had gone too far, Ella? You, who lived with only a rumbling tummy for company?" Callum said.

Lots of people in the city would have thought the Chieftain had gone too far with the price of food, of lodging, the control he wrought over taxes and goods. But he wasn't the one standing in front of us right now. He wasn't here at all, because Odina had paid the carters who'd helped move my loom to dig a hole in the road leading from the Chieftain's house, so it was impassible. Callum wasn't going to get a chance at him tonight.

"You're right, Callum," I said and lowered my head, let my chin fall to my chest. "He's gone too far."

"See? You see now, don't you? Once I'm the patron god of this city, things will be different. Light, exhilarating! Beautiful!"

"We'll live with abandon?" I asked.

He rushed forward and clasped my hands between his, and I stopped myself from flinching. "Yes, Ella, yes. You feel it don't you? The thrill of it buzzing in your belly?"

I nodded, even though the only thing buzzing in my belly was sour bile.

"And you, Odina?" Callum's smiled widened. "Will you embrace it now, after all these years?"

Tears ran down her cheeks and she nodded. "Yes, yes . . . I'm tired of fighting it."

She was very convincing. I would have been worried, if not for the pressure of her shoe on my boot, hidden by the volume of our skirts.

Callum took one of her hands too, threw back his head, laughed with Lugh's deep voice.

The drums thrummed and the pipes cried and the strings twanged. We spun, the three of us, Odina and I letting our heads fall back to mimic Callum. Abandon. This was what he wanted, this loosening of muscles, of troubles from the mind. I almost enjoyed it, the freedom of it, for just a moment.

But this would never lead to real freedom from all the hard things in my life. Callum wanted that only for himself. He wanted payment for the glimpse of a better life he offered.

It was more than I was willing to give.

I opened my eyes. Odina stared at Callum as we spun, dizzyingly, in front of the unnatural tree. He dipped his own head and his eyes were icy blue. Bright, piercing. It worked this time;

with both our dresses against his one suit, the Bean-Nighe's magic was amplified. Callum was beguiled.

I caught Odina's eye, heart pounding, hands slick with sweat. "We don't know for how long. Grab the shroud and a needle and the thread . . . and the shears!" I said and let go of Callum and Odina's grip.

Callum stumbled and fell on the carpet, laughing.

Odina dove for the silk and stuck her hand into the sewing basket.

"Callum, come with me. Let's play a game," I said.

He grinned. "I love games."

"I know."

I took his warm, warm hand and recognized how familiar it felt, even though I hadn't known him all that long. Somehow, in that time, my own hand had memorized the smooth skin of his palm, the dip where his thumb met his wrist, the little mole on the side of his pinky finger. But it was because I knew him even better now that I had to destroy him.

We left the dining room arm in arm, a saunter in our step as I pulled him along, with Odina behind us. There was a way we could make him weak. As powerful as the gods may be with their magic, they relied on us to give it to them. A god without anyone to worship them was nothing but a hollowed husk. They needed the statues and the carvings and the gifts. That was why Callum had asked Odina to commission the carving of Lugh in the gallery—so he'd be stronger here.

The problem was, wood could be chipped away. It wasn't a very reliable font of power; that was why Lugh wanted to be patron god of the city—to take root in people's hearts. People can be stubborn, and they don't often give up the gods they brought oatcakes to as a child. But I was going to make sure that god was never Lugh in Eidyn Crag.

I left Callum dancing to the dregs of music from the open doors of the ballroom and took the shears from Odina.

"Watch him."

I wrapped my hands around the pointed ends of the scissors and ran up the stairs to the gallery, my breath burning in my throat. The statue of Lugh and his worshippers—or perhaps his prisoners—smiled out at me, sending shivers through my arms and legs. Were they trapped like Odina was, like the Bean-Nighe? Rage frayed me, pulled me apart. I channeled it, brought it all into my pin-pricked fingers as I gripped the shears. Then I plunged the tip right into Lugh's carved face. I scraped and pulled. Wood peeled and fell away in chunks.

"Ella!" Odina yelled.

I stared out over the edge of the railing but kept digging, digging, digging Lugh out of the scene. This needed to be done, this was the only way to weaken him. I couldn't see them yet—they must have been coming down from the dining room. The wood cracked under the blades of the shears. Odina and Callum finally rounded the corner into the hall, her leading him by the hand. He was still trapped in the magic. I paused in my digging, watching, gulping in air. Callum's fingers flinched against Odina's. Not slack. Not as they should be.

"Odina!"

Callum bent his head forward and rammed it into Odina, slamming her back against one of the big wooden doors and pinning her there with his horns. I screamed, dropped the shears, and flew to the top of the stairs. Callum glanced over at me. The blue in his eyes receded, swallowed by a brown so dark it was almost black.

"Ella!" Odina called again, but this time her voice gave out halfway through.

"No, stop!" I said.

Callum grinned. "Come get me then."

I lunged for the top stair and then stopped, my legs shaking in restraint. This is what he wanted, for me to go down there so he could overpower both Odina and me. He was still stronger, was still a god. He stared up at me with that look in his eyes, like a dare. But I turned back to the railing and jammed the shears in the wood, hacking at it. Slivers slipped under my papery skin. My swollen knuckles screamed, and I almost lost my grip on the shears. I chipped away Lugh's face last—his wild eyes and wide, toothy sneer. With each bit of wood, I imagined Callum's face might be there underneath. But it wasn't. Splinters filled the space where Lugh's lips had once been, and they wounded the place in my heart that held on to our first kiss.

A rasp reached my ears and brought me back to the wood all around me, the shears in my hands, Callum and Odina.

*Odina.*

I sat up to look over the railing. Callum drooped against her. He seemed to have lost some of himself. Without the carving, he was weaker, but he still held Odina's neck in place with his horns. Her eyes bulged and her lips were tinted blue. Panic exploded in my chest.

"Odina!" I leapt down the stairs two at a time and ran to them, gripping the shears in my fist. When I was close enough, I slammed the metal points into Callum's neck. They didn't go in far, and I let go of the metal as soon as the ends of the scissors hit something hard and my skin touched his. I shivered, my stomach sour. There wasn't any blood, not like with Andrew, but the wound seemed graver somehow. In the neck. Near the beating blue veins just under the skin. Callum moaned, eyes closed, and fell backward. He grabbed at the shears and pulled them free. Blood poured from his skin then. He convulsed, hands on his neck, trying to staunch the bleeding.

I gasped, my entire body cold. The horns on Callum's head drained of their red color and his eyes went dull. Not dead, no. I placed a finger on his sticky, bloodied neck. Still warm. A sob broke through me. If he'd just died, this would have been over. I could have left him behind, tried to forget. Instead, I had to stop myself from shaking and take the man who'd stolen a piece of my heart to his grave.

Odina dropped to her knees, rubbing her neck and coughing. I knelt down beside her and fumbled for her hands.

"Are you okay?"

"Just get the shroud," she rasped.

She'd dropped it near the door when Callum surprised her. I pulled the silk into my hands and let it pool around my fingers. Odina grabbed one end and together we slipped it over Callum's prone figure. I passed her a needle and she deftly threaded it, then another, with the Bean-Nighe's unbreakable thread. Callum grunted as we started stitching the shroud around his legs. His skin was gray now, with the dark blue veins bulging underneath. What muscle he'd had withered away so his suit hung limply from his body.

With precise, quick movements, we closed Callum up in it. I dropped a memory of him into each stitch, tied them up so they'd sink into the water too and leave me be. My tears stained the silk—so did Odina's. Together the drops made a pattern like rain.

Finally, we brought the cloth up around Callum's face and veiled him from view.

"To the river?" Odina asked as she tied off her knot.

I hesitated, my stomach knotting around the sadness there. It had never been *him*. It had been a dream of what could be. The idea of being loved. I blew out a slow breath and turned to Odina. She smiled and it lit up her eyes. We were almost there.

"To the river."

∽

He wasn't as heavy as he should have been. I took the side where his shoulders were and Odina took his feet. We stumbled down the hill toward the water and dropped him on the rocky shore.

"Bean-Nighe!" I called into the wind.

Only the singing of frogs answered. I pulled in a deeper breath.

"Bean-Nighe!"

Odina put a hand on my arm. "You don't know that she wants to come back."

363

But at that moment, she slipped from the veil. First the hem of her skirt, then her faded bodice and the new, fuller hair. The smell of wet earth stuck in my throat.

She stared at Callum's form. "What have you done?"

"We've ended it. Lugh doesn't have any power over you anymore, or any of us."

The Bean-Nighe dropped the shirt soaked with my blood to the ground. "And me? Who will turn me back?"

The thought hit me like a thunderclap. In my rush to save myself, I hadn't considered how we might turn the Bean-Nighe back into a girl.

"There must be something," I said, running my silk skirt through my fingers.

Odina touched my arm. "There isn't. There never was. He wouldn't have done it, not without leaving you in her place."

The Bean-Nighe let out a whimper, a heartbreaking mewl. "I'm stuck like this?"

My chest tightened. "I'm so sorry."

Odina stepped forward. "You have your strength back. He can't make you human again so you can't stay here forever, but you're no longer his servant. You're a fae now. You have the whole world of the veil to explore."

The Bean-Nighe flicked her eyes back and forth between me and Odina. Shame spread through me and heated my cheeks. I should have thought about her, and I hadn't. There wasn't any excuse for that.

"I'm so sorry," I said. "I thought . . . hoped you'd just turn back once we destroyed the carving and got Callum—Lugh—in the shroud."

She laughed and the wet-earth smell got stronger.

"At least I have a bit of your life, girl," she said. "I thought you might be trying to do something like this when you asked for the unbreakable thread. I may not get to come back to the human world, but your years here won't be as long as they would have been. Look at your hands, your hair, the wrinkles at your face. Do you find it hard to move? Are you often tired? You think you saved yourself, but did you really?"

I stared down at my gnarled hands and took in a burning breath, my lungs hurting after carrying Callum all this way. These things might never go away. I understood that. I could live with it if it meant I got to live the rest of my life the way I wanted to, without the weight of debt around my neck or the fear of an empty belly.

"I'm sorry," I said again, because it was all I *could* say.

"Let's get him in the water," Odina said, wiping her hands on her skirt as though she would wipe all this away—the Bean-Nighe, Callum, the shroud full of magic. Lugh's magic, ultimately. Used against him in the end.

The Bean-Nighe caught my eye and gave me a look full of heavy sadness. I almost reached for her, but my hands were empty—I had nothing to offer. She turned, shimmered, and slipped back through the veil, leaving the scent of fresh gardens and new opportunities behind. We both had our lives now, whatever they may look like.

Odina and I rolled Callum toward the water and he went in with a splash. We waded up to our knees and pushed him into the deeper part of the river. Odina pulled out the bag of steel knitting needles she'd taken from the house and handed me a few. I submerged myself in the water and opened my eyes to the brown murk. Feeling my way, I stabbed the first needle through the shroud and forced it deep into the riverbed with my boot. Odina did the same. When we'd secured the shroud over Callum's body, I pulled stones from the bank with my freezing hands and buried Callum, trapping him there in the river. If he ever woke, if people *did* give him the worship he so desperately needed, the only game he'd be able to play would be to count the fish admiring the beautiful silk surrounding him.

# Chapter Forty~Five

The silk butterflies spun and glittered in the breeze let in by the open door. We hung them up in the window because they attracted so many customers.

"I'm thinking a purple one next," Odina said.

We'd been avoiding purple in our creations. It was the Players' color and we didn't need any more reminders of Callum. Each time I rubbed my sore knuckles or lost my breath walking up the hill to the marketplace was reminder enough.

"Are you sure?" I asked.

Odina nodded. "It used to be my favorite color. I don't want to let him take that from me anymore."

My stomach soured a little but I smiled. I would try to think of purple as *her* color, not Callum's. And anyway, I'd kept my purple paste jewel. It sat in a little dish in the show window, where the sun made it glitter.

"People will be flocking for them. We'll have to ask Margaret to come in a few extra days next week to keep the butterflies on the shelves," I said.

"She'll be happy for the money."

Margaret was an eager apprentice, but I refused to let her

work every day, despite her requests. I wasn't going to let her sight grow dim or her fingers turn bent and crooked so we could keep the shop stocked.

That night, after we submerged Callum in the river, we'd trudged up the hill to the empty house. And then Odina and I had decided what to do. No one was coming to claim it, no family. I didn't know Callum's relationship with the other gods, couldn't even fathom it, but I suspected none of them would care about a house on the edge of a human city.

We sold both it and Odina's house. She said she never wanted to sleep there again, in the place Callum had kept her prisoner. The money we got for them both was good, and we put some aside and made a deposit for rent on a tiny shop squeezed in between two others along the main street of the marketplace. The inside was narrow, but it had a good window to let in the light and show the fabrics.

I couldn't weave anymore, not really. I worked with my hands, squeezing them around apples to try to get my knuckles to bend more easily. They still burned when I held the shuttle and I was much slower than I used to be. It didn't make sense to rely on me to stock the store, but Odina and Margaret did a good job at that. Bryn kept the books for us. We'd offered her the job right away, and she was grateful for the chance. I understood why she'd been scared to let go of Gregory's protection before. She hadn't wanted to be back on the streets, and I couldn't blame her for that.

Odina learned to weave quickly, and soon I didn't need to stand over her shoulder anymore to coach her through a bolt of silk. I sourced the materials—paid for up front with money from the sale of Callum's house—and made suggestions on colors and patterns. Odina was a natural at selecting spools of silk that complimented each other too.

I spent a lot of my time taking care of the business. Papa had taught me a lot, and I hadn't even always realized I was learning at the time. I was good with the customers, knowing their names and taking an interest in the bits of their lives they told me about. Helping people select a good sturdy wool for winter or an eye-catching silk for a wedding suit made me happy. I wove sometimes, slowly, just for me. Mostly blues and greens and patterns of waves.

"What do you think of this?" Odina asked one day, when the spring light stretched into the evening, and we were alone in the quiet shop. She showed me a spool of gray wool thread.

"For who?"

"Mister Miller. He wants the material for a summer coat."

I took the spool from her and bent it toward the light. This gray would wash the pale-featured man out.

"I've told you before. For someone as colorless as that, you need to use darker wools or they'll look like ghosts."

Odina's mouth went slack, and her eyes hardened. Immediately, I wanted to suck my words back in. There was no need to be impatient; she was still learning. But if she'd made the gray bolt for him without asking, and he'd worn it and looked terrible and told people where it had come from . . . well, that was our reputation at risk.

But as Odina frowned and dropped the spool of thread to her side, I realized that didn't really matter. Things were different now. I had more than one client and whether or not I could eat wasn't dependent on whether a single person liked our work.

"You've got a good eye for color, I know that. I'm sorry. Use whatever you think is best."

She grinned and put the spool on the large wooden table strewn with shears and ribbons and thread of every hue. A colorful buffet of supplies.

"You know, you're getting better at understanding it," she said.

"What?"

I slid a blue ribbon off the table and ran its silky length through my fingers. I knew what she meant, but it was still hard to say out loud.

Odina took two steps around the table and pulled the ribbon from my hands.

"I like *you*. Not the silks we make, not the glow in the customers' eyes when they see our creations for the first time, not the compliments that come with the work you taught me to do. *You*. I like how you laugh with your held tilted back and how you press your hand under your chin when you're thinking. I like the way you tell me stories of your papa when we sit around the fire, and how you listen to my stories with just as much intensity. I like how you ask me how I am in the morning, how you boil eggs for us both."

Tears slipped from my eyes and ran down my face, around my nose, into my mouth. I'd told myself I was worth more than the silks so many times since we'd left Callum at the bottom of the river. I didn't need to be the best at something to be wanted.

We left the shop that evening arm in arm. Odina had a little package tied up in thin linen and a bow the color of blood under her arm. We strolled down the wide cobbled street and dipped our heads to the familiar faces passing by. Home wasn't far away. We rented two rooms plus a sitting room, just enough for us each to have some privacy but still be together if we wished. We bought our suppers from ordinaries—chicken and mushroom pie was my favorite—or Odina made pork stew and bannock in the hearth.

We talked a lot. She told me all about her life before she crossed the sea to get here, and I told her about Papa and debtor's prison and my time in my tiny room in the crooked building. It had been long before either I or Papa had been born when Odina sailed here—she'd spent a very long time as the Bean-Nighe. She never talked about that part, and we both avoided the subject of the girl we left behind, the one who still lived beyond the veil.

Neither of us knew how to save her, and we were both to blame for not figuring it out before throwing Callum in the river. That was why we walked right past the studded wood door to our building and along down the hill. We passed through my old courtyard, and I thought about the time Papa had brought me down here and we'd spent a happy sun-soaked hour rolling an empty spool back and forth to each other over the cobbles.

He'd wanted me to be a weaver so he could give me his loom, so I could make money for both of us while he grew old. I used to resent that. Now I realized he'd given me a gift. Papa gave me a skill, but he also taught me more than that. He taught me to think on my feet, to look beyond what was right in front of me. It just took me a long time to recognize that.

"Come on, Ella. I smell rain." Odina broke free from my arm and hurried toward the muddy bank. Winter held on with its frosted fingers, but a few blades of green mingled with the yellow grass on the crest of the bank. I stepped carefully on the rocks I knew well, down to the water. Odina, ahead of me, bent down and deposited her package on a flat stone—perfect for slapping laundry against. She pulled on the red ribbon and revealed one of her silk butterflies, green with gold sequins edging the wings.

"It's for you," she said.

No one answered, but I smelled wet earth.

"Let's go, Odina. We should get home."

A few adventurous raindrops, the scouts ahead of the army, landed on my nose. Odina looked up toward the gray clouds and took my arm again. We scaled the bank and found our way back to the road.

"You're getting better at the butterflies," Odina said, lacing her fingers in mine. "That one is really good. The green is the perfect color . . . like new grass. And the sequins look like gold armor on the wings."

I smiled, and I didn't need to force it to be wide. Yes, I was still learning and that was all right. No, she hadn't called the butterfly *beautiful* or *gorgeous*—and that was fine too. Learning to make the butterflies made me happy. Odina teaching me made me happy. The shop, and the new customers and all the possibilities before me made me happy. I wasn't trying to fill myself up with other people's praise anymore. I was full, solid, all on my own.

# Acknowledgments

This is my second published book and the third I've ever written. The only reason it's in your hands now is thanks to feedback and support from my incredible critique partners and friends, my fantastic and intuitive editor, Emily Daluga, and my ever-supportive agent, Chloe Seager. Thank you to everyone who read and helped me grow through their feedback—Rachel Greenlaw, Catherine Bakewell, Gabriela Romero Lacruz, Lyndall Clipstone, Katherine Lapierre, and Susan Wallach.

I wrote and edited this book while preparing for the launch of my first book, and things were busy. To my husband and partner in this life, Misha, thank you for supporting me and our children and helping me carve out time to write books.

To Mom, Dad, Mama, Papa, Devon, Michelle, Wayne, Katie, Peter, Brandy, Richard, and Grandma, your support is so special to me, thank you.

To all the Llamas and the 21ders and the Monsters and Magic Society—what a wonderful community this place can be. I'm so appreciative of all of you.

It takes many people to turn a manuscript into a book, and I'm so thankful to all of my publishing team at Amulet and Abrams—Marie Oishi, Kathy Lovisolo, Maggie Moore, Erin

Vandeveer, Margo Winton Parodi, Penelope Cray, Jenny Choy, Megan Evans, Patricia McNamara O'Neill, Brooke Shearouse, and Hallie Patterson. Thank you to Deena Fleming and artist Colin Verdi for an absolutely beautiful cover.

And finally, to readers—thank you for diving into Ella's story. I hope you enjoyed the journey.